Awaken Online
Tarot Book 1: Ember

Travis Bagwell

Copyright © 2019 by Travis Bagwell
All rights reserved.

To my wife… For the last time, I swear I didn't kill you off in this book and then search and replace your name.

Contents

Prologue	7
Chapter 1 - Crippled	12
Chapter 2 - Intrigued	22
Chapter 3 - Fortunate	27
Chapter 4 - Weighed	37
Chapter 5 - Educated	48
Chapter 6 - Enlightened	58
Chapter 7 - Studious	70
Chapter 8 - Magical	81
Chapter 9 - Converted	94
Chapter 10 - Clueless	104
Chapter 11 - Creative	113
Chapter 12 - Popular	123
Chapter 13 - Modified	131
Chapter 14 - Physical	140
Chapter 15 - Durable	147
Chapter 16 - Deadly	158
Chapter 17 - Sneaky	171
Chapter 18 - Distracted	182
Chapter 19 - Focused	198
Chapter 20 - Pivotal	210

Chapter 21 - Armed	**221**
Chapter 22 - Studious	**231**
Chapter 23 - Fiery	**239**
Chapter 24 - Controlling	**252**
Chapter 25 - Unaware	**260**
Chapter 26 - Fleetfooted	**269**
Chapter 27 - Focused	**280**
Chapter 28 - Thrifty	**292**
Chapter 29 - Subtle	**303**
Chapter 30 - Infamous	**310**
Chapter 31 - Cheater	**316**
Chapter 32 - Vengeful	**329**
Chapter 33 - Violent	**339**
Chapter 34 - Sturdy	**350**
Chapter 35 - Soiled	**361**
Chapter 36 - Shaky	**371**
Chapter 37 - Frigid	**378**
Chapter 38 - Hesitant	**392**
Chapter 39 - Final	**403**
Chapter 40 - Compelling	**408**
Chapter 41 - Blazing	**418**
Chapter 42 - Triumphant	**430**
Chapter 43 - Resolved	**435**

Epilogue **440**

Prologue

Finn Harris looked out the window, watching as the other vehicles and buildings sped past. The sun had long since set, and the passing structures were merely a blur of colored lights. Faint technicolor streaks amid the darkness that vanished almost as quickly as they appeared. He could feel the gentle hum of the car's engine below them, but the shocks and soundproofing dampened most of the road noise.

"Penny for your thoughts?" Rachael asked, snuggling up beside him and draping his arm across her shoulders. He could feel the smooth fabric of her dress, a fanciful affair perfect for the award ceremony they had just left.

Finn grimaced, his eyes still on the window. He couldn't fight the heavy feeling that lingered in the pit of his stomach. It wasn't tangible. There wasn't any reason for it.

Something just felt off.

He felt Rachael tickle his ribs, and he let out a very manly yelp. Mock glaring at his wife, he said, "Behave. At my age, I'm likely to break a hip or something."

A tinkling laugh. "You aren't quite that old yet. There might still be a little fire left in you," she retorted, looking up at him.

The foreboding feeling receded slightly as he met her gaze. Glorious brown eyes framed by auburn-colored hair tinged with faint traces of gray. Rachael had never felt the need to color it. She was just who she was – without any shame or reservation. Even if they had long since crossed the half-century mark and had decades of married life behind them, she hadn't changed a bit. She was still the same captivating, gorgeous, rebellious woman he had married.

"And besides," she continued with a grin and a mischievous twinkle in her eye, "when you kick the bucket, I already have a young gentleman lined up and ready to go. I even have the French villa picked out. The life insurance should be just enough to cover it."

"Is that so?" Finn replied with a raised eyebrow. He rose to her challenge, cupping the back of her head and drawing her toward him. Rachael smiled as their lips met. He might not be twenty anymore, but he could still make a point.

When they withdrew a few minutes later, slightly breathless and flushed, there was a different sparkle in Rachael's eye, one that Finn knew well. "So, is there a way to speed this thing up?" she asked. "I hear you might know a guy..."

Finn snorted softly. He could feel the sharp edge of his most recent award digging into his back. He had designed this vehicle. Well, at least the software that helped navigate both their autonomous car and the many others that surrounded them. These new vehicles were revolutionary. They were much more efficient, allowing for travel in a fraction of the time of their conventional counterparts. They removed the need for separate lanes, traffic lights, and stop signs. Once his company helped repurpose the ancient interstate highway system and this technology spread, people would be able to travel well past the previous speed limits, rivaling even train and air travel.

The mechanical hurdles had been tricky, but the linchpin was the new software controller. Finn liked to think of the new traffic system as water flowing through a pipe, except his software allowed them to track every molecule in real-time. Cars wove into traffic without pause. The AI controller he had designed allowed for incredibly small variances in the distance between vehicles, and it was able to dynamically adjust the velocity of an entire chain of cars – all while making split-second judgment calls. The AI was supposed to be safer since the software never got tired or distracted. There was still the risk of mechanical defects, of course, but the *software* was sound.

They had even given him an award for the achievement.

Well, technically, several awards.

"You know it doesn't work that way. I can't just hit the gas on *this* car," Finn replied, looking down at his wife, his expression somber. The same ominous feeling had returned when she mentioned the vehicle.

"It was just a joke," Rachael replied, looking at him

with a confused glance. "What's up with you tonight? You seem like you are a million miles away and you've had this perpetual frown on your face, even while you were accepting your award."

"And here I thought I was doing a good job of hiding it," Finn muttered.

"Nope. Terrible. Stick to computers because acting definitely isn't your strong suit."

"I'll keep that in mind," Finn replied with a half-hearted chuckle. He shook his head. "Honestly, I don't know what it is. I just have a bad feeling…"

Rachael sighed, rolling her eyes. "I know you want to pull up the terminal and look. Just do it, and then we can get back to where we left off."

Finn smiled ruefully. She knew him too well. He had been compulsively checking the system every few minutes since it had gone live a few days ago. Right now, there was just this small strip of highway between two cities – a test case for the larger rollout. However, plans were already in the works for rapid expansion into every major city center within the next five years. The introduction of a massive federal grant had accelerated what had initially been a simple test project into a full-blown renovation of the country's transportation system within a matter of months.

He tapped at a hidden panel beneath his seat, and a part of the cabin wall shifted, opening to reveal a recessed display. The logo for Cerillion Logistics flashed across the screen, and the system requested login credentials. Finn tapped at the screen, and a moment later, a grid showing the stream of traffic appeared in front of him, data scrawling down the margin. He suddenly wished he was sitting in front of his real workstation instead of this tiny little display.

Everything *looked* okay. The system was maintaining proper distances between the vehicles, and he didn't see any immediate issues – at least nothing nearby. He panned out and looked farther down the highway. A juncture was approaching ahead of them, and they were only about a minute out at their current speed.

A frown tugged at Finn's lips. The system was

reporting that everything was okay, cars merging and diverging seamlessly. However, the data seemed to be telling a slightly different story. A slight millisecond delay, here and there. But even that small variance shouldn't have been happening. He sensed a pattern in the data, but his mind couldn't quite piece it together.

"What's wrong?" Rachael asked, noting his frown.

Finn looked over at her, opening his mouth to speak.

That was when he felt the tremor. Just a small irregularity. Most people probably wouldn't have noticed it. But he shouldn't have felt anything.

He looked back at the screen, and his perspective shifted slightly. "Oh shit, it's…"

He never got to finish that sentence.

Several things happened at once. The tremor grew dramatically more violent, causing the vehicle to sway. Finn tried to throw himself over Rachael, even though he knew that it was pointless. Already his mind was doing some rough calculations – the car's velocity, mass, momentum, and the tensile strength of the steel cage that surrounded them. Then he factored in the other vehicles on the highway. The kinetic dampening foam installed in the walls hadn't been tested to withstand the numbers that were tumbling through his head.

The damage would be catastrophic.

"Finn," Rachael shouted, looking up at him, her eyes wide and panicked.

The world seemed to list sideways, like an angry giant had just thrown their car, sending it tumbling through the air. The muted screeching grind of metal on metal echoed through the chamber, and they were suddenly weightless. Yet Finn's only focus was Rachael, keeping hold of her even as her auburn locks floated around her face.

He saw the fear in her eyes.

In that moment, Finn knew despair. It was a primal thing that flashed through his brain. He wanted to fight, to run, to *fix* this. Yet he knew it was impossible. It was the inevitability of that moment that caused the panic to settle in his mind. He couldn't do anything. He was trapped. *They* were trapped.

Then they slammed into something, the force of the impact throwing him across the cabin and ripping Rachael away from him. Finn's back struck the wall with a muted crack, a blinding pain erupting along his spine.

They were suddenly weightless again. The top of the vehicle had been ripped off in a shower of sparks and a thunderous crack of noise, the system trying vainly to seal the opening with a thick pink foam. Yet it was moving slowly – far too slowly. Finn reached for Rachael, his fingers stretching through the air, almost touching hers.

She met his eyes one last time, her mouth moving, but he heard nothing.

He screamed then, straining with every fiber of his being.

It was futile. Rachael was sucked out of the opening and into the dark expanse on the other side.

Chapter 1 - Crippled

October 3, 2076: 2 days after the release of Awaken Online.

"No!" Finn screamed.

His heart was beating rapidly, his pulse pounding in his ears. It felt like he was drowning, a heavy weight settling on his chest. With great heaving breaths, he tried to suck in air. His arm was outstretched, his fingers twitching as he strained to save a ghost.

All at once, Finn realized he was sitting in his bed. In his home. There was no car. There was no accident. That had happened a long time ago. More than a decade now.

These facts settled in his mind, each one feeling like a heavy blow. In some ways, they were even more painful than his dream. They meant that it had been real. That he was alive, and his wife was…

His hand automatically reached for the familiar spot beside him. It was empty. Of course, it was empty. Yet that hadn't stopped him from making the same feeble gesture every time he had that dream.

"Fuck," he muttered. He felt something wet trickle down his cheek and soon tasted salt on his lips.

A soft chime echoed through the air, and light slowly began to filter into the room. Windows lined the wall behind the bed. The thick metal shutters opened automatically with a faint hiss of hydraulics, letting the morning sunlight trickle through the bulletproof glass that lined the windows on the other side.

"Good morning, sir. Are you alright? The dream again?" a male voice spoke up, his voice thick with compassion. A translucent ball of sapphire light appeared beside the bed, projected from hidden cameras embedded in the walls.

Finn just rubbed at his face without responding.

There was little genuine sympathy in the AI's voice. He knew it was fake. He had programmed it, after all. It was an attempt to simulate emotion – it didn't actually *feel*. It was

Pavlovian. Like a digital dog. It picked up on his behavior. The shout. His heartbeat and respiration recorded by the chips installed under his skin. The gesture toward the empty half of his bed. The AI knew that this combination of behaviors meant that it needed to act a certain way. But it didn't – it couldn't – *understand* his pain.

"Yes, Daniel," Finn croaked. He had named the AI. It had made things easier.

"Would you like a moment?" Daniel asked.

Another canned response. The AI was on-script this morning.

Finn shook his head. "No. I just need to get moving."

A soft chime in response and a chair wheeled into the room, gliding over toward the edge of the bed.

"Would you like any help, sir?" Daniel asked.

"I'm good," Finn grunted, as he did every morning. Someday he would have to accept the AI's assistance – when his body finally grew too old and feeble to do this on his own. But it damned sure wouldn't be today. He would live with the full weight of his mistakes for as long as he could.

Finn gripped his legs, feeling nothing as his fingers touched the bare skin. He forcefully shoved the dead limbs to the edge of the bed and then managed to maneuver himself into the chair with practiced movements. He knew the next steps. Wheel himself to the bathroom, brush his teeth, shower – that was always hard. Then the task of pulling on his clothes. The ritual was familiar. He even knew exactly how long it would take, plus or minus about 90 seconds.

Yet today, he paused, staring down at his legs.

This was the price he had paid. After the accident, the doctors had offered him several options. He could have regrown the damaged nerve-endings in his spine, replaced his legs with advanced robotics, connecting cold metal wires into what was left of his damaged nervous system, or a half-dozen other possibilities he couldn't remember anymore. He had turned them all down. His wife hadn't had any of those options. So, he would live with this.

As a reminder.

"Sir?" Daniel asked, giving off a faint blue pulse as he

spoke. Another canned response. He had been sitting still for too long. Even now, he could visualize the branching dialogue tree from here. He knew exactly what Daniel would say if he didn't start moving.

"I'm fine," Finn said again, as though saying it out loud would make it true.

He didn't sound very convincing, even to himself.

With a sigh, he began wheeling himself toward the bathroom. 1 hour and 37 minutes. That's how long it would take to get ready. Then he could start his day.

* * *

1 hour, 37 minutes, and 47 seconds later, Finn wheeled himself into the kitchen, palming the metal bars on the wheels. He refused to use the chair's electronics. He needed the exercise anyway. The old man that had stared back at him in the mirror had looked rather pale and thin, and it had been a struggle to lift himself in and out of the shower this morning.

The lights immediately came on, Daniel drifting into the room like some sort of overprotective blue angel. However, Finn was forced to do a double take. Something about his routine was off. There was the familiar tang of coffee in the air, but he could also smell food cooking on the stove.

He wheeled himself further into the room. Daniel had been busy. Piles of bacon and eggs were lined up on the counter. Mechanical arms stretched out of the backsplash – stirring and flipping as they prepared another batch of food on the stovetop.

"What is this, Daniel?" Finn asked. "You know I prefer to make my own breakfast."

"Sir, it is October 3rd," Daniel replied.

"I know what day it is," Finn snapped. "Why is that significant?"

"Your children are scheduled to arrive in the next five minutes..." Daniel trailed off, the cloudy blue haze flashing.

"Correction, your son and his family have just pulled into the drive," the AI reported. "Shall I disable the building's security measures?"

Finn bit back a frustrated response. Daniel hadn't given him a warning yesterday evening or this morning. He sensed his son's – or more likely, his daughter's – manipulations behind this. Although to be fair, he had rescheduled the breakfast about a dozen times now. Apparently, Gracen and Julia had decided to take matters into their own hands.

"Fine, let them in. Also, set a reminder for me to overhaul your user permissions," Finn grumbled. He could immediately hear the muted grating sound of metal on metal as the AI released the reinforced shielding on the front door.

"Of course, sir. However, I have been instructed to inform you that your firewall also needs some work and that you are slipping in your old age," Daniel replied. For a moment, Finn almost thought he detected amusement in the AI's voice, but that couldn't have been possible. Not unless he had put it there.

Damn it. Definitely Julia, he thought.

Sighing, Finn wheeled himself over to the kitchen table. Daniel was already transforming the surface, the tabletop expanding and chairs emerging from the floor to accommodate the crowd that would soon be disturbing his home. He closed his eyes, willing himself to stay calm. He needed to keep up the act today. He was fine. Just *fine*.

He didn't have to wait long.

He heard the front door click open a few seconds later. It would take them approximately 60 seconds to walk from the front door to the kitchen. Even now, he could hear footsteps down the hallway.

"Hi, Dad," Gracen said.

Finn opened his eyes to see his son looking at him, failing badly at hiding his concern. His wife stepped into the room behind him, their two young children in tow. Finn did his best to plaster a smile on his wrinkled lips.

"Hey there, sport," he said, as his son stooped to give him a hug. "Sarah," he said with a smile as he greeted his daughter-in-law.

"Wow, have you two gotten bigger!" Finn said, eyeing

his grandchildren as he gave another round of hugs. Rachael would have loved to see them. She had always wanted grandkids. Just that brief thought caused the memory of his dream to return, and he had to bite back a grimace.

"Come on, gang. Get off Grandpa and let's get you something to eat," Sarah said, herding the kids over to the counter with an apologetic look at Finn.

She must have misinterpreted Finn's reaction – assuming the kids had hurt him or something. Damn it. He needed to keep it together. He rounded on his son, looking for a distraction. "What did you do to Daniel?" he asked.

Gracen looked a little nervous, biting at his lip. Sarah glanced over at him in confusion, but her attention was quickly refocused on heaping some food onto the kids' plates and finding them a place at the table. "Well, I just set an appointment for this morning," Gracen offered tentatively.

"Uh-huh. With no reminders," Finn continued dryly. "That seems a bit beyond your capabilities. I sense your sister's hand in this. Where is she, by the way?"

"Julia should be here shortly," Gracen replied cautiously. "She said she was caught in traffic."

"Managed to find a shortcut!" Finn's daughter said, poking her head into the room. Of course, Daniel hadn't announced her presence. Finn couldn't help but glare at the floating blue cloud that hovered in the corner of the room. The lack of reminders had been a minor annoyance, but this was another matter entirely. Julia had somehow circumvented all of the security protocols built into Daniel's systems.

"Hey, Dad," Julia said, giving him a peck on the cheek.

She pulled away, noting the sour look on his face. "What's wrong? Aren't you happy to see me?" He saw her brown eyes flash mischievously. Yet he could only see Rachael in her face. It was the hair and the eyes that got him every time.

"You've been messing with Daniel's programming again, haven't you?" Finn grumbled. "And it sounds like you roped your brother into it this time."

"Didn't have a choice after you removed my remote

access. Besides, I only made a few little tweaks here and there. Daniel needed a little more *personality*. Especially if he's your only companion in your self-imposed exile," Julia replied unapologetically, settling down into the chair beside him and kicking her feet up on the table.

Suddenly, Daniel's glib tone earlier made sense.

"I gave you two remote access to my network so that you could get in touch in case of an emergency," Finn reprimanded Julia. Although he was struggling to maintain his frustration. He was somewhat impressed. Even with a remote login, it would have been an undertaking to hack his system. Julia had gotten a lot better.

"Yeah, well, there was a *boring* emergency in here," she replied, arching an eyebrow.

"Here you go," Sarah said, depositing plates in front of the two and interrupting Finn's next barbed comment. The rest of the group had settled down around the table.

"So, what have you been up to lately?" Gracen asked his father, clearly trying to switch the subject. "Any cool projects or upgrades to the Fortress?" He asked this while gesturing at the house.

Finn grimaced, rubbing at his neck. "Nothing really. Just regular maintenance and a few upgrades around the *house*. Although, it sounds like I'm going to be spending some time running diagnostics on Daniel this afternoon," he added dryly, glancing at his daughter. He just received a grin in response.

"Huh. Well, one of your old colleagues at Cerillion contacted me the other day," Gracen offered. "Said something about having trouble getting in touch with you. He thought he had something that you might be interested in."

"I'm good," Finn replied curtly. He had blocked most public network access for a reason.

"You don't even know what it is. Besides, it could also be a good reason to get out of the house a little..." Gracen offered, trailing off as he saw his father's expression.

"I've got more than enough to keep me busy," Finn grumbled before shoving another forkful of food into his mouth.

His entire family looked at him skeptically. Even Sarah's expression indicated that she thought he was full of shit. This was precisely why he avoided these gatherings! They just had to go and try and help him, fix him, force him to move on. Next, they would probably tell him it wasn't his fault. Just a mechanical glitch. A bit of faulty wiring that had cascaded into a devastating accident.

But he couldn't forgive himself. He just couldn't.

After the accident, Finn had tried to stop the implementation of autonomous vehicles, but it was already too late. He had expected a public outcry, people screaming about the dangers of this new technology. However, he had vastly underestimated the power and influence that Cerillion Logistics' parent company exercised.

The company had spun the story so hard that it had made Finn dizzy. They had pointed out how the accident actually demonstrated how much *safer* the cars were. Very few people had died in the collision due to the additional safety features that had been built into each vehicle. The system – his system – had managed to protect nearly everyone. Besides, they couldn't prevent *all* accidents. And the system was still infinitely safer than manually operated vehicles.

For others, this had been a compelling argument, though the statistics rang hollow for Finn. His wife wasn't just a number on a page. His complaints and concerns had landed on deaf ears. The bean counters didn't want to hear about defects in a product that would make them billions.

He had turned to the government then, trying to stop the federal grant. Yet that had just been another dead end. He had been confronted by senators acting in lockstep. He'd received condolences and handshakes, but nothing more. A little bit of digging had revealed that the company was one of the largest political contributors in the country. No one in their right mind was going to speak out against them – it would have been political suicide.

In the face of this monstrous *thing* that he had created and its overwhelming momentum, he had been forced to give up. He was just one broken man who once again found himself along for the ride. The company had gently nudged him into early retirement, citing mental health issues. The younger executives looking for a rotation in the old guard had been more than happy to help speed that process along.

Disenchanted and disgusted with the world, Finn had sold his shares in the company, taken the golden parachute, and built this house – locking himself away behind several inches of reinforced steel and a nearly impenetrable firewall.

He was now a self-imposed hermit amid an ocean of people.

"I'm fine," Finn murmured, snapping back to attention. The others were all looking at him, concern lingering in their eyes.

"I'm not sure you even know what that word means anymore," Julia groused at him. She waved at the floating blue AI. "It's like talking to Daniel. You're saying the right words, but there's nothing behind it."

"Julia," her brother hissed. "Take it easy."

"Hey, it's the truth," she insisted. She glared at Gracen. "He's getting worse."

Finn didn't miss the way his son motioned at his wife to take the kids into the other room. Sarah spared Finn a sympathetic look as she left, mouthing the words, "I'm sorry." He just wished she would take *him* with her.

Julia turned to face her father. He saw determination there. She knew she was right, and she wasn't going to back down. Damn it, as much as it pained him to admit it, Rachael would have been proud. "When was the last time you left this cyber fortress you've built for yourself?" his daughter demanded.

"Umm..." Finn honestly couldn't remember. Maybe a few months? Everything he needed was delivered, and Daniel took care of practically everything else. There wasn't really any reason to leave.

"The answer is a year," Julia said. "I checked while I was rooting around Daniel's operating system. How about the last time you talked to someone besides Daniel?"

Shit, he thought to himself. Why couldn't he have dropped these brats on their heads when they were younger?

Two human vegetables hooked up to a ventilator would have been much easier to manage.

"Yeah, I thought so," Julia continued, taking his silence as an admission.

"This isn't how we talked about handling this," Gracen muttered.

"So, there was a plan behind this ambush and tirade?" Finn asked sourly. "Was this supposed to be an intervention or something?"

"Definitely *or something*," his son grumbled under his breath.

"Yeah, actually. That's exactly what it is. An intervention," Julia said, glaring at her brother. "And we also brought your stubborn, ungrateful ass a present. Let me just go grab it. I left it by the door." She hopped out of her chair and headed for the front entryway.

"Hey, I'm sorry about this," Gracen said to Finn as his sister left the room. "Honestly, I didn't think she was going to be so harsh."

Finn could only laugh at that. "You didn't expect your sister to speak her mind – bluntly and without reservation? Maybe I'm not the one that's out of touch." This earned him a small smile from Gracen.

Julia stepped back into the room, carrying a simple white box, and set it down in front of her father. Finn's eyes drifted across the surface and stopped on the simple logo on the front, a few words scrawled underneath. They were enough to make his stomach churn.

Cerillion Entertainment.

It seemed that George had created a new division. Go figure. The bastard had always been enterprising. Cerillion this and Cerillion that. Spreading his damn brand across so many industries that Finn had lost count. He wouldn't be surprised if the cunning asshole had developed a new way to deceive and corrupt young minds under the guise of "entertainment."

"No," Finn said.

"You don't even know what it is," Julia demanded.

"I know who made it," Finn retorted.

"You do. I also know you blame yourself for what happened with Mom – which is stupid by the way." She held up a hand to ward off his angry response. "But I'm not going to fight you on that. You think this company is the devil, and you signed on the dotted line. I get it.

"But after an old friend reached out to Gracen, I did some digging of my own. I've heard rumblings about this new VR hardware and this game they're calling Awaken Online. The beta and development lasted for years and underwent extensive testing. They passed with flying colors. Actually, the study results seem too perfect. Let's just say that something is off here," Julia said, her expression somber.

"That's kind of vague," Gracen added.

"Yeah, well, I may not have acquired all of this information through legal means," Julia replied, a grin tugging at her lips.

"You want me to look into a videogame?" Finn asked, skepticism coloring his voice.

His daughter turned back to Finn. "This isn't like any other game you've seen before. That's beside the point, though. I know you feel guilty and you hate these people. Well, maybe you can kill two birds with one stone," she offered, nudging the box toward him.

Julia leaned forward. "Check out this new product. Best case, you figure out some defect that may help some people. Worst case, you might find it entertaining – a way to leave this jail cell without *actually* leaving. Almost like a compromise!"

Julia's eyes twinkled, her eyes challenging. He remembered that look. He had seen a similar one only hours ago – in his dreams. "Unless you think you're not up to it?" she taunted.

Chapter 2 - Intrigued

After he had kicked his two ungrateful children out on their collective asses – or rather, they voluntarily chose to leave after eating all his food – Finn wheeled himself into his workshop on the second floor of his home. As he entered the room, his workstation came to life. It was a thing of beauty, a dozen or more floating blue screens creating a sphere of information detailing every aspect of the house. Finn palmed the wheels of his chair until he came to rest in the center of the globe.

His mind was still working through the conversation with his children. Well, calling it a *conversation* was a little misleading. It was more like a verbal lynching. And against a crippled old man at that!

"Sir, where would you like for me to place your package," Daniel said, interrupting Finn's dark thoughts. The house's AI had floated into the room. Beside him, a small all-purpose drone hovered in the air, the plain white box clutched in a mechanical claw.

"How about the garbage?" Finn grunted.

"I'm sorry, sir, but I cannot fulfill that order. Her Supreme Majesty Julia has commanded that I keep the package and protect it. I was also ordered to use force if you don't try it at least once," Daniel replied.

Finn could only stare at the AI. "What the f..." He trailed off, shaking his head.

Instead of yelling at Daniel, he decided to just fix this problem. "Pull up the system log for AI Controller Build G2.3," Finn snapped.

The screens around him shifted, showing various parts of Daniel's operating system. A display floated down in front of Finn and listed off the recent changes to the AI's operating system. As soon as Finn moved to scroll down the log, a notice suddenly appeared, flashing across every screen. It could have only been left by his daughter.

It was the heart emojis that gave it away.

> **System Notice**
>
> I buried the changes to Daniel's code pretty deep. I may have also made a few other alterations to slow you down. This should take even *you* a while to fix!
>
> Or... you could give the game a try. I'm asking for five minutes. As soon as the headset is connected to the public network and registers a login, a detailed list of my changes will be emailed to you directly. Since you will already be out on the scary interwebs, it shouldn't be too hard for you to actually check your email for once.
>
> XOXO
> Her Supreme Majesty Julia

Finn rubbed at his eyes. *Damn it.*

What was most frustrating was that he wasn't sure whether he was angry or impressed. An involuntary smile crept across his face as he looked back up at the notice. However, it abruptly faded as the drone floated into his field of view, still holding that stupid white box.

He supposed he had a decision to make.

He could spend who knows how long trying to ferret out every little change his daughter had made. There was no guaranteeing that she had stopped with Daniel. He was half expecting for there to be no hot water and his stove to stop working too.

Or he could capitulate. Although he didn't love the precedent that would set.

Yet some part of him also responded to the challenge. Julia had thrown down the gauntlet when they had been sitting in the kitchen. That look in her eye that challenged whether he was up to this. It was the same taunting implication the notice repeated now. Could he find whatever problem she had detected with this new VR technology and game?

If he was being honest with himself, he was intrigued.

Sort of. Grudgingly. Maybe he had been more bored than he realized.

"Okay, fine," Finn grumbled.

"Sir?" Daniel asked.

"Just hand me the damn box."

The AI promptly obliged, the drone dropping it into his hands. "Her Majesty instructed me to tell you that you have chosen wisely."

Finn was grinding his teeth together before he realized it.

Yet his fingers still pulled open the cardboard, revealing a plain black headset. It looked a bit like an old-fashioned motorcycle helmet. He lifted it out of the case, his curiosity overcoming his irritation as that familiar analytical part of his brain took over.

Before he just stuck it on his head, he needed to see what he was dealing with.

So, Finn proceeded to take the headset apart.

Daniel assisted him, using the drone to move a table closer and hand Finn various tools. He then plugged the individual components into his workstation and ran his own diagnostics, watching the data stream down the screens that hovered around him. Once he had the pieces all neatly laid out on the counter and had inspected each one carefully, he put it all back together. The process must have taken hours, although he barely noticed.

When he was finally finished, Finn was left looking at the same black helmet – which now had a few scratches and was now plugged into his workstation. He understood the basics of how this thing worked. Essentially, it was a combination of an incredibly powerful, portable MRI and a wireless router. The helmet sent electric impulses directly into the user's brain, stimulating clusters of neurons. Frankly, he was impressed.

And more importantly, intrigued. Although, this was the moment of truth.

Was he going to put the thing on?

His daughter's taunting expression flitted through his mind's eye once more, and her notice still flashed in the corner of his many screens. He would play her game. And then that would be the end of it.

However, he also hadn't forgotten Julia's cryptic warning.

"Daniel, please allow the IP address for this headset to access the public network and give me a secure connection. Initiate 'Fortress' security protocols. I don't want any outside traffic touching your system or the house. I also want all traffic and activity on the headset logged locally to my workstation. Got it?"

"Yes, sir," Daniel replied.

Finn grimaced and tugged the helmet over his head, his vision suddenly obscured by darkness. At the same time, he powered the headset on by tapping at the side of the helmet. A screen flickered into existence in front of him.

System Initializing
Scanning User... Please Wait.

"Oh, and Daniel?" Finn said, his voice sounding muted through the helmet.

"Yes, sir?" the AI replied.

"If you detect elevated vitals or irregular network activity, cut the connection immediately," Finn instructed.

"Of course, sir. With respect to your vitals, what..." The AI never got a chance to finish its question. Another prompt suddenly appeared in front of Finn.

System Initialized
Scanning complete. Initiating boot sequence. Welcome to Awaken Online!

Before Finn could question what was happening, the

notice abruptly disappeared, and blinding white light flooded his vision.

I really hope I don't regret this...

Chapter 3 - Fortunate

Finn opened his eyes and paused for a moment in shock. He was second-guessing whether he had really logged into the game because the scene around him certainly looked real. He could even feel a faint breeze on his skin.

He still sat in his wheelchair, but he was now inside what appeared to be a large tent, ruddy orange sunlight drifting in from the flap behind him. The leather walls buckled and shifted, and he could hear wind whistling across its surface. Puffs of what looked like sand drifted into the room, swirling and spiraling in the air. The interior of the tent had been adorned with antique furniture and intricate Persian rugs. Colorful tapestries and gossamer silks hung from the ceiling, drifting down into the room.

On the far end of the tent, Finn could see a small table. Not knowing what else to do, he wheeled his way forward. He quickly realized that whoever had designed this place hadn't been focused on making it wheelchair accessible. He kept getting caught in the thick carpets, and the hanging silks slapped him in the face as he passed.

By the time he had made it across the room, Finn was breathing heavily, and his arms burned from the effort. It was all rather astounding. The tactile feedback, movements, and physics of this environment were almost indistinguishable from the real world. Whoever had built this place had created something amazing.

Finn pushed his way up to the table, realizing that no chair lingered on his side. The only thing lying on the surface was a stack of large black rectangular cards, resting face-down. What captured his attention, however, was the tapestry that hung behind the table. It was nearly twelve feet wide, and its surface was painted with orange and red flames, showing what appeared to be a phoenix being consumed by fire.

"What is this?" Finn murmured to himself. He had played quite a few games back in college – although, admittedly that had been a few decades ago. Normally, he would expect a tutorial and some sort of validation of the game's controls and UI. Does the player know how to move around? Can he interact with the environment?

Maybe that's what this was?

"This is a beginning," a voice spoke up from behind the tapestry. A moment later, a woman stepped out from behind the cloth. Her skin was a dark olive, and she walked with an almost unnatural grace, as though she was simply floating. Her face and body were covered in thick purple silks, leaving only her eyes visible and making it difficult to place her age.

"Hello, Finn," she greeted him, bowing her head slightly. "I've been waiting for you."

For his part, Finn was just staring at this woman, dumbfounded. This couldn't be a player. As they'd discussed the game, his daughter had been clear that if he inspected someone, there should be a tag indicating whether he was speaking to another living person. Which meant this woman was an NPC, a digital puppet directed by the game's AI controller.

But damn did she look and sound authentic.

"Hello," Finn replied hesitantly, noticing the woman was still staring at him. "You have me at a disadvantage. You seem to know my name, but I don't know yours." He could only assume that Julia had registered his name when she set up his account.

"I have many names, but you may call me the Seer."

Finn chuckled, glancing around the tent. "That's rather on the nose isn't it? Should we call me the Cripple?"

The Seer cocked her head. "If that is how you choose to view yourself. In many ways, we *are* what we do. There is no shame in that." She leaned forward, peering at him and hummed to herself softly before asking him, "What is it that *you* do, Finn?"

Finn's smile faded. *What the hell?*

He coughed to cover his confusion. Maybe he needed to change the subject. "Okay. So, this is a *beginning*, but what does that entail exactly?"

An arched eyebrow – his attempt to dodge her

question hadn't gone unnoticed. This AI was on point. "I would like to give you a tarot reading, assuming you are *comfortable* having your fortune read," the Seer said, waving at the table.

"Sure," Finn replied.

He had always been a little skeptical of this sort "woo woo" magic stuff, but Rachael had loved it. She had dragged him into more than one fortune teller's shop when they traveled. Frankly, Finn felt that most fortune-tellers were simply con artists – preying on others' pain and passion. Hell, he could easily design an app that would perform a quick look-up on an individual's personal information. Maybe even embed the display in a crystal ball...

The strange woman took a seat on the other side of the table, grasping the cards with nimble fingers and shuffling them with practiced movements. As she worked, Finn noticed something moving the silks that wrapped her body. A moment later, a black python slithered across her shoulder and twisted around her neck, its tongue flicking at the air in Finn's direction.

"Ahh, don't mind Draco. He's harmless – mostly," the Seer murmured, following Finn's gaze. She paused her shuffling for a moment to run a finger across the snake's head.

Dynamic dialogue? Or perhaps this is all carefully scripted? Finn wondered. *The dialogue tree would have to be incredibly complex.*

She set down the deck on the side of the table. "Draw three cards and place them face-down on the table in front of you," the Seer instructed.

Finn followed her orders, plucking three cards from the deck. It might have been Finn's imagination, but it suddenly seemed like a heavy silence lingered in the tent. The tapestries and silks hung limply, the wind no longer rustling them in its wake. Something about this whole exchange felt... off. For a moment, he considered logging out.

Yet the Seer didn't give him a chance.

She flipped the left-most card.

Despite his reservations, Finn peered at the card curiously. An image was painted on the surface in filigreed gold, showing a man with a scepter sitting on a throne. Even more strangely, the throne seemed to be on fire, glimmering flames lapping at his feet.

"The Emperor," the Seer murmured.

"What does it mean?" Finn asked.

The woman peered at him above her silken mask. "It signifies that you are a father. Yet more than that, you seek control and authority – not just over your children but your own life. You hide yourself behind the trappings of routine, an emperor ruling over a solitary kingdom."

Finn could only stare back, his eyes wide. How the hell could this woman – or rather, this *program* – know that? His mind flailed for an answer. Maybe it was picking up information using his IP? Although, his IP should be bouncing across a few dozen VPN connections. He'd always gone to great lengths to hide his personal information.

Maybe Julia? But his daughter would know better than to give out details about him – despite how intrusive she had been lately.

Finn coughed uncomfortably, pulling at his collar. The room felt suddenly warmer than it had a moment ago.

"Do you wish to keep going?" the Seer asked, watching him.

No, not really, he thought, but then felt silly for being nervous about a video game. This was probably just a coincidence. Or maybe the AI was just stereotyping him. If the program had some basic information on Finn like his age, then guessing that he had children would be relatively easy. And it wouldn't be a longshot from there to guess that a crippled old man with adult children felt a little lonely.

"Yeah, go ahead," Finn finally replied.

She flipped over the second card, the material slapping against the table. This image showed a sun, tendrils of flame lancing away from the sphere. However, the scene was upside down, the sun's rays touching the ground at the top of the card.

"The Sun reversed," the Seer murmured, staring down at the image.

She looked back up at Finn, meeting his eyes. For a

moment, he thought he saw a flicker of flames in her pupils, but it vanished almost as quickly as it had appeared. Maybe he had imagined it – or maybe her eyes had just reflected one of the nearby lamps.

"Normally, the sun stands for power and positivity. However, when reversed, the card signifies a... *sadness*," the Seer said softly. "You are depressed. Confused. You lost something incredibly important to you. Something that turned your entire world upside down.

"Perhaps the same thing that drove you to seek control and routine," the strange woman observed, those dark eyes still staring at Finn.

Finn could feel his pulse pounding in his ears now. His other explanations had just gotten tossed out of the window. How the hell could this game know about his wife? The only explanation seemed to be that Julia had told the company, but that didn't make any sense at all. However, Finn froze as another thought occurred to him.

There was technically another explanation. He had carefully studied the VR headset. It would be theoretically possible for it to access other parts of his mind besides sensory input. The headset could possibly pull information from his hippocampus and cerebral cortex – reading his memories like some sort of organic hard drive.

That thought was terrifying.

"Uh, I'm not sure..." Finn began, a bead of sweat dripping down his forehead. He hesitated as he saw that the Seer was already turning over the last card.

The image was of a wand, flames curling away from the tip. However, this card was also upside down, the hand holding the wand stretching away from the top edge. As he stared at the image, Finn could have sworn that he saw the golden flames move, and the hand clench tighter on the hilt.

"Ace of Wands reversed," the Seer said. Her brow was furrowed in a frown now.

Finn once more had to resist the urge to simply log the hell out. Part of him was curious, though, not just at the technical marvel that he was witnessing, but at what this woman was about to tell him.

"You were once creative and passionate," the Seer murmured, staring at the card. There was no mistaking it now; flames danced in her eyes, and the card seemed to respond in turn, fire curling along the wand's shaft.

"You were given the gift of an agile mind, and you used your gifts to *create*, to build, to explore the unknown. You were inspired, and your life burned brightly, a blaze so great that it ignited passion in those around you."

Another frown creased the Seer's forehead. "Yet you lost your way. You lost your heart, bound yourself in the chains of monotony and routine, and fled from the world. And in the process, you lost your passion." As she spoke, the flames around the wand dwindled until they were only faint, dull embers.

The Seer raised her eyes to meet Finn's. It felt like the room had turned into an oven and sweat now freely dripped down his face and drenched the collar of his shirt. He couldn't look away from this woman, her eyes awash in flame and her python hissing at him. This had gone way past anything he had expected, and his thoughts swirled and spun chaotically.

"But this is not the end. Your fire has not yet been completely extinguished. You just need someone – or *something* – to fan it back to life. A purpose. A *passion*."

"What the hell is this?" Finn croaked. "Who are you? *What* are you?"

"As I said before, this is a beginning," the Seer murmured. "Or at least an offer of one.

"As for who I am, I am a god in this world. I am the deity of the flame, the burning fire that resides in the hearts of all men and women. I am that insatiable drive to strike out into the world. To explore. To build towering pyramids. I am the passion to reach for the sun, even if it might burn you. I give life *purpose* and *meaning*."

He had difficulty looking away from the Seer. She leaned forward, her eyes glowing softly. "And I have been waiting a long time for someone like you, Finn."

"What do you mean? What can I possibly offer you? This… this isn't even real," Finn said, confused. How had a game been waiting for him?

The woman chuckled softly. "What does it mean to be real? If you can taste, touch, and see something, is it not real? Can you not feel the heat on your skin? Have the cards not read your past, present, and future? You believe this is merely a technological marvel, but what if you dared to look past that?"

Finn's eyes widened. This woman – this god – was acknowledging that this was a simulation? What the hell was going on here?

"Yes, you are outside your comfort zone. You cannot control this," the Seer murmured. "You cannot explain it." Her eyes blazing. "But isn't that *exciting*? Isn't some part of you intrigued? Compelled to move forward despite the risk?"

"You just read my mind," Finn croaked in surprise, realizing he hadn't been speaking. That was the only remaining evidence he needed. The hardware must be accessing both his short and long-term memory.

"Is that so hard for you to believe?" the Seer replied calmly. "You already figured out the rules of this world a few moments ago. Much, much more quickly than most, I might add. It is that intellect that I need – that hungering curiosity."

The Seer rose from her seat, pacing around the table to stand beside Finn. "Now you face a choice. You can go back to your self-imposed prison and shout about the evils of this world, although I suspect few will listen. You can live out the rest of your years watching your own flame flicker and die.

"Or, you can take a chance at a new beginning. I can offer you a new world to explore and new challenges to overcome. I can give you the opportunity to build and to create again, to let your passion take hold of you like it once did."

She waved her hand, and the silks hanging about the room blew aside as a hot wind swept through the room. A platform rose from the center of the tent, and atop its surface a bright flame ignited from thin air, growing and expanding until it created a roaring inferno, the center of the fire glowing almost white.

"You need only take the first step. A leap of faith," the Seer said, waving at the flames. "Simply step into the flames."

Her voice echoed through the tent as she turned to look back at him.

Finn stared at the fire. His mind was wheeling. Despite the risks that this hardware posed and the fact that he knew this wasn't real, he felt drawn to the flames. What the Seer promised resonated with something deep inside himself, some secret yearning he had buried under a mountain of guilt and pain.

He stared at the platform, realizing that his wheelchair couldn't make the climb. Even as that thought crossed his mind, he thought back to his wife – to his dream. If he accepted the Seer's challenge, would he be betraying Rachael? He couldn't bear the thought of letting her go. He just couldn't…

"You can," the Seer whispered, suddenly standing beside him. Her hand rested on his shoulder, her skin almost uncomfortably warm. "Is this the man that your wife married, mired in his own guilt and self-doubt. Would she have wanted *this* for you?"

Finn shook his head. He didn't want to admit it, but he knew what Rachael would have chosen for him – the same thing her daughter had demanded when she tricked him into entering this game.

Even so, he couldn't walk, couldn't stand up and enter those flames.

"As I said before, you *are* what you do. Do you really think that your condition in your world has any bearing on this one?" the Seer whispered in his ear.

Finn looked at her again. "What are you saying?"

"I am saying that in this world, your only limitation is yourself."

Finn's eyes drifted down to his legs; his brow furrowed in confusion. He ran his fingers across his thighs, and at first, he felt nothing. But then he could sense a small pressure. His eyes widened in shock, and he tried to move his toes – a faint wiggle. He tried to flex his calves next, and the muscles twitched.

The Seer offered him a hand. "Do it. Take the leap," she hissed, her voice more demanding now.

His heart was racing, Finn's breath coming in frantic gasps, and sweat was streaming down his face. Without giving himself time to back out, Finn grabbed her hand and surged to his feet all at once. He stumbled awkwardly, unaccustomed to standing after so long in the chair. Yet he didn't fall.

The Seer stared at him, her eyes triumphant. "Good," she purred. Her fingers stroked Finn's wrist, leaving a burning trail in their wake. Yet she didn't allow him to focus on that, placing another hand against his face and focusing his gaze on her. "Now you need only enter the flames."

Finn looked at the inferno, taking a shambling step forward.

Then another.

And another.

The roaring fire loomed in front of him. The heat was an almost-palpable thing, and the edges of his clothes began to singe, sending streamers of smoke in the air. Sweat streamed down his skin and burned his eyes. Yet he knew he couldn't die – not really – not in this place.

He looked behind him and saw the Seer watching him with flaming eyes, the phoenix tapestry hovering behind her. The image on the cloth moved, the fires now consuming the creature as it let out a silent, desperate scream.

Should I really do this?

Rachael's face flashed through Finn's mind then, that familiar challenging expression taunting him. That twinkle in her eye. He knew what she would say right now. She would have already pushed his stubborn, stupid ass into the flames.

So, Finn took the final step.

The fire surrounded him – swirling and spinning in a dizzying cascade of orange and red. He felt them lap at his clothes and skin, yet he didn't feel any pain. Instead, a tingling, hot sensation washed over him. Then the heat entered his mouth and eyes, the warmth spreading through his limbs until he felt like he was standing in the center of a volcano.

A translucent blue notification crashed down in front of him, framed by the roaring inferno. The text seemed to shift and swim across the window, only resolving into focus when Finn tried to read the prompt.

System Notice
Life has not treated you kindly. It has taken your wife, your life, and your passion from you. But you have been given a chance to be reborn – a chance to start over. Instead of shying away from this challenge, you took a leap of faith. For that, you will be rewarded! You have become a god's chosen, her avatar in this new world. Your only direction is to follow your passion. To burn so brightly that the entire world will turn to watch the blaze, staring in awe at the flames. <div align="center">You have been awarded +100 Fame You have been awarded +5 to Willpower You have been awarded +5 to Intelligence You have been awarded +2 to Endurance You have been awarded +2 to Strength You have been awarded +2 to Dexterity Path of Flame Unlocked Attention of the Seer</div>

This notification soon faded from view, leaving only roaring fire lingering around Finn. Amid this inferno, he heard the Seer's voice. "I will give you one last gift, Finn. In return for your bravery, I will bend the rules a bit for your benefit.

"Enjoy your new life and live it to the fullest."

And then there were only the flames.

Chapter 4 - Weighed

The roaring fires abruptly cleared, and Finn found himself standing in an open courtyard. He felt momentarily disoriented, stumbling slightly and barely managing to grab hold of something to steady himself.

"Hey, watch it, buddy!"

Finn looked up to discover that the "something" had been another person's shoulder. For a second, he was impressed by how solid it felt. The tactile feedback was more muted, perhaps indicating that pain would be as well. But he could still feel the coarse fibers of the man's shirt. Although, Finn suddenly realized he had been awkwardly groping the guy's shoulder for an uncomfortably long time – a point driven home by the man's confused stare.

"Uh, sorry about that," Finn muttered. "Just felt sort of disoriented for a second."

The other guy's expression softened. "No worries. The transition from that weird tutorial to here was a bit... unexpected."

Finn cocked his head. So, this was another player?

However, that question suddenly fled his mind as he went to remove his hand. Finn stopped short, staring at the limb as though it belonged to someone else. It looked different. The wrinkles had smoothed away and the age spots had disappeared. These weren't the hands of a teenager, but they also weren't the gnarled skin of some old fart either.

With cautious fingers, Finn peeled back at the loose beige robes that now wrapped his frame, noticing that his arms were in similar shape.

Was this what the Seer meant by a gift? Did she give me a new body? Or perhaps my own body, but younger? Finn wondered. He'd have to put a pin in that question until he found a mirror.

Even more strangely, Finn noticed a pattern had been tattooed across the top of his right hand, stretching upward across his wrist. There were three tarot cards and a snake wrapping between and around them. The cards showed the same images as the reading in the Seer's tent. The Emperor. The Sun Reversed. Ace of Wands Reversed. He could also vaguely recall that this was where the Seer's fingers had lingered before he stepped into the flames.

A rueful smile tugged at Finn's lips. And here he had thought his days of waking up in a strange place with a random tattoo were far behind him.

Finn's attention shifted back to the courtyard, trying to get a sense of where the hell the fire goddess had teleported him. The area was a rounded enclosure, the walls made of thick clay bricks. It was also hot, but the air wasn't heavy with moisture. It was a dry heat – like Finn was standing in an oven. Only a faint breeze provided some relief, the occasional gust shifting the sand that coated the courtyard.

Finn glanced upward, holding up a hand to blot out the harsh sunlight. There was no roof covering the courtyard, and the sun was just barely cresting the top of the walls that surrounded them. Beyond that, Finn could make out spiraling towers and other structures that loomed around the enclosure – a city of some sort then.

The area was also loud. The courtyard had been packed full of other players, multi-colored rifts tearing open frequently to deposit more confused-looking men and women – all robed in the same drab wraps and sandals. They milled about, talking to each other, and murmuring in confusion. Finn could certainly sympathize. This was an abrupt start to the game.

Just as Finn was wondering what the hell they were supposed to be doing here, a voice spoke up. "Hail, travelers, and welcome to Lahab!"

Finn turned to find an austere man dressed in rich silks addressing the crowd. He stood on a small podium near the back of the enclosure. Intricate tattoos adorned his neck and the bare patches of skin that flashed from beneath his robes. However, he didn't seem to be armed. He was flanked on either side by large men wearing more-practical armor. Massive curved swords were strapped to their backs, and they wore thick mail and metal helmets.

So, this seems like an NPC, Finn thought to himself.

Which must mean that they referred to players as "travelers" here. Clever touch.

"My name is Nefreet, and it is part of my duties to welcome newcomers to our great city," the man continued, his voice booming across the courtyard.

"I am sure you all are confused and have many questions. I assure you that they will be answered in good time. For now, you will need to be tested. In a moment, the doors beside me will open. Please form orderly lines. This will make the sorting process faster." Finn could indeed see that there were large wooden doors installed on either side of the platform. However, none of the players moved to form lines.

"What do you mean by testing?" someone shouted from the crowd.

The man nodded, his expression remaining stoic. "All newcomers to Lahab are tested for their magical aptitude. Those that are shown to have a high affinity are given the privilege of attending our esteemed Mage Guild. All others may pass freely into the city itself."

"I'm guessing that *privilege* isn't optional," a young man beside Finn muttered. The other traveler looked like he couldn't have been older than 20 – maybe even still in high school, with a mop of brown hair and a thin frame.

"What do you mean?" Finn asked.

The young man pointed at the walls ringing the enclosure. "Awful lot of armed guards in this welcome committee." Finn's eyes widened as he suddenly noticed the soldiers ringing the enclosure. He had missed that before. The soldiers were armed with bows, and a few wore robes and held staves. Mages perhaps?

Someone else must have picked up on the same thing because another shout rang out. "And what if we decide not to join this Mage Guild or don't want to be tested?"

Nefreet crossed his arms. "That would be truly unfortunate. Refusal will result in the purge of a traveler's magical ability and immediate exile from Lahab. I suspect any foolish enough to choose this path will not last long among the sands." A surprised murmur rippled across the crowd of players.

"That's bullshit!" someone shouted. "So, we have to join this guild?"

"Or maybe we can just leave!" another shouted. This time, the angry noise came from a traveler near Finn. He was a large, surly-looking man that paced a few steps toward the podium, stabbing a finger at the air. "There are a hundred of us and only a handful of you." More angry murmurs came from the crowd.

"That would be unwise," Nefreet said, unperturbed by the commotion.

"Wow, so this is going to end badly," the young man beside Finn murmured. "We might want to step back a bit."

Finn was quick to agree, and the pair backed against a nearby wall as they watched the angry traveler stalk forward toward Nefreet. "Screw you, you wannabe Jafar! I don't need any of your mystical Aladdin bullshit," the player shouted. "Let me the hell out of here!"

Nefreet barely moved, a subtle twitch of his fingers.

That was the only warning.

Nearly a dozen arrows struck the player at once, a belated hum filling the air. The player stood still for a fraction of a second, wavering on his feet before falling forward and hitting the ground with a dull thump. Blood leaked from the dozen puncture wounds, swiftly pooling in the hot sand. His body rested only a few feet away, his lifeless eyes now staring blankly at Finn.

"Holy shit," Finn whispered. This might be a game, but it looked pretty damn real. That player was dead – definitely dead. He shared a look with the young man beside him, seeing the same shock reflected on his face.

The crowd seemed to have a similar reaction. A sudden silence descended over the courtyard. Into this stillness, Nefreet inserted a single calm question. "Are there any further objections?"

More silence.

"In that case, please form orderly lines in front of each door."

The players were now quick to move into position.

Finn soon found himself standing in line with the young man. "Thanks for the quick thinking," he said quietly.

"No problem," the kid replied before sticking out a hand in greeting. "Name's Kyyle Wibble. That's Kyyle with two 'Y's,' thank you very much."

Finn couldn't help the involuntary chuckle that bubbled to his lips. "Did your parents lose a bet or something?"

Kyyle matched his smile. "I get that a lot. And the answer is yeah, sort of. This is what I get for having trolls for parents, I guess."

"No kidding. Well, I'm Finn. Nice to meet you," Finn said.

He hesitated a moment, his eyes skimming back to the nearby corpse. "So, uh, this might seem like a dumb question, but is this a typical way to start a game nowadays? It's been at least a few decades since I played an RPG, but this seems *intense*..." Finn trailed off. No one had bothered to come clean up the body. Although, with the way the travelers kept glancing at it furtively, Finn suspected Nefreet intended to leave it there as an example.

"A few decades?" Kyyle replied with an arched eyebrow. "You're like what? Maybe forty? Been living under a rock or something?"

Finn had to do a double-take at that. He had forgotten about the Seer's parting "gift" and how strange his hands and arms had looked. However, he better start acting his age – or his appearance, he supposed. So, Finn just shrugged and gave Kyyle a lopsided grin in return. "Sorry, I'm just a little thrown off, by... you know," he offered, gesturing at the corpse.

Kyyle seemed to accept this, grimacing slightly. "Understandable."

The young man let out a sigh. "But to answer your question, not really? AO is supposed to be completely different than any other game on the market. Most start off with a bit of hand-holding and then let you choose your own path. *Open world* and *sandbox* are always the buzzwords."

Kyyle chuckled softly. "Clearly, they went in a different direction here – as though the tutorial or introduction or whatever you want to call it didn't already make that clear," he added with a trace of sarcasm.

Finn cocked his head. "Did you start in a tent too? A tarot reading?"

Kyyle gave him a puzzled look. "Nope. It was weird. Started in some sort of grass field," he replied, shaking his head. His eyes were distant.

Then Kyyle seemed to shake himself out of it, glancing at Finn. "It was kind of intense, and I'm not sure I want to talk about it. Let's just leave it at that."

Okay, so the tutorial is individually tailored, Finn thought to himself. That was impressive. Actually, it was rather frightening. The processing power that would require... Plus, it was clear that the game was picking up on their memories, which meant that the introductions could be rather *impactful*. The game's AI must be incredible. What he wouldn't give to dig into the code behind the game's AI controller.

Finn shook his head, his eyes skimming back to the dead player. "Why would people put up with this, though? Like why not just start over and make a new character?" Hell, he was half-tempted himself.

When Finn looked up, he saw that Kyyle was staring at him in confusion. "Seriously, are you a hermit or something? Didn't you read any of the character creation rules? You get one character and can't reroll another for thirty days.

"In other words, we're stuck here. At least, if we want to keep playing," Kyyle continued. Despite the anxious expressions of the nearby players, a small smile crept across the young man's face. "Sort of exciting, isn't it? Knowing that one fuck-up might completely alter your path through the game?"

Finn wasn't sure how to respond to that. He supposed Kyyle had a point. Real stakes made their decisions more meaningful. Although, it also meant he might end up facedown, with a dozen arrows in his back and his blood pooling on the sand. Not to mention whatever that traveler would face when he eventually respawned.

They stepped forward again. The line was moving quickly. Whatever this test entailed, it must be fast.

"So, if I 'pass' this test—" Finn began.

"Then it looks you're heading to the Mage Guild," Kyyle said with a shrug. "Unless you prefer whatever exile looks like or you find a way to leave or escape. My guess is that both of those options are going to suck, though."

Finn didn't have much longer to ponder on this. The door now loomed in front of them. The portal swung open, and the guards gestured at Kyyle. "Speak of the devil. Looks like it's my turn!" Kyyle murmured.

As the young man passed through, he spared Finn one last look. "Good luck, man. See you on the other side! Maybe..."

Then the doors slammed shut, and Kyyle was gone.

For some reason, Finn felt nervous, which just made him feel like an idiot.

This was a simulation. He *knew* that. These guards weren't real, and neither was the sand that blew across the courtyard. This was all just strings of code pieced together on a server somewhere. Yet that argument rang hollow as he felt the warmth of the sun on his skin, and he stepped up to take his place in front of the doors on completely functional legs.

Finn eyed the wooden doorway that loomed in front of him. It was also clear that his choices in this game mattered and he'd likely only get one shot.

Not unlike real life, he thought grudgingly.

"Next," the guard barked, breaking Finn out of his trance.

The portal opened with the creak of wood.

Finn didn't give himself time to chicken out. He stepped forward quickly, slipping through the doorway and into the small chamber on the other side. He could feel his pulse hammering in his chest, and his palms were sweaty. The doors crashed shut behind Finn with a bang, causing him to jump in surprise.

A single man stood in the small, dark room. The stranger wore dark robes and held a plain wooden staff in one hand. Like Nefreet, his skin was a dark olive, and he sported tattoos on his arms and neck, but Finn didn't understand their significance – if any. His guess was that this man was a mage of some sort – he certainly looked the part – even though he had yet to see anyone cast a spell.

The man gestured at Finn to approach a column in the center of the room. A plain crystal, about the size of a basketball, rested atop the pillar. The surface was polished to a mirror-like shine, and the crystal was almost entirely translucent.

"Please place your hand on the crystal," the man said calmly. "We will be testing for the type and strength of your affinity."

Which is about as clear as mud, Finn thought. *What's an affinity?*

However, Finn did as he was told, approaching the column. As his hand neared the crystal, he noticed orange and red tendrils of energy arc between his palm and the glassy surface. He jerked backward in surprise, although he had felt no pain.

He glanced at the robed man. "Is that normal?"

The man's stoic expression never wavered, but Finn noticed his eyes skim briefly to the strange tattoo on Finn's right hand. For a fraction of a second, Finn thought he saw the man's forehead wrinkle in confusion. "Yes. Now, please touch the crystal."

Finn didn't believe him, but the image of the dead player still lingered in his mind. Best to do as he was told, at least until he learned more about this place.

Moving quickly, he pressed his palm firmly against the crystal.

As soon as his hand touched the surface, darkness encroached on the corners of Finn's vision, growing and expanding until the room faded away.

In an instant, the darkness abruptly receded, and Finn was suddenly standing in a grassy field, a rustic barn lingering nearby. He blinked rapidly, feeling disoriented yet again. The sun shone overhead, and billowing clouds drifted through the air. Yet he was forced to do a double-take as he realized that the surface of the barn was distorted and blurry, as though he was suddenly near-sighted. The building wouldn't quite come into focus.

Yet the scene looked so familiar...

Suddenly, it clicked, a heavy feeling settling in Finn's stomach – a mixture of dread, hope, and longing that felt at once both exquisitely painful and incredible.

Rachael had so desperately wanted a country wedding. It had taken them weeks to find the right dilapidated barn, visiting at least a dozen venues – all located in the middle of nowhere, of course. He had insisted at the time that it was pointless; that he would only have eyes for her when the moment came. They could have gotten married anywhere as far as he was concerned. She had just rolled her eyes and given him an exasperated look.

Finn turned, already knowing what he would see.

Yet his mind still went blank as he took in what lay before him.

His wife Rachael stood there, dressed in her wedding gown, her veil thrown back to reveal her shining eyes. She stared at him as though he was the only person in the universe.

Finn remembered this day. Remembered this look. He could barely make out the pastor and the crowd. Just like the barn, they were nothing more than blurry, half-formed images – splashes of colors in his peripheral vision.

Which meant he had been right.

He had only been able to focus on Rachael that day.

Finn reached for her, but even as he moved, orange and red flickered in the corner of his vision. He glanced to the side and saw fire blooming in the distance, growing at an incredible pace. Within mere seconds, the blaze had swept across the field. Then it was consuming the barn and threatened to overwhelm the pair in a raging inferno.

Finn tried to scream, tried to move, but no sound spilled from his lips. The heat pushed at him like a tangible force, and his limbs wouldn't respond. There was only his wife's shining eyes, framed by roaring flame.

Then the fire consumed them both.

Finn blinked.

He was back in the small room. His heart was pounding in his ears, and he tasted the copper tang of blood. Had he bitten his tongue?

That was just a memory – nothing more, he told himself. Yet his mind was struggling to accept that. To make matters worse, the world was still awash in red and orange. He looked down and realized that it was the crystal. It shone so brightly that it lit the entire room, a fire raging within its core.

"Holy shit," Finn said softly.

He felt a hand tug at his arm, and he looked up. The other man pulled him away from the crystal, the fire dwindling as soon as Finn's hand left the stone. The mage's stoic expression had cracked. He looked worried. Terrified, really.

"What is this?" Finn asked in confusion. "Do I have an affinity?"

The man simply stared at him, incredulously. "Yes. Fire," he said in a clipped voice. He chewed on the inside of his cheek, glancing at the door on the other side of the room. Someone thumped the wood, perhaps a signal to ask whether Finn was ready to move on.

"We don't have much time," the man said, glancing back at Finn. "My name is Abbad. Speak to me once you have gone through the induction ceremony. Tell no one what happened here. Your life depends on it."

Before Finn could respond, a translucent blue prompt appeared in front of him.

New Quest: Curious Capabilities
While undergoing the test of your affinity, something went wrong. The test conjured a powerful memory, and you clearly alarmed the test administrator. Abbad instructed you to keep quiet and approach him once you are inducted into the Mage Guild. He might be able to provide more answers then. **Difficulty:** B **Success:** Find a discreet moment to speak with Abbad. **Failure:** Fail to talk to Abbad, get kicked out of the guild, or die. Or possibly all of the above. There are no "save points" here, buddy. **Reward:** More information on your magical affinity and the results of your test.

Finn opened his mouth, but he didn't get a chance to ask any more questions. Abbad banged on the door once, and it suddenly creaked open. A group of robed men and women stood on the other side, flanked by more mailed guards. The group of mages looked to Abbad as though expecting something.

"Fire affinity, novice rank," Abbad reported, bowing his head and gesturing to Finn.

The group of robed men and women returned the gesture.

"Please come with us," a woman spoke up, addressing Finn.

He obliged, numbly stepping out of the room and his mind still racing. He spared one last look behind him as the doors began to close, meeting Abbad's eyes. He saw concern and fear lingering there, despite the man's attempt to control his expression.

Then the doors slammed shut.

Chapter 5 - Educated

Finn had been in a trance since the strange test. A robed woman silently led him through a series of passages like he was some sort of zombie. His thoughts kept returning to the crystal and the memory of Rachael. He felt conflicted – at war with himself.

Part of him wanted to run back to that testing room. To see her again, just one more time – even though he knew it wasn't real. She was still dead.

He would only be torturing himself.

And then there was the anger.

That whole vision felt like a violation. Like the game was plumbing the depths of his soul. Hell, he didn't even like having his personal information online, much less some sort of program spelunking through his brain. He resolved that this would be the last time he let the game access his memories – at least if he had any control over it.

Then there had been the blazing inferno that burned inside the crystal and the fear in Abbad's eyes. He couldn't explain the man's reaction, or his hastily whispered instructions. What had Finn done wrong? Was he at risk here? If that crystal was intended to measure the intensity of his affinity – whatever that was – then was it strong? If that was a weak reaction, he could only imagine that a "strong" affinity would have caused the damn crystal to explode. So it seemed likely that Abbad had downplayed the instructions he gave the guards.

Finn was also left feeling... intrigued, his curiosity pulling him forward despite his concerns.

"Well, long time no see!"

Finn looked up sharply to find Kyyle grinning at him. At some point, the robed woman had dropped him off. He now stood in a large rectangular room, with globes of light resting on braziers placed at even intervals along the walls. There were at least a few dozen other players milling about the room, their feet scuffing against the bare stone floor. Most spared only a brief glance at Finn as he entered, speaking to one another in hushed voices.

"Hey, Kyyle," Finn said, realizing that he hadn't replied to the young man.

"I take it the test was a little traumatic?" Kyyle asked, arching an eyebrow.

"I guess you could say that," Finn grumbled. "This damn game..."

This earned him a chuckle from the young man. "I'm with you there, but there's still something fascinating about it. I mean, you haven't logged out yet, right?"

Finn had to grudgingly admit that Kyyle had a point. He could have just logged out. He still *could*. But he had never seriously considered it, despite his reservations about how the game was accessing his memories. He still remembered the Seer's offer: a new life – a new passion. Having tasted just a bit of this world, he was already left wanting more.

"Anyway, what were your results? I ended up with earth and novice rank. Although, I have no clue what that means," Kyyle offered with a shrug.

"Fire affinity and novice," Finn replied, omitting the part where the test administrator had looked spooked, and he had lit up the crystal like a Christmas tree. Although, technically, it was more like someone had drenched the tree in lighter fluid and then lit a match.

"So—" Kyyle began but was cut off abruptly as a familiar voice echoed through the chamber.

"Let me have your attention please."

They turned to find Nefreet addressing the group of travelers. This time, he was unaccompanied by any guards. He murmured something under his breath, his hands winding rapidly through a series of intricate gestures. As he finished, the stone floor in the center of the room turned to liquid, pooling and swirling. The players backed away quickly, hovering along the walls. Thick blobs of liquid drifted up into the air and hardened swiftly into dense rock. Only moments later, there were suddenly neat rows of stone benches.

"Please take a seat," Nefreet ordered, his face impassive.

Finn and Kyyle shared a look before finding a spot in the back row. They were both of one mind. Better not to draw attention to themselves, at least until they figured out how this place worked. The memory of that surly player's arrow-studded corpse was still fresh in their minds. Finn was struggling to forget the way the man's dead eyes had stared at him vacantly.

Nefreet waited patiently until all of the players were sitting before addressing them once more. "I imagine you all have many questions. I hope to provide some clarity before you begin your time at the Mage Guild.

"First, some introductions. I am the guild's headmaster," Nefreet explained, placing a hand to his chest. "The courtyard you first entered and this entire complex are part of our guild hall. Please note that you may not leave the compound and enter Lahab until you have graduated from our distinguished program. Anyone attempting to violate this restriction shall have their mana purged and shall be banished into the sands."

He let that explanation sink in before continuing, "You may be asking yourself why travelers first arrive in the Mage Guild and why they are required to undergo testing. The short answer is that mages are dangerous. They wield extreme power over the elements as well as over darkness and light. Even an untrained mage – in a moment of instinct or fear – can cause incredible devastation.

"More than a century ago, the former Emir decreed that everyone in Lahab and the surrounding territories would be tested for magic. Those that demonstrate a natural proclivity for the four elemental affinities are required to attend the Mage Guild – to be properly trained and instructed in the use of their abilities. Those of you that graduate will also be given an opportunity to continue as members of the guild. The most exceptional among you may even be offered a place working with the Emir himself."

A hand shot in the air from the front row, a petite young woman with auburn hair accompanying the limb. Her back was rigid, and her arm held at a perfect 90-degree angle.

"Ugh, I think we found the class kiss-ass already,"

Kyyle muttered under his breath. "Some things never change."

Finn chuckled quietly until he noted Nefreet's eyes skim across them. He quickly covered himself with a cough, but the headmaster didn't look convinced.

Nefreet nodded toward the girl.

"Who is the Emir exactly?" she asked.

"The leader of our great city. Lahab is ruled by the Emir and his royal army. Beneath him are the three guilds, the Mage Guild, Merchant Guild, and Fighter Guild. These groups are charged with governing various aspects of the city."

Another hand rose – lazier this time. It belonged to a hulking man who must have been in his early thirties. He leaned forward as he spoke, "You mentioned training us? And something about graduating? So, this is basically a school?"

"Of sorts," Nefreet answered calmly. "However, you may find the *curriculum* rather grueling compared to your world. Travelers before you have voiced several… complaints."

Oh great, Finn thought to himself, remembering Abbad's concerned expression.

"We will provide classes and instruction on the use of your gifts," Nefreet explained. "Since you are novices, you will be required to attend generalized instruction before moving into more specific topics. Your first objective will be to master the art of summoning your mana and basic spellcasting."

The burly man opened his mouth to ask another question, but Nefreet raised a staying hand. "This may sound normal to you. However, it is the Emir's opinion that competition breeds success. With this in mind, you will also be competing directly with your peers. All students that attend the guild are required to participate in the duels, a weekly gauntlet where you will fight against other students."

Nefreet's gaze swept across the room, his expression impassive.

"For travelers such as yourself, these fights are to the

death."

An uncomfortable silence accompanied this statement.

"The matches will be scored. The lowest 10% of our students are regularly culled at the end of each month," Nefreet explained. No one in the room bothered to ask what it meant to "cull" a player. They could guess from the headmaster's tone. Purging their mana and exile seemed likely – or at least that seemed like Nefreet's go-to punishment.

A hushed silence had now descended over the room, and the players were eyeing each other – their expressions ranging between worry and curiosity. Nefreet had just explained that they would be actively trying to kill each other soon. Some of the other players, such as the large guy that had raised his hand, were openly sizing up the others. He looked somewhat excited at the prospect.

Finn was more hesitant. He wasn't against the idea of PVP. He had played some old-school MMOs, albeit a long time ago. However, AO had been incredibly realistic so far, and he suspected that killing someone in this game would be a different experience. It was one thing to press a button and stab a poorly textured character model, but quite another to feel your enemy's blood trickle between your fingers.

The competitive nature of the duels also had other implications. His classmates weren't "friends" or "teammates." They were potential enemies. Which meant it would be essential to play information regarding his abilities close to the chest. Those details could easily give Finn's opponents an edge.

Nefreet coughed lightly to clear his throat. "I see that you all understand. Although, I note a few concerned expressions. Some of you may be happy to learn that as novices, you will be given two weeks to train before you will be entered into the duels. More details will be revealed then."

As Nefreet finished speaking, another translucent notification popped up in front of Finn, glowing with a soft blue light.

> **New Quest: Cramming**
>
> You have been forcibly inducted into the Mage Guild in Lahab. As part of your training, the headmaster has explained that you will be pitted against the other students in some sort of weekly deathmatch and the poor-performers will be "culled" – talk about a *forced curve*! You have two weeks to prepare, so you better study hard!
>
> **Difficulty:** B
> **Success:** Learn the basics of spellcasting.
> **Failure:** Fail to learn the basics of spellcasting.
> **Reward:** Umm... hopefully you won't get frozen or incinerated by the other students?

Finn snorted softly. It seemed the game's AI had a sense of humor at least. A glance around the room confirmed that the other players looked distracted, their eyes focusing on something he couldn't see. Presumably, they had seen a similar prompt.

"Moving along, I expect you will find your classes similarly grueling," Nefreet continued, oblivious to the students' distraction. "You are travelers. You cannot die – at least not truly. Therefore, we are permitted to exercise more extreme measures to train your minds and harden your bodies to the rigors of spellcasting.

"I suggest you embrace the faculty's instructions and use this initial time wisely," Nefreet said, his voice echoing slightly through the room. "Are there any questions?"

A heavy silence lingered in the air, none of the players – now students – quite daring to breathe. It was clear that they had two weeks before they would be pitted against one another in a duel to the death. Oh, and the headmaster seemed to imply that their teachers would have no compunction about killing or maiming them in the meantime.

Fucking perfect.

What is it with this game? Finn wondered, not for the first time. It seemed to go out of its way to avoid the sort of hand-holding that was common in other games. He *should* be upset. Yet he couldn't help but wonder what it would be like to fling spells around. He was also curious about how he would fare against his classmates. Once upon a time, he had been rather competitive.

"Well, it looks like we can move on then," Nefreet said, waving at the nearby doorway. "The first step will be for you to learn Veridian, the language of mages. Since time is of the essence, we will expedite this process."

Finn's fingers clenched on the edge of the stone bench as he saw Abbad step forward into the room, the stoic man moving to stand beside Nefreet. Although, if Abbad noticed Finn, he made absolutely no sign, staying silent with his arms crossed and his head bowed.

Nefreet gestured at the class suck-up in the front row. She rose and stepped forward, although less enthusiastically this time. As she approached Abbad, he raised a hand and placed two fingers to her temple. She flinched slightly like she wanted to back away, but the girl managed to stay still. Finn could see a flicker of energy pass through the mage's fingers, and her eyes widened in surprise. Although nothing else seemed to happen.

Then Abbad offered his palm face-up. The girl placed her left hand in his, and the man tugged what appeared to be a stylus from beneath his robes. He ran the instrument across the girl's forearm, leaving a dark tattoo in its wake.

As Abbad backed away, Nefreet gestured toward the nearby doorway again. "Once you have learned the language and been given your induction mark, you may leave. You will be provided with a brief respite to become familiar with the school. Your first class will begin tomorrow morning."

The girl stumbled out of the room, muttering to herself, and her eyes looked distant and confused. Then Nefreet gestured at another student. Finn's thoughts were clouded as he watched each student repeat the same process. The tattoo didn't bother him, but the language was another matter. After his experience with the Seer and the testing crystal, he could only assume that Abbad was manipulating each person's memory, basically dumping the language into their mind.

Finn had no interest in letting the mage or this game mess with his head – not again anyway. The image of Rachael's face and their rather fiery wedding was still fresh in his mind.

"Well, this place seems real laidback," Kyyle murmured in a dry tone, interrupting Finn's dark thoughts. "Totally not getting a magical concentration camp vibe or anything."

Finn couldn't help but grin at that. "Agreed, but I have to admit that I am sort of curious about the classes," he replied quietly.

"You mean the ones where the teachers are permitted to beat us to death?" Kyyle asked, trying but failing to stop the smile creeping across his face.

"I have a feeling that I won't be sad to see that happen to some people," Finn commented, watching as the burly man strode up to Abbad.

Kyyle snorted before glancing at Finn out of the corner of his eye. "Speaking of which, you know this is going to get ugly, right? They basically just told us that failure means some sort of expulsion and victory means you get a cushy position in the guild or with that Emir guy. These people are going to be ready to shank each other in two weeks."

Finn nodded. He hadn't missed that.

He also suspected there was another explanation for the competition – not just to encourage the students to try hard. His gaze hovered on Nefreet's face, his expression a perfect, neutral mask. However, it was the headmaster's eyes that drew Finn's attention. They were coldly calculating, weighing and measuring each student that approached Abbad. That was the gaze of a shark – of a predator.

Finn had seen a similar strategy applied to young executives back in the day. Older leadership had intentionally created a competitive environment. Their objective wasn't to improve the company's bottom line – at least, not entirely. Their true goal had been to keep those young bucks fighting each other instead of gunning for their own job. If Finn was right, then this system was likely meant to destabilize a new generation of mages. However, there was some power in numbers, especially when it came to sharing information.

"Truce?" Finn suddenly said, offering Kyyle a hand.

The young man looked back at him in surprise.

"At least until they try to force us to kill each other," he added with a grin.

His smile was matched by Kyyle. The young man shrugged and then accepted his hand. "Fair enough. But I'm not gonna hold back if they eventually pit me against you."

"I never doubted that for a second," Finn replied, meeting Kyyle's eyes evenly. Despite his awkward appearance, the young man had already shown himself to be much more perceptive than the other players. Finn had no doubt he would be a challenging person to fight.

The moment was interrupted as Abbad called Kyyle forward. The young man spared Finn a wink and then stepped up to the front of the room, accepted the language and tattoo, and then quickly exited the room – likely planning to go explore their new school-prison.

And then Finn was alone, the last of the students.

He didn't wait for Abbad to wave him forward and instead stepped up on his own. Finn did his best to control his expression as he approached the pair. Until he knew what had happened in that testing room, he didn't plan to reveal that he knew Abbad – especially not with Nefreet standing right there. He didn't get the sense that the headmaster was on team Finn.

However, as Abbad went to raise his fingers to Finn's temple, he put up a hand. There was also no way in hell he was letting these people mess with his mind again. "I don't want it," he said tersely. Abbad's eyes widened in surprise, and even Nefreet arched an eyebrow.

"You will need this language to cast spells," the headmaster said calmly.

"Is there another way to learn Veridian?" Finn asked. "Perhaps some books or something?"

Nefreet cocked his head, staring at Finn. "There are many books on the language in the library. However, that process will take time – time that is in rather short supply. As I said before, you will only have two weeks before the duels begin, and you will not be granted a reprieve. This decision should not be made lightly."

Finn grimaced. It was easy to pick up on the implication of the headmaster's words. It was safe to say that the others had just had the language dumped into their brain, which would give them a considerable headstart. By the end of the two-week mark, they would likely have mastered multiple spells. In contrast, it was possible that Finn would still be learning the basics. At the same time, he just couldn't go through some sort of mind dump. Not after what he had experienced in the testing room.

He would find another way.

Finn met Nefreet's eyes evenly. "I'm a fast learner."

The headmaster watched him for a heartbeat and then seemed to come to a decision. "Let us hope so." Nefreet waved at Abbad. "Abbad can assist you in finding the right manuals and scrolls. He is one of the guild librarians." The man bowed his head in acknowledgment.

Finn mimicked the movement, bowing to Nefreet. "Thank you, headmaster," he said. There was no sense antagonizing the man, not when he would have considerable power over Finn.

When he looked back up, he saw something that looked like curiosity in Nefreet's gaze. Had he done something wrong by making that gesture?

"Don't thank me yet," the headmaster replied. "You have chosen a more difficult path. Only time will tell whether you come to regret it."

With that, the headmaster strode out of the room without another word. The benches behind Finn slowly sunk back into the floor as Nefreet released his spell. Which left Finn standing with Abbad, at least a dozen questions whirling through his mind.

Perhaps it was time to start answering some of them.

Chapter 6 - Enlightened

"So..." Finn began.

Abbad raised a hand, shaking his head curtly. He then reached for Finn's left hand, tracing a simple pattern with the stylus along his forearm. The instrument left a faint, burning line in its wake, but it wasn't enough to truly hurt and didn't pierce the skin.

As he completed the tattoo, Abbad let Finn go and began heading for the doorway, not saying a word. He merely gestured at Finn to follow and then stepped out of the room.

Finn rubbed at his arm. The tattoo itched slightly. The pattern was a simple star, each point connected by a thin line. He had gone his entire life without getting a tattoo, and yet his digital body seemed to be collecting them at an alarming rate.

His eyes lingered on the doorway for a fraction of a second. Questions swam in Finn's mind. What had he gotten himself into? What had happened with the crystal? Why was Abbad hiding Finn's test results from the other mages? Would following him just make the situation worse? What was the librarian's motive in all of this anyway?

The man's silence and his cautious behavior did little to ease Finn's worry. At the same time, he supposed he had no choice but to follow Abbad if he was going to learn Veridian.

Damn it. With a sigh, Finn followed after the librarian, jogging lightly to catch up.

Only a moment later, Finn's eyes widened in surprise as the hallway opened into a terrace encircling a massive courtyard. A gust of wind whipped at his clothes, the breeze feeling hot on his skin. They were apparently on the third floor of the school, a series of open-air walkways ringing the enclosure at each level. Finn could make out mages walking along the terraces, their forms blurry at this distance.

The inner courtyard was roughly the size of a football field, a rectangular enclosure about 100 yards across. Thick sand coated the area except for a large circular stone platform that rested in the center.

Geez. This place is huge, Finn thought.

He couldn't help but wonder at the purpose of the field and the strange stone stage. Maybe this was where the headmaster addressed the school or something?

The librarian gave him little time to ponder on this. Abbad made a sharp left turn and Finn was forced to follow, soon losing sight of the courtyard. The librarian led him down several flights of stairs and out into an open concourse. Finn could only assume that this was the Mage Guild's main hall, a wide hallway stretching on for hundreds of feet and dozens of staircases leading up into the bowels of the guild.

Throngs of students now streamed past, and Finn was forced to weave his way through the crowd to keep up with the librarian. Strangely, Abbad seemed to have no difficulty making his way through the other students, seamlessly flowing through the mass of limbs and feet with a casual grace.

Finn was only able to distractedly observe the people around him. Many wore different-colored cloth robes. Finn assumed that the colors identified each person's affinity. A uniform of sorts, perhaps? Although, that theory seemed a little tenuous when he noticed that quite a few people were wearing more traditional tunics and pants, while others were garbed in leather and chainmail. A few hasty inspections also revealed that the crowd was composed of a mixture of players and NPCs, although the player population was much larger, the travelers easily identified by the tags floating above their head.

Interestingly, Finn noticed that many people sported tattoos like Abbad and Nefreet. Yet the designs were less elaborate and more spartan – similar to the one on Finn's left arm. Perhaps this was some way to identify a person's rank within the guild?

Finn started to ask Abbad about the tattoos, which seemed like an innocent enough question, but he froze as he caught a flash of light in his peripheral vision.

He turned to find an enormous screen projected above a grand central staircase. The display stretched at least fifty feet into the air. The title line simply said "Novices." Below that, the screen had been divided into two columns – one marked "Travelers" and the other as "Residents." Each row contained a name, a rank, and a numeric score.

Finn suddenly realized he was looking at a leaderboard, most likely reflecting scores in the ongoing duels among the students.

That seemed extreme. It looked like Kyyle had been right. The rivalry among the novices was about to get ugly, especially if the guild broadcast their relative rankings this publicly. Hell, even Finn's programming classes back in the day hadn't been this intense, and his professors had gone out of their way to weed out students.

The leaderboard also raised another question that was far more interesting.

How the hell had they built this thing?

Before he knew it, Finn had approached the display, his curiosity overriding his caution. He soon discovered that what he had thought was a screen was actually a series of colored crystals embedded into the wall. His fingers traced the rough stones. As he inspected them, the crystals flashed and changed color.

Stepping back, Finn could see that the names and numbers had all shifted. They now showed the leaderboard for the "Journeyman" mages.

Fascinating. They are using the crystals like pixels on a screen. So, that must mean that this world's crafting system lets them mimic our technology, Finn thought to himself. He wondered if players could recreate something like this or if this kind of in-game crafting was exclusive to the NPCs.

What could I build with magic crystals?

A cough behind Finn made him jump. He turned to find Abbad staring at him. The man's expression was still perfectly neutral, although a lone eyebrow was twitching slightly. From the little Finn knew about the librarian, he was practically shouting.

He got the unspoken message. No detours.

With another sigh, he followed Abbad, sparing one last longing glance at the display behind him. At least the crystal screen told him one thing: this world was a lot more complex than it appeared on the surface.

A few minutes later, they arrived in front of a pair of massive steel doors. Abbad approached a column beside the door and waved something across the surface. A moment later, the portal creaked open, letting out almost no sound despite its monstrous size.

Abbad waved Finn inside. As soon as the pair crossed the threshold, the doors let out a soft thud as they closed behind them.

Finn was left staring at what he assumed was the guild library. It was a squat, square affair. The center of the room was empty, a smooth stone floor devoid of chairs or tables. Only a single pedestal rested in the very middle of the room. As the pair stepped further inside, Finn spun, taking in the bookcases and cubbies surrounding them, holding all manner of books and ancient, dusty scrolls.

However, he couldn't help but feel underwhelmed.

After everything they had seen, the guild only had a single square room for its library? Why bother with those massive doors then?

"So, uh, is this it?" Finn asked, gesturing at the nearby shelves.

Abbad's response was a single arched eyebrow. Without responding, he paced over to the pedestal and waved something across its surface.

Before Finn had a chance to ask what he was doing, the floor suddenly lurched beneath him. The pair stood upon a square platform in the center of the room, which began to rise at a rapid rate... heading directly toward a very solid-looking stone ceiling.

Finn eyed Abbad nervously, but the librarian made no move to jump off the platform, even as the ceiling approached at a frightening rate.

"Abbad..." Finn began.

Just as they were about to be crushed against the stone, the rock ceiling turned to liquid and rippled away. The stone pooled around the edges of the platform as it smoothly climbed upward, revealing yet another square floor filled with books and scrolls. This time, Finn could see robed men and women moving between the cubbies and shelves – attired similarly to Abbad and dark patterns spiraling across their skin.

Abbad made no move to stop the platform, and they continued to climb. Finn counted at least three levels before the librarian removed his hand from the pedestal. The platform halted and the stone floor slid back into place, sealing them inside what Finn assumed was the fourth floor of the library.

A quick glance around the room revealed that the pair were alone. Finn once more opened his mouth to ask Abbad a question.

The librarian raised a staying hand. His fingers then began to twine through a rapid series of gestures, and the man muttered something under his breath. A gust of wind suddenly blew through the room, tugging at Finn's clothes before whipping and whirling around them. A moment later, the wind stabilized, and a sphere enveloped the two of them, the surface almost invisible, but glowing with a faint yellow light.

"*Now* you may speak," Abbad said plainly, making no effort to lower his voice.

Finn could only stare back and forth at the faintly shimmering globe and Abbad, suddenly realizing that he wasn't even certain where to start with his questions.

"Uh... okay. So, what is this globe?" Finn asked, pointing at the yellow sphere. He tentatively touched at the surface of the orb, and his hand passed through with only slight resistance.

"A sound-dampening spell," Abbad replied calmly, gesturing for the pair to move out of the center of the room. Finn followed his lead, staying well within the circle of yellow energy. "I am an air mage, master rank. We can create barriers of compressed air that prevent sound from passing through."

Abbad's hands darted through another series of gestures, and, as Finn tried to respond, he suddenly found that no sound escaped his mouth. He went cross-eyed trying to look at his lips, and he could just barely see the edges of a smaller, shimmering yellow sphere resting near his mouth.

Abbad made a dismissive gesture and the smaller sphere dissolved.

"Well, that's a cool trick," Finn murmured.

"Indeed," Abbad responded dryly. "Although, applying the spell to a smaller area, especially one that moves around more quickly, is difficult to master. Which reminds me, we need to get to work. We should secure several tomes and scrolls to assist you in your studies. Please follow me."

With that, the librarian took off, winding through the shelves with Finn hot on his heels. Abbad plucked at a few materials as they walked past, handing each one carefully to Finn.

"So, would you mind explaining what happened with that crystal and the test?" Finn asked cautiously.

Abbad spared a glance over his shoulder. "Did you see something when your hand touched the crystal?" he asked calmly, picking up another scroll and passing it to Finn.

"Yes," Finn murmured.

"I take it the image was rather personal?" This didn't really feel like a question.

Finn just nodded.

"That is the crystal's function. It utilizes dark magic to scour a person's memories. It conjured a moment that was impactful – emotional. This is important since the six magical affinities are tied to emotion. Or I suppose you might also call them *personality traits*. Regardless, eliciting strong emotions is the easiest way to test for the type and strength of a person's affinity." Abbad handed him another tome, the pile growing quickly.

"The crystal is one of the few objects that the guild has retained that utilizes dark magic. As the headmaster explained, this guild caters exclusively to the elemental affinities: fire, air, water, and earth."

"I assume there's a reason for that?" Finn asked.

Abbad hesitated for a moment, as though considering his words. "The Emir decided long ago to forgo training dark and light mages. Suffice it to say that the mages of those two schools can be rather difficult to *control*."

That just raised more questions than it answered.

Although there was one thing that Finn had been dying to ask. And he wouldn't be distracted from it – even if he badly wanted to know more about the game's magic system and the guild.

"Okay, so you told me I had the fire affinity, and I'm a novice. But you also seemed pretty nervous, and that crystal was shining like I lit the place on fire…" Finn trailed off, his implicit question hanging in the air.

Abbad gave a curt nod and gestured toward a corner of the room. Finn followed his direction and soon found himself in a small study area, a few rather mundane wooden tables pressed up against a plain stone wall. He carefully placed the pile of books and scrolls on one of the tables before turning to focus on the librarian.

The other man seemed to be struggling to decide where to begin. "I suppose the short answer is that your affinity is quite strong. Much stronger than is normal for someone with your lack of experience," Abbad explained.

"If I had reported the true results, I expect that the guild would have immediately purged your mana and exiled you from the city. You would likely have died of dehydration and exposure among the dunes or been eaten by sandworms." He hesitated. "Although, as a traveler, I expect you would likely have experienced both many times before finally succumbing to despair," the stoic man said this with almost no emotion in his voice, as though it were commonplace.

"Well, thank you, I guess," Finn replied tentatively. "But I guess that raises additional questions. How strong is my affinity exactly? What does that mean? And why try to protect me? Surely that puts you at risk."

Abbad grimaced and nodded slightly, rubbing at his eyes for a moment. "Let's take your questions in order. Your affinity is already expert rank." He looked at Finn sharply. "Although I wouldn't let that go to your head. That doesn't mean you will be able to cast spells easily – you still have much to learn – only that you will exhibit a more significant control over fire mana.

"As for your other questions, to understand my

motive, you would need to first understand more of the history surrounding the formation and purpose of the guild. This is too much to cover in a single sitting," Abbad added.

The librarian's eyes darted to the nearby stacks, as though he were nervous that someone might be watching them. "For the sake of expediency, I'll summarize. This 'school' could be viewed as an elaborate prison or internment camp. The Emir uses it as a way to pit mages against one another, keep track of our movements, and bind us to his service. To this end, it is far easier to cull strong mages early, when they are unable to defend themselves."

Abbad gazed at Finn evenly. "Not all of us agree with that goal."

Finn's eyes widened. It seemed that his earlier skepticism had been justified.

"Well, thank you," Finn said, not needing to fake the sincerity in his voice. NPC or not, this person had taken a risk for Finn – a stranger.

"If you wish to repay my kindness, then do not make my risk in vain. You need to learn how to survive," Abbad said bluntly, pointing at the books on the table. "By denying the gift of Veridian, you have chosen a much more difficult path and have caught the attention of the headmaster. You will need to move quickly and tread carefully from here on out."

Finn's forehead scrunched in confusion. "But doesn't my high affinity mean that this should come more easily?"

"Not necessarily," Abbad replied. "Your affinity for a certain school of magic is effectively a measure of *aptitude*. Think of it like any other trait, such as intelligence or strength. You might have the *potential* to cast more powerful and complex spells, yet you still lack the tools and knowledge to do so. This process typically starts by learning Veridian. Your first classes will then cover how to summon and manipulate your mana."

Well, shit. Finn stared at the books, now suddenly second-guessing his decision. Although, he supposed there was no going back now.

"You mentioned that the affinities are tied to certain

personality traits. What does fire represent?" Finn asked, switching gears.

Abbad nodded. "A good question. In short, *passion*."

"Passion? Really?" Finn replied in an incredulous tone. He had hardly been in a frame of mind to start dating after Rachael. Honestly, he hadn't even given it a thought. As far as he was concerned, there would never be anyone else.

Abbad seemed to pick up on his misunderstanding, faint amusement flitting across his face before he re-assumed his regular stoic facade. "Passion can be quite an expansive emotion. It naturally conjures an image of romantic love, but we find passion in many other things. Building, writing, friendship, combat, and exploration – just to name a few. What these things have in common is that they are enduring and give our life purpose. For example, you might say I have a passion for books, which is why I became a librarian," he explained, gesturing at the nearby shelves.

"Fire mages often tend to be eccentric, competitive, enthusiastic, aggressive, and prone to anger or extreme emotion. These characteristics may seem disjointed, but they share a common root cause – namely, that person's *passion*."

Finn instinctively touched the tattoo on his right arm, recalling his conversation with the Seer before he had stepped into the flames. She had been focused on the same thing: his loss of *purpose* after the accident and his secret yearning for a chance to start over, to build and create again. That tantalizing promise was what had encouraged Finn to make the leap.

Although, he abruptly decided not to reveal that conversation to Abbad. He wasn't certain how the librarian would react if he mentioned that he had spoken to an old lady who claimed to be the goddess of fire. He already had few allies as it was.

"Alright, that makes sense, I suppose," Finn replied tentatively. "So, what does it mean to be *expert rank*, exactly?"

Abbad gestured at the tattoos on his arms and neck. "The guild ranks us according to our abilities. This is a product of both our performance in the duels and our affinity. The ranks are novice, journeyman, expert, master, grandmaster. Mages are then marked by tattoos to denote their skill and affinity level."

He waved at Finn's left forearm. "You have been given the basic guild induction mark. You will be given a true novice mark once you have passed your initial classes."

Finn's eyes widened as he took in the tattoos covering Abbad's arms and neck. That must mean he was talking to a rather experienced mage. Although the man had already made that clear; he was master rank. So Abbad was near the top of the heap.

"Is there a way to quantify my affinity then?" Finn asked, the engineer in him starting to take over. If his abilities and rank were partly tied to his affinity, then it would be helpful to see where he stood numerically.

"Indeed. You can pull up your Character Status to find this information yourself," Abbad explained.

Finn chewed on his lip for a moment as his eyes panned to the system UI that floated in the corner of his vision. He swiped through the menu icons and lists until he found the button for his Character Status. He tapped it, and a translucent blue screen suddenly appeared in front of him.

	Character Status		
Name:	Finn	**Gender:**	Male
Level:	1	**Class:**	
Race:	Human	**Alignment:**	Lawful-Neutral
Fame:	100	**Infamy:**	0
Health:	100	**H-Regen/Sec:**	0.30
Mana:	175	**M-Regen/Sec:**	2.00
Stamina:	120	**S-Regen/Sec:**	1.20
Strength:	12	**Dexterity:**	12
Vitality:	10	**Endurance:**	12
Intelligence:	15	**Willpower:**	15

Affinities			
Dark:	2%	**Light:**	4%
Fire:	37%	**Water:**	5%
Air:	3%	**Earth:**	9%

Alright, so I have stats just like any other game, Finn thought to himself. He also noted that there was a separate section devoted solely to his affinities, the levels denoted in percentages. Indeed, his fire affinity seemed quite high relative to the others. Although, his earth affinity wasn't exactly low either. He just wasn't sure what that meant yet.

Finn looked up to find the librarian staring at him with a serious expression. "As I explained before, it is imperative that you keep this to yourself. Do not show your Character Status to others," Abbad reiterated. "You need to be discreet, both with your classmates and with your teachers. If you have any questions, you should direct them to me and only after I have cast a *Dampening* spell. Do you understand?"

Finn nodded. He didn't exactly plan to go shouting this information from the rooftops.

Abbad rummaged in his robes and pulled out a small circular stone, a simple star symbol emblazoned on the top. He handed it to Finn. "This is a novice token. It will grant you access to the library's lower levels so that you can come here on your own. I will let the other librarians know you will be using this area to study and not to disturb your materials."

"Got it," Finn said, taking the stone. "So, uh, what now?"

"Now, you get to work," Abbad answered curtly. "Your first class begins tomorrow. You might be able to make it through the first few days without knowing Veridian, but this will quickly become an impediment. If you fall too far behind, you will likely be expelled. I suggest you make the most of the time you have."

"A few days," Finn muttered, his eyes on the scrolls that littered the tabletop.

Surely the game would simplify this for him. Maybe

there were just a few catchphrases he needed to memorize or something. It couldn't possibly expect him to learn a complete language... could it?

He glanced up to ask another question, but Abbad had simply vanished – along with the faintly glowing azure sphere. Finn hadn't even heard the man leave. Although, he didn't get long to ponder on this as a new notification popped up in front of him.

Quest Update: Curious Capabilities

Abbad explained that you have an unnaturally high affinity for fire magic. He warned you that revealing this information or drawing attention to yourself may result in your expulsion from the guild and your exile from Lahab. For now, you need to keep your head down and train. That shouldn't be too hard, right?

Difficulty: A
Success: Continue your studies and training.
Failure: Get expelled or draw attention to yourself.
Reward: Uh, you won't get exiled or eaten by sandworms? What more do you want?

Finn grimaced. The quest update provided little clarity, and at least a dozen more questions tumbled through his head – things he hadn't had a chance to ask Abbad. He supposed it didn't matter. He would learn more in time. Right now, he needed to see what he was up against with this magic language.

Letting out a soft sigh, he took a seat at the table. Finn thumbed open the first tome and observed the alien, spiraling symbols that riddled the page. He could feel a weight start to settle in his stomach as he flipped through the pages, his confidence faltering.

Maybe he had made a big mistake...

Chapter 7 - Studious

Finn had figured out a few things over the last few hours.

First, Veridian definitely represented an entire language, replete with its own vocabulary, grammar, and syntax. The written language was somewhat similar to Chinese, each word denoted with an arcane symbol comprised of specific brush strokes. It also appeared that there were certain base symbols and patterns that served as the foundation for other words. That meant he was going to need to memorize a daunting number of unique characters.

Which led Finn to his second realization.

He was an idiot.

An *arrogant* idiot.

Finn leaned back in the chair, causing the wood to groan weakly as he rubbed at his eyes. When he opened them again, Finn glanced at the in-game clock in the corner of his vision, confirming that at least eight hours had passed since Abbad had left.

That's right. He had spent eight hours in a video game studying in a library.

Maybe "idiot" is too nice, he thought to himself.

The table in front of him was carefully crafted chaos, scrolls and tomes placed at seemingly haphazard angles. To an outside observer, it probably looked like he had gone mad. However, there was some order to the insanity. One was a dictionary, another a tome on grammar, and there was at least one scroll that seemed to offer rough English-to-Veridian translations. The whole undertaking had made him yearn for his workstation at home. There was a reason this stuff had all gone digital over time, and he missed the ability to just toss up another screen.

Complaining aside, Finn had to reluctantly admit that he had made a lot of progress. For some reason, his memory felt sharper than usual – bordering on photographic. He only needed to practice a word or the associated brush strokes a time or two before it stuck.

He was even able to read the first few pages from one of the books that Abbad had left for him. Although, he hadn't realized the librarian had left him a *children's book* until he found the illustrations. It was a truly gripping tale about a young girl who had lost her cat in a tree – which did precisely nothing to make him feel less stupid.

In short, this wasn't exactly the gaming experience he remembered from his youth.

As that thought crossed his mind, several notifications flashed in front of Finn.

x4 Level Up!
You have (20) undistributed stat points.

New Skill: Reading
You seem really fond of reading, or at least *trying* to read! Maybe someday – a few years from now, most likely – we can finally find out what happens to that girl's poor cat. More importantly, where the hell are the girl's parents? They just left her unattended with another living creature? That's just plain irresponsible!
Skill Level: Beginner Level 1
Effect 1: 5% increased learning speed while reading.

New Skill: Learning
You have shown remarkable dedication to acquiring new skills and abilities. Masters of this skill become so adept at studying the world around them that they are said to be able to learn new abilities even during combat. You're clearly not there yet, but you have potential.
Skill Level: Beginner Level 1
Effect 1: 5% increased learning speed for skills and spells.

Finn rolled his eyes as he read the prompts.

What intrigued him was the experience gain from studying. Granted, it had been a while since Finn had played an RPG, but most of the older games tended to reward active tasks such as combat, crafting, or exploration. Yet this game was allowing him to level by trying to read a children's book...

Finn shook his head. He would just have to add this to the growing list of mysteries that was Awaken Online.

His gaze skimmed to the level-up notification. He had a few stat points that he could distribute, but he also wasn't quite sure what the various stats did yet. Since he would probably be spending the next few days in the library, it was likely safer to hold on to them for now. Although, that thought made him wince.

Tomorrow would be their group's first class, and Finn hadn't even managed to read a children's book. Despite his heightened learning speed and newfound skills, he doubted he was going to master an entire language in the course of two weeks.

With a sigh, he pushed back from the table and took to his feet. Finn's frustration was only slightly muted by the realization that he had begun pacing instinctively. It was strange how natural the movement felt even after years spent in a wheelchair. Although this wasn't quite enough to distract him from his current problem.

He frowned at the nearby pile of books and scrolls.

There had to be a faster way to learn this language.

To make matters worse, Finn wasn't entirely certain why he was so frustrated. It was a game, after all. Why should he care about learning some made-up language or getting kicked out of a fake magic school? That realization only served to fuel his irritation – making him feel even more silly. Hell, just that morning, he had been reticent to even enter the game, and now he was upset about how little progress he had made?

He had to admit that this world was *tantalizing*, though. The level of detail was incredible, and there was just something about it that kept tugging him forward. Someone had invented an entire magical language, after all!

Maybe it was the mystery of the mark on his hand. Or the Seer's enticing promise. Or seeing Rachael again. Or the teasing glimpses he had been given of this world's magic system. Or maybe it was something else altogether – some feeling that Finn had difficulty putting into words. It felt like the game had issued a challenge.

It seemed to keep asking him, *"Are you good enough?"*

He was surprised by how much he wanted to prove that he was.

However, Finn wasn't given long to ponder on this. A translucent blue screen appeared in front of him, flashing insistently.

System Warning

You have been playing for quite some time now. You should log out to eat and care for your real-world body.

If you ignore this warning, you will be automatically logged out in thirty minutes and a mandatory one-hour waiting period will apply before you will be able to log back in.

"Well, it might be time for a break anyway," Finn grumbled to himself.

Maybe an idea for how to tackle this cramming process would come to him if he put some distance between himself and the problem. That had always helped in the past.

With another sigh, Finn pulled up the system UI with a few quick swipes and pressed "log out." A moment later, he disappeared in a rift of multi-colored energy.

* * *

Returning to the real world was disorienting.

There was simply darkness, the VR headset obscuring his vision and muting any noise behind thick foam insulation. This gave Finn plenty of time to focus on his body. It felt heavier in a subtle way, his heart thudding in his chest and real blood now pumping through his veins. His arms also ached as he moved to take off the headset. Perhaps it was because they hadn't moved in hours.

Yet the most noticeable difference was his legs. It was like someone had shut off a switch at his waist, leaving behind... nothing. There was no feeling at all, which felt strange given the number of hours he had spent in-game. It was startling – and a bit unnerving – how quickly his mind had adapted to a different body.

As he pulled off the helmet, the screens of Finn's workstation flickered into existence, giving off a harsh blue light.

"Hello, sir. Welcome back," Daniel spoke up, his voice echoing through the room as the hazy sapphire cloud that signaled the AI's presence appeared nearby.

"How long was I logged in?" Finn asked, rubbing at his face.

"Approximately three hours," Daniel reported.

Finn froze, peeking at the AI between his fingers. "Say that again?"

"You were logged into the VR hardware for a total of three hours, 16 minutes, and 38 seconds," Daniel repeated, automatically providing more detail.

"That can't be right," Finn murmured, glancing at the screens. He knew he had spent at least ten hours in-game.

"I have double-checked my logs and confirmed the time against two different independent world clocks since I currently have access to the public network. The logged time is accurate," Daniel confirmed.

Finn just shook his head – still refusing to accept what the AI was saying. "Retract the shutters," he ordered, gesturing at the panel of windows along the far wall. Daniel responded immediately, the metal grates that lined the windows tilting until Finn could see early afternoon sunlight trickling through the reinforced glass.

"What the hell?"

There was only one way to explain the time difference. The game must be using a form of time compression – allowing a user to experience the game at approximately three to four times the rate compared to the real world. Finn supposed it was *possible*. The passage of time was relatively subjective, and he knew the hardware could enhance his cognitive function enough to compensate. Yet it was still startling.

The immediate possibilities were also incredible. A person could essentially triple their total effective lifespan if they stayed logged in. At least from their perspective. But honestly, what was the difference? If the user's real body lived for 80 years, they could potentially *experience* 240-320 years in-game...

Finn stared down at the helmet in his hands.

"Who built you?" he said aloud.

Finn's thoughts were interrupted as he heard a chime from his workstation. He glanced at a nearby screen to find that a notification had popped up.

System Notice
Incoming video call from her Supreme Majesty Julia. Accept?

Finn sighed. He assumed Julia had left a tracer somewhere that was monitoring his activity. He had almost forgotten that his daughter had been meddling with his system before he logged into the game – in fact, that had been one of the motivations for him to log in to begin with. The time dilation was throwing him off.

"Would you like to accept the call, sir?" Daniel nudged him.

"Yeah, sure," Finn said, running a hand through his hair and trying to gather his fraying thoughts. Dealing with Julia could be... draining.

A moment later, the screens condensed into a single image, his daughter making an appearance. She was lounging at her own workstation, leaning back in her chair, and gnawing on the straw sticking out of a massive Styrofoam cup. She looked up as the call connected, dropping her beverage on the desk.

"Hey, old man," she said, a small smirk on her lips. "So, you logged three-plus hours here in the real world and closer to a dozen in-game huh? Found something interesting, I take it?"

"I'm still trying to wrap my head around the time compression," Finn muttered, shaking his head. "That one kind of threw me." He spared a glare at the screen. "You could have warned me."

Her smile widened. "I *could* have, but where's the fun in that?" Julia waved a dismissive hand. "Besides, all of that information is available online. I bet you just didn't bother to check. You probably took the damn headset apart and put it back together, but didn't bother to watch a two-minute trailer..."

Finn ground his teeth together. She had him dead to rights.

"You didn't, did you?" Julia asked, her eyes widening. "Wow. That must have been a trip then. Real tactile feedback. Perma-locked characters. Time compression. Enhanced learning speed—"

"Wait, go back to that last one," Finn interjected.

Julia arched an eyebrow. "Well, the game enhances your memory retention and recall. As a result, it is much easier to learn new skills. You can pick up stuff quite quickly actually."

A few pieces of the puzzle began to click into place. Finn had noticed that it was much easier to learn Veridian – it took less time to memorize the new vocabulary, and his recall was much faster. It was uncomfortably close to accessing his memories, but he supposed that the game hadn't quite crossed that line.

"Why do you ask?" Julia offered, curiosity coloring her voice. "You trying to learn something in-game?"

Finn's attention snapped back to his daughter. "Something like that. I got dropped in some random city, and then I was... well... conscripted into the Mage Guild there."

Julia's eyes widened slightly at that.

"Basically, I'm an idiot," Finn said. He raised a hand to forestall the joke he knew was coming, a grin already painted on his daughter's face. "Not just because I didn't watch the trailer first. I'm actually trying to learn the game's spellcasting language from scratch. In two weeks..."

Julia had been in the middle of taking another large swig of her drink and almost spit it out. She swallowed hard. "Two weeks to learn an entire language? Why didn't you just let the game do the whole memory dump thing?"

"You know about that?" Finn asked in surprise.

His daughter waved a dismissive hand. "Sure, sure. I was in the beta. You could say I'm just a bit further along than the average player. But you're deflecting. Why didn't you accept the memory dump?"

Finn rubbed at his neck, looking away. "It just makes me uncomfortable. I don't like that the game is messing with my memory." He didn't really want to go into detail about his confrontation with the fire god or the memory of Rachael. At least, not right now.

"Hmm, fair enough. The game does have a tendency to get a little *personal*, I suppose," Julia said, and he saw some understanding in her eyes. He was curious about what her tutorial had been like. Yet he didn't get a chance to ask.

"Anyway," Julia said, shaking off the gloomy cloud that suddenly hung over the conversation. "That timeline is going to be tight, even with the game helping you. But I'm sure you'll figure out a way. Unless you're losing your edge, of course."

It was Finn's turn to raise an eyebrow. "Uh huh. Speaking of which, don't think I've forgotten what you did to my system. I believe I should be expecting an email soon."

Julia laughed. "Already on its way! And on that note, I'll leave you to it. I have this sneaking suspicion that you already want to log back in."

Finn just grumbled under his breath.

"Oh, one last thing!" Julia said before he could cut the connection. "What's the name of your starting city?"

"It's called Lahab. Why?"

"No reason. Talk to you later!" Julia said, a wide grin on her face and then the screen winked out of existence.

Finn just stared at the empty space the screen had

occupied a moment before. Why had he decided to have children again?

Yet, despite the irritating conversation with his daughter, she had been right. Even now, he was already thinking about logging in and getting back to work. First, though, he needed to come up with a plan. He couldn't just flail around blindly trying to learn Veridian. He only had two weeks.

Finn pulled up another screen, and a translucent keyboard suddenly hovered in his lap. His fingers danced across the keys as he pulled up some information on real-world language courses. He grimaced at the data that scrolled across the screen. Basic fluency in simpler languages typically took approximately 48 days – assuming he trained for 10 hours a day. More complicated languages could take up to 72 days. And Veridian definitely fell into the complicated category. So that was roughly 720 hours as a benchmark.

His mind immediately started working through the calculations.

He had two weeks, minus half a day. 324 hours total.

Finn would also likely need to attend classes and undergo other training during that time. He could probably assume that would take at least 3 hours each day. 39 hours total, not counting the first day.

Then he needed to eat and sleep in the real world. And each eight-hour sleep cycle could cost him up to 24 hours in-game due to the time compression. Over the course of four real-world days, he would lose roughly 96 hours.

That left him with 189 in-game hours.

Compared to the estimated 720 hours needed for basic fluency.

Finn could feel a weight settle in his stomach. To obtain even basic fluency, he had about a fourth of the suggested time. That seemed impossible, even with the enhanced learning speed in-game.

He rubbed at his eyes with one hand. There had to be some way to shorten that time further. He could almost sense an idea in the corner of his mind, but he couldn't quite grasp it – the feeling elusive and hard to pin down.

"Damn it," he muttered, giving up. He would just have to wait for the idea to gel.

In the meantime, maybe he could at least have the AI work on the problem in the background. "Daniel, can you please run a search of all language training programs? I'm looking for programs with the fastest average learning speed."

"I am already seeing that much of this software requires a paid license," the AI replied only moments later, a screen flickering to life and listing a number of courses.

"Then purchase them all," Finn replied, not bothering to look at the prices. "It might not hurt for you to run through the code too – once you've downloaded everything. We might be able to find a few good examples and then refine from there to build our own version." Assuming that worked, Finn would be able to keep training in the real world while he was taking care of routine tasks. It wasn't much, but it was something.

"Yes, sir. I will get started right away," Daniel replied, the blue cloud giving off a faint pulse.

As Finn glared in frustration at the nearby screens, a familiar question nagged at him.

Why was he struggling after this impossible, pointless goal?

It didn't take long to find the answer. The challenge excited him. It had been so long since he had been confronted with a problem that he wasn't certain how to solve. And there was still that damned idea that kept circling the edges of his mind – teasing and tormenting him. He remembered that feeling. It conjured memories of his time in college, tackling complicated programming assignments. Or his initial work building the AI for Cerillion Logistics. It was as though his subconscious had already started tackling the problem and his waking mind just hadn't quite caught up yet.

This feeling was the precursor to that moment when everything finally "clicked." When inspiration struck like a two-by-four to the forehead.

Besides, his daughter's words kept tormenting him. It was the same taunting question the game kept throwing in his face.

Had he lost his edge?
He honestly wasn't sure.
But he planned to find out.

Chapter 8 - Magical

Breathing heavily, Finn entered the room – only to have a few dozen pairs of eyes turn to stare at him panting in the doorway. The other students sat on familiar stone pews facing a podium on the far end of the classroom.

"What is your name?" a stern voice carried across the room.

A rather-severe woman was looking at him, her expression expectant. Brilliant sapphire robes made of rich silk were wrapped around her lithe frame, the cloth not quite enough to cover the tattoos that spiraled up from her wrists and twisted around the base of her neck. Her skin was a dark auburn, and black hair flowed down her back.

His instructor then.

"Uh, Finn," he managed, suddenly feeling self-conscious under the combined scrutiny. "Is the first class for beginning mages?"

"It is. Although, it started five minutes ago," the instructor replied tersely.

"I'm sorry, I had a little trouble finding the place," Finn murmured.

A skeptical eyebrow. "Indeed. Take a seat." The teacher waved at the pews.

Finn's eyes skimmed the stone benches until he spotted Kyyle near the back, an empty spot resting beside him. He quickly slid into place, sharing a look with the other novice mage.

"For those of you who may have missed it, my name is Magus Lamia." She spared a pointed expression at Finn at this remark. "This is also a learning opportunity. Your position within the guild is tenuous. By design, this is intended to ensure that you do not become complacent. Only your dedication and punctuality will maintain your position here, and the alternative is… not *ideal*."

Finn grimaced, feeling his cheeks heat slightly – both at the unwanted attention and the implied threat. He had often heard his peers mention that they wish they could go back to high school and college – to experience those periods in their lives through the lens of greater experience. They would go on and on about how they would do things differently. Take more chances. How they would be immune to the pressure of their peers.

That was pure, unmitigated bullshit.

School just sucked, no matter how you sliced it. Sticking humans in an enclosed environment and forcing them to interact just bred drama and judgment. That position was only reinforced by the smirks he was receiving from some of the other adult students. He abruptly decided that anyone who claimed they were somehow immune to the judgment of other people was either insane or a sociopath – or possibly both.

"Where have you been?" Kyyle whispered.

Finn shot the gangly youth a harried look. "Just studying in the library. I may have done something stupid yesterday," he replied under his breath. That was the understatement of the year. Finn had completely lost track of time while trying to cram as much of this magic language into his head as possible. He had been at it for hours.

He noticed Lamia's gaze flit across the pair, and Finn's mouth snapped shut. He'd already failed horribly at the one task that Abbad had given him – to stay below the radar. No need to make it worse.

"I see some of you are anxious to get started," the stern woman observed. "So, let us begin."

She took a deep breath. "You will all be taking your initial classes together for the first two weeks, after which you will be divided into classes better befitting your affinity and talents." She paused. "Assuming, of course, that you pass your initial classes. Many students never make it to the duels, and I suspect there will be missing faces in the coming weeks."

Lamia let this sink in, her eyes skimming the class.

"Yet we may as well *attempt* to train you. There are two primary components to casting a spell: summoning and manipulating your mana and reciting the requisite incantation for the spell in question. Today, we will be focusing on the first step.

"But before we launch into the lesson itself, I suspect you will require some background regarding your *gifts*," Lamia continued. "You have each been tested and found to have a relatively high affinity for a certain school of magic. Like any skill or trait, that affinity can be cultivated by acting in a way that is consistent with your school of magic."

A confused murmur rippled through the group of students and Lamia arched an eyebrow. Finn wasn't particularly surprised, having been prepared by Abbad's impromptu lecture the day before.

"Several of you appear lost, so let me elaborate," Lamia said, not able to entirely remove the exasperation from her voice. "Each school of magic is tied to a certain trait. These traits are as follows."

The woman's fingers swept across the top of the podium, and a screen flickered to life behind her, flashing with multicolored lights. Finn suspected that the display used the same technology he had seen in the main hall – crystals embedded into the stone wall which acted as makeshift pixels. However, he hadn't realized the displays were so malleable or common.

Lamia's hands darted across the top of the podium, and the display shifted, showing six rows, naming the affinity and the corresponding trait.

Fire: Passion
Earth: Peace
Air: Happiness
Water: Acceptance
Light: Confidence
Dark: Desire

"So, if we're happy, we're better at air magic?" one of the students asked, skepticism practically dripping from his voice. He looked to be in his mid-twenties.

Lamia cocked her head at the student. "I would appreciate you raising your hand to indicate a question," she snapped. The student's eyes widened slightly, but he gave a curt nod in response, which at least made Finn feel a little less stupid for arriving late.

She's just a lovely person, got it.

"It isn't quite that simple," Lamia replied. "You would need to act in a way to foster *happiness*. Many air mages believe that this involves living in the moment, and some even go so far as to let fortune decide their actions – using dice or a coin toss to make decisions. Others take this a bit too far, succumbing to hedonistic distractions." A grimace flitted across her face. "Suffice it to say, there is rarely one definitive approach.

"Either way, these affinities are important, as they indicate the level of control that you are able to exhibit over your own mana." Her eyes skimmed the crowd. "Which leads us to today's lesson. The first step to casting is to learn to summon and control your mana. This is a skill referred to as *Mana Mastery*.

"Each of you holds mana in your bodies, keyed to your specific affinity. This mana can be directed with a series of specific hand gestures, directing the mana out of your body and allowing you to then control that mana outside yourself," Lamia explained.

"The first step is to visualize your own mana pool. I find that for water mana, it is easier to visualize an open-faced well or bowl." Lamia placed her index fingers and thumbs together, forming a rough triangle. "Form this pattern with your hands and imagine that there is a cup in the center. Then imagine that you are pouring a few drops of your mana from your well into that cup."

As she finished speaking, a cloud of blue particles began to form in the air above Lamia's hands. As Finn and the class looked on, the vapor condensed until a brilliant, perfectly symmetrical shard of ice rested above her outstretched fingers, slowly twirling in the air.

"For some of you, this may require using most of your well. And don't be concerned if the summoning is not as—"

Lamia was cut off as a blinding crackle of light illuminated the room, followed closely by a thunderclap that left Finn's ears ringing. It felt like a bomb had gone off on one side of the room, the noise amplified by the hard, stone walls of the classroom.

Finn blinked rapidly to try to clear his vision. As the room resolved back into focus, he was able to see what had happened.

One of the novices – a young woman – appeared to be on fire. Burns riddled her skin and her hair, and part of her clothes were still aflame. The girl might have been screaming, her mouth open and tears streaming down her cheeks, but Finn couldn't make out the sound over the ringing in his ears.

Their teacher acted quickly. With a few swift gestures, moisture accumulated out of the air, forming a massive globe of liquid that promptly splashed the screaming girl. The flames extinguished into streamers of smoke and steam, and the girl slumped to the ground, shaking slightly.

"Hmm," Lamia said, confirming that Finn's hearing was beginning to return. The teacher looked down at the injured girl calmly, noting the gnarled wounds along her skin. Although, on reflection, Finn supposed she might have been looking at the water that now drenched the floor. She didn't seem overly concerned about the girl.

Lamia noted the class was now staring at her, many with their mouths hanging open. "As I was about to say, the goal here is concentration and stability. At first, you may find your mana difficult to control. Start slowly and then ramp up."

No one in the group made any move, sitting still as statutes.

"What exactly are you waiting for? Begin!" Lamia ordered.

Finn and Kyyle shared another look.

"Right, sure. Let's just try not to blow ourselves up..." Kyyle muttered.

Finn shared his skepticism. In part, because he could still hear the girl sobbing slightly and Lamia cursing as she stepped out into the hall to summon some help. A moment later, a pair of green-robed mages entered the room and lifted the girl to her feet, half-carrying her out of the classroom. As she passed him, Finn noted with some relief that the girl's injuries had already begun to heal, although her eyes were still distant and confused. He suspected the game must have also muted the pain feedback. It was likely the surprise that had left her in shock.

At least, he *hoped* so.

Finn glanced around the room and saw the other students cautiously going through the practice exercise, although they seemed to be struggling a little. Whether that was from fear or a function of having less control over their mana, he couldn't be sure.

Not knowing what else to do, Finn cautiously formed a triangle with his fingers and closed his eyes, trying to tamp down on the worry in the pit of his stomach. He most assuredly did not want to end up like that girl...

Okay, now visualize my own mana.

Almost instantly, Finn's thoughts returned to the raging inferno he had seen in the Seer's tent – the flames dancing and roaring in his mind's eye. It felt almost comforting to watch the fire, his concerns bleeding away and replaced by a faint hum of excitement that seemed to spread through his veins with a glowing warmth. The feeling was inexplicable. Like he was a child on Christmas morning, filled with energy and too anxious to sit still. He wanted to scale a mountain, build something, jump up from his seat and shout his excitement.

It took most of his willpower to remain still.

Finn forced himself to focus on the task at hand, suppressing the strange energy that flowed through him. The next step was to visualize a cup between his fingers. Although, he realized that probably wasn't going to work with the way he had imagined his own mana. How did you *pour* a bonfire? Instead, he visualized a single piece of straw floating between his fingers.

Now came the tricky part.

Finn had learned his lesson from the girl's mistake, and he could practically hear Abbad growling in his ear. He could *not* make a scene here or blow them all to kingdom come. He was going to use a spark – the smallest one possible.

Ever so carefully, he visualized a single flickering ember drifting from the flames and resting against the tip of the straw. Almost immediately, the material caught fire, flames sweeping through the dry stalk.

Finn opened his eyes slowly.

A small tendril of flame flickered between his hands, carefully contained, and floating in mid-air. His fingers shielded the small orb of fire from the view of the rest of the class. At the same time, a prompt appeared in his peripheral vision.

New Skill: Mana Mastery
Your body contains natural mana, and you have a high affinity for fire magic. Through training, you have learned to summon your mana. Continued study will allow you to master this trait, to the point where conjuring your own mana will be as natural as breathing.
Skill Level: Beginner Level 1
Effect: -1% to the mana cost of spells.

"Wow, that was fast," Kyyle said.

Finn jumped, having forgotten that the gangly youth was sitting beside him. Abruptly, the flame sputtered out.

"Shit, you surprised me," Finn said.

"Yeah, I saw that," the young man replied with an amused smile. "How did you do that so quick? Besides the girl that blew herself up, the rest of the class seems to be struggling."

Finn shrugged. "I'm not sure. I just did what the teacher said."

As though he had summoned her, Lamia's voice rang across the room. "Really? None of you have managed to summon your mana yet? I thought I'd never see the day that an entire class gets expelled.

"Perhaps you simply lack incentive," Lamia murmured, eyeing the class. "The first student who manages to summon their mana – in a controlled way – will be given their first spell," she said.

Immediately, the students scrambled to try again, some of their reservation at the girl's injury fading in the face of

Lamia's reward. Finn could only shake his head. Their instructor's offer seemed pretty transparent from his point of view.

"You already managed to..." Kyyle began, but Finn cut him off.

"Quiet. I don't want credit," Finn said quickly.

Mostly, he didn't want to get on Lamia's radar. He had already messed up by showing up to class late. He'd prefer if she never knew his name. Besides, he suspected the teacher's reward would either involve dumping the spell's information into his brain or would highlight the fact that he didn't know the mage language. He wanted to avoid the former and sure as hell didn't want to broadcast the latter.

However, Kyyle seemed to draw a different conclusion, his brow furrowing as he glanced back and forth between Finn and the rest of the class. "You don't want them to know your affinity, do you? Since we'll ultimately be competing against each other, that would give them an advantage?"

Finn cocked his head. He supposed that explanation made sense. Actually, now that Kyyle had said it aloud, that was actually a pretty good reason to keep that sort of information close to the vest. Their affinity and the spells they were capable of casting would soon become valuable information.

However, he was saved from responding when a shout went up from the front of the class. The overachiever from their orientation had risen from her seat, a small ball of water held between her hands – the mana stable.

Go figure, Finn thought dryly.

"Well, it seems we have a winner. Someone managed the very basics of spellcasting. Let's all celebrate this mundane victory," Lamia said, clapping her hands in a bored rhythm. "What's your name, girl?"

"Vanessa," she replied, a glowing smile on her face as she stared at the ball of water mana – despite Lamia's sour tone.

With a swipe of her hand, Lamia immediately dispelled the mana, the water disintegrating into small tendrils of mist. Then her fingers darted forward and touched Vanessa's temple, a trickle of sapphire energy seeping through the skin.

Vanessa blinked rapidly, tilting her head to the side with a curious expression on her face.

"Go ahead, cast the spell," Lamia urged her. The entire class was watching anxiously.

Slowly, Vanessa's hands began to twine through a series of gestures, the girl muttering words under her breath. Finn watched her fingers carefully, noting that there seemed to be a pattern to the way they moved. Tendrils of vapor condensed in the air in front of the girl, swiftly forming a shard of ice that grew until it was nearly a foot long and the tip was jagged and sharp. With a final gesture, Vanessa released the spell.

The bolt launched across the room, students diving out of the way, before crashing into the stone wall on the other side of the room. The spear of ice fractured into dozens of pieces, some of the frozen shards bouncing off Finn's shirt.

"That is the type of power you all are striving to achieve," Lamia said softly into the hushed silence that followed. "And this is merely the first step. With dedication and training, Vanessa can summon a swirling vortex of ice and snow that could level entire towns or freeze a charging warrior in place. This is what it means to be a *mage*."

Lamia's eyes swept back across the class. "Now, who else can conjure their mana?"

*   *   *

The class lasted another two hours.

Nearly all of the students had managed to summon their mana – although, many were less controlled than Vanessa, the energy sputtering out quickly or exploding violently. Luckily, no one had been injured as severely as the first air mage.

Finn had steadfastly refused to summon the flame again.

He was among the handful of students that had

"failed" to achieve the task.

When she finally grew impatient with the slower students, Lamia had moved on to teach them about the hand gestures that controlled their mana. There were a simple set of basic gestures that directed the flow of mana and specific spells used certain combinations of those gestures. This explained the movements that Vanessa's fingers had made when she cast the *Ice Bolt*.

Finn emulated each gesture with his fingers, carefully practicing the movements. Yet he still refused to summon his own mana again. He resolved to attempt the process in private once he was able to return to the library. There was no sense in drawing any more attention.

"We'll conclude here for today. Go and practice," Lamia called out, interrupting the latest practice session. "We will meet again in two days. I expect you all to have advanced to at least beginner level 5 in *Mana Mastery* by that time. You should repeat the basic hand gestures until they are second nature."

This was met with a murmur of noise as the students began to disperse. Finn noticed that some of the other students were already beginning to collect into groups. For example, a few students had approached Vanessa, and Finn noticed the burly man from their "orientation" was huddled with a group of guys. It seemed that cliques had already started to form.

Shaking his head, Finn lifted himself from his seat. Yet he hesitated when he noticed that Kyyle hadn't moved. The young man was staring into space, his hands dancing in the air.

"What are you doing?" Finn asked.

Kyyle barely spared him a glance, before his eyes flitted to the other students. He gestured for Finn to move closer and he sat back down on the bench.

"I'm creating a journal," Kyyle said in a whisper. "After I noticed you hiding your mana earlier, I decided to start tracking each person's name, affinity, rank, and known spells."

Finn didn't have to ask why. He had to admit that this

was useful information, especially with the upcoming duels. That might also go a long way towards explaining why Kyyle had done his best to imitate Finn during the class. The young man had managed to summon a small ball of earth but had immediately dismissed the mana.

"It's a good idea," Finn acknowledged. "But how exactly are you recording that information? It just looks like you're waving at the air."

Kyyle paused, staring at him incredulously. "I'm using the in-game console," he said. "Seriously, did you read anything about the game before logging in?"

Finn's eyes widened, completely ignoring Kyyle's teasing. With a few quick swipes, he brought up his system UI and scrolled down the menus until he found the console. He tapped the icon, and a translucent blue screen and keyboard appeared in front of him. Finn could only stare at the console numbly.

Holy shit. A few ideas for how to tackle his language training were already tumbling through his brain.

"...so the headset connects to the public network and simulates a normal workstation here. Hey, are you listening?" Kyyle snapped, forcing Finn to look at him.

"Uh, sorry. I just got distracted trying to find the console," he replied. "Isn't this immersion-breaking, being able to access the public network in-game?"

Kyyle shrugged. "It's probably more about convenience. Adding this sort of feature keeps us in-game longer since we don't need to log out to answer an email or look something up."

"I guess that makes sense..." Finn murmured distractedly.

The idea that had been hovering at the edges of Finn's mind was back with a vengeance, suddenly shifting from an ephemeral thought to something far more tangible. "What's to stop someone from abusing the console or using it to aid them in-game?" he suddenly asked.

"What do you mean?" Kyyle asked.

"What if a player tried to modify the game's code, for example?"

Kyyle just stared at him with a deadpan expression.

"Wait, are you serious?"

"Sure, why not?" Finn asked.

"Uh, because this is a horribly sophisticated game system and the AI is cutting edge," Kyyle answered immediately. "It would take a really experienced programmer to mess with the code. Besides, I bet the AI would shut that down hard and fast. I remember reading something somewhere about Cerillion Entertainment holding an open invitation to hack its software during the beta. They had like a two-million-dollar prize."

"And?" Finn asked.

"And no one beat it. No one," Kyyle answered. "Forget regular anti-cheat protections. This game is unhackable."

Finn ran a hand through his hair, his thoughts already spinning. "Yeah, but what if we didn't try to *cheat*? Older games used to have approved UI mods for example – most were just for convenience or to better keep track of information. Isn't that what you're doing with the in-game console right now? Using it to jot down information?"

"Well, I mean, I guess that's sort of the same idea," Kyyle said, glancing between Finn and a screen he couldn't see. "But—"

Kyyle stopped talking abruptly, his eyes centering on something over Finn's shoulder.

He turned to find their teacher standing behind him, her eyes watching him calmly. Most of the other students had already emptied from the room, giving Lamia a wide berth. There was something about their instructor that was a little… well, terrifying. Maybe it was the feeling that she would freeze someone alive without a second thought.

"Well, if it isn't our tardy student. I couldn't help but notice that you didn't manage to summon your mana during class," Lamia said, judgment lacing her voice.

Kyyle opened his mouth, and Finn stepped on his foot discreetly, the younger man biting back a yelp. "It was challenging, but I will keep practicing," Finn replied, bowing his head as he had seen Abbad do with Nefreet.

"See that you do," Lamia replied. "Otherwise, I may need to make an example of you for the rest of the class."

When Finn looked up, he found a broad, terrifying smile on the woman's face. There was something off about it, as though it showed too much teeth. Or maybe it was the malicious glint in her eye.

"I find an early expulsion always encourages the other students to work harder."

With that, she turned on her heel and strode out of the room, leaving the pair alone.

"Wow, that woman gives me the creeps," Kyyle muttered.

"Yeah, you and me both," Finn replied.

A weight had settled in his stomach. He was treading a precarious path here. He needed to be cautious about revealing his high affinity, but it appeared he had erred too far in the other direction – indicating that he was the weak and injured animal in the pack. And Lamia had just looked very much like a lion, waiting for a single misstep.

He could always reveal his ability to summon mana, but that wouldn't change the fact that he didn't know Veridian. It would become obvious soon just how far behind the others he really was. And Lamia was already watching – waiting for him to give her a reason to "make an example of him."

Finn glanced back at Kyyle, who was already tapping away at his notes again. Maybe Finn could remedy the situation. After discovering the in-game console, an idea was beginning to take shape in his mind. There might be a way to possibly catch back up with the others.

He just hoped it would work.

Chapter 9 - Converted

Finn stepped off the lift on the fourth floor of the library and made a beeline toward his study area on the far side of the floor. He was anxious to get started and had been forced to resist the urge to jog through the Mage Guild.

As soon as he reached the table, he cleared off some space, shoving the books and scrolls out of the way before taking a seat in one of the hard, wooden chairs. Finn then pulled up his system UI. Within moments, he had found the in-game console again, a translucent blue screen flashing into existence in front of him.

Now he needed to explore a little.

Finn began digging through the console. Part of him expected to find a super streamlined workstation, with limits placed on his public network access and the console's integration with the headset hardware. However, his eyes widened only minutes later when he realized there were precious few restrictions placed on the in-game console. Hell, he could still connect to the local network in his lab!

That moment of hesitation didn't last long.

Finn's hands flew over the translucent keyboard as he established a connection to his personal workstation. A few seconds later, a prompt popped up.

System Notice
You are preparing to connect your personal workstation to Awaken Online. Are you willing to grant permissions to allow the game world and local hardware to access your personal workstation? [Yes/No]

Finn tapped "yes." He knew Daniel would take steps to protect his home network and encrypt the connection automatically.

A moment later, the prompt disappeared. Now he needed to take the next step. With the connection established, Finn could finally call for some reinforcements. Another few seconds passed, and a translucent blue cloud suddenly began to form in the air beside Finn, an inadvertent grin creeping across his face.

"Hello, sir," Daniel reported, bobbing slightly in the air.

"Hello, Daniel," Finn replied, excitement lacing his voice. If he was able to use his own AI controller, this opened up quite a few possibilities. However, his smile abruptly disappeared as Daniel froze in mid-air and a cage of green light suddenly encircled the AI.

Another notice appeared before Finn could question what was happening.

System Notice

A foreign and unauthenticated AI controller has accessed the game system.

The foreign AI controller's system privileges have been automatically restricted to prevent any security breach to the game system or harm to other players.

If you wish to access the foreign AI controller inside AO, it will need to be integrated into the environment and grant System Controller XC239.90 full administrative privileges within the game world.

Do you accept?

[Yes/No]

"Shit," Finn muttered. Perhaps he had underestimated just how sophisticated the game's AI really was. It had caught the foreign software intrusion immediately.

The question now was whether to allow the game's controller to have full admin privileges over Daniel. Grimacing, Finn swept the notice to the side and his fingers danced across the keyboard once again. Before he was going to grant those permissions, he needed to put some protections in place. He backed up Daniel's core processes and then built a limited firewall between his local network and the game world.

He was essentially instancing Daniel – creating a home version and a game version, with limited communication between the two. The core processes would be roughly the same – assuming the game's AI didn't make any radical changes. But this would also ensure that Finn didn't inadvertently give the game's AI any control over his home network.

Once he finished, Finn glanced back at the prompt. There was only one way to see if this would work.

With a sigh, he hit "Accept."

The green cage around Daniel fragmented and broke away in a cascade of small particles. The blue wisp then pulsed rhythmically, flashing and spinning in place. Suddenly, the AI changed color, sapphire giving away to varied hues of orange and red. Even more interesting, Daniel seemed to be emitting heat, the air rippling and warping around him.

Only a few short seconds later, another prompt popped up.

System Notice

Subsystem AI Controller A100.01 (code-named "Daniel") has been authenticated and integrated into the game world.

Daniel is now classified as an in-game pet, specifically a fledgling *fire elemental*. Lacking a corporeal form, Daniel is unable to harm other creatures or players. He is currently classified as a "non-combat pet." However, he can still perform tasks and assist the player.

Well, that works, Finn thought to himself.

"Alright, are you operational now, Daniel?" he asked tentatively, staring at the orange ball of flame.

"Yes... yes, sir," the AI responded, his voice sounding slightly confused. That was odd. Finn couldn't help but wonder if a few changes had been made to this instance's code.

"Okay. How much progress have you made on downloading and analyzing the software training courses?" Finn asked. This would test whether this instanced version had retained restricted access to Finn's home network.

"I was at nearly 87%, although I note that my access to those files is now restricted," Daniel replied.

Perfect, Finn thought. His fingers were already dancing across the terminal's keyboard again – working to restore the in-game instance's access to the local files.

"Don't worry about it, I'll make sure you have access again," Finn reassured the AI. He glanced at the books and scrolls that were still strewn about the table. "I think I have a first assignment for you in the meantime."

"Sir?" Daniel queried.

"Can you scan the contents of these documents?" Finn asked, pointing at the materials on the table. "I'd like to be able to view digital versions using the in-game console."

"Give me just a moment," Daniel replied.

The wisp then swept forward, the paper and pages rustling as the AI passed over them. Daniel flitted to a book, and a thin beam of light was projected from his core, the pages flipping slowly as the AI scanned each page. Finn was just about to mention something about Daniel's scanning speed when his pace suddenly picked up.

The pages flew past in a blur of motion, and the beam of light stuttered erratically. Within only a few moments, Daniel had completed one book and moved on to the next. Finn spared a nervous glance through the nearby stacks, hoping no one would notice the strobe lights flashing in this small dingy corner of the library. The last thing he needed was a librarian checking out some sort of impromptu rave.

However, Daniel made swift progress. Within only a few minutes, he had scanned all of the materials, letting out a faint chirp. "Task completed!"

Did he just sound excited? Finn stared at the AI for a second, noting the way the wisp danced in place as though happy to have finished his assignment.

As though Julia's meddling wasn't bad enough... Now some foreign AI is messing with Daniel. At least I had the foresight to instance this version before integrating him.

Finn let out a sigh. "Uh, thanks, Daniel," he said, and the wisp flashed with a bright pulse of orange light. Finn spared a nervous glance at the materials on the desk, but the AI hadn't accidentally set any of the books or scrolls on fire.

"Is there anything else I can do for you?" Daniel asked.

"Actually, yes," Finn replied slowly.

Scanning the materials was helpful, but it was just a short-term thing. He was just reading the page contents off a screen instead of a scroll. It was better than nothing – at least for now, but he ultimately needed to find a way to streamline his studies.

"I've provided you with limited access to my home network. You should now be able to access the language software," Finn explained. "Once your local instance has finished compiling the code from the various software tools, can you upload the contents of the documents you just scanned? I want to create language learning software for Veridian."

Daniel pulsed softly as though considering this question. "I can help with this! Based on the local instance's progress, it should take approximately 6 hours, real-world time, to accomplish this task."

Finn grimaced. Which meant he would have to make do for the next 18-24 hours in-game. He supposed he could live with that – at least for now.

"Is there anything else I can help you with, Master?" Daniel chirped again.

"Master?" Finn asked in an incredulous voice. He definitely hadn't added that dialogue.

"Would you prefer I call you something else?" Daniel

chirped again. "Your highness, your excellency, lord code-monkey, your majesty, your honor…"

Did he just say lord code-monkey?

"Okay, stop," Finn snapped, interrupting the AI. "*Sir* is just fine."

"Of course, sir. Is there anything else I can help you with?" Daniel replied, although this time, he sounded a little despondent.

Damn it. Why do I feel bad for barking at a flaming ball of AI crazy?

"Uh, no, I think I'm good for now," Finn replied, giving the AI a confused glance.

"Okay, I guess I'll just leave then…" Daniel said in a morose voice. Before Finn could respond, he winked out of existence in a flash of light.

Finn just stared at the blank spot the AI had occupied. When he caught a free moment, he would have to try to remember to review the AI's code. Something weird had obviously happened during that integration process.

Shaking his head, Finn turned back to the screen hovering in the air in front of him. An emotionally sensitive AI aside, he needed to get to work. He stood abruptly, and, with a flick of his wrist, he pulled up multiple screens. A dictionary, grammar rulebook, translations materials all settled into place around him. A familiar story took center stage, a picture of a cat caught in a tree easily visible on-screen.

Finn had to resist the urge to sigh. Maybe if he could make some progress, he could move on to a more interesting story. The children's book really was just a slap in the face.

"Okay, Mittens. Let's see if you ever make it out of that tree…"

* * *

Finn rubbed at his eyes, his vision wavering slightly as he tried to focus on the shimmering blue screens in front of him. He had lost track of time while studying. All that occupied his mind were an endless string of nouns, verbs, and adjectives. Although, he wasn't sure what was worse, the sheer amount of memorization this language required or the horribly obtuse grammar rules.

He had learned enough basic vocabulary at this point that he had come to an awkward revelation. In short, most sentences in Veridian were formed in *rhyming couplets*. It was like the language had been created by a drunken Chinese bard who was just a little too fond of Shakespeare. A least that's what Finn chose to believe. It was either that or the game was intentionally torturing him.

"I see you are hard at work," Abbad commented, appearing from behind a stack of books. Finn hadn't even heard the man approach.

"I guess so," Finn replied tiredly, slumping back against the table, and waving the screens out of the way to give his eyes a break. Some part of him knew that they weren't real – eye strain probably wasn't a thing here. But who knew? AO was realistic enough that it would probably create some sort of debuff.

"How did the first class go?" the librarian asked.

Finn let out another sigh. "I think I may have caught the attention of our teacher. I was trying to downplay my affinity in order to stay at the bottom of the pack, but she took it as an opportunity to make an example of me. Apparently, one slip-up and I'm going to be out on my ass."

Abbad's expression was impassive. "Then you will simply need to do better."

Finn couldn't help the incredulous huff that escaped his throat. "Yeah, I only need to learn a new language in two weeks, and learn how to summon and control my mana, and prepare to fight in a series of deadly duels with the other students."

"You can only try," Abbad answered calmly, unperturbed by his tone.

Finn supposed that was true. He would probably fail – the odds certainly seemed impossible. But it wouldn't be for lack of effort.

"Perhaps I can offer some assistance in that regard," Abbad said.

Finn looked up at him sharply. "What do you mean?"

"Well, for example, I watched you for a moment before I made my presence known. You are only focused on one task. There is a more efficient course of action," the librarian suggested.

"Such as?" Finn asked, confused. If there was a more efficient way to learn Veridian, then he was all ears.

"You could be training your *Mana Mastery* at the same time," Abbad answered.

Finn just stared at the stoic man.

Had he just heard that right? Abbad wanted him to learn Veridian while *also* training his *Mana Mastery*?

He must have been looking at the librarian like he was crazy since the man tried to elaborate. "Your hands are idle while you practice Veridian. You could be summoning and learning to control your mana at the same time."

That seemed... well, impossible. "Okay," he began slowly, "but Lamia had us walk through this whole visualization technique—"

"That is merely a tool for beginners," Abbad interjected. "You do not need to go through that process each time. Simply remember the *feeling* of your mana while making the requisite gestures and you should be able to summon it. With your high affinity, you may find that this comes more easily than you expect."

Finn tilted his head. It had been pretty simple to summon the flame during class. With a shrug, he formed a triangle with his fingers. However, this time, instead of visualizing the flames and the straw, he focused on the excitement he had experienced when he summoned his mana the first time.

Almost instantly, the flame appeared between his fingers, dancing in the air.

"Well, shit..." Finn muttered.

"Did Lamia teach you the basic gestures?" Abbad asked.

"Uh, yeah," Finn replied, refocusing on the librarian.

"I suggest you work through them in sequence as fast as you can. Once this becomes second nature, then alter that sequence in a different rhythm. When that becomes tiresome, you should find more *creative* applications."

"For example..." the librarian murmured, trailing off.

His fingers formed the initial triangle, a spark of lightning arcing between them. With a swift series of gestures, the librarian sent the small bolt of energy arcing through the air, bouncing off a nearby glass pane, catching it seamlessly and then tossing it again.

In between the next catch and release, Abbad introduced another bolt.

And then another.

And then another.

The small corner of the library was soon filled with small electrical arcs, Abbad effectively performing an incredibly dangerous juggling act. Abruptly, his fingers swept forward, neatly snatching the bolts from the air – the energy dissipating harmlessly.

"I think that might be just a bit beyond my abilities," Finn replied dryly, his mind wheeling as he watched the exchange. Abbad hadn't even cast a spell. That was just what he could do summoning and manipulating the flow of his own mana?

"For now," Abbad replied evenly. "That is why you need practice. Start with a single ball of flame. Once it feels natural to control its movements, try adding another."

"Or I'll set the library on fire," Finn retorted, waving at the books.

A rare smile tugged at Abbad's lips. "I would not be so negligent as to leave our materials unwarded. You do not need to be concerned about damaging the books." As he spoke, Abbad's fingers were a blur of motion. Within seconds, a sphere of air enveloped Finn, glimmering with a faint yellow light.

"This should be more than sufficient to stop a wayward orb," Abbad commented, a hint of amusement lacing his voice.

Finn chewed on the inside of his cheek, glancing first at the barrier of air and then down at the flame still lingering between his fingers. It looked like he was out of excuses.

Could he really pull off the same little juggling act? While also studying Veridian? He had to admit that the language training was coming along more easily than he had expected, but this still seemed crazy.

Yet his mana still surged through his veins, his doubt giving way to a tantalizing mixture of excitement and curiosity. He had to admit that a part of him wanted to find out if he could manage the feat.

He supposed there was only one way to find out.

"Alright—" Finn began but stopped short as he realized that Abbad had disappeared just as silently as he arrived. He grumbled under his breath. It seemed that their brief conversation was over. And as always, Abbad had left him with more homework.

"I didn't actually want to go back to school…" Finn muttered to himself.

However, there was only one way forward. His gaze turned to the screens around him, shifting them in the air with a flick of his wrist. It was time to get back to work.

Even as his eyes started skimming the first line, his fingers formed a familiar triangle, that same warmth seeping into his limbs and a renewed surge of energy coursing through his veins. Finn began to twist his fingers through the series of basic gestures, doing his best to concentrate on the words flowing across the screen as an orb of fire slowly began to orbit him. It was challenging… but not *impossible*.

He could work with that.

Chapter 10 - Clueless

A sudden chime echoed through the library, interrupting Finn's concentration.

"Hello, sir!" Daniel chirped, his orange form suddenly popping into existence a few inches away from Finn's head.

Typically, this sort of abrupt interruption wouldn't be a problem. Of course, Finn usually wasn't trying to juggle flaming orbs while studying an arcane language either.

Two fiery spheres encircled Finn, swiftly rotating inward and outward as he controlled the movement with a series of hand gestures. Unfortunately, just before Daniel appeared, he had inverted the movement, sending the flaming balls hurtling back toward himself.

His eyes widened in shock.

"Oh shit," Finn managed to mutter. With the unexpected interruption, he didn't have time to stop the orbs.

So, he did the next best thing. Finn dropped to the ground, the air rushing from his lungs even as he felt the heat of the spheres race past him. A moment later, the balls crashed against the wind barrier that Abbad had created, and it whisked away the oxygen surrounding each orb. They soon sputtered out in a rather anti-climatic fashion.

"Sir, are you alright?" Daniel asked, concern lacing his voice.

"I'm fine," Finn groaned from the ground, slowly pushing himself back to his feet. Small tendrils of smoke drifted away from the hem of his robe, evidence that one of the orbs had struck a glancing blow. He had learned over the last couple of days that the orbs weren't enough to deal real damage, but they sure stung when they hit.

"What is it?" he snapped, glaring at the AI's flaming form.

"You told me to give you a fifteen-minute warning before your next class!" Daniel replied, his voice just a little too cheery. Had the AI surprised him on purpose? Maybe as payback for their last exchange? Finn shook his head. He had to be imagining that.

He glanced at the in-game clock in the corner of his vision. Indeed, hours had passed since he had last looked up. Honestly, he had barely noticed. Training both his *Mana Mastery* and Veridian at the same time took up all of his concentration. He couldn't even remember the last time he had taken a break.

Rubbing at his eyes, Finn leaned back against the nearby table, trying to gather his thoughts. He expected this next class was going to be rough. He had already managed to paint a target on his back with Lamia, and he suspected that they were going to be learning new spells today. Hopefully, he had learned enough to let him fake it for a day.

Speaking of which, he ought to check on his progress.

Opening his eyes, Finn brought up his in-game prompts with a flick of his wrist. He had disabled the notifications while training – you know, to avoid accidentally charbroiling himself mid-lesson. Not that Daniel seemed to notice that fact…

x6 Level Up!
You have (50) undistributed stat points.

x5 Skill Rank Up: Reading
Skill Level: Beginner Level 6
Effect 1: 10% increased learning speed while reading.

x3 Skill Rank Up: Learning
Skill Level: Beginner Level 4
Effect 1: 8% increased learning speed for skills and spells.

x4 Skill Rank Up: Mana Mastery
Skill Level: Beginner Level 5
Effect: -3% to the mana cost of spells.

At least he had made decent progress. He had met Lamia's requirements for *Mana Mastery* on top of gaining another six levels. He still wasn't quite certain what to do with his stat points, so he resolved to hold onto them, even though he was tempted to dump them into either *Intelligence* or *Willpower*. If AO was anything like games he had played in the past, he suspected those stats would increase his total mana pool and regeneration, which would make it easier to train *Mana Mastery*.

"Sir, you only have 10 minutes left," Daniel reminded him.

With a sigh, Finn swept the prompts aside. He knew he was just stalling. He'd much rather stay here in the library and keep training, but that didn't seem to be in the cards.

He shoved himself away from the table. "Alright, let's go and try not to get expelled."

*   *   *

When Finn stepped into the classroom a few minutes later, it was abuzz with students talking and lounging around the stone benches. He spared a glance at the other mages. It seemed his observation the day before had been accurate. Groups had begun to form, the students acting far more familiar with each other.

Although, Finn suspected those relationships probably wouldn't last long, not with the duels approaching swiftly. His gaze panned to the burly guy he had seen during the initial guild induction ceremony. He was already surrounded by a band of other guys, sitting in the middle of the pack, and letting their chatter pass around him. Their gaze met briefly, and the other player smirked before glancing away dismissively.

Well, except for *some* groups. A few of the players would likely be able to maintain the newfound relationships by force. His perspective shifted as he watched the other students, now noticing the tension in their shoulders and the way they side-eyed each other with an appraising expression. Suddenly, Finn couldn't decide if the clusters of students felt like benign social cliques or more like fledgling prison gangs.

Although, he also wasn't sure if there was really a difference.

"I find it ironic that I just left high school a few years ago, just to be shoved back into a magical version," Kyyle observed dryly, popping up beside Finn.

"It doesn't get better once you get out of college. Trust me," Finn grumbled, slumping down onto a nearby bench. "The judgmental bullshit and social pecking order are still there. The only difference is that people get a little better about smiling at you while they're screwing you over. Oh, and they typically have more money and power."

"Well, aren't you just a ray of sunshine," Kyyle replied with a chuckle. His expression sobered, and he lowered his voice. "Although, you might not be entirely wrong. You hear about the break-in and the disappearances?"

Kyyle now had Finn's undivided attention. "No, I haven't. What happened?"

"You know how I've been keeping tabs on the students?" Kyyle asked, earning him a nod from Finn. "Well, a few just vanished overnight," he offered, gesturing at the room. "Although, no one seems to be making a big deal about it."

"Maybe they just stopped logging back in?" Finn suggested.

"Possibly," Kyyle replied. He hesitated. "Or they got expelled…"

He let that thought linger in the air. That wasn't a confidence-inspiring idea. Could multiple students have been expelled within the first few days? And why hadn't Finn been on the list? It seemed like Lamia held no love for him.

"Anyway," Kyyle said, interrupting his thoughts. "I also overheard some members of the faculty talking about how several novices have been attacked lately. Their equipment was stolen too. They weren't sure whether it was some sort of inside job or maybe one of the other guilds. I got the impression that there isn't a lot of love lost between the mages, the fighters, and the merchants."

Finn grimaced. Yet another complication. He supposed he would just need to learn to watch his back while he was navigating the school. Maybe the prison analogy hadn't been too far off the mark.

"Well shit," Finn muttered. "This place just gets more and more interesting by the day."

Kyyle grunted in agreement before glancing at Finn, noticing his rumpled clothing and the circles under his eyes. "Gossip aside, you look like shit," he observed. "What have you been up to?"

"Studying," Finn replied, rubbing at his eyes again. Now that he wasn't focused solely on training, the fatigue was beginning to kick in. He could feel a small headache coming on, and he idly wondered if this game had its own version of coffee.

Actually, what would eating be like in-game? He shook his head. That was a rabbit hole he didn't want to tumble down right now. He needed to be focused if he was going to make it through this class. He was already treading on thin ice – pun intended.

As though his thoughts had summoned her, Lamia marched into the room a moment later to the swish of her silk robes. She didn't even glance at the students as she approached the podium on the far end of the room.

For their part, the players froze in place as soon as they caught sight of their teacher, slowly slinking back to their seats. It was rather impressive, considering the confrontation in the starting plaza. Finn could only marvel at how quickly people got used to order and routine.

"Alright, there's no need to sugarcoat this. Today we will be teaching you your first spell. Well, a first for some of you," Lamia acknowledged, sparing a nod toward Vanessa who sat up straighter and tried (poorly) to suppress the smile on her face.

Kyyle let out an amused snort beside Finn.

"But before that, I have a quick announcement." Lamia's eyes swept across the class, hesitating briefly on each face. "There have been reports of novices being mugged in the hallways. They were uninjured, but their equipment was stolen." This earned her a few surprised and wide-eyed glances from the students.

"This may be an opportune time to explain that any violence perpetrated against other students outside of the duels will not be tolerated. If a student is found to have assaulted or killed another mage, trust me when I say that he or she will not enjoy the repercussions. In this case, exile would look like a mercy." Lamia's eyes flashed at this last statement, glowing a faint sapphire.

"Furthermore, if you observe any suspicious or unusual behavior, please report the conduct to the faculty," Lamia added.

She let this announcement linger in the air for a few seconds as she watched the students. Lamia almost seemed to be gauging their reaction. Finn glanced at Kyyle, their eyes meeting briefly. Well, they could confirm that this wasn't just a rumor then.

"Now," Lamia said sharply, switching gears, "with that out of the way, let's start on today's lesson. Since we have members of most affinities present, I'll put the spells up on the board, along with a list of the sequence of requisite hand gestures. For simplicity, we'll simply number the basic gestures," Lamia continued, her hands dancing across the podium.

The display behind their instructor flashed into existence. The screen was now broken into six rows, providing a spell name, an incantation, and a sequence of numbers. Finn's eyes skimmed down the list until he found the fire spell.

Magma Armor, huh? he thought to himself. A glance at the other spells confirmed that they sounded like defensive spells as well, one for each affinity type.

With a swipe of his wrist, Finn brought up his control panel and typed out the list of information beside the spell. He could always practice it later. He noted that a few others did the same, their hands pawing at the air. It seemed some of the players were already starting to identify and take advantage of the tools at their disposal – not that this was a particularly good sign.

"As you've no doubt noticed, these are all defensive spells. Our goal today will be to provide you with one of the basic tools to protect yourselves. Plus, this particular type of spell also allows me to teach you another important skill –

namely, how to act and cast quickly." A small, cruel smile lingered on Lamia's lips at this statement.

A hand rose into the air, accompanied by Zane's burly form. Lamia nodded at him. "Why can't you simply do what you did with Vanessa yesterday or what Nefreet did with Veridian? You know, just download the spell into our heads?" Zane asked.

Lamia tilted her head. "Looking for the easy path, hmm? To be expected of travelers," she bit out. A pause and a brief sigh followed. "Although, we may as well address this fundamental as well. The answer is that there is a limit to how much information a person can learn through that method. Generally speaking, most students can only learn five or six spells or skills by memory transfer."

Finn raised an eyebrow. Now that was interesting. He doubted there was a plausible reason for that limit. He suspected it had much more to do with not wanting to harm the players. Tampering with their memory could likely have unexpected results.

Lamia continued, "Most mages hoard those memorizations, reserving them for extremely difficult high-level spells or more complex skills. They can be quite valuable. That method of training provides not just the raw information needed to master a spell or ability, but the corresponding muscle memory. A single memorization can remove dozens – if not hundreds – of hours of work and study."

Yeah, no shit. Finn might just be a little bitter about that point right now, even if he readily acknowledged it was his own damn fault.

Zane nodded, seemingly content with that answer.

"Now, I'll give you all a few minutes to practice the spells on the board," Lamia said, gesturing at the display. "Then we'll attempt some more *hands-on* training."

Given the evil grin on the woman's face, Finn suspected that was going to be painful.

"It's a shame they didn't teach us an invisibility spell," Kyyle commented dryly. "I'd sure love a way to sneak out of this class right now."

Finn let out a chuckle before shifting his attention to the row of information for *Magma Armor*. The hand gestures were pretty straightforward. His fingers could already easily twine through the sequence after the hours he had spent training in the library.

However, the incantation was another matter entirely. The text looked like it was written in a foreign language – which it was, of course. He could make out a few terms. Something about "heat" and "hard," but that was about it. The problem was that he simply didn't have the vocabulary to identify the other symbols.

For a moment, he considered calling Daniel to help translate, but hesitated, his eyes skimming the room. Did he really want to give away that he had essentially created an in-game pet? At the same time, if he couldn't cast this spell, would Lamia try to expel him?

To make matters worse, the other students didn't seem to be having a problem. Kyyle had already managed to turn his right arm to stone, the skin turning a dark, solid gray. Across the room, Finn could see that Vanessa appeared to be summoning a block of ice which swiftly formed a wall of frozen water in front of her.

"Alright, time's up," Lamia called out. The students stilled and returned to their seats.

Damn it, he thought to himself.

"Learning a defensive spell is merely the first step in your training," their teacher continued. "Casting that spell needs to become second nature. You will rarely have time to consult a spellbook or plan ahead in the middle of a fight. Your reaction needs to be instinctive."

A smile crept across her face again. "With that in mind, the best way to train is to simulate real combat."

Lamia's gaze skimmed the class. "Does anyone want to go first?"

The silence that lingered in the room was almost deafening. You could have heard a pin drop. No one raised a hand, and most of the students seemed to slink down in their seats, avoiding eye contact with Lamia. Even Vanessa and Zane seemed unnaturally quiet.

Finn followed their lead and edged downward in his seat. It was one thing to show up to a class or test unprepared – he suspected everyone had experienced that dread realization at some point. However, in the real world, the worst that could happen was that you would get embarrassed or fail the exam. Finn wasn't so sure he was going to get off with a bit of public humiliation if Lamia chose him.

"What? Have you all suddenly lost your tongues? You were so chatty when I came in earlier. What happened?" Lamia asked, her voice thick with sarcasm.

"In that case, I'll just have to choose someone myself," she continued.

Finn was actually wondering if there was a way to discreetly hide behind his bench when Lamia's eyes landed on him. He could feel a dead weight settle in the bottom of his stomach. Maybe it was the predatory gleam in her eye or the way her fingers twitched, as though eager to start casting.

"Finn, why don't you come show us what you've got?" Lamia suggested, gesturing at the front of the classroom, although it was clear that the offer wasn't up for debate.

As Finn reluctantly rose to his feet, Kyyle spared him a sympathetic look.

Finn marched up to the front of the room like he was stepping up to a gas chamber. He could feel the eyes of the other students on him. In other circumstances, he might have appreciated the irony here. This was like a classic schoolroom scene. Come to the front of the room and write something on the board, right? Except for the part where he was pretty sure Lamia was about to horribly maim him in front of the entire class.

I guess we'll get to see how the pain feedback works in-game.

As Finn squared off with their teacher, her smile widened further. "So, uh, what do you need for me to do?" Finn asked cautiously.

"Oh, that's simple," she replied calmly, her eyes beginning to glow with a soft sapphire light. "You just need to survive."

Chapter 11 - Creative

Lamia didn't give Finn a chance to question her teaching style.

Instead, her hands began moving as she whispered arcane words under her breath. Finn could feel his pulse pounding in his ears, and his hands clenched reflexively. It might have been the adrenaline, but it felt like the teacher was taking her time. Her fingers twined through the gestures slowly, as though she was savoring this moment and the fear that must be shining in his eyes.

Shit. What the hell do I do? There was no way he was going to be able to cast *Magma Armor* – at least not without some uninterrupted time to study and translate the incantation.

That was time he didn't have.

Moisture was already accumulating in the air beside Lamia, the droplets thickening and freezing until they formed a spear of ice – similar to the one that Vanessa had cast the day before. However, this icy shard wasn't being cast by an amateur.

"Hey, this seems..." Finn began, holding up his hands.

Lamia didn't wait for him to finish.

The ice spear launched forward toward Finn at an incredible speed. He jumped to the side but moved just a hair too slow. He felt something rip through the fabric of his robes, and a line of burning pain bloomed along his arm. The lance struck the wall behind him a moment later, fragments of ice showering the floor.

A notification flashed in the corner of Finn's vision.

-15 Damage (Glancing).

"Fuck," Finn muttered, his fingers touching at the rip in his robes. They came away covered in blood. He was surprised by the dull ache that radiated from the wound. It didn't have the sharp sting of a real injury – feeling more muted. Although, he decided right then and there that he didn't love getting hit in-game.

More important, that single glancing blow had shaved off 10% of his current health. Despite the panic he felt flooding his mind, it set to work analyzing his situation. There were two takeaways here. First, the game's damage system seemed realistic, modifying the damage based on where and how he was hit. A shard to the face would probably kill him, but a scratch along his arm would just leave him wounded.

Second, he could probably only take one or two direct hits before he died.

Lamia observed him coldly as Finn stared at the blood on his fingers. "You didn't even try to cast your defensive spell," she observed, her voice eerily calm. "Have you even managed to summon your mana after the first class?"

Finn gritted his teeth. This was what he got for trying to hide his abilities. Lamia thought he was an idiot. He had thought the woman cruel before, but something about channeling her mana had changed her – and for the worse. Those cold, glowing eyes watched him with detached disinterest, as though he was a bug in a jar. There was no animosity there, but also no remorse.

"Our guild is no place for the weak," Lamia stated in that same impassive voice. "I need to make an example of you to show the others that the stakes here are very real." Even as she spoke, her fingers were moving again, ominous moisture already beginning to accumulate around her.

"However, in the interest of fairness, I will make you a deal," the ice mage continued. "If you aren't able to defend yourself, then you will be expelled – immediately. Your mana purged and you will be forced to wander the sands."

"And if I manage to defend myself?" Finn asked, although the possibility seemed hopeless. It didn't help that he could hear the anxious murmur of his classmates. They had just increased the stakes of this little "lesson."

Lamia smiled, but the expression didn't reach her frigid eyes. "I'll let you stay in the school. I'll even go ahead and pass you from the beginning class with flying colors."

She didn't give him time to respond. A second icy shard formed in the air beside Lamia, a pair of frozen lances now floating on either side of her.

Finn's eyes widened.

The spears launched forward, and he dove to the side, hitting the ground hard. He felt a rush of air as one of the lances raced past, slamming into the wall behind him and shattering explosively. Yet he never heard the second shard hit the stone. It took a fraction of a second before he realized what had happened, muted pain rippling from his thigh.

He looked down to see the shard embedded in his skin; the ice was at least a few inches deep. Finn stared at the wound in horror, feeling the pain radiate from the injury and his mind flailing. The flashing notification that had appeared in the corner of his vision didn't help either.

-110 Damage.

He was nearly dead.

Even worse, Finn could only stare at the shard. He remembered the last time he had felt this sort of pain – the vague image of tumbling car upholstery and a feeling of weightlessness returning to him. He could feel his breath coming in ragged, frantic gasps. It felt like he was drowning, gulping at the air like a dying man.

Rachael's face returned to him. He saw her eyes, pleading. Frantic. The way her hand reached for him. He remembered the feeling of helpless despair – the same feeling that settled in his stomach right now.

"You stand on death's door, and yet you still do not act," Lamia observed with icy precision. "And this is what the Emir and our headmaster fear? Travelers who are too afraid to even fight back?" She sounded confused, a trace of disgust entering her voice.

At her words, Finn suddenly felt... angry. She mocked his helplessness, the same way he had tortured himself for years. He hadn't been able to protect Rachael. And he was too weak to stand up to Lamia now. Yet hearing it coming from her felt different. It gave him a target for his anger.

Although he hadn't summoned it, the familiar warmth of his mana seeped through his limbs, flowing through his veins, and settling in his chest. This feeling was different. It wasn't the soft glow of a candle's flame. It was a roaring, angry fire that crackled and popped.

Before he knew what he was doing, Finn grabbed the icy shard embedded in his thigh. With a quick jerk and a hissing breath, he yanked it free, blood pooling around the wound. Then with a grunt, he shifted his weight, struggling to push himself to his feet with his injured, unresponsive leg. Yet he was used to that feeling. He had lived with it for years now.

Then he met Lamia's sharp gaze. He could still feel the rage burning in his chest, urging him to fight back. To do *something*, even in the face of impossible odds. It gave him strength, and he clung to that fiery sensation.

"Ahh, I see your spirit isn't entirely broken," Lamia said, tilting her head as she observed him. "Yet it doesn't matter."

Finn watched, almost in slow motion, as her fingers began to curl into another intricate pattern. He needed a plan. He couldn't cast *Magma Armor,* and he doubted Lamia was going to let him dodge again. Even a glancing blow might kill him now – a point that was driven home by the red notifications that continued to flash in his peripheral vision.

What did he have left?

Could he cast *anything*?

Finn's thoughts abruptly returned to the library, remembering how he had summoned the orbs of flames – even without the incantation for a spell. He also remembered how the girl had injured herself during their first class, summoning a massive blast of lightning. Behind Lamia, he could still see the board flashing with multi-colored lights, the indecipherable words of *Magma Shield* mocking him.

Even as Finn noticed moisture beginning to accumulate around Lamia in a dense cloud, an idea tickled at the edges of his mind, a thought born of desperation and pain and anger. The words of the spell had a structure, one he hadn't quite noticed before. Almost like it was a rhyming couplet. A magical haiku with its own internal syntax and restrictions. He also knew a few words – a child's magical vocabulary, but maybe it was enough.

What if he created something of his own?

That question swam through his mind. Challenging him. Taunting him.

Shards of ice were forming around Lamia now, at least a dozen lances materializing in the air like a deadly hailstorm, the tips of each frozen spear homing in on Finn's position.

He was running out of time.

Finn's hands began to move. His fingers twined through a set of now-familiar gestures. He didn't hold anything back this time. Instead of a small tendril of warmth, he fed the spell the molten anger that surged through his veins. The burning sensation in his chest only grew hotter in response, the flames pushing away any lingering doubt or reservation.

At the same time, he began muttering arcane words under his breath. He drew on the vocabulary he knew – words that conjured an image of flames and fire. Aura. Area. Hot. Heat. It wasn't artful. It was an incantation born of desperation.

A ball of flame emerged between Finn's hands, the flames lapping at the air hungrily. He wasn't able to focus on anything else anymore. The world bled away until all he saw was the flicker and dance of the orange flames. They weren't nearly enough. So, he fed it more. The fire grew, expanding rapidly until the air around Finn began to ripple with heat.

And still, he gave it more.

The flames began to encircle him, the fire burning brightly.

Finn was having difficulty breathing now, his lungs heaving frantically but filling only with superheated air that burned his throat. New notifications were flashing in the corner of his vision. Yet he didn't let himself stop or become distracted.

Finn looked up then. He saw Lamia facing him, her sapphire eyes wide as she took in the globe of fire between his hands and the tendrils of flames that now encircled him. She quickly launched the icy projectiles toward him.

And then he was done, the final words of the spell

slipping past his lips.

The world exploded around Finn.

He saw nothing but fiery flames and felt torrential heat engulf him. The fire didn't burn him – at least, not really. But he still couldn't breathe, slowly suffocating amid his own flames. His vision swam and danced in time with the fire. For a fraction of a second, he thought he saw a familiar face staring back at him, burning eyes set above a silken veil. However, as he tried to focus on the image, it disappeared, and darkness crept into the corners of his vision.

And then Finn finally let go...

*   *   *

Finn woke to the sensation of icy cold water splashing across his face. He sat up abruptly, sputtering and coughing, feeling suddenly disoriented and confused.

He pawed at his face, trying to clear the water from his eyes.

"Are you alright?" someone asked. Finn glanced at the source of the noise, a familiar face hovering in his vision. It took his mind a moment to connect the dots. This was Vanessa – the water mage. Possibly the reason he was very wet right now?

"Uh, I think so?" Finn croaked. His voice sounded dry and hoarse, and his throat felt like he had swallowed sandpaper.

Then he saw the scene around him, and his mind went blank.

Finn sat in the center of a ring of charred stone, the material burned a stark black. Around this circle was a wall of half-melted ice. Even as he looked on, the frozen barrier was breaking apart, revealing that most of the class was now pushed back against the far wall of the classroom. Although, they were creeping closer now that no one was flinging spells around the room.

"What happened?" Finn choked out.

"A question I'd like answered as well," a voice bit out.

Finn glanced over to find Lamia standing next to the

classroom's ruined podium. She looked like she had just run through flames, her robes charred and stray tendrils of smoke still curling into the air. As he looked on, she patted at her arm to put out a stray ember.

"What was that you cast?" Lamia demanded, her eyes focused on Finn. He saw anger there and something else that he was having trouble putting a name to. Fear maybe? "I just barely managed to protect myself and the rest of the classroom."

"I-I'm not sure," Finn replied, not even sure he could answer that question himself. He remembered coming up with words for a spell – a *new* spell, potentially. However, he sure as hell wasn't going to say that. Even in his disoriented state, he could recall that he was supposed to be keeping a low profile.

Although, as his eyes skimmed back across the ruined classroom, he could feel an uneasy weight settle in his stomach.

It seems like I bungled that goal. Even if Lamia doesn't kill me right now, Abbad will probably be waiting in line.

"Well, you better get sure quickly," Lamia snapped, stalking toward him. "Are you a spy from another guild? A foreign mage?"

He needed an explanation that Lamia would buy. Finn glanced at Vanessa out of the corner of his eyes, the winner of their little *Mana Mastery* challenge the day before. A sudden thought occurred to him.

Finn looked back at Lamia, meeting her eyes and trying to sound confused and naive. That wasn't as hard as it sounded under the circumstances. "I was... I was desperate. I thought you were going to kill me. So, I just summoned my mana – all of it. Like that girl that blew herself up did the other day."

Lamia stared at him, and Finn had to resist the urge to hold his breath. Had she noticed him chanting under his breath? Seen his mouth moving maybe? Or had the flames obscured him from sight?

She looked away, gritting her teeth. "That does seem more plausible than you somehow infiltrating the guild," she said at last.

Her eyes refocused on his face, anger flashing. "Although, I should kill you right now for endangering the rest of the class and myself. That was reckless. Stupid. I'll make sure you never get out of this beginning class—"

A cough interrupted her tirade. "Uh, if I might interject," Kyyle said, stepping forward. "You mentioned that if Finn was able to defend himself that you would automatically pass him."

Finn looked at the gangly youth in surprise. He did sort of remember that. Although it felt hazy after everything that had happened.

"You did say that," Vanessa offered hesitantly.

"It might also look bad for you to kill an unarmed student after he clearly passed your test," Kyyle added, gesturing at the other students. "That might be the sort of thing that riles up the other travelers."

Lamia froze, her eyes narrowing slightly. Then her gaze shifted to the remainder of the class that lingered at the back of the room – the group watching anxiously. Anger flared in her eyes again, but she forcefully tamped down on it. She had clearly been backed into a corner.

"Fine," she bit out suddenly. Her voice grew a bit louder so that the other students could hear, "Finn has passed."

She whirled back to the remainder of the novices. "As for today's class, it is over. I will need to see to the repair of the classroom. Go and practice the spells that we discussed today," she barked, trying to regain some semblance of control.

"Tomorrow you will all be meeting in the courtyard for physical training. We will regroup in two days," Lamia barked.

When she saw that no one had moved, she grimaced. "You are dismissed," she reiterated, waving toward the door. The novices must have taken this as a sign to retreat. Finn had never seen the students disappear so quickly. They practically bolted for the door, with the exception of Vanessa and Kyyle.

Vanessa spared Finn a serious look. "Congratulations

on passing the class," she said, although Finn noted some reluctance in her voice. "I look forward to meeting you in the duels." Then she walked out without another word.

Kyyle was more sympathetic. He offered Finn a hand up, which he accepted gratefully. However, as soon as he regained his feet, he let out a yelp of pain, accidentally putting pressure on his injured leg.

"Need some help?" Kyyle offered. "I bet it's going to take a few minutes for the wound to heal."

"Yeah, I guess so," Finn replied.

The youth threw one of Finn's arms around his shoulder. The pair then limped toward the door. As they made their way forward, Finn finally noticed the notification lingering in the corner of his vision.

> **New Spell: Fire Nova**
> In your desperation, you created your first spell, allowing you to summon a ring of flame that erupts outward from your body. This spell should only be used as a last resort, as the flames will make it difficult to breathe and may devastate the area around you, harming friend and foe alike.
> **Skill Level:** Beginner Level 1
> **Cost:** 50% of your mana
> **Cooldown:** 60 minutes.
> **Effect 1:** Creates an explosion of flame centered around the caster. Deals 100 + (INT x 200%) damage.

Holy shit, Finn thought. So, he really had created a spell!

The implications of that were already cascading through his brain. If he could create this spell, could he build others? Were there any limits? Had any other players discovered this? The possibilities seemed incredible.

Finn was so enmeshed in his own thoughts that he didn't catch Lamia's parting glance. She leaned against the podium as the last pair of students left the room, staring at Finn's back. There was no anger in her expression, only a perfect clinical detachment, her glowing sapphire eyes appraising.

Chapter 12 - Popular

"Okay, what the hell was that?"

Finn turned to find Kyyle staring at him, his gaze containing an awkward mixture of curiosity and accusation.

"Uh, what do you mean?" Finn tried to dissemble.

"You're really going to go with *playing stupid*, huh?" Kyyle replied. Despite his tone, Finn noted that the young man looked a little hurt.

"I wouldn't say that our friend here is stupid," another voice spoke up.

Finn felt someone clap him on the back roughly, almost sending him toppling forward with his bad leg. He discovered that his new "friend" was none other than Zane, the large man giving him an appraising look. His crew lingered around them, eyeing Finn as though he might explode at any moment. Other students edged around the group warily. They likely expected a fight to break out.

"I mean he is the earliest graduate of our little tutorial classes," Zane offered with a grin. "That takes some brains, not to mention balls of brass."

"More like I painted a target on my back," Finn muttered, shrugging off the larger man's arm. "What exactly do you want?" he asked, doubting this was a social visit.

"I like a man who gets to the point. I actually wanted to extend an olive branch," Zane offered, spreading his hands widely. "What you did in the class was pretty impressive – even if it wasn't exactly controlled."

Finn noticed that Kyyle was glaring at the man skeptically.

"Well, consider the branch extended—" Finn began.

Zane cut him off, leaning forward and his eyes gleaming. "I suspect you've already noticed players beginning to group up. Information and allies are important here – even more so once the duels begin. I think you'd make a great fit with our crew," he offered, gesturing at the pack of players that loomed around them.

"We have big plans once we get out of this wannabe

magic school. We're going to form a guild. Maybe focus on PVP, if you catch my drift," Zane offered, his smile widening.

"You mean you plan to kill people and steal their shit," Kyyle muttered.

Zane's eyes flashed angrily as his gaze swept to the gangly earth mage. Yet he controlled his expression quickly, a grin tugging at his lips. "I prefer to think of it like re-allocating resources. I'm more of a socialist gamer, I suppose you could say," he added with a chuckle – laughter that was echoed by members of his crew.

"Yeah, and have you given any thought to what it's going to be like to kill other people in this *game*?" Kyyle demanded. "It's pretty authentic. You saw that girl that electrified herself. The burns along her arms... Yet you don't seem too worried about that part."

His accusation hung heavy in the air and Finn noted that Zane's hands clenched involuntarily. "It's still just a game. It isn't real. No one really gets hurt. Besides, we'll be doing much worse to each other soon, and we won't be given much choice then. I guess we'll see if you're able to get off that moral high horse."

Zane's attention snapped back to Finn. "It's clear that this is a dog-eat-dog world and having *powerful* friends would be a blessing," he said, the implicit insult to Kyyle not going unnoticed. "So, what do you say," Zane asked, offering a hand. "Interested in joining our crew?"

Finn hesitated for a moment. Some of what Zane was saying rang true. This world seemed to operate much like the real one – which meant it wasn't fair. Not at all. Just like their little class of novice mages, people would likely fall back into a natural rhythm. The strong would prey on the weak. People would band together for protection. Zane's offer was blunt and heavy-handed, but he also wasn't wrong.

At the same time, Finn didn't like the hungry glint in the man's eye. He'd seen that same look in the corporate world. They might not burn each other alive, but business was a different form of battle – one where most players were willing to go to any lengths to win. However, that wasn't Finn. Not anymore, anyway.

"I think I'm good actually," he said, meeting Zane's eyes evenly. "I appreciate the offer, but I think it might be a bit early to start picking sides."

Zane barely reacted, his face remaining neutral. Yet Finn still picked up on the way his eyes crinkled at the corners as he struggled to control his expression. "Well, I'll leave the offer open." A brief glance at Kyyle. "But it won't be on the table forever. You'll need to choose your friends wisely."

"I plan to," Finn replied, unperturbed by the man's posturing.

With a jerk of his chin, Zane motioned to his crew, and the group strode down the hallway, leaving Finn and Kyyle standing there.

"What an asshole," Kyyle muttered.

Finn just shook his head, watching as the group walked away. "He's not wrong, though. He just might be one of the first players to realize what's happening here."

"Which is?" Kyyle asked, his anger giving way to puzzlement.

"I think this place is a hell of a lot more real than we first thought," Finn said aloud, almost talking more to himself than to the earth mage. "This world isn't handing us pre-prepared spells or asking us to mash a single button like an idiot. It's asking for a hell of a lot more."

"Like creating your own spells?" Kyyle demanded, although he kept his voice at a discreet volume.

Finn glanced at him, noticing the look on his face.

"What? It's an obvious deduction," Kyyle added when he saw Finn's reaction. "You were able to summon your mana easily the other day, far faster than anyone else in the class. I doubt you suddenly *lost control*. Which only leaves one other answer."

"I could have just thought I was about to die. Stress does strange things to people," Finn offered. He ran a hand through his hair, trying to pull his fraying thoughts together and come up with a reasonable-sounding excuse. To make matters worse, his thigh still ached from where Lamia had impaled it. The pain, even muted, was distracting.

"You don't strike me as the sort of person who loses

your cool," Kyyle replied immediately, waving down the hall in the direction of Zane's crew. "So are you going to level with me or what?"

Finn sighed. "Alright, I'm not sure what I did. I *might* have created something new. Maybe. But I'm not sure what that means or how to recreate it."

"I bet that won't take too long," another voice chimed in from behind him, this one distinctly feminine – and oddly familiar.

Oh, who the hell is it this time? Finn thought to himself.

When Finn turned around, he froze in place, his jaw going slack. A pair of mischievous brown eyes met his from under a deep hood. Despite the heavy fabric, he could still see stray locks of auburn hair framing her face. Even more strangely, she wore a familiar set of pale-blue robes.

"J-julia?" Finn asked.

"Hey there, Old Fart," she replied with a grin before taking in Finn's battered and bloodstained appearance. "You look like shit."

This earned a chuckle from Kyyle. "I said something similar."

Finn could only stare dumbly as his brain tried to reboot. Was his daughter a student at the school? That didn't seem right. He also couldn't help but remember her seemingly innocuous question the day before about which city he had started in. Had she followed him here? How the hell had she even found him? He looked much younger and was walking around on two fully functioning legs.

"Uh, not to interrupt this moment or whatever?" Kyyle interjected. "But are you going to introduce me?" He nudged Finn.

"Um, so this is Julia. She's a...ah... a friend of mine," Finn choked out. Julia's grin widened. "And this guy propping me up is Kyyle."

"Pleasure to meet you," Julia offered, her eyes flitting to Kyyle. "It looks like you've been taking good care of my *friend* here."

Even in his surprised state, Finn noticed that Kyyle looked a little tongue-tied at that comment, his eyes darting between Julia and Finn with a questioning look. It seemed like he might have taken away the wrong message from Finn's hesitation.

"So how did you guys meet?" Kyyle asked.

Finn opened his mouth to answer, but Julia beat him to it. "I'm actually in another entering mage class," she explained smoothly. "We ran into each other randomly. Turns out we have a connection in the real world. Go figure," she added, rolling her eyes.

"Huh, okay..." Kyyle offered, confused by the weird tension between the pair.

"Would you mind if I spoke with Julia for a bit?" Finn asked Kyyle. The young man arched an eyebrow and Finn continued quickly, "I haven't forgotten our conversation. I promise. I'll try to explain more. I just need a second."

Kyyle's eyes bounced between the pair, and Julia smiled at him sweetly – which was usually Finn's signal to start running. Meanwhile, Finn could already see Kyyle's mental wheels turning. The young man was too damned perceptive for his own good. "Yeah, no problem," Kyyle said slowly and extricated himself from Finn's grip, letting him lean against the nearby wall. "I guess I'll see you at the physical training thing tomorrow."

"Sounds good. Thank you," Finn replied.

As Kyyle walked away, Julia slumped against the wall beside Finn. "Seems like a smart guy. Sort of cute, in an awkward kind of way. Plus, he didn't buy your bullshit story. I already like him."

"What are you doing here?" Finn hissed under his breath. "And don't try to feed me that bullshit about being a student. I didn't believe that the first time."

"Ahh, so little faith in your darling daughter," Julia replied with a grin. As Finn glared at her, she let out a sigh. "Fine, I might have snuck in when you mentioned you were stuck in the Mage Guild."

"Snuck in," Finn echoed, suddenly remembering what Lamia had told them at the beginning of class. "You didn't..."

"Knock out some idiot mages and steal their shit?" Julia asked. "Maybe." She flicked an object at Finn. He barely caught it, and when he unfurled his fingers, he found a small chit, much like the one Abbad had given him to access the library.

"Not a terribly secure system if you ask me," Julia offered.

"If they find you in here, there's going to be hell to pay."

"Then let's hope they don't find me," Julia replied with another grin.

Finn sighed again, rubbing at his temples. At some point, this day had taken a hard-left turn into crazy-land.

"Why exactly are you here?" Finn asked, glancing at Julia again.

"Can't I just be checking on my dear old dad?"

Finn stared at her with a deadpan expression.

Julia shrugged. "Hey, I actually did want to check up on you. You know this is basically a prison, right?" she added, waving at the hall.

"Well, it's more like a school…" Finn began.

His daughter arched an eyebrow. "It has guards and walls, and you can't leave." She hesitated. "Although, I guess the same could be said of my high school back in the day. Huh, damn." She refocused on Finn. "Either way, I'm not sure you completely understand what you stumbled into."

"And you do?" Finn asked skeptically.

"Maybe not all of it, but more than you," Julia replied with a dry voice. "There's a ton of shit going on out there beyond the walls of this place. People are saying the Emir is sick and might be going a little batty. The guilds are in an uproar. People are already talking about the line of succession. It feels like there's something big brewing."

She met his eyes, her expression more serious. "And you're stuck in this prison, which isn't exactly ideal."

"And you know all this how?" Finn asked, handing back the chit as he tried to maintain his composure. Julia had just dropped yet another bomb on him. There was a growing power struggle outside the guild? That wasn't great – not at all.

Julia shrugged. "I like to keep my eyes and ears open.

Plus, my particular skill set adapted well to this world." As she said this last part, Julia flicked the chit, and it disappeared before Finn's eyes. He also caught a flash of what appeared to be leather armor beneath her robes. What exactly had Julia been up to in-game?

Julia noted his confused expression, another grin tweaking her lips. "I was always good at getting into places where I shouldn't be and learning things I shouldn't know.

"Although, I'll admit that finding you was more challenging than I thought. I wasn't expecting the makeover. Although, the legs should have been an obvious point," she added ruefully, gesturing at his appearance. "It wasn't until I heard a bunch of students talking about how some guy named Finn blew up a classroom that I was able to find you."

Finn grimaced. Great. The rumors were already starting to spread. He wondered idly if Abbad would kill him quickly or draw it out.

"I also overheard the conversation with your boy," Julia continued when he didn't speak. "You created something new, didn't you?" Her eyes darted to his, sparkling with curiosity. "I'm not exactly surprised, but I feel like I deserve details."

Before he could figure out how to respond, her fingers plucked at the cuff of his robe, noting the tattoo on his right wrist. "This looks new, and the other novices don't seem to have one. I bet there's a story there too."

Finn was saved from responding as he heard a commotion farther down the corridor. The pair turned to look, only to find a group of three robed mages making their way down the hallway. Their robes were higher quality than the students and the tattoos that spiraled up their arms and encircled their necks indicated that they were much higher-ranked. They stopped to accost a student, and Finn noticed one mage pull out a crystal, holding it toward the novice. It soon glowed with a bright-green light.

The group immediately dismissed the student and moved to the next one.

Shit. Finn assumed they were somehow testing students for their magical affinity. They must be searching for whoever broke into the school.

"You need to get out of here," Finn whispered.

"Yeah, it does look like it's time to make a hasty retreat." Julia's eyes flitted back to Finn, and she smirked. "But don't think I've forgotten our little conversation. I'll be back, and I'm going to expect some answers."

"Fine, fine. Just go," Finn replied, the mages already stalking closer. "If you need to find me, I'll likely be in the library – fourth floor."

"Huh, I haven't broken into a magical library yet. That should be fun!"

Finn turned to snap at Julia; this wasn't the time to be cracking jokes. However, she had already vanished, only a faint chuckle echoing through the hall. He quickly covered up his irritation as he saw the guards approaching, re-assuming a genial mask and giving them a polite nod.

Nothing to see here, he thought. *Definitely not breaking multiple rules or anything.*

They gave him a quick pass with the crystal and then passed him by. As they marched away, Finn let out a sigh of relief, slumping back against the wall.

What the hell had he gotten himself into?

Chapter 13 - Modified

Finn leaned back in his chair, taking in the tomes and scrolls that riddled the tabletop before him. He had made it back to his haven in the library – managing to skirt past the mages that patrolled the guild's hallways. Yet even in the relative peace of the library, his thoughts were a chaotic whirlwind, fluttering about wildly.

To sum things up: he had somehow created a new spell, accidentally blown up a classroom, revealed his abilities to the other students, likely made a permanent enemy of one of the guild's faculty, and turned down an emerging gang leader. Then his daughter had shown up – revealing herself as the person who had been breaking into the guild and assaulting students. He was still struggling with her role in all of this, much less the news she had revealed of some impending power struggle in the city outside the Mage Guild.

He rubbed at his eyes.

Oh, and he still had that tiny little problem involving his need to learn Veridian, and the clock was still ticking on the upcoming duels.

Finn could feel his pulse thumping in his ears. It had been a long time since he had felt this sort of stress – not since his days back in college and working at Cerillion Logistics. How had he managed to make it through those moments when he just felt overwhelmed by the endless list of tasks and problems before him?

The answer came to him immediately, Rachael's face flashing through his mind's eye. He had always found her a calming presence. A hand that set down a steaming mug of tea in the corner of his vision. A kiss on the forehead. And when he was truly struggling, she had been the person to make him step away from the work for a moment – just long enough to take a walk or stretch.

She had given him perspective.

She had helped him find his center again.

Finn felt a hollow ache in his stomach – like a gnawing void had formed there that could never be filled. Rachael was gone now. He was on his own. Yet, for some reason, as painful as those memories were, they were still calming. He knew what she would say if she were standing beside him in this strange new world.

Rachael would likely rest a hand on his shoulder. "Everything will be okay," she'd say. "Just focus on one thing at a time." For a second, he could almost feel the weight of that hand on his arm.

Finn's eyes fluttered open. There was no one there. He was alone. Just a trick of his mind. He let out another sigh.

However, the phantom advice still helped.

He just needed to focus on one task. The first step was to rule out things he couldn't control. Finn couldn't do anything about whatever was happening outside the school, and he couldn't change what had happened during the class. And he sure as hell couldn't keep Julia out of trouble. Right now, he needed to learn more spells, and he needed to get out of this guild. Those should be his only goals.

And both were accomplished by finishing his studies. Which meant he needed to learn Veridian and see if he could replicate how he had created the *Fire Nova*.

A thought suddenly occurred to Finn. It was a moment of clarity that left him sitting there in stunned silence for a moment – like he had been staring at a half-finished jigsaw puzzle and finally realized he had been holding the piece he needed in his hands the whole time.

Maybe he could kill two birds with one stone.

"Daniel," he said aloud.

In a flash, a ball of flame erupted in the air beside Finn. Tendrils of fire licked at the air, causing it to ripple from the heat. "You summoned me?" Daniel replied.

"Did you finish compiling the language training software?" Finn asked.

"Yes, sir. I have also uploaded the vocabulary and syntax for this new language, and I have taken the liberty of creating a custom framework for a new iteration of the software. Would you like for me to show you what I've done so far?" Daniel asked.

Finn's eyes widened. Well, that was one spot of good news.

"Yes, please," he replied.

The ball of flame flashed, and a half-dozen displays suddenly appeared in the air in front of Finn, the translucent blue screens shimmering in the light cast by Daniel's form. Complicated lines of code skittered down one screen, and another showed a modular view of the program's codebase. However, Finn's gaze focused on the rough simulation of the program's UI.

Finn chewed on his lip as he examined the display, his wrist occasionally flicking at the air. The tantalizing idea at the edge of his mind had now fully come into focus – especially after the incident in the classroom earlier. Learning Veridian was critical to spellcasting in this world – both in terms of memorizing existing spells and creating new ones. However, that was just the first step.

His thoughts drifted back a few decades to when he had been in college. He had spent far too many hours sitting in front of a screen mindlessly clicking away at some MMO. Finn could barely remember the game itself. The reason for that was because he had gotten distracted working on mods for the game.

He had spent countless hours designing various UI and gameplay improvements. He had built mods that mapped out dungeons and detailed boss attack patterns. Mods that added additional information – mob threat, teammate DPS, healing assistance that auto-targeted injured teammates. Complex macros that automated his actions with pinpoint precision. It had become an almost-bottomless rabbit hole filled with legit and not-so-legit modifications to the game world.

It was part of what had gotten him into programming in the first place.

A small grin crept across Finn's face as he looked at the displays. Now he had a chance to build something similar. Although this challenge was on an entirely different level. Lucky for him, he had come a long way since the days of a ramen-only diet and all-nighters.

He could already visualize what he needed to create. The game world came with a default UI – although it was quite barebones. Finn's health, mana, and stamina gauges all hovered in the top left corner of his vision and tended to bleed away and become transparent unless he focused on them. The chat and system menus were similar and had clearly been designed with minimalism in mind. There was really no heads-up display, and there was no targeting reticle at all.

What if he wanted to change that? Would the game's AI permit him to mod the in-game UI and possibly create a custom HUD?

There was only one way to find out. He cracked his knuckles, and a translucent keyboard appeared in front of him. He felt his doubt and hesitation bleed away, replaced by excitement at the programming challenge in front of him and a grin lingering on his lips.

Then his fingers began to dance across the keys, and Finn lost himself in his work.

* * *

System Warning
You have been playing for quite some time. You should log out to eat and care for your body. If you ignore this warning, you will be automatically logged out in thirty minutes and a mandatory one-hour waiting period will apply before you will be able to log back in.

Finn let out a frustrated growl, swiping away the irritating notification.

However, the flashing notice had already knocked him out of his programming fugue. He glanced at the in-game clock in the corner of his vision, letting out a low whistle. Hours had passed in an instant. His attention had been focused solely on the flickering screens before him.

His eyes flitted back to the code that streamed across a

nearby screen. He almost had something he could work with. Daniel had done much of the time-consuming part of this project already – creating a database for the new language and compiling a new iteration of the language training software. Finn had been able to build on that as a foundation. And now he had created version 1.0 of a new in-game mod.

"It's time to give you a little test run," Finn murmured. He needed to move quickly before the game kicked him out.

His fingers danced across the keyboard as he uploaded his new program into the game world – much as he had tried to do with Daniel. The screens shimmered briefly, and then a notification appeared.

System Message
All modifications to the game world or the player UI must be reviewed and approved by System Controller XC239.90 to ensure that the modification does not unduly interfere with the operation of the game world or affect the experience of other players. You have submitted a player-made mod for administrator approval, code-named "Icarus Incantations V1.0." Please wait...

Finn rubbed at his neck, watching the screen.

He hadn't realized he had been holding his breath until another notice popped up.

System Message
Icarus Incantations V1.0 has been approved. Your in-game mods are now accessible through the system menu.

"Hot damn," Finn muttered aloud, an excited smile creeping across his face.

However, this was the moment of truth.

Finn swiped away the various screens and then pulled up his system menu. Indeed, there was now a new menu option, which opened into a submenu showing his single mod.

His fingers shook slightly as he tapped the icon.

A series of semi-translucent guidelines suddenly overlaid Finn's vision.

"Language training," he said aloud.

Immediately the lines shifted, forming a series of panes that spread out in front of Finn. There was a rough Veridian dictionary and grammar rulebook. He also had a basic set of workbooks and reading materials – although he still only had the children's books Abbad had given him. He'd have to remedy that at some point.

This feature, however, had been the easy part.

"Spellbook," Finn ordered next.

The language training display immediately disappeared, and the translucent guidelines popped back up. His two spells were listed in a nearby pane. Finn had taken the liberty of uploading the incantations and hand gestures for both *Magma Armor* and *Fire Nova*. Finn glanced at the defensive spell for a moment, and the program immediately acknowledged his selection. Casting instructions appeared on the left-hand side of his vision that showed the spell's full incantation, the phonetic pronunciations of each word, and highlighted the word he was on. The right-hand side of his screen provided a rough English translation. At the same time, his fingers twisted through a series of gestures as he summoned his mana.

His pronunciation was awkward, and his movements were slow.

However, only a few seconds later, a shield of molten energy slid along Finn's right arm from his wrist up to his shoulder. The surface of the armor soon solidified in the cool air, forming a rough armor, but the substance below stayed fluid and malleable so that it didn't hinder his movements.

The air above the shield shimmered from the heat. Yet, he only felt a tingling warmth where the armor touched his skin.

At the same time, a notification popped up.

New Spell: Magma Armor
You have summoned a barrier of molten energy, the mana condensing into a hardened shield. This spell can be used to deflect incoming attacks. It is less effective against ice or water-based magical effects but can be used to absorb kinetic energy as well as other elemental attacks. Higher ranks of this spell make the shield more resilient and increase the coverage.
Skill Level: Beginner Level 1
Cost: 50 Mana
Effect 1: Creates a damage shield capable of absorbing 100 damage (50 damage if water/ice).

"Well, hello there," Finn murmured.

He had only been able to cast the spell because of the assistance provided by the mod and because he had memorized the requisite gestures ahead of time. He had found it difficult to create an easy visualization for the hand gestures, and he suspected he was simply going to have to learn to handle that part by "feel" or rely on a number system similar to what Lamia had provided.

However, this still wasn't the feature he was excited about. One was basically a simple language training program, and the spellcasting module was little more than magical training wheels until Finn got his feet under him. These two features weren't that novel.

He had left the best for last.

"Icarus," Finn said, initiating the mod's final mode.

The casting directions for *Magma Armor* abruptly disappeared.

Then Finn spoke the Veridian word for "Flame."

The UI elements shifted. The symbol representing "flame" now hovered in the air in the left-hand side of Finn's vision, blank spaces indicating a projected length for the incantation. To his right, a word cluster formed in the air, showing various symbols in Veridian. As Finn focused on a specific word, it shifted in the air, growing larger and more prominent. These were connecting words supplied by the mod. He chose another word, and it was added to the incantation. At the same time, the word cloud shifted, new options cropping up.

Finn had analyzed the structure of *Fire Nova* and *Magma Armor* and had noticed a similar syntax. It was the same pattern he had picked up when he had intuitively cast *Fire Nova*. However, he didn't want to rely on instinct alone. He needed to understand the underlying system so that he could reliably create new spells. His theory was that all spells created in-game had a pattern. They were almost like magical haikus – each spell comprised of a rhyming couplet with a certain number of brush strokes per line.

The mod was designed to meet these basic requirements.

Finn doubted he had caught all of the relevant rules by applying a pattern analysis to only two spells. That sample size was pretty small. There might also be different types of spells that used a different pattern. For example, Lamia had already alluded to higher-level incantations that were more challenging to master. Either way, he expected there would be a *lot* of trial and error – with particular emphasis on the error part. If he could eventually get his hands on a real spellbook that would help immensely.

However, the two spells he knew were at least enough for him to realize that there was a formal spellcasting system at work here. And this mod was a first stab at developing software that would allow him to dynamically create spells. The software was then designed to store a successful incantation for future practice, adding it to his digital spellbook. For now, it would work best as a way to experiment in private. The process would likely be far too slow to pull off reliably mid-battle.

Finn stared at the mod's UI, a warm feeling drifting through his chest. He had effectively created a testing environment to build new spells. In many ways, it was similar to developing a new programming language – a spell bounded by certain syntax and commands. Although, that thought made him chuckle. Was he becoming some sort of programming wizard?

"At least Julia will be jealous," he commented dryly. Daniel just flashed slightly in response from where he hovered nearby.

Joking aside, Finn doubted many other players had yet noticed the intricacies of the game's magic system, much less figured out a way to manipulate them. Honestly, he wasn't sure he would have noticed if he hadn't been actively learning Veridian. This new mod might be the sort of thing that would give him an edge in the coming duels.

Finn moved to start experimenting but was interrupted by another notice.

System Warning
Your thirty minutes has expired. You are now being logged out. You will be unable to log back in for a real-world hour.

Before Finn could react, the world around him bled away, darkness creeping across his vision until he floated in an endless black void. He struggled to tamp down on his irritation. He had little desire to return to his crippled aged body that was entirely incapable of hurling magical spells. What he wanted was to keep going – to continue his studies and tinker with his new mod.

He could only hope the hour passed quickly.

Chapter 14 - Physical

Finn blinked blearily, holding up a hand to block out the harsh light that speared down into his eyes. His poor pupils were struggling to transition after the hours he had spent in the dreary library.

After logging out the night before, he had taken care of his real-world body and tried to lie down for a few hours. Yet no matter how hard he tried to sleep, it eluded him. The only thing he could think about was logging back in.

Eventually, he had given up on sleep entirely, wheeling himself back to his workroom and donning the heavy plastic headset. He wanted to create new spells, but Finn had quickly discovered that his limited vocabulary seemed to be holding him back. The mod could only assist him so much. So, with a sigh, he had switched gears, moving back to his language training. The hours had flown by. Before he knew it, it was already time to attend his next class.

He now stood in the sandy area that rested in the Mage Guild's inner courtyard. Sunlight reflected off the sands, and the occasional gust of wind caused the particles to dance in the air. At ground level, the field felt even larger, spanning at least a hundred yards.

"About time you showed up," Kyyle said as he approached, smacking Finn on the back. "I almost thought you were going to bail since you're too cool for Lamia's class now."

Kyyle stared at him expectantly. "Get it? Too cool? Because she shoots ice..." He noted Finn's sober expression. "You know what, it's not funny if I have to explain it."

"I'm not sure it was that funny to begin with," Finn replied dryly, although he felt an inadvertent smile tug at his lips.

Kyyle placed a hand to his heart. "You really know how to hurt a guy?" Then his eyes darted back to the rest of the crowd of students that filled the field. There were a few dozen of them milling about the sands.

Finn picked out Zane and his crew immediately. The

man gave him a curt nod as their eyes met. It was also clear that the others had grouped up as well, only a few stragglers standing alone in the center of the courtyard.

"So, what do you think this is going to involve?" Kyyle asked. "Some pushups? Maybe a few laps around the sand courtyard."

Finn glanced at him skeptically. "You think this is going to be some sort of mundane P.E. class? Lamia tried to *kill* me yesterday," he replied.

"I mean, you're right. But I can hope," Kyyle offered with a shrug. "Although, the audience does poke a few holes in my theory," he added, gesturing at the multi-story terraces that ringed the inner courtyard.

As Finn followed his gaze, he saw that other students lingered along the railings, watching the group of novices. The crowd continued to grow even as he looked on, as though some spectacle was about to take place on the sands.

What do they know that we don't?

Finn grimaced. He had been so focused on his studies that he hadn't given a lot of thought to what this class might entail. He suddenly remembered the sensation of the icy shard impaling his thigh and the feel of his own blood dripping down his skin. The injury hadn't been permanent since his in-game body's natural health regeneration had eventually healed the wound. But he wasn't looking forward to getting hit again.

He could only imagine what it would feel like to die in-game.

"Alright, whelps, group up!"

Finn turned to find a hulking man striding across the sands. In lieu of the typical robes, he wore a light tunic and trousers. This only served to highlight the intricate pattern of tattoos that spiraled up his forearms and twisted around his neck. His hair was shortly cropped, and a faint shadow of stubble lingered on his chin. Even more strangely, Finn noted that a longsword hung from the man's waist. This was actually the first weapon he had seen a mage wear.

A master mage maybe? Finn thought as the students formed a group in front of the man. The tattoos pointed in that direction, but the weapon was an odd touch. Could this physical training involve combat?

The man's eyes lingered on them, skimming across each novice as though weighing and measuring them. As his gaze drifted to Finn, he felt his eyes linger for a hair longer, although it may have been his imagination. Their instructor let the silence lengthen and stretch until the students began to shuffle nervously in the sand.

"My name is Brutus, and I've been charged with whipping you lot into shape," he finally barked. "Although, what I see before me is going to need some work. Most of you look soft – like you will fold at the bite of a single arrow or sword. That won't do at all.

"But first, let's cover some essential information. I've been told my teaching style isn't sufficiently *educational*... What can I say? I prefer a more hands-on approach!"

"Wait, so are there teacher surveys?" Kyyle murmured, a grin creeping across his face. Finn started to whisper something back but stopped as he saw Brutus' eyes sweep across them.

"Let's start with the basics. You're probably asking yourselves why you need any sort of physical training," Brutus continued, crossing his massive arms as he spoke. "You can hurl devastating balls of magical fury, after all. Who could possibly stand against your might?" He posed this clearly rhetorical question in a voice just as dry as the sand they were standing upon.

"Right now, you can barely waggle your fingers in sequence, but in just a little over a week, you are going to be facing real combat. You are going to learn the hard way that a caster rarely gets a chance to sit in one place and cast freely. In the heat of battle, there are spells, arrows, swords – an endless tide of distractions that will force you to move, dodge, and reposition. Or simply drop the spell and reach for a real weapon." He said this last part while patting the longsword that hung from his waist.

"To make matters worse, our lot tend to place all of their stat points into *Intelligence* and *Willpower*," Brutus spat distastefully.

Finn had already started raising his hand before he realized it. Too late, he realized he was just drawing more unnecessary attention to himself. However, he saw Brutus' gaze flit to him and jerk his chin to acknowledge Finn's question.

Oh, well. Might as well ask now.

"What exactly does each stat do?" Finn asked.

"Not the worst question," Brutus replied grudgingly. "In total there are six attributes, which you've likely noticed if you've bothered to pull up your Character Status."

The mage rubbed at the stubble on his chin. "Most are intuitive. *Strength* increases just that – physical power. This allows you to swing harder, run faster, and carry more. *Dexterity* is more about finesse. This stat affects things like accuracy and balance.

"*Vitality* improves your total health as well as your resilience to certain physical conditions. It helps with things like broken bones, blindness, poisons, and illness. *Endurance* increases your stamina. In short, it allows you to keep moving for longer and is vital for the use of certain martial combat skills."

Brutus' eyes skimmed across the group of students, many of whom gestured at the air as they surveyed their Character Status. "Which brings us to *Intelligence* and *Willpower*. Both stats increase your total mana, although *Intelligence* to a lesser extent. The primary difference is that *Intelligence* increases spell damage as well as learning speed. *Willpower*, on the other hand, provides a much more substantial increase to mana and makes the caster harder to sway. It can provide resistances to mind-altering effects, and you will find it easier to focus.

"Most mages tend to allocate their stat points toward *Intelligence* and *Willpower* since these statistics are difficult to train and directly improve their spellcasting. However, that means that their physical abilities tend to be rather... lacking," Brutus said distastefully.

"There are two ways to help address this shortfall. The first is equipment," he explained, holding up a calloused finger. "The second is physical training." Another finger rose into the air.

"The difficulty with the first option is that you're giving up the casting stats you could have put on your gear." Brutus leaned forward, his eyes glinting in the sun. "This means *training* is the best way to improve those other stats – since you give up nothing but your blood, sweat, and tears. And the more, the better! The longer you keep at it, the more difficult it will become to raise those stats and the more demanding your training will need to become."

Finn – as well as the rest of the class – were now staring at Brutus wide-eyed. The logic of his statements each landed like a sword strike. In short, they could dump their stat points in *Intelligence* and *Willpower*, but they would need to train like a fiend to keep their physical stats at a reasonable level. Finn was suddenly glad he had decided to hold on to his initial points.

At that thought, he glanced at his notifications and Character Status.

x3 Level Up!
You have (65) undistributed stat points.

x2 Skill Rank Up: Reading
Skill Level: Beginner Level 8
Effect 1: 12% increased learning speed while reading.

x1 Skill Rank Up: Learning
Skill Level: Beginner Level 5
Effect 1: 9% increased learning speed for skills and spells.

x2 Skill Rank Up: Mana Mastery
Skill Level: Beginner Level 7
Effect: -4% of the mana cost of spells.

He had already noted that his experience gain and skill growth had started to slow slightly, which seemed to indicate that they had diminishing returns. Finn idly wondered if he could also improve skill growth by increasing the hardship of his training. It was certainly an interesting idea and something he should probably ask Abbad. Assuming, of course, that the librarian didn't kill him the next time they spoke.

Finn had managed to avoid explaining the encounter with Lamia. At least for now.

"Alright," Brutus barked, clapping his palms together loudly, "that's more than enough talking and staring into space. I already feel like I'm coddling you with these lectures. In my opinion, people learn best by doing. Particularly, you travelers. I find I need to beat the common sense into at least a few of you."

A smile began to creep across Brutus' face. "So, let's start the first and most important lesson that you will ever learn."

As he finished speaking, the burly man's fingers twined through a complicated series of gestures. Finn's brow furrowed as he noticed a few patterns he hadn't learned yet, but it was the incantation tumbling out of the mage's mouth that captured his focus. He only caught the occasional word. Something about flames and construction – or maybe construct? The syntax was also strange. The words flowed together in multiple lines, creating a much more complicated incantation than for a spell like *Magma Armor* or *Fire Nova*.

"What is he casting?" Finn murmured.

He didn't have to wait long to find out.

Flames suddenly erupted along the edge of the field, the fire lancing nearly twenty feet into the air and swiftly blocking out the sight of the guild hall. Although, Finn could still barely make out other students watching from the terrace that ringed the field. The group let out a cheer as they saw the fire rise into the air. The inferno roared with blazing force, swiftly melting the sand on the edges of the courtyard into liquid glass.

Then the sands in the interior of the courtyard began to shift and swirl as flames ignited in erratic pockets across the field, erupting from the ground like miniature volcanoes. One such fountain of heat started to form near Finn's feet, and he and Kyyle backpedaled quickly, trying to put some distance between themselves and whatever the hell was happening.

Some sort of flaming volcano maybe? Finn thought frantically.

He was wrong. Oh, so, very wrong.

The sands spiraled up into the air, lifted by the heat and fire. These particles were soon melted down and combined to form a glowing red mound of liquid glass. From each of these magma pools, hulking creatures rose – swiftly taking shape. They climbed nearly seven feet into the air, their body a mass of superheated glass.

Finn's mind went blank as he realized he was looking at some sort of glass golem.

They must cool off in the air, he thought to himself. If they stepped out of the flames, their bodies should become rigid and fragile.

Yet that guess was disproved a moment later as the nearby golem lumbered out of the pool of molten glass and ambled toward Finn and Kyyle. Its body did indeed cool in the air, creating a hard, skin-like surface. However, the golem's limbs were still semi-translucent, which allowed Finn to see that an angry red core of heat still burned in its chest and along the center of each limb, keeping the glass malleable enough to allow it to move freely.

"I have one last piece of advice for this lesson," Brutus' voice boomed across the courtyard. Finn looked over to find the mage awash in flame, his eyes a blazing red and orange as streamers of fire encircled him. Meanwhile, more and more golems were still emerging from the sands.

"Run!" Brutus declared.

Chapter 15 - Durable

The glass golem shifted forward, planting a charred foot into the sands with enough force to cause the ground to shake and yellow particles to launch into the air. Finn and Kyyle backpedaled quickly, keeping an eye on their newfound opponent. Meanwhile, a similar scene played out across the field. At least a half-dozen of the creatures had pulled themselves from the sandy courtyard and now faced off against the scattered students.

"How the hell are we going to kill this?" Kyyle shouted at Finn, trying to make himself heard over the screams of the other students.

Finn just shook his head. Brutus had boxed them in – unless they wanted to try braving the inferno that now ringed the courtyard. His gaze skimmed to the walls of fire, noting that the flames were so dense that he couldn't see through them.

Okay, that's not an option.

Finn's attention darted back to the golem. He quickly inspected the creature.

Glass Golem (Summoned) – Level ???
Health – Unknown
Mana – Unknown
Equipment – Unknown
Resistances – Unknown

Finn's guess was that the golem was so much more powerful than the novice mages that they simply couldn't see its level. He could feel a heavy weight settle in his stomach, and his mind wheeled.

Finn didn't have long to ponder on this.

The golem pulled back its arm, the surface starting to glow a bright red as it seemed to superheat the limb. It almost looked like the golem was winding up for a pitch and Finn's eyes suddenly widened in surprise.

"Spellbook!" he said aloud. Immediately, the new

guidelines appeared in Finn's field of view. He began casting *Magma Armor*, silently thanking his earlier self for having the foresight to practice the spell.

Just as he finished casting, Finn shouted at Kyyle, "Get behind me!" The young man didn't hesitate and dove behind Finn.

A barrier of molten energy swept up Finn's arm, thickening with each second that ticked past. He turned to the side, holding his arm in front of him like a shield as the barrier glowed with an angry red-and-orange light.

Finn just hoped it would be enough.

The golem let loose, its arm arcing forward with surprising speed. Time seemed to slow for a moment, and Finn saw that the creature's arm had turned entirely into molten glass, a red-hot blob where its hand used to be. The momentum of the swing caused a ball of glass the size of a basketball to detach, sending it hurtling toward Finn and Kyyle.

"Oh shit," Finn murmured, dropping to a crouch and bracing himself.

The molten glass crashed against his shield, and his arm trembled from the force of the impact. Even worse, the magma broke apart as it struck, spraying the area with glowing red droplets. His shield didn't provide enough coverage to avoid the splash, and he felt a dozen hot pinpricks strike his clothes, burning through the flimsy cloth before eating into his skin.

Finn let out a hissing breath, watching his health dip precariously in the corner of his vision. They could only take one or two more hits like that. He dismissed the remaining fragments of his *Magma Armor* and yanked Kyyle to his feet in one movement.

"We need to put some distance between us," he shouted over the roaring flames and the shouts of the other students. The golem was already advancing again – the only small mercy being that the creature was slow, stumbling in the shifting sands of the courtyard.

Kyyle nodded numbly, and then his gaze swept back to the golem. "I-I can buy us some time," he murmured.

Before Finn could ask him what he was doing, the young man's fingers twined through a rapid series of gestures as arcane words drifted from his lips.

Finn didn't wait to see what happened. As soon as Kyyle finished casting, he grabbed his arm and yanked him along after him, the two jogging across the sands of the courtyard.

When they had created some distance, Finn finally spared a glance behind him. He saw the golem suddenly lurch as it took its next step. Its foot plunged into the sand as though the ground had given way. Finn blinked in confusion and suddenly realized that this was exactly what had happened. Kyyle had caved in a portion of the courtyard. The golem stumbled forward before crashing into the hole, its body half-embedded in the sand.

Maybe this is a way to...

Finn never got to complete the thought. The sands around the golem turned an angry red as a pulse of heat rippled through its body. Within only moments, the creature was swimming in a miniature lake of molten glass. Finn doubted that would hold the creature for long, but at least they had bought themselves a few seconds of breathing room.

"Fuck," Finn muttered.

"We need a plan," Kyyle panted beside Finn.

He could only nod in response, although nothing came to him immediately. Finn glanced at the gauge for his health, mana, and stamina in the corner of his vision. Blocking a single strike and running away had left him almost half-empty. He doubted the others were faring much better.

With that thought, Finn's attention turned to the rest of the class. His stray thought didn't do the carnage justice. Corpses already riddled the courtyard, many of the bodies still smoking as molten glass continued to eat into their flesh. Only about a dozen students remained, and the golems were following them relentlessly.

As Finn watched, he noticed a student attempting to run away from a golem, clutching at a burnt arm and stumbling in the shifting sands. His foot landed wrong, and he suddenly fell hard on his side, looking at the golem pursuing him with fear-filled eyes as his fingers stumbled through some sort of spell. He finally finished casting, a shard of ice rocketing through the air and slamming into the golem's body. The ice carved a furrow in the creature's glass skin, causing the rigid substance to fracture. Yet the golem simply shrugged off the blow. Its glass flesh glowed an angry red before melting back together.

In his haste, the mage hadn't noticed that he had walked into the path of another golem – its glowing form pursuing a mage that was sprinting toward the wall of flame that encircled the courtyard. The golem suddenly seemed to notice the fallen novice and switched course. The prone player must have felt a tremor reverberate through the sand since he glanced to the side. His mouth dropped open in surprise, and he tried to move.

But it was too late.

The golem's foot came down on the player's chest, and Finn could hear the crack of his ribs despite the distance. If the blow hadn't killed him, the pulse of heat that rippled through the golem's foot and speared into the player's body surely did. Only a moment later, another half-melted corpse had been added to the field.

Finn tried to marshal his flailing thoughts – his own fear and adrenaline clouding his mind. Acting on instinct, he summoned his fire mana, feeling the warm energy burn through his chest. His perspective suddenly shifted, the fear receding and replaced by a boiling excitement. This was just another problem to be solved!

His gaze shifted back to the player's prone corpse, his thoughts more clinical and detached. The player hadn't had a chance against the golem. That much was clear. But his death had indicated that the creatures could switch targets, likely choosing whoever was closest. Which sort of made sense if they were being maintained by Brutus.

Finn's thoughts abruptly trailed off, his eyes widening. He suddenly whirled to the spot where Brutus had been standing. He now saw that the master mage was standing inside a circle of swirling flames. He didn't seem to be speaking, but his hands moved steadily. The obvious deduction was that he was somehow controlling the golems and the wall of fire that ringed the courtyard.

"If we could distract him..." Finn muttered, the bones of a plan beginning to form in his mind.

"Distract who?" Kyyle snapped, jerking at Finn's arm. "If you have a plan, now is the damn time. We don't have much longer," he added, pointing at the golem that had initially attacked them. The creature had managed to pull itself from the glowing red lake of molten glass, a fresh coating now covering its body. If anything, Kyyle had just made it even larger.

Finn's gaze focused on Kyyle. "Brutus. But we'll need some help. You have your notes, right? You've been watching the other novices?"

Kyyle just nodded, his expression confused. His eyes kept darting to the approaching golem.

"Okay, of the students that are left, I need a water mage with an area-of-effect spell and someone that can hit hard. Like a physical attack," Finn ordered. "Hurry," he insisted when he saw that Kyyle wasn't moving.

The young man's fingers trembled as he brought up his in-game terminal, his eyes skimming down an invisible list and occasionally darting back to the field. A few precious seconds later, he pointed out two students.

"Zane and Vanessa should work," he said. "Vanessa has a spell called *Frozen Orb*, and Zane can cast *Earth Spikes*. He's an earth mage too," Kyyle replied to Finn's unspoken question.

Finn nodded, mentally marking the locations. He noticed that the pair were together and were slowly circling the wall of fire, using their spells to slow the golems. Smart thinking, but it wouldn't last forever.

"Okay, here's what we're going to do," Finn said, turning his attention back to Kyyle. "I need you to stay away from the golems so that you don't draw their attention. When I give the signal, you need to use that pit spell against Brutus," he said, tilting his head in the direction of their instructor.

Kyyle's eyebrows rose. "You want me to do what now?"

"Make a pit just below his feet. You just need to distract him for a second." Finn glanced up and saw the golem was still approaching. At least his natural regeneration had recovered his health, mana, and stamina. He was going to need it.

"You got it?" Finn asked.

Kyyle gave an uncertain nod. "Sure... but what about the signal?"

"You'll know it when you see it," Finn said with a lopsided grin.

He should be panicking. What he was planning to do next was insane. Yet with the fire mana burning through his veins, he could only feel excitement boiling in his chest. He wondered if it would work.

However, he didn't have any time to lose. He could see that more of the remaining students had already fallen, leaving only Finn, Kyyle, Zane, and Vanessa. Most of the golems were already following the other pair since they were closer. He needed to hurry.

"Good luck," Finn said to Kyyle and then shot off across the sands.

He ran straight at the golem that was approaching them, his legs pumping hard. The creature seemed almost surprised by Finn's change of tactics. As he neared, it swept a hand at him. Finn rolled under the blow and shot back to his feet, stumbling slightly but managing to catch his balance. He could feel a searing line across his back where droplets of molten glass had splashed him, and notifications flashed in the corner of his vision.

Then he was past the golem and sprinting toward Zane and Vanessa. They were circling around the courtyard toward Kyyle's position. He could feel the ground shake as the golem behind Finn turned to follow him.

Good. They aggro based on proximity, he thought to himself. That was one less assumption to worry about. Two more to go.

Within a few seconds, Finn was beside Vanessa and Zane.

Zane spared him a frantic look as Finn appeared next

to him. He looked terrible. Burns riddled one arm, glass having cooled against his skin and giving it a mottled appearance amid the charred flesh. He seemed to have been covering for Vanessa – who wasn't injured but looked exhausted.

"Huddle up, quickly," Finn shouted at the pair. His hands then began moving through another *Magma Armor*. He could see the pack of golems following them beginning to wind up for another attack, and he needed to give the pair a few seconds to regenerate their mana.

They stared at him blankly before they noticed the shield forming along his arm. Then they slowly moved toward him, crouching behind his small shield.

"I have a plan," Finn grunted as he finished casting his spell, preparing to accept the next blow. He hoped he could withstand the attack he knew was coming.

Zane barked out a harsh laugh. "A plan? We're fucked."

"Don't be so sure," Finn retorted, giving him a grin. His mana was still burning through his limbs, and his eyes danced with orange flames. Zane seemed slightly taken aback by his crazed smile. With that, he began casting another shield, reinforcing the first one behind an even thicker layer of molten energy.

I just need to keep my mana above 50%. Which meant Finn could just barely afford to cast the two shields.

"What's this plan?" Vanessa asked as he finished the second spell, eyeing the pack of golems as they prepared to send another wind-up pitch of molten glass, even as the sixth ambled up behind them.

"I'm going to take this hit," Finn said. "Once they launch their attack, you two run away and get some distance. Don't move any closer to the golem behind us or he'll aggro."

Zane opened his mouth to ask a question, but Finn snapped at him. "No time.

"Assuming I survive this, I'm going to do something crazy. His eyes focused on Vanessa. "When the golems glow red, strike with *Frozen Orb*."

"How do you –?"

Finn cut her off, turning to look at Zane. "Then you cast *Earth Spikes* right afterward. You'll only have a window of a few seconds. Got it?" he demanded.

The two just stared at him. "Do you understand?" Finn demanded. "We don't have much longer."

They both nodded.

Finn turned his attention back to the golems. As they prepared to strike, their hands glowed an angry red. Their arms moved backward and then arced forward rapidly as Finn braced himself.

Shit, this is going to hurt.

That was an understatement.

Multiple blasts of molten glass smashed into Finn's reinforced *Magma Armor*. The momentum alone was so powerful that it sent the group stumbling backward a few feet. Finn was certain he would have toppled over completely – leaving his body exposed to the follow-up globs – if it hadn't been for Zane and Vanessa.

Droplets of the molten substance ate through Finn's shields, swiftly eroding the armor. At the same time, the terrible liquid sprayed outward around the edges of the shield. Yet Finn didn't back away. He needed to take most of this blow. He felt the burning substance splash against his arms and face. His skin felt like it was on fire, the glowing red substance burning through his flesh at an alarming rate before rapidly cooling and hardening.

Notifications flashed in Finn's peripheral vision, and stars danced in his eyes. Yet he was alive. If only barely – a sliver of health still visible on his health gauge.

"Run!" he croaked, sparing one last look at Zane and Vanessa. They hesitated for a fraction of a second, taking in Finn's ruined arms and the glass riddling his skin. Then they sprinted for safety.

Leaving Finn alone.

Six golems lumbered toward him, their hulking forms surrounding him and trudging ever closer. After that last barrage, he would have a few seconds. After watching the other students get demolished, his guess was there was some sort of cooldown on that "molten pitch" attack. If they followed the same pattern, they would try to move into melee range now.

Which was right where Finn needed them.

He struggled to his feet, the process made difficult by his arms. They felt rigid and inflexible, half-cooled glass practically coating his skin.

Yet a moment later, he stood upon the sands.

The golems were only a few yards away now and slowly trudging forward.

Finn forced his burned fingers to move, words escaping his lips. His mod immediately filled in the remaining incantation for *Fire Nova*, Finn focusing on those flowing symbols like a lifeline. As he cast, flames appeared in the air around him, dancing like wraiths. The fires swiftly grew until the golems were hazy dark outlines, growing ever larger as they loomed around him. Although, this time, Finn was prepared. He had held his breath – preventing himself from passing out until he cast the spell.

For a fraction of a second, Finn hesitated. He thought he saw an image in the flames. It almost looked like a woman's face. She looked eerily familiar – her eyes challenging him in the way only Rachael could.

Then he blinked, and the face was gone.

And Finn spoke the last word of the spell.

The *Fire Nova* raced away from him in a fantastic cascade of fire and flame, crashing through the golems that lingered around Finn. At the same time, Finn sunk to his knees, suddenly unable to stay standing. The blast pushed the golems back and superheated their glass bodies until all six shone brightly, liquid glass dripping down their limbs.

Yet the creatures didn't stop. They still lumbered toward him, glass droplets splattering against the sands of the courtyard.

A grin stretched across Finn's face, his eyes awash in orange energy.

Those same glowing eyes turned to look at Brutus. The mage was watching the scene intently, his hands still moving through a rapid-fire series of gestures.

"Checkmate, mother fucker," Finn mouthed at him.

Then the fire magic master suddenly dropped out of sight, falling into the sand as it disappeared below him. Finn would never forget the look of shock and disbelief on his face.

Several things happened at once.

An orb of ice suddenly crashed into the middle of the pack of golems, before exploding in a shower of icy fragments. The miniature avalanche was consumed by the molten bodies of the golems, streamers of steam arcing into the air. However, the ice rapidly cooled the glass golems, their limbs growing suddenly rigid and fractures appearing along their skin as a result of the makeshift tempering process.

The blast of icy energy was soon followed by lances of earth that speared out of the ground, smashing into the golems. After the rapid heating and cooling, the earthen spears caused the brittle golems to explode in a shower of glass fragments. Their bodies blasted apart so forcefully that it rocked Finn where he sat in the middle of the maelstrom.

Steam, glass, and rock shards filled the air and rained down upon him. He could feel stray fragments pelt his fragile body and impale his ruined flesh, his own blood leaking down his skin and staining the sands.

Yet the pain felt muted and distant enough that he barely paid attention to it. His thoughts were focused on that face he had seen in the flames. He had endured far worse than this. This pain was only physical, after all. It wouldn't last forever.

He knew from firsthand experience that there were some wounds that never healed.

As the last of his health finally disappeared, a triumphant smile was still painted on Finn's face, and flames danced in his eyes. A single thought roared through his brain, even though he was no longer able to say the words aloud.

It had worked!

Then the world went dark, and a single translucent blue notice filled his vision.

System Message
You have died.

Thanks for playing Awaken Online!

Chapter 16 - Deadly

Finn blinked as the world suddenly popped back into focus.

He let out a heaving gasp as he clawed at his arms. He looked down, expecting to see ruined, burnt flesh mottled with cooled glass. Yet his fingers only met solid, healthy skin. Despite the evidence that he was whole and uninjured, it took Finn's mind a minute or two to catch up.

When his pulse slowed, and he no longer felt phantom burns along his forearms, Finn was finally able to take stock of his surroundings. He was standing in the field once again. However, his surroundings were... different. The scene looked washed out. Sunlight still shone down on the yellow sand, but it was like someone had forgotten to add the bloom or had reduced the saturation on the world. Even more strangely, Finn noticed nearly transparent motes of sapphire energy drift down around him like ash. He held out a hand, but the substance passed through his palm.

"Alright, whelps, group up!" a familiar voice barked. Finn whirled to find Brutus addressing a crowd of students.

"What the hell?" Finn murmured.

His eyes widened as he noticed himself standing in the crowd. Finn probably wouldn't have recognized himself if not for Kyyle standing beside him. He looked younger in-game – a *lot* younger. Finn suddenly realized he hadn't had a chance to survey his new appearance in a mirror. He placed his own age in the early forties, graying stubble dotting his chin and his hair chopped short in the same no-nonsense style he had maintained for decades.

Finn pulled his attention away from examining his doppelganger as flames suddenly erupted around the edge of the field, and the golems once more began to pull themselves from pools of molten glass as the battle played out once again.

Although "massacre" might have been more appropriate.

He could only assume this was some sort of deathscape that allowed him to view a replay of how he had died. Finn had to admit it was an interesting concept. In a game that focused on realism, it would be helpful to analyze how you had fucked up.

"I wish real life had a replay button," he muttered to himself, his voice sounding muffled like his words were being swallowed up as they left his lips.

The scene continued.

Finn watched as he and Kyyle ran away from the golem and as the other students were gunned down by balls of molten glass. The strange part was that parts of the scene were blurry, only odd shapes and washed-out colors. It was like someone had taken a paintbrush and smeared together part of the picture. It took him a second to realize what was happening.

He could only view a replay of things that had happened in his line of sight.

It was easier to see if Finn walked over to his clone and faced the same direction. As his perspective shifted, so did the focus of the replay.

"Interesting. So, I can only view things that I actually saw."

At first, this seemed like a major limitation. Then Finn realized that he could see details that he hadn't focused on in the heat of battle. For example, he could see the other students fighting in the distance, even though he hadn't really focused on them at the time. He would have to remember this. Maybe he could think of some way to expand his visibility when he died – that might offer invaluable information later.

Even while he had walked around the field muttering to himself, the battle had continued to rage across the field. He soon saw his other self huddled with Kyyle and then his mad sprint across the sands toward Zane and Vanessa.

Finn watched in silence as he saw himself cast *Fire Nova*, the flames exploding outward in concentric rings, and the golems glowing red hot. Vanessa's *Frozen Orb* struck next, crashing into the cluster of golems like a frozen grenade. And hot on its heels came Zane's *Earth Spikes*, causing the magical creatures to explode in a torrent of stone, ice, and shards of glass. Finn remembered that part vividly and he instinctively clutched at his arms, feeling his heart race.

Then the scene faded away, restarting from the beginning.

Finn rubbed at his chin for a moment. Now that he was dead, he had a bit more time to think about the fight. How had Vanessa and Zane known those spells? He doubted that they had invented them on the fly. Now that he thought about it, he realized that Kyyle had already known about them – otherwise, Finn couldn't have come up with that plan. He'd have to remember to ask Kyyle when he respawned.

There was also one incredibly interesting variable on the field.

As the scene played out a second time, Finn's gaze shifted to Brutus. He hadn't had eyes on the fire mage the entire fight, his form blurring out during certain portions. But he had usually been in his line of sight – even if Finn hadn't had time to watch him closely.

Finn now noted the way the man's hands twisted together, moving so quickly that he almost had difficulty following the movements. At the same time, Brutus mouthed the incantations. A thought suddenly occurred to him, and he pulled up his in-game console, taking notes. He doubted he could recreate the fire wall or golem spells, but he might as well record what he could. Although, as he watched Brutus' hands, he noticed something strange. The rhythm felt off. It took Finn a few seconds to figure out why.

The fire mage was actually moving each hand independently!

Is this like some sort of ambidextrous casting? he wondered. If so, then that was incredible. He'd have to add that to his list of questions for Abbad.

Unfortunately, Finn hadn't managed to catch every word that Brutus had said over the screams and shouts of the players racing across the field, but he transcribed the incantations as best he could. They might be useful later.

Then the scene shifted again, starting to play the battle's climactic finish.

However, Finn's attention was solely on Brutus. The ground opened up under the mage, and he plummeted downward, his eyes widening in shock. Surprisingly, the image only began to blur as Brutus fell below the lip of the sandy pit that Kyyle had formed. Finn glanced back at himself where he stood surrounded by the golems. His eyes were pointed in the same direction of Brutus.

"Interesting."

What happened next, however, was enough to make Finn's jaw go slack.

Brutus soon reappeared above the lip of the pit. At first, Finn couldn't see how he had managed the feat – not until his feet crested the edge. Then he noticed the nearly translucent discs of still-cooling glass that had formed in the air, the fragile material exploding as Brutus' feet struck home. Brutus had formed these small platforms quickly, using them like a staircase to run out of the hole.

"Holy shit," Finn murmured.

"How did you…" He trailed off, turning his attention back to Brutus' face. He looked calm, his eyes blazing with orange energy.

How had the mage maintained the fire wall, the golems, and managed to cast this new spell? Finn glanced back at himself, inspecting the scene more carefully. He almost didn't catch the detail before the scene reset again. However, he did see the fire inside the golems dim and then wink out just before he died.

Then darkness descended upon the field.

Finn stood there in the void, his thoughts whirling.

What had Brutus been casting before Kyyle sprang his trap? Their instructor had already summoned the fire wall and the golems, so why were his hands moving? Was he actively channeling mana into the spells? And to what end? This seemed at odds with how Finn had cast his spells – namely his *Magma Armor* and *Fire Nova*. He simply recited the incantation and performed the gestures and then let'em rip.

Finn chewed on the inside of his cheek. Something more had been going on there – which would explain why the fires inside the golems had dwindled when Brutus had cast a new spell to get himself out of Kyyle's trap. Even more disconcerting was that the fire mage had never stopped casting nor lost his balance. He hadn't even looked harried.

As the world flashed back into existence and Brutus' harsh voice once more echoed across the field, Finn was still numbly trying to process what he had just seen. Despite his questions, one thing was clear. Brutus was on an entirely different level. It was his mastery of multiple spells, the ambidextrous casting, the physical prowess needed to pull off that recovery – all while maintaining his composure and thinking through his steps logically.

There was one easy takeaway from all of this.

Finn had a *long* way to go.

*   *   *

Finn appeared on the field in a flash of multi-colored energy. The sudden change was mildly disorienting, but he was growing more accustomed to the abrupt transitions. A glance around the courtyard confirmed that phantom ash no longer rained from the sky.

He was back in the regular game world.

Several tears formed in the air around Finn, flashing with multi-colored light. As these rifts disappeared, the members of Finn's class stood in their place. A rift ripped open beside Finn, and he stepped aside to avoid the flash of energy.

A moment later, Kyyle stood beside him, the young man blinking rapidly and raising a hand to blot out the harsh light that shone down on the field. Then he suddenly noticed Finn beside him and their eyes met.

Finn arched an eyebrow, not needing to ask his unspoken question aloud.

Kyyle grimaced, rubbing at his neck. "Yeah, so we all died right after you. It was... pretty bad. I can honestly say that I was never curious to experience being burned alive." He hesitated. "Or *melted* alive, I guess. Although, that doesn't have the same ring to it..."

Finn wasn't surprised. After what he had observed in the deathscape, he was surprised they had lasted as long as they had. The only answer he could come up with was that the golems were rather "stupid" – possibly a product of Brutus casting multiple spells.

That or the mage hadn't meant to kill them immediately.

"Well, we tried," Finn finally added.

"Welcome back!" Brutus barked, interrupting the students.

Finn and Kyyle turned to find the man lounging on a glass throne in the center of the field. At some point, he must have gone to retrieve an umbrella and what appeared to be a glass of lemonade.

"If you all want to gather round, we can review today's lesson," Brutus continued. His voice sounded positively cheery, particularly after his more-foreboding tone at the beginning of the class. Not to mention the part where he had killed them all.

"So, I imagine you all have some questions regarding the point of that little exercise," Brutus began once the students had grouped up in front of him.

He shrugged. "I might not have been entirely upfront, and I'll be the first to admit that. Just yelling 'run' was probably a bit vague. However, this first lesson is important, and I can assure you I'm not just a sadist. Anyone want to take a stab at the goal here?"

Vanessa raised her hand. "Were you trying to emphasize the importance of physical skills while casting? We sure did a lot of running away." She couldn't entirely keep the bitterness out of her voice.

Brutus cocked his head. "That's a good takeaway. As I mentioned before, your opponents likely won't let you stand still and cast to your heart's content. But that wasn't the primary purpose of the lesson. Anyone else?"

The burly mage frowned as he saw the novices all look away. "Hmm, no takers? Then I guess we'll get to call on some people."

Brutus' eyes skimmed across the crowd before locking on Finn. "How about you?" the fire mage said, stabbing a finger at him. "What do you think the true goal of this lesson was?"

Finn grimaced. He had actually given that some thought. Brutus had opened the class by talking about the need for physical training. But there were likely more productive ways to show the benefits of improving their bodies. He hadn't needed to kill them all.

Finn hesitated at that thought.

"You wanted us to know what it feels like to die," he said softly. The other students looked at Finn in shock, their attention bouncing back and forth between Finn and Brutus.

A broad, knowing smile crept across the fire mage's face. "Indeed. This is a valuable lesson. As travelers, you can't die – not truly. As such that puts me in an interesting predicament. How do I properly *motivate* you?"

He let the question linger in the air. "With the residents of this world, I don't really need to answer that question. They want to survive. They understand pain, hardship, and injury. But I have found it much harder to convey this point with your kind. It's the sort of thing you can only understand firsthand."

"Y-you killed us just so we could *appreciate* what it feels like?" another student sputtered, anger tinging her voice.

"Yes, I did," Brutus replied matter-of-factly. "And I bet you now understand the importance of your training. You'll also likely make an effort to avoid dying in the future. Besides, if it's any consolation, I was actually going easy on you. In a real fight, your opponent will be trying to kill you much faster." The student just stared at him. Her brow was furrowed and her mouth opened and closed, but no words escaped her throat.

Finn had to admit the man's logic did make a certain amount of sense. He suspected he might have tried a little harder in high school PE if he had been chased by golems hurling molten glass.

"There were other lessons to be learned here, however," Brutus acknowledged, taking a sip from his lemonade and nodding at Vanessa. "Your physical training is indeed vital to your survival. You also saw what a mage can do in an environment tailored to their magic. You can use the terrain to your advantage. That would have gone quite a bit differently if the fight had taken place on a ship or in a forest, for example."

His smile widened as he noticed many of the students glaring at him. "Anyway, the death was the stick. The carrot is those oh-so-sweet skill and stat gains," Brutus explained. "But I'm sure you all have diligently checked your notifications..."

Almost as one, the class of students all stared off into space, idly swiping at the air. As Finn checked his own notifications, he was surprised by his progress.

Stat Increases:
+3 Strength +7 Dexterity +7 Endurance

x1 Level Up!
You have (70) undistributed stat points.

x1 Spell Rank Up: Magma Armor
Skill Level: Beginner Level 2
Cost: 55 Mana
Effect 1: Creates a damage shield capable of absorbing 120 damage (60 damage if water/ice).

"As I'm certain you've noticed by now, this sort of training provides experience and allows you to rank your skills. The same applies to the duels," Brutus added. "The regular competitions are an important way to both rank members of the guild as well as provide invaluable combat experience and training."

That shit-eating grin was back on his face as Brutus continued. "So, let's recap. You need this training if you don't want to die – which I understand isn't exactly *pleasant* – and this is also one of the easiest ways for you to get stronger. Feeling motivated yet?"

A few students still seemed upset, but the majority were now watching Brutus with an appraising expression. More than one novice was also openly assessing their peers with hunger in their eyes. Not that Finn blamed them. Brutus had basically just explained that they could grow stronger by killing their classmates.

"Now there's one last thing I'd like to address before we wrap up for the day," Brutus barked. "Specifically, some of you learned a lesson that wasn't exactly on my syllabus. I suppose we can turn this into a *teachable moment*."

Brutus leaned forward, setting his drink down, and his expression sobering. "More specifically, some of you learned the importance of working together – which, admittedly, is not a skill our guild tends to cultivate in its students – but it is a useful lesson for the world outside these walls."

Brutus' eyes flashed a bright orange as he channeled his mana, his otherwise-friendly demeanor washing away entirely. "So, on that note, who came up with that *clever* little plan to drop me in a hole and try to destroy my golems?"

Fuck, Finn thought. *Fuck, fuck fuck.*

He had just gone and painted yet another target on his back. What was his damn problem? He watched as Brutus' eyes danced across the four members of that conspiracy, lingering on him for a fraction of a second. Finn's thoughts raced as he tried to think of a way to dig himself out of this hole.

"I did," Kyyle said loudly, his voice echoing across the field.

Everyone whirled to look at the gangly youth, including Brutus and Finn.

"Really?" Brutus replied slowly, skepticism practically dripping from his voice.

"Yes," Kyyle said more firmly. "I saw that you were casting multiple spells and how resilient your golems were. The obvious play was to distract you while hitting the golems hard enough that they couldn't repair themselves."

Brutus glanced at the three other members of the conspiracy. "Is that right? Our skinny little mage over here came up with this master plan?"

They all nodded numbly.

"Hmph. Well, what's your name, boy?" Brutus asked, turning his attention back to Kyyle and flames dancing in his eyes.

"Kyyle," he replied, barely managing to keep his voice even.

"Well, congratulations then. I'll have to keep an eye on you. Someone with your aptitude deserves some *special* attention."

Finn could actually *hear* Kyyle gulp at that comment.

"Alright," Brutus announced, leaning back and snatching at his lemonade – the weight of his attention abruptly disappearing. He waved a hand at them. "Anyway, class is dismissed! See you all tomorrow. Our next class is going to be a real *killer*, so get yourselves mentally prepared," he added with a grin.

Not a single chuckle escaped the group of students, nor did anyone make any move to leave, eyeing Brutus cautiously. However, when no flames erupted from the ground, they decided to beat a hasty retreat. Finn swore he heard Brutus grumble something about "novice mages" and "no sense of humor" as the students rushed to get away from him.

Finn and Kyyle stood in silence for a moment, a sudden awkwardness hanging over them as they looked at each other and the flock of other students that were passing around them. Finn finally opened his mouth to speak but was interrupted.

Zane approached and smacked the youth on the back. "Not a bad plan! I mean, we all died anyway, but it might have worked out under other circumstances. I guess I underestimated you."

Finn was surprised to see that Vanessa was walking with Zane, her expression more severe – as though she was mentally berating herself. "Yes… yes, it was a good plan," she bit out reluctantly. "Although, it did ultimately fail."

I guess this is the second time our wannabe class valedictorian has gotten shown up, Finn thought dryly. *She doesn't seem to be taking it well.*

"Uh, thanks I guess," Kyyle said, running a hand

through his hair to cover his awkwardness.

"Anyway, we're going to get back to it," Zane continued. "You guys take it easy."

With that, the two of them strode off.

Kyyle looked at Finn, but he held up a hand. "Thanks. I certainly don't need more attention right now."

The young man let out a sigh of relief. "I'm glad you're okay with me taking credit. I saw the look of panic on your face and just sort of acted – wasn't sure it was the right move."

He gave Kyyle a lopsided smile. "It's more than fine. Besides, I wouldn't have been able to pull it off without you." Finn hesitated, remembering the question that had been bugging him in the deathscape. "Although, I was meaning to ask, how did Vanessa and Zane learn those new spells?"

Kyyle immediately looked guilty again, kicking at the sand as he looked away. "Well, last class Lamia taught us all three basic spells…"

Finn just stared at him, anger suddenly simmering in his veins as he realized that Lamia had cut him out from learning new spells. She must have known that Finn would miss out by *graduating* from her class early. "That cold-hearted—"

"—beauty!" Kyyle interjected, looking pointedly at a group of passing students. "I know, she's pretty hot, right."

In a lower-pitch voice, Kyyle continued. "I wouldn't talk badly of the teachers in public. They seem to hold a grudge, if you know what I mean."

Finn did – firsthand. But he ground his teeth together as the pair started heading back to the main guild. Between the harsh reality check that Brutus' "lesson" had given him and missing out on new spells, Finn needed to haul some serious ass if he was going to keep up with his classmates.

* * *

Brutus took another sip of his lemonade as he watched that boy, Kyyle, walking away. He spoke to an older novice who walked with him. He had caught the man's name in passing.

Finn.

There was something in that older man's eyes that unsettled Brutus – although, he was reluctant to admit it. Maybe it was the way Finn seemed to analyze and measure everything around him. He hadn't seen any fear shining in his eyes during the lesson even while the others panicked. Only a calm precision and even a flicker of excitement. That plan to distract him might have even worked had the group of novices been a bit more experienced.

"What do you think?" a quiet voice asked. Abbad suddenly appeared beside Brutus' makeshift glass throne, his body shimmering as he dropped the reflective shield of air that had kept him hidden from sight.

"I don't buy that kid's bullshit story," Brutus grumbled.

"Loyalty is an admirable quality, as well as the ability to engender it in others," Abbad replied in a neutral voice. "And what of the older student?"

Brutus hesitated. "He has potential, but he hesitated to take credit for his plan. I wonder whether he has the spine to do what needs to be done." Brutus spared a glance at Abbad. "You know as well as I do how grueling the duels can be."

Abbad gave a curt nod. Yet he stayed still, as though waiting for something.

"I also noticed the mark on his hand – his sleeve slid back during the fight," Brutus murmured, grinding his teeth together. That symbol was a bad omen.

More silence.

"Can you not train him yourself?" the fire mage asked when it was clear that Abbad didn't plan to speak.

"You know that my skills and temperament are better suited for... *other* activities," the librarian replied.

Brutus let out an incredulous snort. "I've seen you in a fight. You're selling yourself short by a mile."

Abbad simply cocked his head but didn't say anything.

Brutus knew that the so-called librarian was just waiting for an answer. And he already knew the one he would give. A man's debts needed to be repaid.

Brutus finally let out a frustrated sigh. "Fine. I'll train him. But after this, we're even." A brief pause as he chewed on his next words. "How… how is she?"

"She is doing well," Abbad said simply and began to walk back toward the guild building, taking the same route as Finn and Kyyle.

Brutus was glad for the librarian's quick movement; it spared him the need to control his expression. He choked back at the sudden lump that had settled at the base of his throat. "Why are you taking such a large gamble on this one?" he asked as Abbad walked away. "You know what the others will do if they find out you're meddling."

The librarian hesitated, stopping in place. "Because I can imagine a different world," he said softly. "One where we're more than slaves."

Then Abbad disappeared as though a mirror had swept in front of his body, only hot sand visible where he had been standing a moment before. Brutus could just barely make out the faint ripple of light that marked the edge of the condensed pocket of air – a limitation of the librarian's school of magic. Light and water mages could craft illusions that were far superior. Although, they lacked some of Abbad's other talents.

Brutus' gaze returned to Finn. He hoped Abbad was right, but he couldn't shake the feeling that something was off here. The Crone's Mark hadn't appeared in more than a century, and it never came without a cost. He'd only seen that symbol in books, alongside entries and accounts that chilled even his blood.

"Let's hope you're tough enough to handle what's coming," he murmured.

Chapter 17 - Sneaky

Finn sighed, letting his mana lapse as his fingers stilled. The balls of flame that hovered around him winked out of existence. He was getting better. He could maintain three orbs at the same time now, letting them revolve around him and alternating their rhythm at will and he no longer required Abbad's shield to protect the room around him. On top of that, the hand gestures had become almost entirely instinct.

His ability to actually cast spells... now that was another matter altogether.

"Icarus," Finn said aloud, bringing up the spell creation UI he had designed.

Translucent guidelines soon hovered in his field of view. A new window opened, showing a list of his most recent failures. It was a rather long list.

After Brutus' sadistic training exercise, it had become clear that Finn's primary problem was a lack of spells. He couldn't depend on the abilities of other students to bail him out of a situation – at least, not during the upcoming duels. Finn needed to become more flexible, which meant he needed more weapons in his magical arsenal.

However, he seemed to be missing something.

No matter how many different variations he tried, he couldn't replicate what he had done with *Fire Nova*. He wasn't sure what was missing. However, after his time in the deathscape, it was clear that there were different tiers of spells. The golems that Brutus had summoned had involved a much more complex incantation. The trouble was that with just his two simple spells and the fragments of the spells that Brutus had cast, Finn was having difficulty finding the problem. His sample size was simply too small.

"I need a real spellbook," Finn murmured, skimming the list of failed spells.

"Oh, really? Well, there are plenty of books in here. Have you tried checking the stacks?" a voice chirped from over Finn's shoulder.

Acting almost entirely on instinct, Finn fumbled to cast his *Magma Armor*, the hot liquid belatedly forming a barrier along his arm even as he whirled to face whoever had snuck up on him. The stranger wore dark-blue robes, the hood drawn over their face and long sleeves covering their tattoos.

"Well, that's a little dramatic," the woman said, pushing back her hood to reveal Julia's mocking grin. "Although that shield is pretty cool – or *hot*, I guess," she amended, tapping at her lips thoughtfully.

"You scared the shit out of me," Finn hissed, letting his spell lapse.

"You do seem jumpy," Julia replied with a smile. "Maybe because a rather large man killed you and an entire class of students earlier?"

Finn let out another frustrated sigh, leaning against the table and rubbing at his face. "How do you know about that? Actually, how the hell did you even get in here?"

Julia paced in front of him, rolling what appeared to be a novice token across her knuckles with a speed and precision that Finn found a little frightening.

I hope she didn't hurt anyone to steal that, he thought to himself.

"I told you already, I have a knack for getting into places," Julia said, waving a dismissive hand. "Especially if I haven't been invited. I'm like... the opposite of a vampire."

"So, you're a stalker?" Finn asked in a dry voice.

Julia shrugged. "Ego much? It's not all about *you*. I'm trying to find a chink in this place's armor. Maybe a way to smuggle your dumb ass out of here."

"Might I suggest the same way you keep getting in?" Finn offered.

She grimaced. "I'm not sure you would enjoy that." Julia's attention returned to Finn once more. "Besides, I don't think you have the skill to pull it off. Not without a lot of training and a few more levels anyway."

"She's correct," a familiar voice said. Finn felt a dull weight settle in his stomach as he observed Abbad step out from behind the stacks. "You would not be able to take the same path as the thief."

Julia tensed but made no overt move to reach for a weapon. Instead, she painted a woeful expression on her face. "A thief? I am just a lowly street urchin. I stumbled in here... I-I think I may have gotten lost."

Abbad didn't react to her theatrics. As he approached her, he rested a hand on her shoulder. "Save the sob story for someone more gullible, child."

What happened next was a bit difficult for Finn to follow, the movements practically a blur of motion.

Julia flicked a dagger out of the sleeve of her robe while simultaneously flinging the same arm forward. Abbad didn't move; he merely twitched the fingers of his left hand. The dagger stopped short as though it had hit an invisible wall.

Yet Julia wasn't done. She seemed to expect the blow to be blocked, pushing off the wall of compressed air and whirling into a counterattack, another blade suddenly appearing in her other hand.

Abbad finally moved, a gust of air shoving him forward and inside Julia's guard. He grabbed at her arm, twisting it up and behind her back until he held her pinned.

The entire engagement took about two seconds.

"Submit, or I will be forced to break your arm," the librarian said calmly.

"Really?" Julia gasped. "Because you better look down." Finn could see that Julia still held the first dagger in her free hand, the blade pressed against Abbad's abdomen.

The hint of a smile tugged at Abbad's lips. "Feel free to try."

Julia snarled and tried to stab the blade forward. However, it slid across an invisible barrier. Finn only then noticed that Abbad's free hand was still dancing through a series of gestures.

Holy crap his reflexes are incredible, Finn thought to himself.

"Please don't harm her," he offered, trying to defuse the situation. "She's a friend."

Abbad glanced at Finn and then suddenly released Julia, pushing her across the small space with a sudden gust of wind to create some distance. "I am aware that you and the thief are acquainted. If she can keep her blades to herself, she can remain."

Julia rubbed at her arm, glaring at Abbad. "Stop calling me a thief."

"We are what we do. Did you not steal those robes as well as the token in your front pocket?" Abbad answered.

Finn's daughter gritted her teeth and her fingers clenched around the dagger still resting in her palm. Finn decided he needed to intervene.

"Hey, let's all relax for a moment," he interjected. Finn glanced at Julia and then pointedly at her weapon. "And maybe put down the dagger? Abbad is a friend. He has helped... well, *guide* me since I was admitted to the guild."

Julia looked skeptical and spared one last glare at Abbad. However, she reluctantly slid the dagger back under her robes. "A friend, huh? Sounds more like Stockholm Syndrome to me. This is just another one of your prison guards."

Abbad's normally passive expression broke for a moment, his eyes flashing – a fact that didn't go unnoticed by Finn. It lasted only a heartbeat before his neutral mask fell into place once more. "I am not responsible for keeping Finn here. In fact, it is my wish to see him set free."

"See, we're all on the same side," Finn offered, glancing between the pair.

"Hmph." Julia let out a snort. Yet she leaned against the table, some of the tension leaving her shoulders. "We'll see."

Abbad simply arched an eyebrow, shifting his attention back to Finn. The librarian's unspoken question hung in the air. Finn had been dreading this confrontation, having violated the librarian's instructions at nearly every turn.

"So, I know I haven't exactly been keeping a low profile like you asked," Finn began hesitantly.

He wasn't certain what sort of reaction he expected from Abbad. However, Finn wasn't anticipating the abrupt laugh that bubbled from the man's lips.

"Low profile?" the librarian echoed. "Let's see. Since we last spoke, you torched a classroom, were ejected from Lamia's class, and helped the other novices fight Brutus. Although, I'll admit the ploy was clever." He noted Finn's surprise. "Do you think he bought your friend's excuse? Other people were watching that fight, after all."

Finn's eyes widened. He could suddenly remember that there had been onlookers standing on the terraces ringing the guild's inner courtyard.

Shit.

Abbad's gaze flicked back to Julia. "On top of that, you seem to be conspiring with the thief who has been terrorizing the guild for the last few days. That alone would be enough for the headmaster to order that your mana be purged and to expel you into the sands.

"Did I miss anything?" Abbad asked.

Finn grimaced. "No, that sounds about right," he answered softly.

Abbad let out a sigh, his fingers idly running across a nearby book. "There is little we can do to change the past. We can only move forward. As such, a change of strategy may be in order," he explained.

"That seems unnecessarily cryptic," Julia groused. "Is he always like this?" she asked Finn. He just shrugged noncommittally.

"I will explain shortly—"

Abbad was cut off as Julia kept going. "Hey, mysterious librarian dude, before we get to whatever overly complicated plan you've concocted, how about explaining why you are even bothering to help—"

Julia was abruptly cut off, a faintly glowing yellow sphere enveloping her mouth. She struggled to speak, but no words came out. Julia felt at her throat and then went cross-eyed, trying to stare down at her mouth.

When she saw the yellow-tinged sphere, Julia tried to lunge at Abbad, her daggers reappearing in her hands. A sudden gust of wind blasted through the library, knocking her backward until she fell into a nearby chair. Finn could see shimmering bands of air wrap around her wrists and ankles, locking her in place.

"That is much better," Abbad said in a dry voice before turning back to Finn. "Now, as I was saying, I think a change of plans is in order. My attempt at caution may have been short-sighted. I underestimated your ability to attract chaos," he added, with a glance at Julia, who was struggling against her bonds and glaring at the librarian.

"So, what are you proposing?" Finn asked, trying to ignore the pleading look Julia kept giving him. He had to admit that some part of him wished he could use that magical duct tape trick in the real world – which didn't make him feel *too* guilty. He still hadn't forgotten what Julia had done to his AI.

"My original hope was to sneak you through your training and the duels, allowing you to graduate without incident. However, I expect that is no longer an option."

"Why not?" Finn replied. "I mean, I could just keep my head down…"

"Because most of the guild is already talking about you," Abbad interrupted. "Do you think your actions in Lamia's class went unnoticed or that the other students bought the story you fed Brutus? You are now the primary competitor for nearly every novice about to enter the duels. To make matters worse, you also alerted the faculty to your potential. And their directive is to put upstart mages in their place."

Finn tensed, his fingers tracing the pattern on his right wrist. He could suddenly remember Lamia's cold-eyed stare and the malice that lingered in her eyes. Finn had accidentally pissed off one of the guards.

"I see that you are starting to understand the weight of the situation," the librarian continued, observing Finn's expression. "The faculty may not act directly for fear of alarming the other students. However, that does not mean that they won't go out of their way to undermine you more subtly."

"Like Lamia not teaching me those two new spells," Finn murmured.

"Precisely," Abbad said with a nod.

"Okay," Finn said slowly. "I get it. We need to change tactics. What did you have in mind?" he asked hopefully.

It was Abbad's turn to grimace. "You need to train harder. We're not aiming for the middle of the pack anymore. With the way you've drawn attention to yourself, many will be watching you. However, that attention also provides a peculiar sort of safety. If you are in the public eye, then it will be more difficult for the headmaster and the others to act against you.

"In short, we're aiming for the top of the leaderboard now."

Finn coughed. "Wait, what? Are you serious? I haven't even learned Veridian yet!"

"Then I advise you to study," Abbad replied curtly.

"Fortunately, I've also found someone who can help teach you," he continued. "However, neither myself nor your new instructor can be seen as playing favorites, so do not expect any special treatment."

"Who exactly is this new instructor?" Finn asked.

"Brutus," Abbad answered immediately.

Finn just stared at him in shock. "You mean the guy that killed me today? The one I also helped drop into a hole in the ground?"

A faint smile tugged at Abbad's lips. "Indeed. I suspect he won't go easy on you."

"Yeah, no shit," Finn murmured.

"In any event, for now, act as though nothing has changed. Continue your studies and be certain to attend your next class with Brutus. I am sure he will find a suitable time to pull you aside for additional instruction," Abbad explained.

The librarian turned his attention back to Julia where she was still struggling against his bindings. "Now we need to decide what to do with you, thief. I suppose I should turn you in – which would likely result in imprisonment or exile," the librarian murmured, tapping at his lips. "I understand imprisonment is especially problematic for your kind."

Julia's eyes widened in alarm and Finn moved to speak, yet Abbad continued, ignoring them both. "However, you have proven rather resourceful. I also sense that you care for Finn – which might make you useful."

The librarian's fingers twitched, and the sphere hovering over Julia's mouth disappeared. "I'll kill you—" she growled.

Abbad cut her off. "Unlikely. But I suggest you stay silent unless you wish for me to gag you again."

Julia's jaw snapped shut with an almost-audible click.

"Good. At least you learn quickly. Now, I will set you free, and you may keep your disguise and the novice token you stole. However, I will not be able to protect you if you are caught," Abbad explained.

"I don't need your help," Julia replied with a glare.

"Let us hope that is the case," Abbad replied, unperturbed by her tone.

His fingers danced through a new pattern, and Abbad murmured an incantation under his breath. Julia's bindings soon disappeared, and she took to her feet. Although, she appeared more cautious now, keeping a watchful eye on the librarian.

"And what do you want in return for these *gifts*?" Julia grumbled. "Don't tell me you're helping me out of the kindness of your heart."

Abbad nodded. "Indeed, your freedom comes with a price. It always does. In this case, I only ask that you continue watching Finn. I expect he may need a second set of eyes in the coming days. As well as a hidden blade or two," the librarian replied, his tone ominous.

Julia cocked her head, eyeing the man in confusion.

Abbad glanced at Finn. "I have other matters to attend to, so I will leave you to it. Train hard and don't hold back. You only have a short time left to prepare."

With that, the librarian stepped back toward the stacks, soon disappearing among the books and scrolls. Which left Finn and Julia standing beside the table, each of them trying to process the encounter.

"I like him," Julia finally said, breaking the silence.

Finn just stared at her incredulously. "He gagged you and tied you to a chair."

Julia shrugged. "I'd have done the same."

She shifted her attention to Finn, peering at him. "Although, that conversation raised a few interesting questions. Like why is our super-serious new friend so interested in you, specifically? Also, he seemed pretty familiar with what happened in the courtyard, but I don't remember seeing him there. How did he obtain that information so fast?"

Finn looked at her in surprise. He wasn't exactly certain why Abbad was interested in him. The man didn't seem to be acting out of altruism – at least, not entirely. Which made Finn wonder what purpose the librarian felt he could serve. His thoughts flashed back to his conversation with the Seer, but he quickly discarded that image. There was no way the librarian could know about his conversation with the god. For now, he supposed Abbad's motives didn't really matter. Their immediate interests were aligned, and that was enough.

However, Julia's second question was more intriguing. Finn supposed Abbad could have discovered what happened with Brutus from the other students, yet he seemed to have firsthand knowledge of the fight. Yet how had Abbad witnessed the battle if Julia hadn't seen him there? Perhaps the librarian had a few other talents that he had yet to reveal to Finn. He'd make a mental note of that.

"I'm not sure," Finn finally answered, shaking his head.

Julia shrugged, a grin creeping across her face. "Perhaps you aren't *positive* you know the answer to either question, but I have a feeling you know more than you're telling me," she retorted. Finn moved to object, but she put up a hand. "Nah, don't ruin it or try to lie. You're not terribly good at it. Besides, I like a good mystery. It's more fun figuring it out on my own."

She started to saunter back toward the nearby bookshelves, pulling up her hood to hide her face. Then Julia hesitated, stopping in place and her back still to Finn. "However, that windy asshole is right about one thing, you seem to be collecting enemies here."

In a flash of movement, Julia pulled something from her robes, whirled, and flung it at him. A dagger embedded itself in the nearby table, the blade still quivering. "I know you're learning this magic stuff, but you should still have a weapon. Keep it close. I can't guarantee I'll be there to cover your ass if shit goes down."

And then Julia disappeared.

Finn slumped back against the table, his eyes on the dagger. He was surprised at how normal this all felt. He had died today, witnessed a mage subdue his daughter and tie her to a chair with bands of compressed air, and then that same daughter had given him a dagger as a present.

"Just another day inside AO," he muttered.

As though on cue, a screen popped up in front of him.

Quest Update: Curious Capabilities

You failed miserably at keeping a low profile, and Abbad decided to change tactics. You have already painted a big target on your back, but you may still be able to maintain your position in the guild by showing everyone that you're the most badass SOB around. You know what, this really is feeling more and more like a prison...

In order to make that happen, you need to double down on your training, which will somehow involve Brutus. If you thought your studies were tough before, then you're really going to hate what's coming next.

Difficulty: B
Success: Continue your studies and begin training with Brutus.
Failure: Get expelled.
Reward: Same reward. Not getting killed or exiled. Aren't you grateful? You should definitely be grateful.

Finn let out an amused snort as he read through the prompt. Although the game's AI was right about one thing – he needed to get back to work if he was going to survive.

He sighed, swiped away the quest notification, and

pulled up his mod interface, loading the next language lesson. Even as the symbols began to swim down the UI, his fingers were already twining through a familiar pattern, a tingling heat burning in his chest as he summoned his mana to continue training his *Mana Mastery*.

Hopefully, his training would be enough.

Chapter 18 - Distracted

"Alright, that's a wrap for today," Brutus barked.

The novices all dropped to the sand.

Even the searing, sun-drenched particles felt like heaven after the last few grueling hours. The fire mage had them running laps across the shifting sands, sprinting through a glass obstacle course whose razor-sharp edges were now stained a dark crimson, and balancing for an hour on a glass pole about ten feet over the sands. He had topped it all off by having them hold a plank position for about 15 minutes above a pool of molten glass.

Finn supposed none of that would have been too terrible, except Brutus had appointed himself "Head Motivator" – which only seemed to entail creating large pits of molten glass around whatever activity they were doing and throwing *Fireballs* in their direction when they wavered or slowed down.

"He's a fucking sadist," Kyyle groaned from beside Finn. The young man's robes, like most of the students', were singed and burned. Luckily, their novice equipment seemed to recover each time they logged back in.

Finn just grunted, letting his depleted stamina gauge slowly refill. This was one of those moments when he wondered why the game needed to feel so realistic. He could feel his limbs ache, and his muscles throb and burn in a far-too-authentic sort of way.

To make matters worse, he had spent the entire afternoon waiting for the axe to drop – that moment when Brutus would pull him aside and introduce him to his own individually tailored version of hell. Abbad had promised as much.

Yet that moment never came.

And, at this stage, he was struggling to see how it could possibly be worse...

"You know we have another week of this, right?" Kyyle groused from beside Finn, slowly heaving himself to his feet with a groan. "I'm starting to think I might just risk the sandworms."

"At least there was that five-minute break in the middle?" Finn offered.

"He had to go refill his drink," Kyyle snapped, pointing at Brutus' makeshift glass throne – replete with umbrella and a pitcher of lemonade. "And he summoned those stupid glass golems while he was gone."

"But they're slow," Finn said with a grin while pushing himself to a sitting position.

"Now I know you're messing with me," Kyyle grumbled.

"Finn," a familiar voice barked.

Both of them winced. They didn't have to look to see who was calling Finn. They had already heard that voice enough to last a lifetime.

"You have been summoned by our overlord," Kyyle muttered.

"I'll let him know you said hi," Finn shot back.

He hauled himself to his feet, idly noting that most of the class was still struggling to stand up, before trudging over to Brutus. Finn already suspected what was coming, but it didn't make it any easier.

"Your performance was complete crap today," Brutus said when Finn neared. The man's voice boomed across the courtyard – loud enough for the other students to hear him.

"I'm sorry," Finn replied evenly.

"Which means exactly zilch to me," Brutus retorted with a broad, knowing smile. "I don't know if it's your age or just lack of effort, but it doesn't really matter. You'll be tackling some extra lessons from now on until you manage to catch up with the others."

Finn could hear a few stifled laughs behind him and couldn't help but grind his teeth together. He shouldn't give two shits what these other people thought – not at his age anyway. And he knew this was just an act. At the same time, Brutus didn't need to lay it on so thick.

"As you wish," Finn bit out, glaring at Brutus.

"I did, and I do. Let's get to it. Follow me," the fire mage instructed, winking at Finn as he hopped up from his glass throne. With a wave of his hand, the chair melted back into the sand and Brutus set off toward the southern side of the guild hall.

Kyyle shot Finn a sympathetic glance as he passed. "Sorry," he mouthed.

Finn just shrugged and tried to look miserable.

Luckily, he didn't need to fake that.

* * *

The pair wound through the northern portion of the guild hall. Strangely, this part of the complex seemed deserted, and Finn observed far fewer students wandering its halls. If anything, many of the structures and rooms they passed looked dilapidated, with boarded-up doors and trash littering the floor.

"What is this place?" Finn asked Brutus.

"This northern annex used to house the school's crafting division," Brutus grunted. "Once upon a time, we had a full-fledged forge, a crystal growing room, an enchantment wing – the works basically."

Finn's eyes widened. That sounded amazing. Although, that did little to explain the condition of the buildings. "What happened? This place looks like it should be condemned."

Brutus grimaced. "The Emir and the headmaster closed it down."

"But why—?" Finn began.

The fire mage cut him off, giving him a sober look. "Because they chose to. This is one of those things you shouldn't dig at." He hesitated, his eyes clouding over as they passed what appeared to be a ruined forge. "Although, I'll leave you with a question."

Brutus glanced back at Finn. "Why wouldn't the people in charge want mages to have access to powerful weapons and armor?"

Finn's brow furrowed. So, this was intentional? The obvious implication of Brutus' question was that this sort of activity would make the mages too large of a threat. Finn shook his head. But that also meant the Emir had chosen to give up an edge in equipping his own troops and people in favor of suppressing a single group. That seemed crazy. Did Lahab not have any enemies *outside* its own walls?

The pair came to a stop in front of a plain stone room. There were no windows and only the single entrance, a massive circular steel door. Although, the hinges of the door looked rusted through. Even more oddly, the locking mechanism was on the inside.

At a gesture from Brutus, Finn stepped inside. At first glance, Finn didn't see anything impressive about the room until he examined one of the walls more closely. He noticed indentations in the stone and scraped away a thick coating of dust.

"These are Veridian runes," Finn murmured, stepping back to survey the symbols. "They've been etched into the wall itself."

"Enchantments," Brutus grunted. "This used to be used as a testing room a long time ago. Mages would bring new contraptions and projects here to avoid accidentally blowing apart their own workshop."

The mage snorted as he examined the walls. "Obviously, it isn't seeing any use now, but it makes for a great training room. We don't need to worry about causing any damage. There are also suppression spells built into the walls. No matter how much noise you make down here, no one will hear. Besides, this area doesn't get much foot traffic nowadays, so it's pretty private."

Brutus glanced over at Finn. "In short, this is your new training room."

"What about the library?" Finn asked.

"Abbad said it was too public. Any old librarian or student could wander through that area. This room is safer as you progress in power," Brutus explained. "You'll be coming here to train when you aren't attending a class."

"So, you're really planning to train me?" Finn asked skeptically, finally addressing the flaming elephant in the room.

A grin swept across Brutus' face. "Ahh, that's cute.

Training." He laughed. "By the time I'm done, I'm sure you'll be referring to it as *torture*."

The fire mage clapped his hands together. "Anyway, we should get to work. As a first step, let's take a look at your stats and skills – I need to know what I'm working with. Go ahead and pull up your Character Status.

Finn did as he was asked, noting that he had a stat notification from that afternoon's training in the courtyard:

Stat Increases:
+6 Strength +8 Dexterity +11 Endurance

Character Status			
Name:	Finn	**Gender:**	Male
Level:	15	**Class:**	
Race:	Human	**Alignment:**	Lawful-Neutral
Fame:	100	**Infamy:**	0
Health:	170	**H-Regen/Sec:**	0.30
Mana:	245	**M-Regen/Sec:**	2.00
Stamina:	370	**S-Regen/Sec:**	3.00
Strength:	21	**Dexterity:**	27
Vitality:	10	**Endurance:**	30
Intelligence:	15	**Willpower:**	15

Affinities			
Dark:	2%	**Light:**	4%
Fire:	37%	**Water:**	5%
Air:	3%	**Earth:**	9%

"Hmm," Brutus murmured, staring at the translucent screen. He glanced at Finn. "You've leveled a lot for a novice, but you haven't distributed any stat points?"

"I didn't have a good understanding of what the stats did until your last class. I just forgot to assign points last night since I was studying."

"Well, you can go ahead and put everything in *Intelligence*. That will benefit you the most right now – increasing your learning speed, mana, and mana regeneration rate. Damage isn't really a priority," Brutus murmured.

Finn had to admit that made sense and went along with what he had been thinking already. He promptly allocated his 70 stat points to *Intelligence*. This caused his mana to jump to 595 and his regen to increase to 12.50/second. That should make training his *Mana Mastery* much easier. He had just been summoning the flaming orbs until he ran out of mana and then focusing on his language studies while his mana regenerated.

Brutus must have been reading his mind. "What is your *Mana Mastery* at now?"

Finn chewed on the inside of his cheek as he brought up the skill panel.

Mana Mastery
Skill Level: Intermediate Level 1
Effect 1: -4% to the mana cost of spells.
Effect 2: 1% faster cast rate.

Finn was somewhat surprised to see that he had reached Intermediate Level 1 already. He had disabled his skill notifications temporarily since they kept interrupting his studies. He would need to remember to check on his progress more regularly.

"Intermediate Level 1," Finn reported.

"Hot damn, what has Abbad been having you do?" Brutus asked in surprise.

Finn wasn't really sure how to respond. "He's just been having me channel my mana constantly. He said to create orbs and then direct them in specific patterns while I'm studying Veridian."

Brutus simply stared at him. "How many orbs can you control at once?"

"I'm up to three now," Finn replied cautiously, not certain whether this was a positive or negative thing.

"Three!?" Brutus exclaimed. He ran a hand through his hair, shaking his head at the same time. "Have you been doing this every waking moment since you joined the guild?"

Finn grimaced. "Uh, basically."

"Well that changes things," Brutus replied, his eyes distant – considering something.

The fire mage's attention snapped back into focus, honing in on Finn. He clapped his hands together. "Alright, we can definitely work with this."

Brutus sighed, glancing at the doorway leading into the training room. "First things first, you can come on out now, thief girl!"

There was only silence for a few seconds, and then Julia seemed to step out of a shadow near the doorway. "How did you know I was here?"

"Let's just say it was a lucky guess," Brutus answered dryly. "I take it you're the one that gave him that little pig-sticker he's got hidden under his robes?"

Julia nodded.

Meanwhile, Finn was still trying to figure out how Julia had managed to blend into the shadows like that. And how Brutus had noticed. And how the fire mage had also somehow figured out that he had the dagger. He looked at Brutus with newfound respect. The man might be a sadist, but he was also observant and skilled.

Perhaps there was some method to his madness.

"And I assume you have no clue how to use that little blade?" Brutus asked, whirling back toward Finn.

A grudging shake of his head.

"Great. Then the thief will be useful as a training partner. You could say this is a match made in hell," Brutus said, rubbing his hands together and chuckling at his own joke.

Finn and Julia shared a look. What exactly had they just signed up for?

"Alright, let's cover some basics, and then we can get to the real training," Brutus began. He waved at Julia. "We don't need you quite yet, thief. You can either stay out of the way and watch or go step out in the hall and stand guard."

"I'm not a thief," Julia grumbled, but moved back against the chamber wall, hovering near the door. After her encounter with Abbad, she seemed to be a bit more wary of mages.

Brutus ignored her, his attention focusing on Finn as the pair faced off in the center of the room. "Your *Mana Mastery* is high enough that I can teach you a new trick. Watch my hands closely."

That was all the warning Finn got. Brutus' fingers exploded into movement, twining through a series of gestures so fast that Finn had difficulty following the movements. Only a moment later, *Magma Armor* materialized along Brutus' arm. Although, Brutus' version was much larger than Finn's, spiraling all the way up to his shoulder before lancing out into the air.

What was more strange was that Brutus' hands hadn't stopped. They continued their rhythm, and a ball of flame began to manifest next to the fire mage, growing rapidly in size until the heat forced Finn back a step. The *Fireball* lingered in the air, simply hovering beside the fire mage for several long seconds even after the spell had finished.

Without warning, Brutus hurled the *Fireball* at Finn. His body acted on instinct as he dove to the side – only managing the feat due to the time he had spent running the fire mage's obstacle course. Just like the other students, Finn had learned the hard way that he couldn't drop his guard around Brutus.

Finn hit the stone ground hard, managing to stumble into a roll and regain his feet even as a massive blast of flame struck the back wall of the room. The fires smashed against the stone, blooming outward before peeling back in on themselves.

A moment later, Finn once more stood in front of

Brutus, watching the fire mage warily. His shoulder ached, and he quickly patted at his sleeve to put out the fresh embers that had blossomed there.

"Alright, what did you learn?" Brutus asked, gesturing at the wall and the massive *Magma Armor* still stretched along his arm.

That you're an asshole, Finn thought but bit back that response.

He tried to collect his thoughts, thinking back to what he'd just seen. For some reason, his eyes kept drifting back and forth between the shield of molten energy and the scorched wall. It took a second for it to click.

"You cast two spells at once – or at least their cast time seemed to overlap," Finn murmured. He shook his head. "Although, that doesn't seem quite right."

A grin tugged at Brutus' lips, but he kept quiet, clearly waiting for more.

Finn felt like he was close. He closed his eyes, mentally inventorying Brutus' hand gestures. The large man had cast the original spell using both hands, but once that *Magma Armor* had been summoned, something had changed. It helped that Finn had seen the same ability during his time in the deathscape. The man's hands had begun acting independently after the first spell, with Brutus' right hand shifting into a different rhythm.

"You cast the first spell with both hands, and then cast the *Fireball* with just your right hand…" he said, half talking to himself. "But why did your left hand keep moving, and how did you manage to make the *Fireball* hover beside you?"

"Good," Brutus replied curtly. "You caught it faster than many students. I call this *Multi-Casting*. The skill allows you to chain cast spells quite quickly. It has some limitations, of course. Apart from being difficult to learn, the second spell casts slower since it is harder to control the flow of mana with one hand."

Finn just shook his head. Even Julia was staring at Brutus skeptically. "Is this ability common?" He was grappling with the speed and concentration required to pull that off. It was one thing to be ambidextrous, quite another to perform two intricate tasks simultaneously.

"Not exactly," Brutus said, grimacing. "Almost all other mages can only cast or maintain one spell at a time. Although, to fully appreciate the benefits of *Multi-Casting*, you will need to learn a little more about *mana channeling*. That's why my left hand kept moving after I finished casting *Magma Armor*. I suspect you missed this lesson, having graduated from Lamia's class *early*," he added, sarcasm lacing his voice.

Finn just raised an eyebrow.

"It may be easier to show you what I mean than to try to explain it. Let's take your *Magma Armor* as an example. Go ahead and cast the spell," Brutus instructed.

Finn did as he was told, his fingers twining through the requisite gestures as the incantation tumbled from his lips. The warm molten substance soon coated his right arm up to the shoulder, although it was a much more fragile-looking version of Brutus' shield.

"Alright," the fire mage continued, "now continue to move your hands, directing your mana into the shield. This isn't an exact science, just try to visualize your mana flowing into the spell."

Finn did as he was told, his fingers dancing through the air as he frowned in concentration. It took him a few tries, but he finally got the hang of it. Brutus was right. It was more of a *feeling* than a strict set of gestures. Yet after hours spent practicing his *Mana Mastery*, the process felt intuitive to Finn. As he directed mana into his *Magma Armor*, he could have sworn he saw the shield along his arm pulse an alternating red and orange, and then a notification appeared in front of him.

Spell: Magma Armor
Skill Level: Beginner Level 2
Cost: 55 Mana
Effect: Creates a damage shield capable of absorbing 120 damage (60 damage if water/ice).
Channel Effect: Repairs the shield at a rate of 40 damage/second at a mana cost of 10 mana/second.

Finn was so surprised that he accidentally let the

channel drop. The spell had a secondary effect if he continuously channeled his mana into it? Did that only apply to this spell or *all* spells? The implications were already tumbling through his mind in a wave.

"Huh," Finn said aloud. He could already see some of the advantages of mana channeling. "So, I could effectively block more strikes without needing to recast."

"Exactly!" Brutus replied. "It's a useful and efficient trick. As for other spells like *Fireball*, mana channeling allows you to form the spell and then hold it without firing. Channeling can also be used to charge or empower certain spells."

Finn just shook his head, glancing back at Brutus' hands and the shield winding up his arm. He was mentally reviewing the steps the mage had taken to cast *Magma Armor* and then the *Fireball*. He had summoned the shield with both hands, then only his right hand had switched to a new pattern.

"So, you cast the *Magma Armor*, continued to channel mana into that spell, and then cast the *Fireball* with your right hand – shifting to a channel on that spell once it was complete," Finn said slowly.

A broad smile lingered on Brutus' face. "Indeed. *Multi-Casting* allows you to cast more quickly, and, when combined with mana channeling, it potentially allows you to channel two spells at once. For example, you could summon and maintain two *Fireballs* at the same time, waiting for an opportunity to strike. In short, this skill not only increases your ability to cast more rapidly, but it provides more flexibility."

Something I could definitely use, Finn thought, thinking back to the fight against Brutus in the courtyard. However, another question was still bugging him.

"Why doesn't everyone learn how to do this?" Finn finally asked.

Brutus smirked. "Because it's difficult. It requires a high affinity, advanced *Mana Mastery*, and quite a bit of practice to get good at it.

"Frankly, it's usually easier for a mage to cheat," he continued. "Staves or wands can replicate the same channeling effect without as much effort, using crystals embedded in the weapon to maintain the channel. So, your typical mage will cast a spell and then shift the channel to their staff. The weakness is that they can't maintain two channels at once." He hesitated. "Although, I suppose there are myths of staves and wands that could channel two or more spells at the same time."

Brutus waved at the door leading back to the ruined crafting rooms, a frown plastered on his face. "Suffice it to say, there aren't many of those weapons anymore.

"You should also be wary of an opponent using melee or ranged weapons – such as a sword or bow. Certain mana-infused skills use the weapons as a focal point, allowing the mage to cast with a single hand or no hand gestures. The limitation there is that the mage typically can't sustain a channel at the same time.

"In other words, just because the person is holding a sword doesn't mean that they aren't a mage. They're just working with different limitations."

Brutus could see he was losing Finn and Julia, both of them staring at him with a puzzled expression. "Okay, let me simplify. If the mage has a staff or wand, then they are usually going to be able to maintain one channel, and they can only cast one spell at a time – but they can also fight with that staff or wand in the meantime.

"If they have a melee or ranged weapon, they'll still be able to cast a spell, but they can't channel. Although, they are probably going to be deadly with that weapon. These opponents will often try to get in a position to use their weapon instead of relying on casting."

"And if I'm *Multi-Casting*, I can't carry a weapon, but I can cast more quickly and channel two spells at once," Finn murmured.

Brutus cracked his knuckles. "You've got it! There are tradeoffs to each setup. However, for the spell-slinging purist, there are quite a few advantages to using my approach, assuming you can learn the skill. We can cast much faster, we can maintain more spells, and it keeps the hands free." He wiggled his fingers. "Which means you will be much more agile. Lugging around some fancy staff or sword restricts your ability to move and dodge."

His smile widened. "Also keep in mind that we can still drop the channels at any time and reach for a weapon. So, we'll always be the most flexible in a fight.

Finn stood there in silence for a moment, mulling on Brutus' explanation. He could indeed see the advantage of *Multi-Casting*, especially now that he understood that he could actively channel mana into his spells.

"But all of that is just theory right now." Brutus grinned at Finn. "First, you've got to learn how to *Multi-Cast*. Start by casting *Magma Armor* as your first spell and then shift the channel to just your left hand."

Easier said than done, Finn thought, still skeptical that he could pull it off.

Yet he was curious. Could he manage it? Things seemed to come easier to him in-game; his memory and reflexes were sharper. He had also been practicing a lot with maintaining and controlling his mana, and he was able to manipulate multiple orbs now. It seemed *possible*...

I guess there's only one way to find out.

Finn closed his eyes, lifting his hands and focusing his attention entirely on his fingers. He slowly began the gestures of *Magma Armor* even as he summoned his mana. The burning sensation soon seeped into his limbs, and his hesitation and doubt bled away – replaced by an excited, simmering anticipation.

He held himself back. Finn didn't need to focus on speed – that would come later. He just needed to keep it slow and steady. Maintain the pattern.

A few seconds later, he could feel the warmth of the *Magma Armor* trickle up his left arm, a solid barrier against his skin. Here was the difficult part. He abruptly shifted the channel to his left hand, his fingers fumbling for a moment under the strain of trying to keep up with the spell. However, days spent juggling burning orbs finally paid off, allowing him to pull off the feat with only a brief stumble.

Now for the next part.

Finn began moving the fingers of his right hand. The

movements felt awkward. His fingers were forced to wind through double the number of gestures required to cast the spell, and he could feel the muscles ache from the effort. This was made even harder by maintaining the *Magma Armor* with his left hand.

Yet Finn could feel a single flaming orb beginning to form – a simple manifestation of his mana. He fed it more energy. Gingerly. Trying to keep up the steady rhythm with his left hand. And then he felt it complete.

Finn's eyes snapped open.

The shield still lingered along his arm and a single ball of flame orbited in front of him. A triumphant smile crept across his face, and the flame wavered and flickered erratically as Finn lost his focus. He steadied it a moment later, his right hand picking up the rhythm of the channel. Beads of sweat already lingered on his forehead, the concentration needed to maintain both spells taking its toll.

"I did it," he murmured, staring at the orb.

"Fantastic!" Brutus said.

"Now dodge!"

"Wait, what?" Finn croaked, glancing at the fire mage in alarm.

He looked up just in time to see another massive *Fireball* hurtling toward his head. Finn barely lifted his shielded arm in time. Even so, his fledgling armor wasn't nearly enough. The force of Brutus' spell sent him hurtling backward, and he could feel his *Magma Armor* crumble and then break apart.

Finn's back crashed against the stone wall, the wind escaping his lungs in a rush as flames lapped at his body, leaving burnt flesh in their wake. As the spell dissipated, he slumped to the floor, landing on his chest and gasping for air. He lay there for a moment, red notifications flashing in his peripheral vision. He couldn't bring himself to look at his arm. Judging from the throbbing pain, it was a mess.

The sounds around him were warped and garbled, his ears ringing.

"What... kill him..." he heard someone shouting, but it sounded far away.

"...wasn't... too much..."

Finn groaned.

"You see? He's fine," Brutus said, his voice snapping back into focus. "I told you I adjusted the force to make sure I didn't kill him."

"You came pretty damn close," Julia snapped at him.

Finn pushed at the ground feebly, barely managing to push himself to a sitting position. His left hand and arm were a gnarled mess of burnt flesh, his blood dripping onto the stone from the open welts, but the skin was already beginning to repair as his natural regeneration healed the wounds.

However, his attention wasn't focused on Brutus and Julia, the pain, or the many crimson warnings flashing in his peripheral vision.

His eyes lingered on two blue skill notifications.

New Skill: Concentration
Prolonged study and practice have gifted you with an uncanny ability to concentrate – even going so far as to allow you to split your focus between more than one task. With further practice, it will be almost impossible to interrupt or disrupt your incantations. Higher ranks of this skill may also enable the user to perform phenomenal feats of mental agility.
Skill Level: Beginner Level 1
Effect: Ability to split your focus between [2] tasks.

New Skill: Multi-Casting
Through intensive training of your mana (and the help of a sadistic instructor), you have learned to cast and maintain two spells at once. Experts of this skill were once rumored to be a force of nature, capable of slinging spells with such ferocity and speed that they could level armies singlehandedly. Or, well, with *both hands*, technically... anyway, you get the point.
Skill Level: Beginner Level 1
Effect: -50% casting speed on second spell.

Finn grinned, wiping at the mixture of sweat and

blood along his forehead with the back of his hand.

Assuming he mastered these new skills and figured out whatever was blocking his ability to create new spells, the possibilities were almost endless. A dozen ideas were already swimming through Finn's head, and he could feel his mana respond, the fire in his chest roaring in response to his excitement. Despite his injuries and having run Brutus' hellish gauntlet all afternoon, a sudden surge of energy swept through him.

With a grunt, Finn heaved himself back to his feet, wavering for only a moment before he steadied himself. The burns were only a dull ache now. A manageable distraction.

Brutus and Julia abruptly stopped arguing, turning to stare at him in surprise.

"Alright," Finn said, cracking his knuckles. "Let's go again."

Chapter 19 - Focused

Julia lunged forward, her blade sweeping through the air with a soft hum.

Finn shifted his weight, raising his left arm to block the strike and feeling the comforting warmth of his *Magma Armor* pulse along the limb. He was keeping a watchful eye out for a counter strike. Julia was fast – really fast. And he had learned that the hard way. More than one blade had sliced through his skin over the last week that they had spent training in-game.

The dagger's blade skittered against the molten barrier, carving off chunks of the half-cooled substance. Yet Finn's fingers never stopped moving; his left hand continued its regular rhythm and quickly repaired the damage as he channeled more mana into the barrier.

Finn grimaced. Julia had bested him in nearly every duel. The story was always the same, she slowly beat him down, whittling away at his health and armor with small cuts to critical areas until he couldn't keep up anymore.

This time around, he intended to do something unexpected.

Instead of reaching for his own weapon or backpedaling to avoid the counter-attack he knew was coming, Finn summoned a second *Magma Armor* and stepped into Julia's follow-up attack. Within seconds, he could already feel the tingling warmth drift up his right arm as the armor slid into place.

Julia's eyes widened slightly as her other blade skittered against the barrier that was still forming along Finn's right arm. He used that brief hesitation and swung. His fingers had abruptly stopped their continuous movement, and his left fist connected with her face.

His right hand also swept forward, dropping its cast and grabbing at his dagger.

However, his next swipe only struck air.

His daughter anticipated the blow. She had recovered quickly, using the force of Finn's punch to fall backward into a backflip. At the same time, two throwing knives suddenly arced through the air. Time seemed to slow slightly as the blades flipped end over end. Finn batted the weapons aside, sparks flashing in the air as the metal skittered along his armored arms.

"Damn, you punched me in the nose," Julia said a moment later, standing a few yards away and rubbing at her face. Her voice came out a little nasally, and a trickle of blood emerged from between her fingers.

"More like your nose hit my hand," Finn taunted. This was a small victory. He knew the punch had barely hurt her. In a real fight, it would have been nothing more than a distraction.

Julia mock-glared at him. The injury was shallow and impermanent. They both knew that it would heal soon. "Still. Punching your own daughter in the face," she said, a smile tugging at her lips. "Pretty sure this is child abuse."

"You're definitely not a child anymore, and have you forgotten how many times you've stabbed me over the last few days?" Finn retorted. A sudden grin crept across his face. "Speaking of which, maybe I should start calling you, Old Lady. I was actually meaning to mention that I saw a few wrinkles forming."

Julia's eyes widened. "Oh, you fucking take that back..." she began.

A slow clap suddenly interrupted Julia's tirade. The noise came from the doorway, and the pair turned to find Brutus leaning against the frame. "You're getting better," he grunted at Finn. "It doesn't seem like you're struggling with *Multi-Casting* now and you're weaving spells into your normal movements."

"I guess so, but I still don't have any real way to fight back," Finn muttered as he released his spells and relaxed his posture. As the molten armor along his arms disappeared, he rubbed at his forehead with the back of his hand, his skin coming away slick with sweat.

Julia arched an eyebrow. "True, but you're getting to be a real pain in the ass to hit," she muttered, wiping away the blood still trickling from her nose and looking at the droplets staining her fingers.

"Which was the goal of this training," Brutus commented. "The most important lesson for a mage to learn is how to avoid getting hit. Everything else is really secondary."

Finn supposed he might be right. He had gotten pretty good at avoiding attacks and using his armor, but that was only half the battle. The duels were to the *death* – which meant he needed a way to inflict some damage. He still lacked a decent way to attack short of casting *Fire Nova* or reaching for his dagger, and both of those options had severe limitations. They required him to get close, and *Fire Nova* ate mana like crazy.

"In any event, I might be able to help you boost your offensive capabilities soon enough," Brutus added. "Unless you've forgotten what's coming tomorrow…"

The fire mage trailed off, the implication of his words hanging in the air. It only took Finn's tired brain a few seconds to catch on. He glanced at the clock in the corner of his UI, his eyes widening in surprise as he saw the calendar readout below the time.

"Oh, damn," he murmured.

Tomorrow was the last day before the duels began.

Finn had been so absorbed in his training that it almost felt like no time had passed – which was only made worse by the time compression in-game. A week in AO was just a few days in the real world.

It also didn't help that the last week had been one painful, exhausting blur. He had attended Brutus' class almost every day, followed by more *personal* instruction – by which he meant that Brutus kicked his ass for an hour or two. The fire mage usually just blasted away at Finn while he tried vainly to avoid the blows. After his beating, Finn shifted gears, continuing his language and *Mana Mastery* training, interspersed with the slightly more reasonable bouts with Julia.

"I expected a happier reaction," Brutus offered with an arched eyebrow. "You look like I just kicked your dog."

Finn grimaced, shaking his head. "I'm not ready yet."

The pair just stared at him skeptically. "Are you

kidding?" Julia asked.

"No. No, I'm not," Finn replied. "I haven't mastered Veridian, and I'm sure the other students have been busy in the meantime. I mean, I know two spells?"

"You've been training continuously for weeks," Julia retorted. "And I mean *continuously* – like day and night in-game." She glanced furtively at Brutus, before continuing, "Hell, I had to remind you to log off the other day since it had been at least eight real-world hours since you took a break."

Now that she mentioned it, Finn had noticed that the log-off warnings had slowed down considerably. Which only made him wonder how many more hours he could squeeze in before tomorrow.

"And yet I bet you're thinking about how much longer you could train tonight…" Julia accused, stabbing a finger at him.

Finn tried not to look guilty, but he wasn't sure how well that worked.

"Well, I don't want to interrupt this little spat," Brutus said with a chuckle. "I just wanted to pop in and say that Finn needs to show up in the courtyard tomorrow at noon. There'll be a ceremony to celebrate the passage of the newest class of novices."

The fire mage's expression sobered, his eyes clouding over. "I also hear there's supposed to be a rather large announcement." His gaze snapped back to Finn. "You shouldn't miss that ceremony."

Finn nodded, cocking his head at their instructor's serious tone. The man was clearly a sadist – that had been firmly decided – but he was usually a *jovial* sadist. If he was worried, then there was definitely some cause for concern.

Brutus turned to leave but hesitated. He glanced back at Finn. "Just my two cents, but you should take the thief's advice. Some rest would do you well. This might be the last opportunity you get for a while." With that, Brutus stepped out of the room, leaving Julia and Finn alone.

"See, even the flaming asshole agrees with me," Julia said, her arms crossed and her foot tapping insistently. She hadn't even reacted when the fire mage called her a thief, which meant she was really on the warpath now. "Do you even remember the last time you logged out?"

Finn ran a hand through his hair, his mind flailing for the answer. "I'm honestly not sure. Maybe yesterday?"

"Are you asking me?" Julia demanded. She shook her head, letting out a frustrated sigh. "I thought you were supposed to be the parent, but here I am nagging you to put down your videogame and go to bed."

Finn barked out a laugh. "I thought that was how it worked. You change your kids' diapers, and then they do the same for you when you get older."

"You aren't quite that old yet," Julia observed dryly, although she was struggling not to smile now. "Besides, I'll leave diaper duty to Daniel, thank you for very much. Maybe I can program a 'parent protocol' for him…"

They both laughed at that.

Julia's expression sobered. "Seriously, though. You need to get some rest."

"I will. I will," Finn agreed, although he didn't sound super convincing even to his own ears.

"Hmph. We'll see." Julia sheathed her blades, her eyes skimming to her own UI. "Ahh, shit. Speaking of which, I've got to get going."

She stabbed a finger at Finn. "Thirty more minutes or I'm going to have Daniel yank you out of here kicking and screaming."

Finn just gave her a thumbs up.

Then Julia disappeared in a rift of multi-colored energy.

Finn stood there for a moment, watching the rainbow tendrils slowly dissipate. For all the angry bluster and banter, he suddenly realized that he had missed this.

It had been a long time since he and Julia had spent this much time together. When she had left for college, they had become more distant. He supposed that was natural. Although, Rachael's death certainly hadn't helped. He had pulled away even more after that. He had been like some wounded creature, crawling into his cyber cave and shutting the door firmly. Yet now AO had brought them back together, and he had spent most of the last week with Julia.

At least one good thing had come from his recent training.

Finn cracked his knuckles. Speaking of which, now that he had no distractions, he could finally get back to work.

"Language training," Finn said aloud. His UI shifted, presenting him with multiple screens, a line of symbols now floating in front of him. However, Finn had no difficulty reading the patterns now. His studies had progressed quickly – especially since he had sunk more points into *Intelligence* and his *Learning* and *Reading* skills had advanced.

At this stage, he only had to see a new symbol once, and it would "stick" in his brain.

"Next lesson," Finn ordered.

Yet the UI didn't change.

His brow furrowed in confusion. He didn't want to waste time digging through the program or the code to see what was wrong – not with less than a day left.

"Daniel," Finn said aloud. The AI popped into existence a moment later, a glowing ball of flame dancing in the air.

"Yes, sir?" the AI asked.

"What's wrong with the training software? It won't load the next lesson."

The ball of flame flashed, changing from orange to a dark red and then back again. A few seconds later, Daniel's voice echoed through the training room. "You have completed all of the available lessons," he explained.

"Wait, what?" Finn asked. How was that even possible? He had been making better progress, but that was still much faster than he'd expected.

"I double-checked, and you have completed all training courses available," Daniel replied a moment later. "If you would like, I could prepare additional lessons."

"But I haven't even gotten the language notification..." Finn murmured to himself.

Then he hesitated.

Now that he thought about it, he hadn't gotten any notifications recently. It only took him a few seconds to realize why.

"Wow, I'm an idiot," he said, rubbing at his face. Or maybe he was more tired than he realized – although he shied away from that idea. That would mean Julia was right.

Sighing, Finn pulled up his system UI, and with a flick of his wrist, he swiftly navigated the menus. A moment later, he turned his notifications back on—

—and was promptly met with a barrage of blue windows.

x10 Level Up!
You have (50) undistributed stat points.

Stat Increases:
+21 Strength +32 Dexterity +40 Endurance

x6 Spell Rank Up: Magma Armor
Skill Level: Beginner Level 8
Cost: 85 Mana
Effect: Creates a damage shield capable of absorbing 240 damage (120 damage if water/ice).
Channel Effect: Repairs the shield at a rate of 40 damage/second at a mana cost of 10 mana/second.

x3 Skill Rank Up: Reading
Skill Level: Intermediate Level 1
Effect 1: 15% increased learning speed while reading.
Effect 2: 5% increased memorization.

x4 Skill Rank Up: Learning
Skill Level: Beginner Level 9
Effect: 13% increased learning speed for skills and spells.

x3 Skill Rank Up: Mana Mastery
Skill Level: Intermediate Level 4
Effect 1: -7.5% to the mana cost of spells.
Effect 2: 2.5% faster cast rate.

x7 Skill Rank Up: Dodge
Skill Level: Beginner Level 8
Effect: 4.5% increased speed and reaction time.

x4 Skill Rank Up: Small Blades
Skill Level: Beginner Level 5
Effect: 9% increased damage and accuracy with daggers and throwing knives.

x3 Skill Rank Up: Toughness
Skill Level: Beginner Level 4
Effect: 2.5% reduced damage and increased pain tolerance.

x5 Skill Rank Up: Concentration
Skill Level: Beginner Level 6
Effect: Ability to split your focus between [2] tasks.

x7 Skill Rank Up: Multi-Casting
Skill Level: Beginner Level 8
Effect: -46.5% casting speed on second spell.

x4 Skill Rank Up: Sprint
Skill Level: Beginner Level 5
Effect: 7% increased movement speed.
Cost: 7.5 Stamina / Second

"Holy shit," Finn muttered. That was the only appropriate reaction to a week's worth of notifications. Despite the barrage of windows, there was one final prompt that caught his attention, his heart skipping a beat as he saw the title.

System Notice: Veridian Language Learned

> After extensive training, you have learned a new language: Veridian!
>
> You are currently considered [Fluent].
>
> You can now read, write, and speak Veridian at a high-school level, although further progress can still be made to master the language.

Finn could only stare at the translucent blue screen for a moment.

He had done it.

He had learned Veridian – or at least enough to get by. And he had done it in two weeks! Finn almost couldn't believe it.

Although, that accomplishment had other implications. The last couple of weeks had highlighted that this *game* allowed him to pick up new skills and abilities at a frightening pace. Could this learning enhancement be applied to real-world applications? Learning calculus? Woodworking? Martial arts? Economics? A person could basically plug themselves in and learn *anything* in a fraction of the normal time – not even accounting for the time compression.

Not for the first time, Finn was left marveling at what the developers and engineers had built here. He also expected he wouldn't be the first person to start asking these questions. What would happen when other players discovered this? He wasn't certain whether to be excited or terrified...

His thoughts were interrupted as another notification flashed in front of Finn.

> **Quest Complete: Cramming**
>
> Through intensive training, you managed to learn Veridian and the basic mechanics of spellcasting! Although, we don't exactly have a reward for you. Isn't the accomplishment

> reward enough, though? It's the intangible "achievement" that matters, that shiny notification that will be forever hidden in the depths of your account profile and no one will ever see...
>
> Uh, anyway, congratulations!

Finn barked out a laugh as he read the quest completion prompt. To be fair, he'd never been a fan of "completionists" – who just strove after in-game achievements for no reward. What was the point of bragging rights in a game? It was nice for the AI to acknowledge that this was a silly way to motivate people. In Finn's case, the rewards of his training were much more tangible. He could easily quantify and measure his progress.

Speaking of which, the other notifications still flashed in Finn's peripheral vision, reminding him that he needed to review the rest of his progress.

As his eyes skimmed down the list of skill notifications, Finn noticed that he had ranked skills that he didn't remember acquiring – likely because he had the notifications turned off. For example, *Sprint* and *Toughness* seemed like an obvious result of running Brutus' insane obstacle course and letting both the fire mage and Julia beat the hell out of him in the training room.

Finn could see that some skills were slowing down. For example, *Mana Mastery* had been much more difficult to rank since hitting Intermediate. He had also gained far less experience for his skill training than at first. To top it all off, as he looked back over his feed carefully, he realized that his stat gains from Brutus' training had dwindled.

He supposed that made sense. There was a limit to how far a player could progress with training alone. The game seemed to be pushing people toward interacting with the world instead of spending all their time sitting in a library.

Or in a hidden, condemned training room...

Finn swept the skill notifications aside and turned his attention to the additional stat points he had earned. Brutus had urged him to allocate his original points toward *Intelligence* – which had given him more mana and regeneration, as well as further increasing his skill learning speed. Presumably. His other stats all seemed respectable at this point, apart from *Vitality* and *Willpower*.

However, *Willpower* seemed a bit redundant with *Intelligence* – at least for how he was building his character. On the other hand, a few more hit points might be helpful with the upcoming duels. When combined with his *Magma Armor*, he could have a respectable amount of health for a mage.

Finn chewed on his lip for a moment and then abruptly made a decision. He stuck another twenty points into *Intelligence* and placed the remaining thirty into *Vitality*. Then he pulled up his Character Status.

Character Status			
Name:	Finn	**Gender:**	Male
Level:	25	**Class:**	
Race:	Human	**Alignment:**	Lawful-Neutral
Fame:	465	**Infamy:**	0
Health:	520	**H-Regen/Sec:**	1.80
Mana:	745	**M-Regen/Sec:**	15.50
Stamina:	820	**S-Regen/Sec:**	7.00
Strength:	42	**Dexterity:**	59
Vitality:	40	**Endurance:**	70
Intelligence:	105	**Willpower:**	15

Affinities			
Dark:	2%	**Light:**	8%
Fire:	39%	**Water:**	5%
Air:	3%	**Earth:**	10%

Finn had grown considerably.

With his damage shields, he could get close to 1,000 effective health – assuming he took hits on his arms. The points in *Vitality* also helped increase his natural health regeneration, which might come in handy. If he also considered his ability to channel more mana into the shields with *Multi-Casting*, he would be pretty resilient.

The only remaining problem was his offensive abilities. Right now, it looked like he was bringing a knife to some sort of magical gunfight. He could still vividly recall the *Frozen Orb* and *Stone Spikes* that Vanessa and Zane had used during that first encounter with Brutus, and it was unlikely that they had spent the last week goofing off.

However, despite his shortcomings, a part of Finn was excited to find out how far his peers had come along in such a short time. How would he measure up against the other novices in a one-on-one fight?

Finn's thoughts were interrupted as he let out an inadvertent yawn, blinking his eyes blearily.

"Sir, it has been approximately 7.5 hours real-world time since you last logged out," Daniel interjected in a worried voice. "You really should take Julia's advice and consider returning to your world."

Finn glared at the glowing orange ball of light. Now even the AI was nagging him? After Julia's teasing about building a "parent protocol" for Daniel, he idly wondered if she had already hacked his system again. But that seemed unlikely. The AI was probably just picking up obvious behavioral cues for fatigue.

"Fine, fine," Finn muttered. Now that he wasn't frantically training, he could finally feel just how tired he was – his eyes drooping and his limbs feeling stiff and heavy.

He swept aside his screens and brought up the system menu. Perhaps he should take everyone's advice. Tomorrow would be a big day.

The duels were coming, after all.

With that final thought, Finn hit the "log out" button and vanished in a flash of multi-colored light.

Chapter 20 - Pivotal

It feels strange to be standing here, Finn thought.

He stood amid a mass of other students in the courtyard. There had to be at least a hundred students in their initial novice class. It occurred to Finn that these were likely some of the first players to start AO, be inducted into the guild, and make it through the initial training. A sort of excited tension hung in the air, reminding him of a high school graduation. That sense that the students were pushing at the gates, just waiting to be set free.

And yet they hadn't graduated from anything.

They had barely passed the tutorial.

"Geez, there are a lot of people here," Kyyle said, coming up behind Finn.

"Yeah, I didn't realize there were this many students," Finn murmured.

If this represented just their novice class, how many mages attended the guild? The number felt hard to pin down with so many players in attendance, especially since the playerbase varied based on who was logged in at that moment. Although, judging from the throng of players ringing the terrace, Finn guessed that there were quite a few.

"Or teachers," Kyyle observed, pointing at the stone platform in the center of the courtyard. "I don't recognize most of those people."

Finn could see that Kyyle was right. He could pick out Brutus' massive form and Lamia's stern glare, but the rest of the faculty were just nameless faces lined up behind Nefreet.

"By the way, how have you been?" Finn asked, turning back to Kyyle. "It feels like I haven't seen you in days, Brutus' stupid obstacle course aside..." The fire mage's training regime hadn't left room for much conversation, and Finn had been rather distracted.

Kyyle shrugged. "Studying just like everyone else, I suppose." He side-eyed Finn. "How have the extra special training sessions been going?"

Finn grimaced. "About how you would expect.

Brutus is... well, Brutus."

A laugh. "You feeling nervous about the duels?"

A few students immediately glanced at Kyyle when he mentioned that word, and even Finn had to resist the urge to flinch. Everything they had been doing over the last few weeks was leading to that competition. And the stakes were still real – Nefreet holding an axe over the heads of the bottom 10%. Just mentioning the duels had almost become taboo among the novices.

Finn glanced at Kyyle. "I'd like to lie and say no, but I'm not cool enough to pull that off. Yeah, it's going to be difficult. I can't imagine what it will be like to fight another player for real."

He just had to hope his training was enough.

"Hello," Nefreet said, his voice carrying across the field. The crowd of students immediately stilled, a hushed silence filling the air.

"Congratulations are in order. You have all made it this far, your first step along the path. Hopefully, one of many."

Nefreet paused, his eyes skimming the crowd. "From this point forward, you all are full-fledged members of the guild. This comes with a few advantages: the award of your mage class, access to the guild requisition officer, greater access to our library, and more advanced instructions." The students murmured among themselves at the mention of possible rewards.

"However, while exciting, this also represents a pivotal turning point. Guild membership comes with a cost. We ask for none other than complete excellence. It is that prestige and accomplishment that has allowed the guild to flourish for over a hundred years and to become the gem of Lahab.

"And the cornerstone of that accomplishment is the duels."

At this statement, the silence returned abruptly, as though Abbad had just cast a *Suppression* spell on the crowd.

"As I mentioned when you were first inducted into the guild," Nefreet continued, "these duels pit mage against mage, allowing the best of us to rise and to shed the dead weight of those that cannot keep up. Our motto is simple:

"Victory or death."

Nefreet let this statement echo through the air, pausing to take in the crowd.

"In keeping with this tradition, we have an important announcement to make." Nefreet turned to look at the students ringing the terraces. "This is a message that affects not just this novice class, but the guild as a whole." Finn noticed that many of the faculty behind Nefreet shuffled nervously at this introduction, more than one glaring at the man's back with an accusing expression.

Yet the headmaster seemed unaffected by the faculty's judgment. He continued in an even voice, "Within the seclusion of these walls, you all may not be aware that our Emir has grown sick. He also has no offspring or natural successor, which has created a question regarding who shall be appointed as the next Emir."

He paused as the students and faculty listened in anticipation, more than one brow furrowed in confusion. "Within the last 48 hours, the Emir passed a royal decree to each of the three guilds. He has declared a competition the likes of which our great city has never seen.

"Each of the three great guilds has been ordered to host a tournament to choose a single competitor to represent their guild. This person must be selected from among the guild novices and may either be a resident of Lahab or a traveler. These three champions will then be given the opportunity to compete to become the next Emir."

Nefreet looked across the crowd of students. "Which means one of our novices may qualify to rule our great city."

Holy shit. Finn could see that same thought echoed across the face of every student in the courtyard and could hear the nervous murmurs from the balcony ringing the courtyard. The sour expression on the faces of many of the faculty also made sense now. Finn saw Lamia glaring daggers at Nefreet. The prospect of an uneducated student given the opportunity to rise above them in power couldn't be easy to accept.

Finn frowned. He had to admit that the conditions

were strange. Why a novice? Perhaps the Emir wanted to select someone untainted by the city's politics? Or maybe this had all been set up by the developers as a way to induct the players into the game world?

"Now, of course, your class is not the only group of novices attending the Mage Guild," Nefreet continued, turning back to the fledgling mages filling the courtyard and speaking through the incredulous stares of the students and faculty alike. "There are those who passed the initial training before you, but who have not yet risen to the rank of journeyman.

"Therefore, the faculty and I have reached a decision regarding how best to structure our guild's tournament. Starting tomorrow, a new competition shall begin, and the novice leaderboard shall be wiped clean. Travelers and residents shall compete separately, adopting the same rules that we use for our duels."

Nefreet hesitated for a moment, glancing back at the faculty. "The Emir has imposed a two-week time limit on this competition, and so we have been forced to change our regular schedule for the duels. Students may now initiate a challenge at will. The victor of each challenge shall receive 10 points. Their opponent shall lose 5 points. Points earned in the tournament shall continue to be redeemable at the guild requisition officer."

The what now? Finn thought. Nefreet had mentioned this requisition officer twice now. He'd have to remember to ask Brutus or Abbad about that.

Although, that wasn't really the biggest takeaway from Nefreet's explanation. Finn immediately glanced at Zane, noting the large smile on his face. Finn could only assume that their up-and-coming gang leader was thinking the same thing as him. If the students could initiate a duel, that meant they could challenge their friends and have them throw the fight, beefing up their own score.

Nefreet seemed to anticipate this issue as well. "To prevent potential abuse, we are also instituting a new system for how the duels are assigned." Finn noticed Zane's expression fall.

"Each novice will be given a token," Nefreet explained. His hands moved rapidly, and two dozen thin columns of stone rose around the dais, creating a circle around the headmaster. "That token will be tuned to these pedestals and the gate to the challenge arena. To initiate a duel, you need only tap a column beside me with your token. Your opponent will be chosen randomly, and their token will then light up, giving each party fifteen minutes to prepare and make it to the courtyard. For the travelers, only those present in our world will be selected."

Nefreet took a deep breath. "If your opponent fails to appear, the initiator will immediately be counted as the victor."

Finn's mind was racing. That was a better system, he had to admit. But it also left some wiggle room for abuse. Another glance at Zane confirmed that the earth mage had already caught on to that nuance, a subtle grin replacing the frustration on his face.

This is about to get really ugly, Finn thought.

"With that out of the way, the tournament shall begin tomorrow morning at 8:00am and shall last for two weeks."

The headmaster raised a hand to forestall the murmurs that were already rising from the students. "Although there is one final matter. Since we have permitted this practice for the existing novices, our teaching staff has urged me to allow faculty sponsors for each new group of mages that make it through their initial training. These represent students that have shown exceptional aptitude or dedication during their initial studies. Sponsorship grants each student a starting score of 100 points."

Nefreet looked at the crowd, his face solemn. "Good luck. I expect nothing less than perfection from our students, and I look forward to discovering who will carry the torch for our guild."

The headmaster stepped back, the crowd still staring at him in shock.

Into this stunned silence, Brutus' booming voice broke over the crowd as he took the stage. "Alright! I bet you all are still reeling from that revelation. Our headmaster is a hard act to follow – promising the possibility of ruling a city and all." No one reacted, and the fire mage frowned, murmuring to one of the other faculty, "Tough crowd, am I right?"

"Anyway, I guess it's time to announce some sponsors!" Brutus continued. "I'll just list the teacher and the student that they've chosen. If you hear your name called, then please approach the platform. Once we're done, the *losers*... ahem, other students can line up to accept your tokens and class change," he added, motioning to a group of mages that were standing along the edge of the field.

"First up, Magus Lamia. Vanessa," Brutus called out.

"Big surprise," Kyyle commented sarcastically as Vanessa approached the stage.

Lamia stepped forward to greet the student. Her fingers twined through a complicated series of gestures as a globe of water formed in the air. Within only a few seconds, the orb had expanded until it was nearly six feet in diameter. Vanessa strode calmly into the sphere, unperturbed by the lack of air. There was a blinding flash of sapphire energy, and when it dissipated, the water was gone.

Vanessa nodded at Lamia and then moved off the stage.

"So... uh, I guess we're competing to be the ruler of a city now," Kyyle offered awkwardly as Brutus continued calling out names.

"I guess we are," Finn replied, unsure of what to say. It had been bad enough worrying about getting kicked out of the guild – now the students were all going to be ferociously gunning for the top spot.

"Not sure how to ask this tactfully, so I'm just gonna throw it out there. Does our truce still stand?" Kyyle asked. "I'm not really loving the idea of treating *everyone* as an enemy for the next two weeks."

Finn eyed the earth mage in surprise. "Yeah, of course." Then he hesitated. "Unless we get paired, I guess."

Kyyle grimaced.

Zane's name was called, along with someone named Magus Jax. The pair both immediately turned to the stage, their eyes widening as they saw Zane's sponsor. The man was robed in straps of cloth that concealed his face and body. Even more strangely, nearly a dozen weapons were strapped to Jax's body.

"What school of magic does he use?" Finn wondered aloud.

"Beats me," Kyyle murmured. "Maybe a mummy affinity? I've been keeping careful track of everyone I meet, but that's the first time I've seen that teacher."

Yet the surprises didn't end there.

"Magus Gaius. Kyyle," Brutus barked out.

"Hey, you've been holding out on me!" Finn joked playfully, punching Kyyle's shoulder. "Clearly, you've been more than just a little busy."

Kyyle winked at Finn as he started toward the platform. "Hey, a guy has to have some secrets."

Brutus continued to call out names as students stepped toward the stage, each instructor soon standing beside a chosen student. Within only a few minutes, none of the faculty stood unaccompanied.

"Well, looks like we're done!" Brutus announced. "*Finally*," he muttered to himself, yet his booming voice still carried partway across the field.

Finn actually felt disappointed. Not that he expected to be sponsored by an instructor he'd never met, but he had been kind of half-hoping that Brutus himself would throw him a bone, especially after the fire mage had spent the better part of two weeks beating the ever-living shit out of him.

"Ahh, damn! I just remembered!" Brutus shouted. "I forgot to pick my own student."

His eyes roamed the crowd as he made an act of searching for someone. "Let's see. Who's the least pathetic one here…"

Then his eyes centered on Finn.

"Hmm, I guess you'll do," Brutus said, pointing at him. "Finn, come on up here."

Finn had to resist the urge to sigh. Brutus might have been spending just a bit too much time with Julia. He had clearly leveled up his *Trolling* skill.

With reluctant steps, Finn approached Brutus.

The fire mage clapped him on the back as he neared, leaning close. "Joking aside, you've done good, kid," he said, lowering his voice.

"I'm older than you," Finn replied with a deadpan expression.

"Well, that's just what people say at a moment like this, isn't it?" Brutus asked.

"You don't pick many students to sponsor, do you?" Finn murmured.

"How'd you guess?"

Finn sighed. "Let's just get on with it. We're holding all these people up."

"Fine, fine," Brutus replied, backing away and ignoring the exasperated look on Finn's face. His fingers twined through a rapid series of gestures, a small flame igniting in the air beside Finn. As the seconds ticked past, the blaze grew, the heat expanding outward in almost-visible waves that warped the air.

Once the flame towered nearly eight feet in the air, Finn knew what to do next.

Yet he hesitated, staring into the raging inferno.

Finn had the strangest sense of déjà vu. He had stood in this spot once before in the Seer's tent, although that seemed like ages ago. In that moment, he had taken a risk – literally leaping into another world.

His gaze panned back to the students watching in the field, their gaze weighing him; measuring him. Over the last two weeks, he hadn't given himself a chance to wallow in the omnipresent guilt that lingered at the edges of his thoughts. He had dived into his studies as a distraction. Yet in this moment it all came rushing back. Here he was again, standing on a stage. Receiving a prize. His competition staring at him from the crowd like hungry vultures, just waiting for one misstep.

The last time, he had lost everything that mattered to him.

He could give up. Right now. Just walk away.

He wouldn't have to kill anyone. He didn't have to fight these people. Things were about to get ugly; he could feel it. Did he even want to be Emir? Did he deserve it – deserve this second chance at life? Or should he just return to the safety and solitude of his fortress? To his routine and tedium. Return to his self-imposed prison… where he belonged.

In that moment of hesitation, Finn saw two eyes open amid the flames. They were familiar, the tendrils of fire sliding around the glowing irises like silk. The Seer's face shone back at him, and he could almost hear the fire god's words in his mind – the same question she had asked him in that tent.

Would Rachael have wanted that for you?

Finn took a deep breath. The answer was still the same.

He stepped forward.

The flames washed around Finn, obscuring the rest of the field from sight. His mana responded automatically, crackling in his chest. He felt the sensation burn away his doubt and his guilt, replacing it with that same feeling of weightless freedom that ignited his soul.

It was almost like a drug – the sensation addictive.

"You have done well, Marked One," the Seer's voice sang from the flames around him. "*But now you must keep going. You have only just begun to ignite the flame of inspiration in your heart. We still have a long way to go to build that into a burning blaze.*

"*Your next step is to win this competition.*

"*By any means necessary.*"

With that simple instruction, the flames abruptly disappeared, leaving Finn standing in the courtyard once again. A notification hovered in front of him, this one glowing a vibrant orange, as though the prompt was awash in flame.

Class Change: Fire Mage

You have been granted a class by Brutus himself, becoming a fire mage. During the ceremony, you were approached by the Seer, who urged you to win the competition to represent the Mage Guild in a three-way fight for control of Lahab.

> The gloves are about to come well and truly off. Are you ready?
>
> +20 Intelligence
> +15 Willpower
> Increased Fire Magic Affinity (Currently 41%)

Finn was distracted from the notification, as a residual trace of warmth continued to wind up his arms. He looked down to see that his left arm was now emblazoned with a small wand surrounded by flames, the tattoo marked just above the star symbol denoting his induction into the Mage Guild.

Yet his right arm was different. The skin itched and burned like he was being bitten by a mound of fire ants. Finn pulled back on the sleeve of his robe, and his eyes widened in surprise. Inky-black flames slithered up his skin like a serpent, spreading from the tattoo of the Seer's tarot cards and coiling up his forearm, stopping just below the elbow.

Brutus abruptly stepped forward and pulled down Finn's sleeve. "Keep that hidden," he hissed, sparing a brief glance at the nearby mages. Luckily, no one seemed to have noticed.

"Congratulations!" Brutus said more loudly, smacking Finn on the back hard enough to cause him to stagger forward.

Then the fire mage turned back to the courtyard. "Alright, you lot, that's the end of the show. Go line up to get your classes and tokens!" Brutus instructed, pointing at the row of mages waiting for the other students.

Meanwhile, Finn stood there, his mind reeling as he tried to process what had happened. This was the first time the Seer had contacted him since his start to the game. But why now? What did she gain from this competition? Why had the tattoo changed? What did that mean? The questions swam and danced in his head, reaching no resolution.

Yet one thing was clear. The Seer wanted him to win this competition.

The words of the prompt returned to him, the other questions melting away.

"*Are you ready?*" it had asked.

With his fire mana still surging in his veins, Finn couldn't wait to find out.

Chapter 21 - Armed

"Here you go," Brutus said, gesturing at a nearby door. After the ceremony in the courtyard, the pair had fled the crowds, with Brutus leading Finn along a winding path through the guild hall.

"This doesn't exactly look like a spellbook," Finn retorted, crossing his arms.

Brutus had made a promise when they started Finn's training. Cryptic instructions from a god and some world-shattering competition aside, Finn wasn't going to be distracted from what was really important.

He needed some damn spells – now more than ever.

Finn's instructor arched an eyebrow. "You're gettin' kind of uppity now that you have a class and everything." He cracked his knuckles. "I might just need to beat that out of you."

"Scary," Finn retorted, unperturbed. "But you know that threat gets weaker the more often you do it, right? And it rings kind of hollow now that every novice in the school will be ready to tear each other's throat out starting bright and early tomorrow morning."

Brutus grimaced at that comment, eyeing a group of students as they walked past and dropping his voice. "Some of the faculty weren't too fond of that plan – especially including all novices in the competition," he murmured. "Yet Nefreet wouldn't be swayed. He only sees this as an opportunity to expand the power and influence of the guild."

"And you don't?" Finn asked.

The fire mage ran a hand through his closely cropped hair. "I wonder at the result. It isn't enough for *anyone* to win. That person may become Emir. Which means they will have power over the city and everything inside it – including the Mage Guild. Nefreet and some of the other faculty seem to think that person will be a malleable puppet. I'm less convinced."

Brutus looked away and his brow furrowed. "I've seen what that sort of power does to people firsthand."

Finn could only wonder at that. What exactly had the guild done to him?

Brutus met Finn's eyes. "Anyway, you should watch yourself. Even among Nefreet's camp, there are those that insist that the candidate matters. They have strong views about just *who* should qualify to represent the guild. As for the rest, they don't seem to think that any traveler is good enough."

Finn shot him a questioning glance.

"As I said during my first class, your kind are simply different. You weren't born here, you don't entirely understand our world and culture, and the stakes are very different for the travelers. When you are essentially immortal. Would you place the same value on the lives of this world's residents?"

Finn stared at the man in surprise. Those were actually pretty compelling arguments. Honestly, now that Finn thought about it, he wasn't so sure that a traveler should rule Lahab – or at least not most travelers.

"Like I said, you should be careful," Brutus grunted.

"Aw, it almost sounds like you care," Finn replied dryly. Despite his carefree tone, Finn was already weighing the subtext of Brutus' words. It seemed like the burly fire mage suspected the other faculty and students might interfere in the competition.

"I care about the future of this place, even if the likes of you or Abbad might claim otherwise," Brutus snapped, his eyes flashing as he inadvertently summoned his fire mana. "We mages have lived too long as…" He trailed off as more students passed, making a visible effort to calm himself.

"It doesn't matter," he grunted finally. "If I had to pick someone, it might as well be you. At least you don't shrink from a fight. Plus, you have some big flaming balls on you – which you're going to need."

Finn was surprised. Those were some of the few words of kindness he had heard pass Brutus' lips. Despite the man's surly attitude and constant attempts to kill or maim him, he had helped Finn immensely. Training him. Sponsoring him. Although, that also reminded him of how

Brutus had tried to hide Finn's tattoo – presumably to protect him from *something*.

"And would that reason have something to do with this tattoo?" Finn asked, touching his right arm, but not pulling back the sleeve.

Brutus grimaced, lowering his voice. "You should take care with that mark. Many might not recognize it for what it is. But there are still mages here that remember the old gods. They will not take kindly to a *Marked One*."

Finn's eyes widened. Brutus knew that the Seer had given him the mark? His questions began bubbling to the surface again. "You know about the Seer?" Finn whispered under his breath.

"Unfortunately," Brutus grunted, before meeting Finn's eyes. "Although, most here call her the Crone. Exercise caution with that one. Her gifts always come with a price. Always."

"But what—" Finn began.

The fire mage shook his head, interrupting him. "You have enough problems right now. You need to focus. Remember what I said. Neither the students nor the faculty are your friends here. I would only speak plainly with Abbad or myself. Or, hell, just keep your secrets to yourself. Better not to trust anyone." That last statement didn't seem entirely for Finn's benefit, Brutus' eyes going distant for a moment.

With a shake of his head, the fire mage smacked Finn on the back. "Now, go on inside and get yourself that damn spellbook." He started down the hall, calling over his shoulder. "And tell Charlotte that I said hello!"

Finn's eyes followed Brutus as he walked away. He felt like he had come no closer to answering any of the questions that were still tumbling through his head. However, the fire mage was right about one thing. He needed to get that spellbook and use the rest of the evening to prepare for the duels tomorrow.

With a sigh, Finn yanked at the nearby door and stepped inside.

Only to stop short in shock.

The room on the other side was complete and

spectacular chaos. Robes fluttered and flew through the air, guided along by streams of current that were almost invisible to the eye, revealed only by a slight shimmer of yellow. The floor of the room wasn't much better. Rows upon rows of wooden shelves displayed all manner of armor, staves, wands, swords, daggers, and trinkets. Yet there was no discernible rhyme or reason to their placement. A massive stone hammer was placed beside a delicate bracelet, but on the other side of the rack was a smoldering staff. The items went on like that for as far as he could see.

The room was also practically filled to the brim with other mages, the crowd perusing the equipment. A dull roar, the product of dozens of voices speaking at once, filled the air. As Finn noted this, a lance of electricity suddenly shot through the room, arcing directly toward him. He dodged to the side quickly, the bolt splashing against the wooden door, but failing to damage the wood.

The room is warded? Finn wondered.

"Sorry!" someone shouted from the crowd.

"What the hell is this?" Finn murmured.

"Hello-and-welcome-to-the-guild-requisition-hall! I-am-part-of-the-requisition-staff!" an energetic young man declared, popping up in front of Finn. He spoke so quickly that Finn struggled to understand him.

The man didn't wait for Finn to respond, tugging at the sleeve of his left arm and revealing his tattoos. "Ahh-a-novice-fire-mage. Recent-by-the-looks-of-the-mark! That-means-you'll-need-to-chat-with-Charlotte-before-you-can-make-any-purchases!

"Come with me!"

And then the aide was winding through the crowd. Finn could at least piece together a few important bits of information from the man's frenetic introduction. This was apparently the guild requisition hall, which meant Finn could possibly purchase gear here...

Or a spellbook.

Not wanting to lose the man in the crowd, Finn hesitated only a second before following the aide. He kept a watchful eye out for the idiot mages around him as they half jogged through the clusters of other students. He didn't love the idea of getting fried trying to purchase equipment. Although, he was distracted by the assortment of gear littering the room; armor and weapons glowed with a faint sheen. His fingers practically itched to get his hands on some of this loot.

I'm surprised Julia hasn't raided the place already, he thought to himself.

His thoughts were interrupted as a guttural growl came from Finn's left. Acting on instinct, he leaped to the side. Claws swiped through the space he had been occupying only a moment before. Finn's eyes went wide as he took in the row of cages along the nearby wall. What appeared to be some sort of miniature chimera glared at him from behind the bars, each of its three heads trained on Finn. Dozens more eyes stared at him from nearby. He saw glowing crystals, slick scales, and thick fur among the shadows of the cages.

"Mind-the-pets-they-can-be-quite-dangerous," the aide said in a rapid-fire pitter-patter of words, before taking back off through the crowd again.

Finn just shook his head. Yet he followed the young man, now giving the cages a wide berth.

A few moments later, the aide deposited him in front of a counter on the far end of the room. "Here-you-are! Have-a-great-day!" he said and then immediately vanished back into the crowd.

"Real pain in the ass, aren't they?" someone groused from behind Finn. He whirled to find a woman sitting behind the counter, resting her chin on one palm, and watching the rest of the room with weary resignation. To Finn's eyes, she must have been in her mid-thirties. Copper hair framed a face that spoke of lack of sleep, heavy circles hanging under her eyes.

"Uh..." he began, not sure what the woman meant by her question.

"The Merchant Guild instituted this new system to provide more *incentive* to our staff," she continued, waving at the room. "The aides now get compensated for each person they help instead of getting paid by the hour. The result is this circus. Fast-talking idiots that dump someone in front of a rack and then take off like a damn dragon is on their ass."

Another spell hurtled across the room, this time a massive *Fireball*, directed straight at the robes that drifted through the air. The woman sighed, her fingers twining through a series of gestures. A sphere of shimmering yellow light suddenly encircled the flaming orb, the fire winking out.

"And this is also how we get travelers accidentally launching spells in my hall," the woman muttered, rubbing at her eyes. "Do you know how much damaged merchandise has resulted from this idiotic policy change? Not that this ridiculous competition has helped matters either..."

"So, you're a member of the Merchant Guild?" Finn asked cautiously as her rant began to die down.

The woman's eyes trained on him once again, her head tilting. "Indeed. The Merchant Guild is responsible for all sales that occur within the city walls – whether magical or mundane. A distribution of power intended to maintain a system of checks and balances. At least, that's how the Emir sold it to the guilds."

She leaned forward, speaking in a hushed voice. "The result is more like a polite cold war. I swear Nefreet would push me out given half a chance. The man would likely rather see you lot beat each other to death with your bare hands than give up an ounce of power to the merchants."

"Huh," Finn said. Between the dilapidated crafting area on the northern side of the campus and Charlotte's explanation, he was beginning to see a pattern. It seemed the Emir was desperate to restrain the mages' power. Although, he also noted that Charlotte seemed to be an air mage. There was apparently some cross-guild recruiting going on as well.

"Anyway, I'm sure you're not here for my bitching. My name is Charlotte. I'm responsible for this shit show, even if I had nothing to do with creating it." She peered at him. "I take it you're a novice? Recent class change?"

"Yeah," Finn said. "Brutus said I could purchase a spellbook here."

Her eyes widened slightly. "Brutus, huh? How is he doing?"

"Uh, alright, I guess," Finn offered noncommittally.

"He told me he says hello."

Charlotte nodded, a small smile tugging at her lips. "Always the gentleman."

Are we talking about the same guy? Finn wondered.

"Anyway, here is your bag," she offered, handing over a plain leather satchel. "Standard issue for all novices." As Finn took the bag, he didn't see anything particularly remarkable about it. Just scuffed leather, like it had seen some prior use.

"It's more interesting than it looks," Charlotte added, noting Finn's skeptical expression. "The interior has been enchanted. It can hold up to about a hundred pounds. Bit bigger on the inside than it looks," she offered, snatching the bag from him, and sticking her arm inside. The limb went in up to her shoulder, which seemed physically impossible given its dimensions. Then she tossed it back to him.

"Anyway, you mentioned a spellbook," she continued as Finn stared at the bag, sticking his hand inside experimentally. Charlotte stepped out from around the counter. "I can show you over to the spellbooks. Just let me ward the room first to make sure they don't burn it down."

Finn stood still – the novelty of the bag forgotten as he stared at Charlotte. His attention was captured by the woman's legs. In place of normal flesh and blood, Charlotte moved along on a set of spider-like mechanical limbs, each tapping at the stone floor and giving off a small shower of sparks. Even more interesting, the mechanical limbs seemed to be connected to her torso and Finn couldn't see that she used any sort of controls. It was almost as though the extremities had been connected directly to her nervous system.

A cough interrupted his thoughts, and Finn looked up to find Charlotte staring at him, her formerly friendly expression now grim. "Eyes up here," she snapped.

Finn raised his hands. "Hey, I'm sorry. I didn't mean any offense. I was just surprised is all. Brutus didn't mention your legs."

He hesitated, his eyes drifting back to the mechanical limbs. "I... I know from personal experience how hard it is to lose a limb," he added his eyes clouding. The limbs only served to remind Finn that his crippled body was hooked up to a headset right now – that this was an illusion.

Charlotte's expression had softened when Finn met her eyes again. "Well, in that case, why don't we just ignore that bit and go find you a spellbook?"

Finn just nodded, catching on to the subtext of her statement. She didn't feel like talking about her legs. He could certainly relate.

"There's just one thing I need to do first…" Charlotte murmured as she turned back to the room, her hands already twining through the gestures of a spell. Wind gusted through the shelves, whipping among the players and NPCs that crowded the racks. Suddenly, the noise vanished, leaving only a deathly silence in its wake. Dozens of heads whipped toward where Charlotte stood, their eyes wide.

"Any of you lot break anything while I'm gone, and I will kill you slowly and painfully," Charlotte said into this silence, her tone even and deadly serious. "Do we all understand each other?"

Nods all around the room.

Charlotte glanced at Finn. "Alright, we're ready to go!"

Finn couldn't help but glance back at the room as Charlotte led the way to a door along the far wall. She had left the spell in place, many people trying to speak or groping at their throats but no sound escaping. He idly considered that she could just as easily have cut off their ability to breathe.

Don't mess with Charlotte. Got it, he thought to himself.

"Here we go," Charlotte offered once they crossed into the side room. "Spellbooks. These are actually copies of the original workbooks. Each one contains a few basic spells. They're also organized by affinity. The novice stuff is all out in the open, which is all you can purchase right now. Each one costs 25 points. Journeyman and higher spellbooks are kept in the back. You won't be able to enter those sections without a token."

"Huh," Finn murmured, eyeing the room. "Why aren't these books in the library?"

He glanced over to find Charlotte looking at him incredulously. "So that any student can just start trying to hurl around whatever spell they feel like? You saw those idiots in there. The whole guild would be a madhouse. Honestly, this is one of the few policies of Nefreet's I actually agree with. You've got to dole out this sort of information slowly."

Finn cocked his head. That sort of made sense, although it made him wonder what purpose the library served then. Clearly, it held other information. For example, it had contained the materials he had used to learn Veridian. However, Abbad had also alluded to restricted levels of the library.

Maybe Nefreet just controlled the type and quantity of spells that were disseminated to the students and those restricted levels contained more detailed information on spellcasting? He would have to try to remember to ask the librarian about that the next time he saw him.

Finn turned his focus back to the books. He picked up a nearby tome, the cover glowing a faint orange. With gentle fingers, he flipped it open to find Veridian scrawled down the page, along with a description of various hand gestures – crude pictures providing more detail. There were also notes scrawled in the margins – along with some diagrams that Finn had never seen before.

Charlotte smacked his hand, snapping the book shut. "There's no reading in the stacks. That's part of why students aren't allowed back here without a chaperone. You can study the books after you've bought them."

Finn grimaced. His eyes skimmed to the rest of the fire spellbooks on the nearby shelf. They all seemed to be copies of the same workbook – at least from what he could tell based on the symbols on the cover. He kept the one in his hand. That was an easy choice.

Yet Finn hesitated as he eyed the books for the other affinities. Should he purchase a few more? If he was going to get his spellcrafting mod to work, he might need a larger sample group of spells. That would likely help him identify what he was doing wrong.

At the same time, each book cost him about three wins' worth of points – points that he might be better off hoarding or spending on other gear. He could still remember the room filled with weapons and armor. He chewed on his lip in indecision. Yet the ability to create new spells was likely worth far more than some novice equipment and might give him an edge over other students.

Making an abrupt decision, Finn grabbed another three books – one for each of the elemental affinities and turned back to Charlotte. She eyed him curiously.

"Okay, this should do it," Finn declared, hefting the stack of books.

Charlotte arched an eyebrow. "You know you likely won't be able to use those other books," she explained. "It's extremely difficult to learn spells outside your primary affinity."

Finn shrugged, trying to think of an excuse. Then it suddenly came to him. "If what you said is true – that Nefreet ensures that only select spells are provided to the students – that means that these books likely contain all of the spells that the novices know." Finn met Charlotte's eyes. "That could give me an edge. If I study these other books, I'll know what spells my opponents will be able to use and their limitations. Information is power, after all."

"Huh, well at least Brutus picked a student with a head on his shoulders," she replied, grudging respect shining in her eyes. "I always enjoyed the fact that he didn't suffer stupid. We have that in common.

"Speaking of which, let's go," Charlotte declared, turning back to the door leading into the requisition hall. "I doubt my spell will keep that lot distracted for long."

Finn followed her, his mind already a million miles away. His thoughts were only on the spellbooks in his hand and the brief glimpse he had caught of those handwritten notes in the margins. His eyes skimmed down to the books.

Maybe he had finally found the key to building his own spells. He hoped so. He suspected he was going to need an edge come tomorrow morning.

Chapter 22 - Studious

Finn sat cross-legged in the middle of the barren training room.

He could feel excitement bubbling in his chest as he opened the fire spellbook. The title of the book was missing, and only the author's first name was listed on the cover. That was a little odd. Finn had expected something that looked like a formal textbook. Perhaps the spellbooks were just copies and the original version had been damaged?

Or maybe Nefreet is trying to hide information, he thought.

Finn's gaze focused on the author's name. "Bilel." A quick glance at the other three books indicated that the same mage had written all three tomes. That was another interesting note. Had the author mastered multiple affinities?

There was only one way to find out.

Finn flipped forward to the first few pages of the fire spellbook, his eyes skimming the contents as he devoured the book hungrily. He soon lost track of time, the world around him bleeding away until his entire universe was a mixture of arcane symbols and poorly scrawled notes. Once he was done with one book, he idly groped for another, losing himself in his studies.

When he looked up again, Finn noticed that hours had passed in-game. He snapped the last book shut. His eyes were distant as he stared blankly at a nearby wall, struggling to process the implications of what he'd read.

First things first.

"Spellbook," Finn said aloud. The mod's UI immediately popped up in his vision.

Finn's fingers began to twine through a new series of gestures, the images from the fire spellbook seemingly burned into his mind's eye. It felt almost effortless to recall the requisite incantation, although he wasn't certain whether this was a product of his enhanced learning abilities in-game or the countless hours spent in training.

As he spoke, a ball of flame suddenly erupted in the air beside Finn, growing quickly until it was almost the size of a basketball. Finn soon completed the spell, his left hand automatically continuing the gestures needed to channel mana into the sphere as he turned to inspect it. The orb was a roiling mass of fire, and the heat was so intense that it caused the surrounding air to ripple and warp.

With a final gesture, Finn sent the *Fireball* hurtling into a nearby wall, the flames dissipating harmlessly against the warded stone. As soon as he completed the spell, a notification appeared in front of him.

> **New Spell: Fireball**
> You have summoned a great flaming ball of fire! Congratulations, you've managed to cast a spell that even the most arcane-challenged fire mages manage to master. Would you like for us to throw you a party or something? Perhaps hand you a participation trophy of some kind?
> **Skill Level:** Beginner Level 1
> **Cost:** 50 Mana
> **Effect:** Creates a ball of flame that deals 100 + (INT x 50%) damage.

Finn snorted in amusement as he read the prompt.

Although, his good humor was short-lived, his eyes dropping back to the spellbooks strewn about the stone floor. The truth was that *Fireball* was the only spell in the novice fire spellbook that he hadn't learned already. The rest of the notes outlined the incantation and gestures for *Magma Armor* and *Fire Nova*.

He couldn't help but feel a little disappointed. *Fireball* would certainly be useful. He needed a ranged attack, after all. However, he had been hoping for something more interesting and versatile.

Finn had also confirmed that the other spellbooks contained only the primary three spells that all mages were taught upon their induction into the Mage Guild. It seemed Nefreet really did intend to dole spells out to novices slowly. Although, the spellbooks had made it abundantly clear that these spells weren't all there was to learn.

There was so much more to this magic system.

The most intriguing part of the spellbooks had been Bilel's handwritten notes. It had quickly become clear that they were actually *workbooks*. Bilel had been creating these spells first-hand – a point made evident by the notes in the margins outlining his many failed attempts. Where Bilel had lacked the requisite affinity, he had conscripted other mages to help him in his studies. However, the fact that the mage had managed to eventually create the spells was definitive proof that it was possible to craft spells in a systematic way.

Finn shook his head. *How could the other students not have noticed this?*

The answer seemed to be that there was typically no need to purchase the novice spellbooks. If the novices were taught these initial spells as part of their introduction to the guild, it would only be people like Finn – who had deviated from the regular path – that would notice these details. Lamia had certainly not gone into any depth regarding how spells were crafted during her classes. His training in Veridian had also likely helped. Even with the memory dump, Finn had noticed that students struggled to read the arcane language. Raw information alone wasn't enough – the knowledge still needed to be put into practice.

Even more fascinating were Bilel's notes regarding the nature of spellcrafting and mana generally. The mage had written at length, positing his theories behind the structure and nature of mana. He had almost treated the workbooks as a series of personal journals, providing his observations and opinions as he had tested different spells.

Notably, Bilel posited that mana existed as ambient energy in the world that permeated all objects. Humans had a naturally high carrying capacity, and the mage's theory helped to explain the way their mana regenerated after casting a spell. A mage effectively absorbed ambient mana from the world around them. Most living and non-living materials then converted that energy into a specific affinity. Bilel hadn't said this explicitly, but he indicated that humans acted as a sort of high-efficiency converter of ambient mana.

The mage had also alluded to a sense that he didn't

create spells, so much as discover *existing* spells. As though he was somehow decoding natural laws as part of his studies. The implications of that were like a shot of adrenaline for Finn. Did that mean that there were a static number of spells in the world? Or perhaps that was misleading. Perhaps the spells weren't finite, there were simply immutable rules behind how they were formed? A sort of magical code for this world?

That would mean that spells were discoverable in a methodical way, wouldn't it?

Finn could feel a familiar burning sensation in his chest, his fire mana responding to his excitement. He wanted to get started.

"Daniel," Finn said aloud.

The AI immediately flashed into existence, a burning orange-and-red ball that danced and spun next to Finn. "Yes, sir. What can I assist you with *today*?" Daniel asked, sounding a bit petulant. Perhaps it had been a while since Finn had last summoned him.

"Scan all four of these books," Finn ordered, resisting the urge to roll his eyes at the AI as he waved at the spellbooks on the floor. "Compile the incantations and hand gestures for all twelve spells. Specifically, I want you to look for patterns in the syntax and diction of the incantations."

"Sure... fine," the AI groused before diving toward the books. In a flash, Daniel had scanned the four books, bobbing and dancing in the air as he processed the information.

"I do notice several patterns," Daniel said a moment later. His voice sounded slightly distracted, as though he was processing the information.

"Show me," Finn ordered.

The UI in front of Finn suddenly shifted. The incantations for all twelve spells floated in front of him, the arcane symbols painted a translucent blue. Daniel began to parse each line of symbols, identifying similarities between the text and highlighting specific phrases and symbols among the various incantations. Many were observations that Finn had made using his small sample set of spells.

Each incantation was broken into a rhyming couplet composed of two lines and a certain number of syllables –

which also translated to brush strokes for the written symbols. Finn's assumption was that more-complicated spells likely contained additional lines, which had been at least partially confirmed by the fragments of Brutus' golem spell he had managed to record.

Then Daniel began highlighting certain specific symbols among the text, showing alternating patterns. The AI didn't propose a theory, only showing similarities in brush strokes, basic symbols, and meaning.

Finn's eyes suddenly widened, something clicking in his head.

"Stop," he ordered. "Go back two patterns."

The AI did as he instructed, words highlighted in each of the twelve incantations.

"Now cluster these spells together," Finn said, tapping at the incantations. Daniel had soon organized the spells into three groups.

"I'm an idiot," Finn muttered to himself.

The answer was staring him in the face.

One category of spells was all single-target. *Fireball*, *Lightning Bolt*, *Ice Bolt*, and *Slow*. Each incantation had incorporated this designator symbol into the body of the spell. Placement didn't seem important, only that the symbol denoting the spell type was included. The same key phrases also appeared in area-of-effect and defensive spells like *Magma Armor* or *Fire Nova*.

In short, each novice spellbook contained one single-target spell, one AOE spell, and one defensive spell and each spell contained a clear designator among the incantation. This was also an interesting takeaway. It meant that nearly all the novice mages would be working with these same basic three categories.

"Shift forward one pattern," Finn said.

New symbols were now highlighted, denoting a specific affinity. For example, all of the fire spells contained a variant of the "fire" symbol, with only minor brush strokes altering the meaning. The same pattern was replicated among the other three spell groups.

Finn couldn't believe that he hadn't noticed this before

– although he supposed it would have been difficult with a sample set of only two spells.

His mind was racing. He now had a basic set of rules. The question was whether this was enough to let him create something new.

There was really only one way to find out.

"Daniel, incorporate these four rules into the mod. Syntax, symbol limits, and these two required keyword types," he instructed, tapping the two spells. "For higher-ranked spells, journeyman-level and above, let's assume we need to add a second couplet as well as at least one new keyword," Finn said slowly, speaking partly to himself.

"Also, identify possible keywords and their synonyms. These will be general categories of spells. Single target, AOE, defense, utility." Finn was already mentally reviewing his vocabulary lessons, and he realized that there were very few synonyms for these categories. Perhaps this was a telling fact.

"Of course, sir," Daniel replied, sounding pleased that he could be helpful. A few seconds passed. "The changes have been made."

Now was the moment of truth.

Finn just needed to decide what he wanted to try to create. He looked down at a book, noting that he had been using the dagger Julia had given him as a bookmark to keep track of one page. A stray idea crossed his mind, and he snatched at the blade.

Finn set the dagger on the stone floor in front of him.

"Icarus," he said aloud. The mod's UI shifted, showing the spell creation panel.

Finn made several assumptions immediately. "Journeyman spell," he instructed. The UI shifted, showing four lines comprised of two couplets.

"Enchantment, fire," Finn said, identifying the affinity and one category keyword. The requisite symbols soon hovered near the first two lines.

What would the second category keyword be? he thought to himself.

"Utility," he said aloud. The word sprang to his lips almost without conscious thought. This keyword now floated near the second couplet along with the symbol for fire again. Daniel must have noticed a pattern in the fragment of Brutus' spell. Finn gave him an appreciative nod and the glowing orange cloud flashed once in response.

"Can you show the different possible iterations with this basic spell structure?" Finn asked, holding his breath. He could practically feel his heart thudding in his ears.

The words shifted as Daniel sorted through dozens of possible incantations. Invalid versions turned red and disappeared at a rapid pace. Soon, only three variants hovered in front of Finn.

Without giving himself time to second-guess his reasoning, Finn's hands began moving as he recited the first incantation. The hand gestures were entirely intuition. Finn knew he needed to direct the flow of mana from his body and into the dagger. That was enough. Or at least he *hoped* it was enough.

As he finished the first incantation, nothing happened.

The dagger still lay there – plain and unchanged.

"Shit," Finn muttered. Then he began the next spell.

This time, the process felt different. He could sense his mana responding to the hand gestures, flowing out of his body. He also felt a subtle "click" as he recited each word as though they were tumblers in some sort of arcane lock. He could see flames begin to materialize around the blade, twisting and writhing like a living thing as the metal began to glow with a dull red light.

Then Finn spoke the final word of the incantation.

The flames squeezed against the blade, becoming a solid mass of fire that burned along the metal. A flaming dagger rested on the cool stone, charring the dust on the floor.

With trembling fingers, Finn reached forward and grabbed the hilt. Despite the flames and the heated metal, it only felt warm to the touch – much like his *Magma Armor*.

Two notifications appeared in his peripheral vision.

New Spell: Imbue Fire
You have discovered a new spell, granting you the ability to imbue weapons with fire. This spell grants

offensive bonuses, causing the blade to deal fire damage. Masters of this art may also imbue objects for defensive purposes, creating flaming armor or altering their environment to their advantage.
Skill Level: Beginner Level 1
Cost: 100 Mana
Effect: Imbues a weapon with fire mana, increasing the weapon's base damage by INT x 5%. Can only be used on unenchanted metal weapons.

New Skill: Spellcrafting
Through intensive study, you have discovered the forgotten art of spellcrafting, allowing you to create new spells. The spellcrafters of old were a fearsome breed, capable of using this world's magical laws to weave together magics in a dazzling array of devastation and carnage. You should keep this skill to yourself, as many of these mages were hunted for the danger they represented to both themselves and to others.
Skill Level: Beginner Level 1
Effect: Ability to create novice and journeyman-ranked spells.

"Spell created successfully," Daniel reported belatedly. Finn's UI updated automatically as the AI added *Imbue Fire* into Finn's regular spellbook.

Finn couldn't help but bark out a laugh, the sound echoing harshly in the empty stone room. The triumphant smile painted across his face was illuminated by the flickering light of the burning dagger in his hand. His feverish study and preparation had finally paid off.

Now it was time to see how he fared in the duels.

Chapter 23 - Fiery

When Finn arrived at the guild courtyard the next morning, he was surprised to see the throng of students already in attendance. Several hundred novices were clustered in the center of the field, their feet kicking up a fine cloud of dust. Hundreds more mages lined the nearby terraces – presumably higher-ranked members of the guild who couldn't compete in the competition.

The tension in the air was palpable. Finn could have sworn that if he squinted, he would be able to see streamers of anxiety, fear, and excitement dancing in the air above the crowd of novices. The group was oddly quiet, the combination of low murmurs and whispers creating a faint, worried buzz.

For his part, Finn didn't feel that concerned. Instead, excitement burned in his chest and it was a struggle to restrain his fire mana. Here was his chance to finally put all his training and study into practice.

Finn scanned the crowd briefly, picking out Kyyle's form nearby. "Hey, how's it going?" he greeted as he approached the earth mage.

"Fantastic, actually," Kyyle replied in a dry voice. "Today, I get to start competing in an ongoing deathmatch for the next two weeks straight. Didn't care for sleeping or eating much anyway," he muttered.

Finn had to chuckle at that. Indeed, with the way the competition was structured, the victor might very well be the player who was able to stay logged in the longest. "But think of what you'll win!" he replied. "An all-expenses-paid trip to some sort of mega-death gauntlet competing against two other guilds for control of this messed-up slave city!"

Kyyle barked out a laugh, the sound seeming out of place among the crowd of worried novices. The other students must have agreed since they glared in their general direction.

A thought occurred to Finn then, something that had been pestering him since he studied the novice spellbooks. He had concluded that the novice mages all knew basically the same three spells. However, the spell that Kyyle had cast in their bout with Brutus was new. The way he had dissolved the sand beneath the golems and their instructor was nothing like any of the spells Finn had found in the workbooks. Thinking back to the monk-like man that had sponsored Kyyle, his guess was that some of the faculty had been bending the rules.

"I've been meaning to ask," Finn began cautiously. "How did you learn that spell you used against Brutus? I haven't met any other earth mages that know that spell."

"So, you've been talking to other students?" Kyyle replied, side-eyeing Finn with a grin. "That seems out of character. I thought you just disappeared in a puff of smoke as soon as you were done with your single class. You've barely spoken to anyone." The earth mage shifted his gaze back to the stone podium in the center of the courtyard. "Maybe I should be asking you what you've been up to in the northern complex. I thought it was abandoned," Kyyle continued.

Damn, this kid is observant. He needed to be more careful in the future.

Finn shrugged, grinning slightly, and trying to dissemble. "What can I say, I'm an enigma wrapped in a mystery." He didn't nudge Kyyle, just let his original question linger in the air.

The other mage sighed. "Okay, I might have found a spellbook that Gaius left lying out," Kyyle said, lowering his voice and glancing at the nearby students.

"And I guess we're assuming this was an accident…" Finn offered, trailing off and letting the implicit question hang there.

Kyyle smiled. "We're actually not going to question that too hard."

So, Gaius was cheating, Finn thought. He supposed Brutus might have done something similar with Finn since he had taught him *Multi-Casting*. That had interesting implications. The faculty had a stake in this competition, after all. Whoever won would not only control the city but the guild as well. Which meant that with the right amount of discretion, the teachers could play favorites and dole out additional spells and skills. That meant that some of the other students might have a few tricks up their sleeves as well.

"Good morning," a voice whispered through the air. Finn whirled. It almost felt like the person was speaking over his shoulder, yet there was nothing when he turned to look – just other wide-eyed students looking similarly confused.

As his gaze shifted back to the stone platform in the center of the courtyard, Finn saw Abbad standing calmly upon the stone surface, flanked by a group of more veteran mages.

The librarian continued in a normal voice, yet his words were carried upon the wind, making it seem like he was standing right beside each person in the crowd – as though he was speaking just to them. "This morning, we will start the duels. As the headmaster explained, there will be some variations from our normal rules.

"To summarize, anyone may initiate a duel by touching one of the pedestals on the dais with your token. At that point, you will be unable to leave the dais and will be randomly assigned to an opponent. If you have been summoned to a duel, your token will flash with a unique symbol. Once you have been notified of the duel, you will have 15 minutes to return to the courtyard. If you fail to show up to the dais on time, points will automatically be given to whoever initiated the duel. To enter the duel, you and your opponent need only tap your tokens together."

Abbad's gaze swept across the field, meeting Finn's eyes for a fraction of a second. "The competitors will then be teleported to a random environment. Please be aware that these areas are locations within the world, and they may contain ambient wildlife.

"There are only two ways to return: death or your opponent's token. The survivor may tap together the tokens to return to this guild hall. The loser will simply respawn here. Points are awarded to whoever returns first. You may hand the loser's token to the faculty that will be stationed here in the courtyard upon your return."

Silence met these instructions as the players processed

this information. Finn could see the worried tension deepen in the way the novices shuffled about the sand and glanced at each other. He had to admit, this was beginning to feel more real, dampening the excitement that still boiled in his veins.

I'm going to have to kill someone today.

He wasn't exactly certain how he felt about that. He didn't relish the idea of hurting someone else, and he tried vainly to convince himself that it was okay – that the pain and injury weren't permanent. Although, that explanation rang a little hollow given the realism of this world. Finn could only hope that instinct and a healthy dose of fire mana would take care of any reservations he might have.

"With that, the competition has officially commenced," Abbad said calmly. "May you fight for the glory of Lahab and the Emir."

No one moved, as though nervous to be the first.

Out of this silence, Zane emerged from the crowd. He strode up to the dais with carefree steps and placed his token upon one of the stone columns. Immediately a shout of surprise went up as another player's token responded. The novice wove through the other students to reach Zane. Finn noted that he appeared much more hesitant.

Everyone looked on as the two students glanced at each other, their mouths moving but their words inaudible to Finn from this distance. Then the two players tapped their tokens together, and they disappeared in a rift of rainbow energy – not unlike the portals that opened when a player logged in and out of the game.

The start of this first duel seemed to thaw the crowd. All at once, the novices streamed toward the platform, rifts of energy opening in the air as the mages paired off and disappeared.

"Well, good luck, man," Kyyle said, glancing at Finn.

"You too," Finn replied with a nod. "Try not to get wrecked. I'm going to need someone fun to fight."

Kyyle snorted in amusement. "Strong words from the old man who didn't know anything about this game a couple weeks ago."

With that, the earth mage took off for a column,

leaving Finn alone. Taking a deep breath, he approached a nearby pedestal, picking out one of the dozens of columns that ringed the platform that wasn't being thronged by other mages. Just before he touched his token to the pedestal, Finn felt a hand on his shoulder. He turned to find Abbad watching him.

"Come to see me off?" Finn asked.

Abbad gave a nod, gesturing discreetly at the nearby novices. "Only to check on you briefly and perhaps offer some words of wisdom to a student." His point was clear. They needed to be circumspect since they were in public.

"I would gladly accept any advice," Finn replied, wondering what point the librarian was trying to get across here.

"Some of us are blessed with *unique* gifts," Abbad said. "Yet discretion is the better part of valor. These duels are a marathon, not a sprint."

Finn's eyes widened slightly, but he nodded wordlessly.

Abbad departed, and Finn stared down at the token in his hand. He had a sense of what the librarian was trying to say to him. It wasn't about winning just this one match – it was about topping the leaderboards two weeks from now. If he revealed all his abilities quickly, that would only make the successive duels more difficult.

Some of Finn's excitement had dwindled as the flash of multi-colored rifts flickered around him. The reality of what came next was finally beginning to set in. He could feel doubt and hesitation flit through his mind. Could he really do this? Kill another person? And somehow manage the feat without revealing his more advanced abilities?

Finn closed his eyes and instinctively summoned his fire mana. The warm energy surged through his veins and swiftly replaced his newfound anxiety with bubbling anticipation. He reveled in the sensation, letting the excited warmth seep into his bones. This wasn't the time for doubt or hesitation. He needed to think clearly.

Then he abruptly released the energy.

Without giving himself time to chicken out, Finn

placed his token on a nearby column. After a few minutes of hunting through the throng, another student approached him, raising his token to show the symbol to Finn. He was a younger man, maybe in his mid-twenties. The player was dressed in robes and held a staff in hand – one of the few weapons that Finn had seen since arriving in the guild.

Likely a more senior novice, Finn thought to himself. He didn't recognize the man from the small graduation ceremony. Which meant he was either part of another novice class or had completed the beginning courses before Finn. Either way, he was competent if he had sufficient points to purchase the weapon from Charlotte.

"Good luck," Finn said, offering a hand.

The player ignored the gesture. "I don't need luck," he replied, smirking as he looked at Finn's novice attire and lack of weapons.

Finn didn't drop the other player's gaze as he shifted his token forward. It seemed even the pretense at civility was over. They were all competitors now.

So be it, Finn thought, some of his doubt fading away.

Then he touched the other player's token with his own.

The world blurred around Finn, disappearing in a flash of multi-colored energy and darkness encroaching upon the edges of his vision. Within only moments, the courtyard faded from view, and everything went dark.

* * *

The world abruptly snapped back into focus. Harsh sunlight shone down on Finn, and he raised a hand to cover his eyes.

He glanced around, realizing that he was no longer in the courtyard of the Mage Guild. Instead, he stood in an open, level field covered in dry dirt and devoid of practically any vegetation. A lone cactus lingered nearby, standing beside the brittle, stained bones of what might have once been some cow-like creature. This left little to block the hot rays of light that beat down on the field, forcing streamers of heat to rise from the soil.

Finn's thoughts were interrupted by a flash of orange in his peripheral vision. He barely dove out of the way in time. It was only his training with Brutus and Julia that had prepared him to react quickly enough.

He hit the ground hard and rolled, feeling a wave of heat pass over him. A *Fireball* slammed into the ground nearby even as Finn regained his feet.

Apparently, his opponent wasn't as disoriented by the abrupt transition. That confirmed Finn's theory. He was fighting a more veteran player. The other mage stood at least 20 yards away. Holding his staff firmly, tendrils of flame were already beginning to collect in the air again as he readied another *Fireball*.

Fire mage then, Finn thought. That likely limited his opponent's spells to *Fireball*, *Fire Nova*, and *Magma Armor* – at least if he hadn't managed to learn another spell like Kyyle.

Finn didn't hesitate. His eyes glowed as he narrowed his focus and summoned his own mana.

His fingers began twining through an intricate series of gestures, arcane words spilling from his lips. He started toward his opponent while he cast, his feet beating against the dry dirt as he tried to close the distance between them. A moment later, he felt a warm sensation envelop his right arm, his *Magma Armor* sliding into place. The fingers of his left hand kept moving as he continued channeling mana into the shield, and he mimed the gesture with his right – pretending to keep up the channel with both hands.

He hadn't forgotten Abbad's last-minute advice.

For now, he needed to test how hard the other mage could hit.

His opponent smirked at Finn, hurling another *Fireball*. This time, Finn didn't bother to dodge. He simply raised his right arm and dashed through the flames. The energy slammed against his *Magma Armor*, tearing off chunks of the molten substance and almost destroying the shield entirely. The blast sent Finn staggering to the side.

Fuck, he hits like a truck.

Finn managed to stay on his feet – barely. With slightly wobbly steps, he continued his sprint toward the other mage. His opponent's expression faltered as he saw Finn had not only survived the blow, but his shield was repairing itself, the molten energy thickening and expanding until it had regained its former luster.

Maybe his defenses are weaker, Finn said. He would have crossed his fingers, but they were already busy. His right hand was moving rapidly, a ball of flame igniting in the air beside him even as he continued his headlong sprint.

The other fire mage shifted gears, forming his own *Magma Armor*. Then he formed another until both of his arms were coated in the molten material. Yet Finn noted that his opponent didn't keep up the channel once the spell completed. His opponent likely intended to save the channel for his offensive spells.

Finn's right hand directed his *Fireball* at the other mage as he completed the spell, the energy speeding across the field and smashing against the other mage's shield. A flash of flames briefly obscured his opponent, but as it dissipated, Finn saw that his *Fireball* had been weaker, barely carving off the molten energy of his opponent's shield.

Damn it.

He had been given less time to practice the spell since he had only learned it last night; he hadn't had a chance to level it. It appeared the other mage had a higher-level *Magma Armor* as well and likely much better equipment buffing his stats.

The other fire mage seemed to notice the same thing, his smirk returning.

Finn could visualize his thinking.

This was a battle of attrition. Both mages had a limited mana pool, and it was relatively safe to assume that they knew the same three spells, which meant they would just be slamming *Fireballs* against one another until someone caved. However, the more veteran mage had the advantage of gear, levels, and training.

Finn saw another *Fireball* incoming and dove to the side instead of taking the hit. He needed to preserve his mana. He hit the ground and rolled back to his feet. The other mage snorted in frustration.

So, I'm faster, he thought. He supposed that was one more advantage of the brutal weaponless training he had endured at the hands of Brutus and Julia.

Yet Finn needed a strategy if he was going to win.

If he dodged the other mage's spells and used his *Multi-Casting*, he could possibly overwhelm his opponent. However, Abbad's advice still echoed in his head. Right now, he had done little to give away his abilities, and this certainly wouldn't be his last duel.

What do I do then?

Casting another *Fireball*, Finn sent it hurtling at the other mage to buy himself some time to think. Flames soon curled around his opponent's shield, and the other mage faltered briefly, unable to see Finn through the flames.

The other option was for Finn to move in close and use his dagger. He might be able to use a few rapid *Fireballs* to block the other mage's sight. However, his opponent had the advantage of reach with that staff, and his arms were well shielded.

Finn wished he had a way to strike the mage from behind or catch him off guard.

It was then that an idea occurred to him. Finn could feel his mana respond immediately, fiery excitement pulsing through his veins. He wasn't certain if it would work, but he was damned sure curious to find out.

Finn's left hand stopped moving, dropping the channel on his *Magma Armor*.

Then both hands began twining through the gestures of another *Fireball*, an orb of flame appearing beside him. Finn dashed forward toward the other mage. The man's brow furrowed slightly, but he didn't hesitate, forming his own *Fireball* to put pressure on Finn. The bolt would either destroy Finn's shield or force him to dodge and slow him down. The other mage seemed confident that his own shield would be able to absorb Finn's attack.

Finn finished casting his *Fireball*, shifting the channel to his left hand, and holding the ball of flame beside him. Yet the fingers of his right hand never stopped moving. From the other mage's perspective, it likely looked like Finn had cast the one *Fireball* and was simply channeling with both hands. It would be incredibly difficult to see that his fingers weren't moving in sync.

The other mage's spell completed, and a blast of fire raced toward Finn. He didn't hesitate, raising his right arm to block the attack. He could feel his *Magma Armor* shudder and then crumble under the blow, the molten energy melting away from his arm and leaving him defenseless.

As the flames cleared, Finn could see the gloating expression on the other man's face as he summoned another *Fireball*. He likely assumed Finn didn't have time to cast another shield. Technically, he was right.

However, Finn wasn't done yet. He continued to race toward his opponent, swiftly closing the distance.

As the fingers of Finn's right hand completed their spell and shifted into a channel, he launched the *Fireball* he had been holding. His opponent raised his arm almost casually to block the blow, knowing that it wouldn't break his shield. However, it didn't need to; it just needed to obscure the other mage's vision.

Finn lunged forward the last few feet. The other mage swept forward with his staff at the same time, swinging blindly amid the flames, and Finn ducked under the flailing blow and stepped closer. As the flames cleared, the other fire mage's eyes trained on Finn. He shook his head as he raised his staff back to a defensive position. His expression practically gloated.

"Checkmate," Finn murmured.

Then he released his second spell.

A blast of flame crashed into the back of Finn's opponent, burning through his robes, causing him to drop his guard. His expression twisted into a grimace of pain.

Finn didn't give him a chance to recover. Julia's dagger appeared in his right hand, and as he lunged, time seemed to slow.

The other mage tried to raise his staff in time, but he was too slow. Finn dipped below the attack and came up inside the man's guard.

Finn's blade soon cut into the other mage's stomach,

slicing through his robes and sliding into his flesh. The impact rippled up Finn's arm, and he pushed harder against the resistance. At the same time, Finn grabbed the mage's other arm and batted it aside. Then Finn twisted the blade and jerked upward.

Julia had taught him that trick. Even if the first cut didn't kill, the goal was to cause as much damage as possible. Bleeding damage could be quite dangerous.

The other mage coughed, blood splattering his lips. "What? How...?" he croaked.

Finn didn't say a word, his training with Julia taking over. He ripped the blade free and then lashed out with his arm, cutting through the mage's throat before he could recover. Blood sprayed from the wound as the fire mage slumped into the sand. He let out one desperate gasp, his hands trying to claw at his throat. And then his body went still.

Finn stood there, his chest heaving and fire mana burning through his veins in triumph.

His plan had worked!

With the mage lying face-down, Finn could see scorched cloth and burned flesh along the man's back where his second *Fireball* had struck. Finn had gambled that the spell didn't technically need to be conjured beside him, but could be formed at a distance and then maintained with his channel.

The other fire mage hadn't even thought to look behind him – assuming that Finn wouldn't be able to hold two *Fireballs* at once.

And the best part? Even inside the deathscape, Finn's opponent likely wouldn't be able to figure out what had happened. The second *Fireball* had struck from behind – out of the other mage's line of sight, and it would be difficult to detect that Finn's gestures didn't match.

"I'm going to have to practice that trick," Finn murmured to himself. Although, he suspected he would get plenty of chances before the day was over.

He continued to channel his fire mana as he looked down at the corpse, the mage's blood pooling in the dry dirt. He didn't trust himself to handle this next part without the anesthetic effect of his mana.

Finn stooped, his fingers rifling through the man's belongings until he found the other token. Then he wiped his blade off on the dead man's tunic, sheathed the weapon, and forcefully released his mana. He didn't want to accidentally reveal his affinity when he returned to the courtyard.

His preparations complete, Finn took a deep breath and tapped his opponent's token together with his own. Multi-colored energy soon enveloped him, and the world abruptly faded from view.

*　　*　　*

When Finn opened his eyes again, he was back in the courtyard, standing upon the stone dais. He blinked rapidly, although this time the disorientation was less severe. He was growing accustomed to the abrupt teleportation. He supposed that was a good thing. He hadn't forgotten how quickly his opponent had gotten the jump on him.

I need to move faster next time.

He heard murmuring, and Finn turned to find Abbad and the other mages staring at him, as well as dozens of other novices that lingered on the platform. Hundreds of mages still stood on the terraces ringing the courtyard, whispering to each other, and pointing at Finn. On each face, he registered a mixture of surprise and confusion… as well as an emotion that he couldn't quite place.

"How long was I gone?" Finn asked.

One of the instructors beside Abbad coughed, sharing a look with the others before replying. "About two minutes. You were the first to complete your duel."

Finn glanced at Abbad in shock, looking for confirmation. "Technically, 87 seconds by my count," the librarian amended.

Then Abbad turned back to the rest of the crowd, his fingers twining through a series of gestures. "Congratulations to Finn, the first to complete his duel! He has been awarded 10 points," the librarian's voice whispered into each person's ear.

Finn looked at the other novices and mages around him and then down at himself, noting that his clothing was undamaged, and he didn't appear to be injured. He suddenly understood the unfamiliar expression on their faces.

That was *fear* that he saw in their eyes.

While that battle might have *felt* like it had taken longer to Finn, from their perspective, he had won almost instantly. Not only that, but he hadn't taken any injury. In fact, his mana had already regenerated, and he was ready to go again.

Not knowing what else to do, Finn snagged the dead player's token from his pocket and tossed it to Abbad. The air mage master snatched the token from the air with an almost casual grace. Then Finn met the librarian's eyes evenly. He didn't see any fear there. Only the same appraising expression, his eyebrows arched in a silent question.

What now? Abbad was asking.

Finn smacked his token against a nearby column.

"Alright, let's go again."

Chapter 24 - Controlling

"Look what we have here! Sleeping on the job. Typical," someone snapped.

Finn's eyes flickered open, his hand automatically dropping to his dagger. Yet he hesitated as he saw Julia looming over him where he sat with his back to the warded stone wall of the training room. His daughter's eyes danced with amusement. Finn groaned softly before rubbing at his eyes and stumbling back to his feet.

"I've started taking these power naps. It's been letting me stay logged in longer," Finn explained with a yawn. "My theory is that the game condenses a normal sleep pattern, cycling the person between REM and non-REM sleep very quickly."

Julia just stared at him skeptically.

"I guess what I'm saying is that they really do seem to be *power* naps," Finn explained.

"Uh-huh, but what about that part where your real body needs to eat and go to the bathroom?" she retorted. "From what I can tell, you've been logged in for a crazy amount of time now."

Finn grimaced. She was right, of course.

With the ongoing competition, he hadn't logged out much over the last two days in-game – which was close to 12-18 hours in the real world. With the way that the competition was set up, the winner would likely be whoever could stay logged in the longest.

The math was pretty simple. 14 days. 24 hours per day. Accounting for the 15-minute time limit for players to match up and another 5-10 minutes for a duel, that meant he could reasonably manage 3-4 duels per hour. That resulted in 1,008 to 1,344 matches or 10,080 to 13,440 possible points. That was the maximum possible score range assuming he never logged out.

Although Finn had found that this wasn't really realistic. The player population in-game fluctuated with the real-world time zones. It was much harder to find matches during certain times of day or night. So, Finn had taken to using these downtimes to return to the dilapidated training room – napping and training in private. Or logging out briefly to eat a snack. He didn't lose much time this way since other players would queue for the duel and his token would light up when he was matched.

Julia was still glaring at him, and Finn rubbed at his neck, looking away. "Well, I might have had Daniel help with some of those real-world problems," he grumbled.

"What was that?" Julia said. "I didn't quite hear you there. It sounded a lot like, '*I'm an addict, please send help.*'"

Finn chuckled. "Okay, fine. I might have a problem."

"The first step is admitting it," Julia replied with a grin.

Then her expression sobered. "Seriously, though. Do I even want to know how Daniel is *helping* you stay in the game longer?"

It was Finn's turn to smile. "Well, you know how I'm sort of numb from the waist down?"

"I'm going to stop you right there," she interrupted, holding up a hand. "The correct answer was no. That sounds like way too much information."

"Well, you did ask," Finn retorted.

Julia paced the room before glancing back at Finn. Despite her teasing tone, Finn could see concern in her eyes. He had the strangest sense of déjà vu. Rachael used to give him that same look every time he started a new project – a smile covering exasperated worry. He'd lost count of how many times she had brought him something to eat or drink because he had skipped multiple meals or how often she had to remind him to sleep.

The thought alone was enough to create a hollow pit in Finn's stomach – an aching void that he knew couldn't be filled, only covered and patched up by another distraction. He had a sudden strong urge to summon his fire mana, letting the sensation burn away these unpleasant thoughts. Yet he resisted. Barely.

Julia was now looking at him expectantly.

"What was that?" Finn asked, shaking his head. He had missed her last question.

She sighed. "Do you know your rank right now?"

He shook his head. It didn't really matter. He just needed to keep going.

"Number five – and the margins are pretty tight," Julia reported.

"Still not number one," a gruff voice spoke up from the entrance to the room. The pair looked over to find Brutus leaning against the rusted door. "But there's plenty of time to change that. You shouldn't let your guard down."

The fire mage glanced at Finn. "Finn has done well so far. I might have been doing some snooping. Many of the players he's fought can't figure out how he's winning. It's almost like *magic*," Brutus added, dry amusement coloring his voice. "Although, I'm noticing a pattern. Most report getting struck from behind by something. A few have even complained to the faculty that Finn has been cheating."

Julia glanced at Finn, curiosity replacing her worried expression. Both of them were watching him, waiting for an explanation.

"I'm not sure a magician is supposed to reveal his secrets..." Finn began.

"Oh, shut it," Julia snapped at him. "Just tell us what you've been doing."

Brutus laughed. "I like this one. She gets to the point."

"Fine, fine," Finn said, raising a hand. "Abbad cautioned me before the duels began to keep my abilities hidden. So, I didn't want to tip my hand regarding *Multi-Casting* too early." Finn's eyes shifted to Daniel, where he hovered nearby.

Or about how I can create spells, he thought. But he kept his mouth shut on that point. That wasn't something he had revealed to Brutus yet.

"After you killed us all in the courtyard," he continued, gesturing at Brutus, "I discovered that the deathscape doesn't allow you to replay events that you didn't actually see. So, I came up with a way to take out players without revealing my abilities. Although it might be easier to show you than to explain..." Finn trailed off, his fingers twining through a series of gestures.

He summoned his typical one-two combo, a *Fireball* soon hovering in the air beside him. Then Finn shifted his left hand to a channel and summoned another orb with his right. A second *Fireball* soon appeared in the air behind Brutus.

The fire mage master glanced behind himself at the burning globe, an appraising expression on his face. "Clever," he murmured. "So, you use the first bolt as a decoy, let your opponent think you are defenseless, and then strike them from behind to capitalize on the moment of weakness. Most mages don't figure out that trick until they hit journeyman rank."

Brutus snorted, shaking his head. "I doubt that will work for much longer, though. Your opponents will start to wisen up."

"I didn't realize he could summon spells at a distance," Julia observed as Finn dismissed the two spells. "He never did that during our training."

"It just occurred to me in the first duel," Finn offered with a shrug. "I never needed to hide my skills during our sparring matches."

"Part of that is also my fault," Brutus offered with a sigh. "We've been focused solely on training Finn's stats and basic spellcasting abilities, so we haven't really had a chance to delve into magical theory. It's something that is usually covered during more advanced classes.

"Specifically, we haven't talked about caster range and control."

Brutus now had Finn's undivided attention. "Well, there's no time like the present. At least, until someone summons me," he added, gesturing at the token that rested on the floor next to his bag.

"True enough. We might as well start at the beginning," Brutus said, meeting Finn's eyes, his expression serious. "What is fire magic?"

Finn cocked his head. Was that a trick question? It seemed like being a fire mage was just about launching fire-based spells: flaming orbs, shields of molten energy, waves of flames, etc.

Brutus seemed to read his mind. "It's not a rhetorical question. Have you ever wondered *how* or *why* you are able to conjure and control a massive ball of flame? Or how your bolts tend to track a person – shifting slightly in mid-air to hit the target? Or how about the way I summoned the golems and those walls of flame in the courtyard?"

Now that Brutus mentioned it, a fire mage didn't just summon some flames and call it a day. They actually had the ability to actively control that mana outside their bodies. Finn had done that many times, his fingers channeling and guiding his spells. So, was fire magic just the ability to control *fire*?

Finn hesitated. That didn't seem right either. The golems hadn't really been on fire; Brutus had just melted the sand and kept it superheated. And Finn's *Magma Armor* wasn't exactly "fire" per se. Those spells had more to do with *heat*.

His perspective suddenly shifted, and his eyes widened.

"It's the ability to manipulate thermal energy," Finn murmured.

"Exactly," Brutus replied with a grin. "This is the foundation for all fire-based spells. Or rather we could say *heat-based spells*, I suppose," he amended.

"All of the affinities are designed this way," Brutus continued. "At their core, they each represent *control* of a certain type of energy or matter. That word is important. Being a mage is entirely about control. This is also why *Mana Mastery* is such an essential skill. It directly translates into greater command over your mana."

Finn was already processing the implications of that. He spoke slowly, several pieces of the puzzle beginning to click together in his head – a mixture of what he had learned from his instructors and through his own study of *Spellcrafting*. "That would explain why I can form orbs with my *Mana Mastery*. I am directly controlling the mana, but the incantation then gives the mana a shape or form."

"Indeed," Brutus replied. "You can also take manual control of a spell once it has been cast. This is how you can repair your *Magma Armor*. Or how we can hold a *Fireball* suspended, for example. This is basic mana channeling. On the other hand, we could also simply cast the spell –

effectively powering it for a limited time.

"Your *Mana Mastery* and the strength of your affinity represents control of your mana. Period," Brutus explained. "That has several results. For example, it explains how you can maintain several spells at once – much like the orbs that Abbad has you summoning as practice. This is what allowed you to learn *Multi-Casting*.

"Your control also affects your *range*. You can only summon and control mana a certain distance from your body. The greater your *Mana Mastery* and affinity, the farther away you can cast. Right now, you are likely limited to about ten feet or so."

"But his spells don't dissipate once they go past that limit," Julia observed. "Hell, this room is about thirty feet across, and I've seen him launch *Fireballs* from one end to the other."

"This just represents his *control range*, not his *effective range*," Brutus explained. He frowned as he saw the look of confusion on their faces.

"Okay, let's say he casts a *Fireball* in a straight line from one end of the room to the other. Finn could control the *Fireball* up to a certain point – representing his maximum control range. Past that line, he can no longer directly control the mana, and the spell begins to deteriorate and break apart. The farther outside the mage's control range, the faster the deterioration."

The fire mage master eyed the room. "This space is small, and we've spent all of our time training in this room, so you haven't had a chance to really observe this limitation. However, if Finn were to cast a *Fireball* out in the courtyard, it would break apart after a certain distance."

So, there is a hard limit on my control range and some sort of exponential decay on my effective range, Finn thought. He was guessing that with some testing he could probably figure out both the limit of his control range and the mathematical formula behind the mana decay. Then he could update his mod to show his control range and effective range.

That also had other consequences. Finn thought back to his initial encounter with Brutus in the courtyard. If what he was saying was true, then the fire mage master's control range must be incredible. He had been able to continuously channel and control spells across the length of a football field. Was that what Finn could eventually aspire to?

He shook his head. That seemed to be a little out of reach at the moment. Although Brutus' explanation did raise an obvious question.

"How do I increase my control range?" Finn asked.

Brutus smirked. "A question most mages start asking once they hit journeyman and expert rank. The answer is practice. You can modify your *Mana Mastery* exercises to focus on range. You simply summon the same orbs but hold the pattern as far away from you as you can, increasing the distance incrementally."

The large man grimaced. "Unfortunately, you will eventually reach a hard limit. Like I said, control is a function of your mastery *and* affinity. At some point, you will need to increase your fire affinity to keep going. However, with your naturally high affinity, that might take a while."

Finn rubbed at his chin, feeling the coarse stubble beneath his fingers. He could likely modify Abbad's practice routine to train his *Mana Mastery* while also extending the orbs to his full range. For now, he might be able to tackle this inside the training room. Once his control range reached about thirty feet, he'd likely have to take his exercises out to the courtyard.

His thoughts were interrupted by Julia. "Looks like you are being summoned," she observed, pointing at the token on the floor. Finn could indeed see that the small chit was now glowing softly, indicating that another player had initiated a duel.

Julia let out a yawn. "Probably for the best anyway. I've gotta get out of here and get some sleep." She eyed Finn. "You should too. Power naps or not, you need to log out."

Finn arched an eyebrow. "I thought I was supposed to be the parent here."

Julia shrugged. "Then start acting like it." With a grin, she logged off before he could respond, a rift of multi-colored energy tearing open next to him.

"Damn kids," Finn muttered. At this comment, Finn noted that Brutus looked away, a pained grimace flitting across his face.

"You should enjoy it while it lasts," the fire mage offered. "Someday you might find yourself missing these little irritations."

Finn was puzzled by his reaction, although he didn't want to pry. Brutus' words also made him think of Rachael. Perhaps Brutus was right. Maybe he should go a little easier on Julia and try to savor these moments. Finn certainly knew firsthand how easily the people he loved could be torn away from him.

"Fair enough," Finn said. He stopped and grabbed his pack. "Well, better get going. People to kill, points to earn."

Brutus nodded, although his expression was somber. "Like I said before, I've been snooping. The other students are already catching on to that little spellcasting trick. They aren't going to keep falling for it. Besides, your rank is high enough now that people are going to start looking to knock you off your pedestal. The rest of the pack may start sharing notes in an attempt to best the top few students."

There was some truth to Brutus' words, but Finn grinned back at him, trying to lighten the mood. "Well, I'd love to see them try."

The fire mage laughed as they stepped out of the training room. "See, this is why I decided to sponsor you," he offered. "You remind me of myself."

Finn gave him his best deadpan expression. "Ouch. So, you're calling me an arrogant asshole then?"

Brutus paused for a second, tilting his head. "Huh. Yeah, I guess I am."

Chapter 25 - Unaware

Finn padded along the empty halls that made up the northern part of the Mage Guild, his feet whispering against the stone floor as he palmed the glowing token in his hand. Brutus had left him only a few moments ago, claiming he needed to go attend to faculty business – which probably meant that he needed to go torture and harass some students.

Finn had just waved at him distractedly. His thoughts kept returning to Brutus' lecture. For some reason, he kept coming back to the idea that fire magic was really just the control of *thermal energy*. That had some interesting implications.

For example, did that mean the fire was necessary?

In the real world, a flame was a function of combusting oxygen, which gave off heat and light. However, it was entirely possible to have heat without light.

What if Finn cast a *Fireball*, but was able to set the temperature just below the ignition point for oxygen? Of course, that assumed that the game had something akin to oxygen in the air, but Finn did seem to be breathing *something*, and the game world had been quite detailed and authentic so far. So, it seemed possible.

Did that mean he could potentially throw around invisible *Fireballs*?

Finn supposed that they might deal less damage since the burning point for oxygen was roughly 1000 °F. Whereas, most wood fires burned at around 2000+ °F. Typically, heat was largely a function of the combustible material and the amount of energy released. Although, in his case, his mana seemed to be the only thing that mattered.

He suspected that even an invisible *Fireball* would hurt pretty badly, and it would be extremely hard to avoid. It might also allow him to circumvent some of the other classes. For example, couldn't an air mage simply cut off the oxygen to a *Firewall* or *Fireball*? Fighting someone like Abbad seemed like it would be incredibly difficult. Mages might effectively have "counterspells" that could neutralize another element or type of spell. It would be much harder to counteract a spell that didn't rely on combustion.

Finn was so deep in thought that he didn't notice he was in danger until it was too late. Something suddenly struck him in the back of the head.

Hard.

He was sent toppling into a nearby wall, rebounding off the stone, and slamming against the floor. Air escaped his lungs in a whoosh, leaving him gasping. At the same time, his vision swam, and red notifications flashed in his peripheral vision – an indication that he had been stunned. Something wet trickled down the back of his neck.

Blood. That's my blood, he thought feebly.

He felt momentary panic flare in his chest; he felt trapped. Like a cornered animal, his fight-or-flight reflex kicking in with abandon. He responded instinctively and summoned his fire mana, his eyes soon glowing with orange and red flames, the energy burning away his useless emotions and providing a moment of clarity.

He didn't know who or how many people he was fighting or why they had attacked him, but they had already gotten the jump on him. A glance at his health confirmed that the single hit had made a sizable dent and he likely had a concussion. He was going to have difficulty casting in this condition.

He realized with a calm precision that he was likely going to die here in the hallway.

Yet maybe he could at least catch a glimpse of what had attacked him – something to make his death less futile. He struggled to push himself upright, trying to turn to look behind him.

His attacker had a different plan. He felt something heavy land on his back, pressing him back against the floor and smacking his forehead against the stone hard enough to set his ears ringing. Then he felt a hot lance pierce through his back. However, this wasn't his mana. He could feel the blade shift inside him, like a molten rod burrowing through his chest.

It withdrew and then stabbed down again.

And again.

Finn could only lie there, stunned and incapacitated, still gasping for air and the taste of copper lingering in his mouth. The only thing he could see was his glowing token, resting on the floor a few inches away – as though mocking him.

Then the world went dark, and a notice appeared in Finn's vision.

System Message

You have died.

Thanks for playing Awaken Online!

---

* * *

Finn returned to his body abruptly. His lungs were still seizing, and he coughed hard, dropping to his knees. He gripped at his chest with clumsy hands where he had felt the blade impale him repeatedly. His fingers met intact flesh, indicating that he was alive and well.

However, it still took his mind a while to catch up.

"Damn it," Finn croaked when he began to recover.

He looked up to find himself kneeling in the same dark, dusty hallway along the abandoned northern part of the guild hall. Blue motes of energy drifted around him like flecks of ash, signaling that he was inside the game's deathscape. As though on cue, Finn's doppelganger walked around a corner, murmuring to himself as he paced down the hallway.

"*Pay attention, idiot,*" Finn wanted to snap. But he knew it was pointless. The mistake had already been made.

An indistinct blur whizzed out of the darkness and Finn watched himself slam against the wall and then fall to the floor. His clone tried to rise, its eyes glowing with fire mana. However, something dark hovered above him, weighing him down. He couldn't even see what stabbed him – only the look of pain that twisted his features as he was speared repeatedly.

His blood soon pooled beneath him, staining the stone with the thick soupy substance.

Only a moment later, Finn's body went still.

Then the scene dissolved and reset.

Finn – the real Finn – slumped back against a wall, sitting on the cool stone floor as he watched himself round the corner once more.

Frustrated anger simmered in his stomach, and his hands clenched into fists as he watched himself get murdered again. He could still feel the phantom pain of the weapon sliding into his back and that feeling of helpless panic.

Then his eyes centered on the dueling token, the symbol still glowing across its surface. The 45-minute lock-out timer upon death meant that he wouldn't be able to meet his opponent for the duel. So, he had just lost 5 points by default. Technically, he had lost a net 15 points assuming he had won the duel, plus another 10 points assuming he had managed to get paired again. So, the death had likely cost him upwards of 25 points.

Finn closed his eyes, forcing himself to take a deep breath. Maybe as humans had crawled out of the primordial soup, anger had served a purpose; helped them to overcome their fear. Yet despite the pain and despair of Rachael's death, Finn had learned one thing. Anger didn't accomplish a damn thing. Getting angry hadn't brought her back, it hadn't made the loss hurt less, and it sure as hell didn't help him here.

No. Right now he needed to focus on learning what he could.

Finn's eyes popped back open, and his attention returned to the scene of his death, watching carefully for any clues that he might have missed.

He hadn't managed to get a good look at his attacker – or *attackers* since it might very well have been more than one person. They had been careful to stay outside of his line of sight. He also couldn't identify any noise or information that would give away their identity. Perhaps they had learned *Sneak* like Julia or had used a spell to conceal their movements. Although, since he hadn't been paying attention, they might have simply crept up behind him.

Finn also wasn't certain what had struck him. Judging from the wound, it looked like something blunt. Maybe the hilt of a sword or a mace? A sword seemed more likely since something had impaled him repeatedly.

On top of all that, Finn's attackers had chosen a perfect location for an ambush. This area of the school was deserted, and there were no witnesses.

Although, that led to one possible deduction. Whoever had killed Finn had planned this carefully. This likely wasn't an act of impulse. It had been intentional.

The question was *why*.

It could have been something personal; Finn didn't exactly have a lot of friends. Yet his attacker was taking a big risk. Lamia had made it clear that infighting outside the duels would be punished severely – assuming that the attacker got caught, of course. Which meant the reward had to outweigh the risk. That definitely narrowed the field. As far as Finn knew, there was only one reward worth getting expelled for.

Winning the competition.

Finn's eyes widened as a possible explanation struck him. He suddenly realized that there were actually two ways for a person to climb higher on the leaderboards.

The first was to win duels.

The second was to ensure a higher-ranked person lost – as each loss would cost them 5 points. And the easiest way to ensure a loss was to force a person to default. It would be simple enough to follow a player, wait until he was summoned to a duel, and then ambush him on the way. As Finn had already determined, a single death could cost as much as 25 points when factoring in the opportunity cost.

That was the only explanation that made sense.

If Finn was right, then that meant every other top-ranked player could have been the attacker – although, his thoughts instantly turned to Zane. This seemed like the sort of cutthroat tactic that the earth mage would come up with. Although, technically *any* player could be complicit. Even a lower-ranked mage could have an incentive to help a friend.

Finn hesitated. He suddenly realized that this was likely the first attack of many. A single default wouldn't be enough to influence Finn's rank long-term. No, to make a real impact on his score, his attackers would need to *hunt* him. He also suspected it wouldn't take long for other students to catch on to this strategy. The higher he climbed in the rankings, and the longer he stayed there, the larger the target on his back.

Which meant, this was only going to get worse from here.

"Shit," he muttered to himself, rubbing at his eyes. How the hell did he avoid getting murdered in the guild hall with most of the novices gunning for him?

"Okay," he said aloud. "Focus. This is just another problem. Solve it."

Finn's eyes skimmed back to the scene of his death, watching as he bled out on the floor again. If he examined the problem logically, this encounter had emphasized a couple of weaknesses on his part.

The first was that Finn was extremely vulnerable if an opponent got the jump on him. If he were stunned or unable to move, his spells provided no advantage since casting a spell required that he was able to speak, that his hands were free, and that he was able to concentrate.

Finn also had little health or armor. He typically relied on speed and *Magma Armor* to avoid or block attacks. One possible solution was to purchase better equipment, but he didn't want to burn his hard-won points on new gear just yet. Besides, a bit more health wouldn't really solve the problem if his opponent managed to catch him off guard.

Even if he survived the initial attack, it occurred to Finn that he might not really be able to fight back. If he was ambushed, defended himself by slaying the attacker, but left witnesses, he could be expelled for attacking other students. He also needed to assume that he was up against more than one person. Working in packs, the other novices could lie and claim that Finn was the aggressor – that he was hunting *them* and that explained his score. Brutus had already mentioned that there were rumors that he was cheating.

That meant his best strategy was to avoid the battle altogether.

"Okay, the primary goal is avoidance. And my main

problem is someone sneaking up on me," Finn said to himself, his voice echoing slightly in the stone hall. "Which means I need a way to detect the attack sooner."

The first option was to get Julia to help. She could follow him in *Sneak*. However, that wasn't a perfect fix. She couldn't stay logged in all the time, even if he could convince her to act as his full-time bodyguard. Besides, what could she really do? She could potentially kill Finn's attackers, but that really just highlighted the same problem. Besides, if she got caught, Finn doubted Nefreet would go easy on her. That only put Julia at risk. So, at best, she could warn him through the in-game chat.

Finn snorted in irritation as he saw his doppelganger get smacked in the back of the head and topple over once more. He supposed he just needed to grow eyes in the back of his head.

Finn froze at that thought. The "growing eyes" thing was out of the question, but maybe he could increase his awareness of his surroundings. Any advance warning might have allowed Finn to avoid the blow and get away.

"Daniel," Finn said.

A moment later, a flaming orb appeared in the air beside him. "I suppose you want something?" Daniel replied. From his tone, Finn could practically visualize the AI raising an eyebrow. The AI now became progressively more moody if Finn hadn't summoned him in a while, as though upset at being ignored.

Finn quickly put aside Daniel's surly attitude, his mind racing as he stared at the AI. He recalled the prompt he had seen when he integrated Daniel into the game. It had said that the AI couldn't harm other players – meaning that Finn couldn't use him as some sort of living *Fireball*. However, it hadn't said anything about Daniel providing information.

Finn had also seen the pets lined up against the wall in the requisition hall. Presumably, that meant that other mages kept pets or familiars. So, it might not seem strange that Finn had purchased one. He could always explain that Charlotte had played favorites or given him access to a special pet. The most perceptive players might notice that his points hadn't dipped, but so be it. If others were going to cheat, then Finn was more than comfortable bending the rules a bit.

"Daniel, from now on, I want you to stay summoned unless I tell you otherwise," Finn instructed, speaking slowly.

"Really?" Daniel asked, bobbing slightly. He seemed happy at the suggestion.

"Uh, yes," Finn replied, sparing him a confused glance. He shook his head. "I also need for you to watch any direction outside of my direct line of sight at all times and warn me if someone is trying to attack me. In fact, I'd like for you to actively scout or monitor the area around me for enemies." This earned Finn a small bob in response.

Another thought occurred to Finn as he saw the blurred-out form hover over his body once more. Even if Daniel's warning system failed and he died again, it would help to be able to see who the hell had killed Finn. If he knew who was attacking him and how, that would certainly improve his odds of surviving.

Finn gestured at the scene that was replaying. "It would also be helpful if you could record video of my environment."

"Unfortunately, I cannot actively record video," Daniel replied.

Finn's brow furrowed. "What? Why not?"

"Those permissions have been denied by the system controller. Remote video recording is restricted to players with specific endorsements from the development team."

Finn grimaced. *Well, shit.* There went that plan.

However, at least Daniel might be able to alert him to danger more quickly – in theory, anyway. If the attacks escalated, then he would need to come up with something else.

"I can still keep an eye out," Daniel offered, weaving slightly in the air. When Finn didn't reply immediately, the AI asked, "Is there anything else I could do to help?"

Was that anxiety in his voice? Finn idly wondered if Daniel was scared of being dismissed. Yet he discarded that idea immediately. That wasn't possible, at least not the way Finn had initially coded him. Maybe he was just reading into things.

He was about to tell Daniel "no," but Finn hesitated as he saw the scene replay once again. It seemed he was going to be here for a while longer. He glanced at Daniel and then at the hallway, noting that it was at least 60 feet long. Brutus' lecture was still fresh in his mind. Despite his frustration, he might as well make the most of the involuntary downtime.

"Actually, you *can* help me with something," Finn replied as he dropped down onto the floor, sitting cross-legged with his back to the wall. "Pull up the code for our casting mod. We need to make some improvements…"

Orbs of flame soon began to hover around Finn as he channeled his mana. It was time to test his control range and effective range.

Chapter 26 - Fleetfooted

"Damn it, that was close," Finn huffed, leaning against a nearby wall. His lungs burned, and his stamina was just beginning to regenerate. Finn still had a few minutes until he needed to find his dueling partner – time he needed to use to recover from his latest near-death experience.

The interior courtyard lingered nearby, bright sunlight shining down on the sands. That hot, dusty rectangle had become a haven of late – one of the few places that was too densely populated for the other players to launch an attack.

"They're getting more aggressive," Julia reported, dropping from *Sneak* and lounging beside Finn. She seemed relaxed, as though she had just gone for a light stroll, arms folded beneath her robes and her hood drawn to conceal her face. "This is what? The second attempt this morning?"

"This was the third attack this morning and the eighth attack since Finn was originally murdered in the hallway 37 hours ago—" Daniel reported, his flaming body floating nearby.

"Quiet," Finn barked at Daniel, sparing a glance at the nearby players. The AI flashed once in response, and Finn swore he heard him grumbling under his breath. Although, he didn't have attention to spare for the AI right now.

"The plan is working well for now," Finn offered, side-eyeing Julia. "I haven't died or missed a duel yet."

Julia rolled her eyes at Finn beneath her hood. "Your master plan of *running away*? This just doesn't seem sustainable. I can't always be here to help, and I have a feeling that Daniel will struggle on his own as the players continue to escalate their attacks."

Finn let out a mental sigh. She was right. Of course, she was right. Her words just mirrored his thoughts after the first ambush.

Daniel was an okay watchdog, but Julia was better. The AI simply stood out too much, his flaming body making him easy to spot. Although, once the players had realized that Finn had a new pet, he had been able to use Daniel as a decoy on more than one occasion. In contrast, Julia's *Perception* skill and *Sneak* allowed her to effortlessly spot a group of players and then relay their location through the in-game chat without being detected.

"Maybe we shouldn't be running. The best deterrent is *fear*. We could simply make an example of a few of them," Julia offered, her eyes flashing and a dagger suddenly appearing in her hand.

"We've been over this," Finn retorted. "Only as a last resort. It's too risky. They could just as easily frame me for killing another student."

"Well, the other option is to stay out in the open where there are plenty of witnesses," Julia offered, waving at the courtyard where mages milled about the sands. Finn could see that many of the novices had begun to travel in groups. Apparently, he wasn't the only student who had been ambushed lately.

"We also need some privacy to train," Finn replied quietly. "I don't love the idea of creating spells out in the open." Although to be fair, he hadn't really had any time to experiment with his *Spellcrafting*. Between the duels and the attacks, he was barely able to maintain his standing in the rankings.

Julia frowned but held her tongue.

"For now, we just need to keep going," Finn said, pushing away from the wall and glancing back at his daughter.

"Well, we'll see if you change your mind the next time you get brutally murdered," Julia replied, an involuntary grin tugging at her lips. "Don't know about you, but I've tried that a couple times. Didn't love it."

"Thanks for the vote of confidence," Finn replied in a dry voice.

"Anytime!" Julia offered. "But you do need to get moving." She gestured at the token in his hand. "Time is almost up."

Finn grimaced and turned back to the courtyard, eyeing the circular stone podium in the center, dozens of novices lounging around the platform.

"Good luck," Julia called from behind him. When Finn turned to look at her, she had already disappeared – returning to wherever she went when she wasn't busy nagging him and acting as his bodyguard.

With a sigh, he started marching toward the dais. There was no sense in dragging this out. He soon spotted another mage with a similar symbol standing on the stone platform and swiping at the air, likely reviewing her notifications. Finn slowed his steps, taking some time to inspect his opponent carefully. Knowledge was power, after all.

The woman looked to be in her mid-twenties, long brown hair flowing down her back. In lieu of robes, she wore light leather and cloth armor, and a rapier was strapped to her waist. After his time spent sparring with Julia, Finn was also able to pick out a few hidden sheaths tucked away beneath her armor.

Experienced mage. Unknown affinity, he surmised. The gear indicated that the woman had points to spare and her choice of equipment was smart. Quite a few of the novices had dropped the habit of wearing robes that loudly announced their affinity.

Probably because it was stupid as hell.

"Hey there," Finn said in greeting. "Looks like we got matched. The name's Finn," he said, offering a hand.

The woman glanced down at his token to confirm their symbol matched before accepting his grip. "Kat. You ready to do this thing?"

Finn saw no hesitation in her eyes at the mention of his name. Usually, that was enough to make his opponent nervous. Instead, she simply inventoried his equipment, arching an eyebrow as she saw that Finn was still wearing the original gear that the guild had given him. He idly wondered at Kat's rank, although he made it a habit not to check the leaderboards. That information tended to be more distracting than helpful.

"Yep, let's go," Finn replied, offering his token.

Without ceremony, Kat touched her mark to his and the world soon dissolved around them as the sunlight and sand bled away into darkness.

*   *   *

The world abruptly popped back into focus, and Finn found himself standing in a dense forest. Thick tree trunks lingered around him, the trees spaced only a few yards apart. Visibility was an issue, and Finn could barely see more than a dozen or so feet in a straight line. To make matters worse, the sunlight had also been filtered out by a thick canopy of leaves far overhead, creating an artificial gloom.

Fireball may reveal my location, Finn thought to himself as he slunk against a tree, putting his back to the rough bark. The environment could be just as much of a challenge as his opponent. It was always a wildcard since the scenery changed with every duel. Not to mention that the local wildlife had made an appearance on more than one occasion. He had gotten attacked by some sort of acid-spitting snake last time.

He glanced at the AI hovering over his shoulder. The burning ball of flame created a similar problem. He quickly dismissed Daniel. The element of surprise was more important than the AI's ability to warn Finn of danger.

Moving slowly and keeping his voice low, Finn's fingers wound through the gestures to summon *Magma Armor*. The hot, protective substance soon coated his right arm. Out of an abundance of caution, he summoned a second shield along his left arm. Luckily, the faintly glowing armor didn't give off much light.

Finn held his breath – waiting.

This was always the worst part.

The beginning of a duel could be chaotic. Finn didn't know his opponent's affinity, and so he couldn't anticipate how she would attack. If he could survive the initial engagement or get the jump on her, his chances of winning climbed drastically. He had found that patience and caution were helpful virtues, although the way his fire mana hummed in his veins often made it difficult to sit still. His fingers twitched, and he had to forcefully resist the urge to summon a *Fireball*.

As the seconds ticked past, nothing happened.

Finn could only make out the occasional faint chirp among the branches overhead – no telltale crack of wood or rustle of leaves giving away his opponent's position. From experience, he expected that Kat was within 20-30 yards of his location, likely hidden behind another tree trunk and waiting for him to make the first move.

Finn chewed on his lip for a moment in thought. Under other circumstances, he might have simply stepped out from behind the tree, knowing that he could survive the first strike. It was amazing how terrible some players were at combat. He'd encountered quite a few that actually stood in place and shouted the names of their spells as they cast them. However, something about this opponent urged Finn to be more cautious.

He eyed a nearby tree, his UI flickering and changing. He had made a few improvements to his mod after his discussion with Brutus. A small translucent circle now ran along the ground, tracing his control range. He could cast about 12 feet away right now, which was usually enough to get a jump on his opponent from behind with his typical combo – assuming he managed to get close first.

This time, he had another idea.

Finn dropped the channel on his right hand, beginning to cast another spell. A moment later, a *Fireball* flared to life – except the orb hovered beside another tree, as though Finn were hidden behind the trunk.

Then he waited.

A rustle of leaves was the only warning he received before a massive bolt of lightning arced through the air, slamming against the ground beside the trunk. Tendrils of electricity speared through the air, lashing at the nearby bark and vegetation. Amid the gloom, the brilliant light left Finn momentarily blinded.

Air mage. Likely three spells, he thought as he blinked rapidly and rubbed at his eyes. *Lightning Bolt, Lightning Nova, and Blink.*

As his vision began to clear, Finn saw that the decoy tree had been charred black, but the ground and surrounding plants had absorbed most of the damage. That told him a few things. His opponent was smart. She had struck *beside* the tree, hoping to catch Finn in the arc of electricity. She was also close. Bilel's notebook had explained that it was difficult to aim a *Lightning Bolt* the farther it traveled.

He felt a surge of excitement, his mana responding to the challenge. He hadn't fought many air mages, and this person seemed competent. It was all he could do to remain standing there calmly, allowing his vision to fully recover and re-adjust to the low-light conditions.

A few seconds later, Finn peeked out from the trunk and saw Kat hovering behind a tree, her body only partially concealed by the trunk. She caught sight of him at the same time, their eyes meeting and a frown tugging at her lips.

Then there was no time for careful reflection.

Kat dashed out from behind the tree, but instead of running away, she darted directly toward Finn. Acting quickly, he began casting another *Fireball*, keeping it hovering beside him and waiting for Kat to get close.

When she was only a dozen or so feet away, Finn hurled his *Fireball*. Instead of trying to dodge, Kat's form suddenly blurred, her outline glowing with yellow energy. Then she disappeared, reappearing a few feet away from Finn. She immediately yanked her rapier free and stabbed forward in a single fluid motion.

He backpedaled and released his second spell.

The *Fireball* that Finn had formed behind Kat raced toward her. Yet she turned her head at the last second, barely catching sight of the *Fireball*. She abruptly blurred again, flashing away.

Which left Finn in the line of fire of his own spell...

He grimaced, raising his arm and feeling the wave of heat wash over him, his armor cracking slightly under the blow.

"Clever," Finn muttered to himself.

Finn didn't often encounter Kat's style of fighting. With the rapier, he knew she couldn't channel a spell. That meant she must have started casting the second *Blink* as soon as she teleported. At least, he assumed that was the case since he didn't know how she could have anticipated his second *Fireball*.

"That's a neat trick. I bet it usually works, doesn't it?" Kat taunted, now standing more than a dozen or so feet away, her sword raised, and her free hand poised to cast another spell.

She watched Finn with an appraising expression. "Although, I'm curious how you pulled it off. You would have needed to channel two spells. And why aren't you using a staff or wand?"

Finn didn't answer. His mind was racing as he tried to decide how to proceed. She was right, normally that one-two combo worked. But now that she was aware of the trick, she wasn't going to fall for it a second time. Even worse, Kat's loadout was perfect for her affinity. As an air mage, she didn't really need to channel. Her spells were typically one-off casts. It meant that she was going to be fast and dangerous. She could teleport into melee and stab him, or teleport away and blast him with *Lightning Bolts*.

At least, until she ran out of mana.

A conventional mage using a staff would likely struggle against Kat's combat style. She could pressure them from a distance, wait for them to cast, and then teleport into melee. Finn abruptly realized that there was nothing for it – he was going to have to give up his secret if he wanted to win this.

His fingers immediately began moving, summoning two *Fireballs*, the orbs floating nearby as his fingers continued to channel his mana. The *Magma Armor* along one arm was cracked but still intact, and the other hadn't been damaged yet. He could worry about repairing the shields in between casting *Fireballs*.

Kat's eyes widened in surprise as she watched Finn. "How are you—"

Finn didn't wait for her to finish. He sprinted forward, trying to close the distance between them and keep Kat inside his control range. The air mage reacted quickly, her fingers twining through a rapid-fire series of gestures as lightning began to crackle around her.

As the *Lightning Bolt* completed, Finn darted behind a nearby tree and squeezed his eyes shut. The bolt smashed into the wood on the other side but left him unharmed. Finn couldn't afford to take a direct hit. From experience, he knew that his *Magma Armor* wouldn't absorb all the damage. Some of the energy would arc around the shield, striking his chest and face.

Then Finn was moving again.

He darted out from behind the tree, throwing both *Fireballs* at the same time. One of his hands immediately began repairing his left shield, while the other remained free.

Kat saw the two bolts incoming and dodged behind a tree.

One of the *Fireballs* raced past Kat's location, but the other arced in the air as Finn channeled his mana into it, curving around the trunk. He saw a flash of yellow, and Kat appeared only a few feet away. She had blinked out from behind cover to avoid his attack.

Kat stabbed at Finn, but he raised an arm, causing the blade to skitter along the molten armor. He dropped the channel on his shield, both hands summoning another *Fireball* as he moved away from his opponent to create some space. Kat saw the new *Fireball* flare to life, and she backpedaled, glaring at him and sweat shining on her forehead as she let her mana regen.

Finn sympathized. This was rough.

Even with his faster spellcasting, he was starting to realize he had a weakness. He might be able to cast faster, but that was just enough to keep pressure on Kat. He still had a few seconds of downtime after releasing both spells where he was forced to re-cast the *Fireballs*. Kat could use this window to dart forward and attack in melee. If Finn only used one *Fireball*, then Kat could simply pepper him from a distance by staying outside his control range where it was more difficult for him to aim.

To make matters worse, neither of them were using a considerable amount of mana, and they could use the environment to block attacks. Finn expected they were relatively even in terms of attrition.

Which meant he needed to take a risk if he was going to win this fight.

His fire mana surged in his veins as sudden inspiration struck him.

Finn initiated again, running toward Kat as his *Fireballs* hovered nearby. Kat hurled another blast of lightning at him, forcing Finn behind a tree and allowing her to widen the distance between them. She clearly wanted him to commit to an attack with both of his *Fireballs* before she struck. It was just a matter of waiting for that window when he needed to recast.

Finn realized that he would need to simulate that moment if his plan was going to work.

He darted out from behind the tree, sprinting toward Kat, and launching both *Fireballs* forward. Yet his hands kept moving, constantly channeling mana into each projectile as he kept careful track of his control range.

Kat dodged behind a tree, and Finn sent one orb whizzing past her location while he arced the other – just as he had before – tracing Kat's movement. However, he'd never stopped running, and this time, he was still within range.

Kat blinked forward, and Finn automatically raised his arm, expecting the attack. The blade glanced off his shield. Yet he didn't anticipate her next move, his eyes widening as he saw lightning crackling between her fingers.

Oh shit, Finn thought, just barely raising his arms and squeezing his eyes shut.

Lightning slammed into his forearms like a truck, lances of energy stabbing around his shields and leaving a burning trail of welts along his skin. Finn didn't need to look at his UI to know his health had plummeted.

But he also wasn't dead.

And his hands had never stopped moving.

The flaming missiles curved in the air, still well within his control range. Once he had corrected their trajectory, he dropped the channel on both *Fireballs* while simultaneously lowering his arms and stepping close. As he expected, Kat had to close her eyes to avoid blinding herself. He grabbed her by her sword arm to hold her in place, and his free hand started moving again.

She looked at him in shock, and he saw her hand move, trying to cast *Blink*.

She didn't make it in time.

His two *Fireballs* struck Kat from behind, the force of the impact slamming her into his chest and interrupting her spell. She grunted in pain and tried to back away again – this time, more feebly. Yet Finn's grip was like iron and the air around them was already beginning to heat up, shimmering and rippling as tendrils of flame wrapped around his body. His spell was almost complete.

Kat was able to look at him one last time.

Her eyes were round, and he saw fear there.

Then he finished casting *Fire Nova*.

A massive blast of flame rocketed away from Finn's body. He was already holding his breath, having experienced firsthand how the fire made it difficult to breathe. He saw Kat's clothing go up in flames first; her hair ignited, and her mouth opened in a wordless scream. And then there was only fire, orange and red crackling around him in a remorseless maelstrom.

The flames soon dwindled, and Finn released his grip. Kat's charred corpse dropped to the ground with a dull thud, her limbs unmoving. Even with his mana flowing through his veins, Finn couldn't bear to look at her, his eyes shifting instead to the red notifications flashing in his peripheral vision. He only had a hundred health left, and his mana was empty. That last attack had used everything he had.

If he had missed... Or if Kat hadn't been overconfident...

He shook his head. It didn't matter. He had won.

He kept repeating that thought as his mana fled him, exhaustion soon replacing the boiling energy that surged through his veins. Finally looking at the burnt remains of his opponent, a wave of disgust hit him. He couldn't help the involuntary shudder as he saw the extent of the damage. Kat's body was barely recognizable.

The reality of his situation was also finally settling over him. He might have won – if only barely. But his secret was out now.

Chapter 27 - Focused

The door to the training room slammed shut with an ominous thump, the deadbolts sliding into place with the rattle of metal. Finn checked each of the locks, making sure that they were all intact.

The precautions were necessary with the way the attacks had continued to escalate. He had spent some time hunting through the abandoned northern wing of the guild and had eventually found an old can of grease. After a few minutes and a lot of cursing, he had finally managed to get the door working again – although the damn thing was nearly more rust than metal at this point and it let out a grating shriek every time he shouldered it closed.

Finn had been somewhat surprised that the warded room locked from the inside. However, based on Brutus' original explanation, the room had likely been used to test new magical items. In that case, Finn suspected that the locking mechanism was a safety feature designed to prevent people from accidentally walking inside during an experiment.

Either way, it was safer to lock themselves in. He didn't want to get ambushed while sparring with Julia or practicing his *Mana Mastery* and spells.

"I take it the duel didn't go well?" Julia asked, throwing back her hood and observing the sour expression on Finn's face.

"That's one way to put it," he replied, running a hand through his hair. Finn paced the room, feeling too anxious to sit still. "I had to use *Multi-Casting* in front of that air mage," Finn muttered, half to himself.

"Finally!" Julia replied. He looked at her in surprise and was rewarded with an exasperated eye roll. "Were you having fun tricking a bunch of noobs and hitting them in the back of the head with your *Fireballs*? Now that the gloves are off, we can start having some *real* fun."

Finn snorted skeptically. "That *trick* earned me a lot of points, and the duels didn't last long. It's probably going to be more challenging from here on out. You can bet that girl will tell the other players – and many of them already seem to be gunning for me."

Julia waved a hand. "We both knew that wasn't going to last forever. Plus, it was boooring. Now you'll be forced to adapt," she observed.

Finn slowed his pacing, glancing at her. He supposed she was right. Despite his complaint, a part of him did feel… well… excited. What would the new duels look like now that he could finally start using his abilities to their full extent?

"Although, it also looks like that girl did a number on you," Julia added, gesturing at Finn's singed clothing. The burns from Kat's *Lightning Bolt* had long healed, but blood still stained Finn's unmarred skin.

Finn nodded. "That last duel was a close one."

Too close, really.

As a first step, he needed to analyze that last fight to see if he could improve on his technique. Finn swiped at the air, pulling up his combat log and notifications – intending to review the data from the last battle. As he did so, a series of prompts suddenly popped into existence, cascading through the air in a nearly endless stream.

He groaned, realizing that he had disabled the notifications and built up a considerable backlog over the last few days.

x15 Level Up!
You have (75) undistributed stat points.

Stat Increases:
+5 Strength +12 Dexterity +23 Endurance

x3 Spell Rank Up: Magma Armor
Skill Level: Intermediate Level 1

Cost: 100 Mana
Effect 1: Creates a damage shield capable of absorbing 300 damage (150 damage if water/ice).
Effect 2: Damage absorption increased by INT x 25%.
Channel Effect: Repairs the shield at a rate of 50 damage/second at a mana cost of 15 mana/second.

x8 Spell Rank Up: Fireball
Skill Level: Beginner Level 9
Cost: 90 Mana
Effect: Creates a ball of flame that deals 180 + (INT x 50%) damage.
Channel Effect: Controls the Fireball within your control range at a cost of 10 mana/sec.

x1 Skill Rank Up: Learning
Skill Level: Beginner Level 10
Effect: 14% increased learning speed for skills and spells.

x1 Skill Rank Up: Mana Mastery
Skill Level: Intermediate Level 5
Effect 1: -8.0% to the mana cost of spells.
Effect 2: 3.0% faster cast rate.

x2 Skill Rank Up: Dodge
Skill Level: Beginner Level 10
Effect: 5.5% increased speed and reaction time.

x3 Skill Rank Up: Small Blades
Skill Level: Beginner Level 8
Effect: 12% increased damage and accuracy with daggers and throwing knives.

x2 Skill Rank Up: Toughness
Skill Level: Beginner Level 6
Effect: 3.5% reduced damage and increased pain tolerance.

x2 Skill Rank Up: Concentration
Skill Level: Beginner Level 8
Effect: Ability to split your focus between [2] tasks.

x3 Skill Rank Up: Multi-Casting
Skill Level: Intermediate Level 1
Effect 1: -45.0% casting speed on second spell.
Effect 2: -10% reduced channeling cost.

Finn skimmed through the notices quickly, swiping each one aside.

He noticed that he was leveling much more quickly from the duels, but his skill and stat growth had slowed considerably. Whether this was a function of diminishing returns as his skills hit intermediate or a product of more sporadic use, he couldn't be sure.

Although, he supposed it didn't matter. The bonuses from leveling his skills were typically small unless he moved from beginner to intermediate or they represented a prerequisite for something else. Not only that, but some of his skills had begun scaling with his stats, which meant levels were becoming more important. It was the only way he could easily increase *Intelligence*, for example.

His eyes skimming the notices, Finn saw that he had stat points to distribute. Although, he decided to put a pin in that for a moment. First, he needed to review that last fight and decide if he should make changes to his casting style. He was beginning to realize that strategy typically trumped raw strength within AO.

His gaze shifted back to the combat log as he mentally replayed the fight with Kat. The duel had firmly emphasized the tradeoffs between the different casting styles. It was one thing for Brutus to explain the three variants in theory, and another matter entirely to see them in practice. However, the pros and cons of each style were beginning to crystallize in his head.

A conventional mage with a staff or wand could use their weapon to block but still had a channel. This meant that they could repair a shield or hold a spell at the ready. The mage had stronger casting abilities, but still had the simultaneous use of a more limited melee weapon. Although, a mage with a staff typically had trouble casting and fighting at the same time since they needed both hands to use the weapon effectively. A wand solved this problem but made for a pretty flimsy melee weapon. That likely explained why Finn had encountered mostly conventional mages wielding staves.

Kat's casting style was different. She had forgone the channel for the use of a much faster and more agile weapon. Finn suspected that in a fight between Kat and a conventional mage, she had a few advantages. If she could bait the mage into burning his single channel, she could use the subsequent few seconds to close in melee. The mage could still use his staff or wand to block, but Kat had the advantage of speed. She also had the ability to cast easily while attacking with her rapier.

That last *Lightning Bolt* had certainly driven that point home.

However, Finn was different.

Without a weapon, he was reliant solely upon his shields and channeled spells. If he burned both channels, his only option was to dodge and run away until he managed to re-cast the spells or switch back to a style closer to Kat's by drawing his dagger. Even the secondary effect from hitting intermediate in *Multi-Casting* emphasized the strength of his casting style. It provided a reduction to his *channeling* cost.

Finn was only as strong as the spells he was able to channel.

If he continuously channeled mana into his *Magma Armor*, for example, he could be quite resilient – putting aside that he would then have no ability to attack and the armor didn't exactly guarantee his safety. The defensive spell had stopped most of Kat's *Lightning Bolt*, but a decent portion of the energy had actually arced around the molten armor. So that wasn't a surefire defense.

In contrast, the disadvantage of the *Fireballs* was that they were a one-and-done spell. Once he hit something, they were gone, and he needed to recast them. It was only because he had kept Kat within his control range that he had managed to beat her – tricking her into thinking that he needed to recast the *Fireballs*. Even so, he still had a window where Kat could have bested him. Her lightning had ignored part of his armor, and if she had gone for a dagger with her free hand instead of trying to *Blink* away, she might have killed him.

In short, Finn was strongest when he had two channeled spells active. If he could keep the channels up 100% of the time, he could remove that window of vulnerability where he needed to recast. However, both of his spells had shortcomings.

What would be my ideal spell? he asked himself, his perspective shifting.

It would be something that he could channel constantly without recasting. Ideally, it would also be able to shift between offense and defense. It was simple enough to cast his *Magma Armor* at the start of a fight. Yet if Finn could channel a spell that could bolster his defenses while dealing damage, that would be the best of both worlds.

He glanced over at Julia, distracted by the movement in his peripheral vision. She was in the process of juggling several of her throwing knives, tossing the blades into the air and neatly catching them by the tip. The feat was a testament to her high *Dexterity*. Finn was pretty sure his hands would have been cut to ribbons if he tried that trick.

He sometimes envied Julia's abilities. She could easily switch between offense and defense, relying solely on her weapons and agility. She didn't have any lag or pause in making the transition since she wasn't reliant upon whispering an incantation or wiggling her fingers. He had dueled her often enough to know that those throwing knives could also be used both to engage and inflict injury and to create pressure and build space for her to retreat.

He wished he had that sort of flexibility.

If only he could control some sort of blade like he controlled his *Fireballs*...

As that idle thought drifted through his mind, Finn went suddenly still. His mana flared in response to the idea that suddenly ignited in his mind, pulsing through his body in a fiery torrent.

"You've just been staring at me for like a solid minute," Julia observed dryly, glancing at him before turning back to her juggling act. "Also, your eyes are glowing... If you're going to kill me, could you just go ahead and get it over with?"

Finn chuckled. "I'm not sure it would be that easy," he replied.

"Damned straight. At least you're learning," Julia retorted with a grin.

Finn shook his head. "I just had a thought and need to brainstorm something for a second. You remember how Brutus said that fire magic was about controlling thermal energy?"

"Yeah, you've been hurling *Fireballs* around this room often enough to prove his point," she observed dryly. "How is that some major revelation?"

"Just bear with me. What is it about *Fireballs* that allows me to control them?" Finn asked as he paced the stone room.

"The *heat* I would imagine," Julia replied, arching an eyebrow. "You know, *thermal energy*. Seriously, are you okay? Maybe that air mage fried a few brain cells."

"I promise I'm not going senile just yet," Finn said, speaking slowly. "So, if I can control a *Fireball*, it must be because there is sufficient thermal energy. If that's the case, could I control other objects if they were hot enough?"

And there it was. The question that was boiling in his mind.

Julia paused, snatching the blades out of the air with nimble fingers. "Huh. I mean, that does make sense logically..."

That wasn't a no.

"Well, there's one way for us to test this theory," Finn murmured.

He had created the *Imbue Fire* spell a few days ago but had precious little opportunity to use it. There were very few benefits of a flaming dagger in the duels, and the minor damage increase meant that it was almost always more efficient to cast another spell.

Finn glanced over at the makeshift weapon rack that Brutus had helped them install. His sadistic instructor had insisted that he practice fighting against different weapon types. Brutus had even been generous enough to provide some old weapons – courtesy of Charlotte, most likely. They were rusted and chipped, but good enough for Finn to get a flavor of dealing with other weapon styles.

Now Finn stood and grabbed a simple longsword. With a few quick gestures, he cast *Imbue Fire* on the blade, the metal soon awash in brilliant orange flames. He then set the blade down on the stone. Julia stepped over to him, standing beside Finn and watching the weapon with interest.

Instead of simply letting the spell complete, Finn continued to channel his mana into the blade. What would the channel effect on *Imbue Fire* look like exactly? He hadn't thought to try this before, and now he was mentally kicking himself.

He poured his mana into the spell, making the same gestures he used with his *Fireballs* to direct their movement. His fingers twitched, ordering the sword to rise. For a second, he didn't observe any change.

He poured more mana into the channel, now *demanding* the sword to rise.

Finn saw the blade shift slightly, and the metal rattled against the stone floor.

"Well, it moved. Sort of," Julia observed, laughing lightly. "But you'll have to forgive me if I don't run away in fear."

"Thanks for the support," he replied in a dry voice.

Finn grimaced, dropping the spell.

He seemed to be on to something here, but that clearly hadn't worked. Maybe the sword had moved because he was increasing the intensity of the heat? That might have simply caused the rusted and ancient metal to warp slightly.

Finn pulled up the spell information now that he had unlocked the channel effect. Maybe the spell's tooltip would provide some insight.

Spell: Imbue Fire

Skill Level: Beginner Level 1
Cost: 100 Mana
Effect: Imbues a weapon with fire mana, increasing the weapon's base damage by INT x 5%. Can only be used on unenchanted metal weapons.
Channel Effect: Allows the user to direct the weapon within his control range at a cost of 20 mana/sec.

His heart skipped a beat as he saw the updated tooltip.

He had been right about being able to control the weapon if he imbued it with thermal energy. That meant the twitch had likely been the sword attempting to rise. But why hadn't he been able to raise the blade?

"The channel effect indicates that my plan should have worked," Finn said.

Julia just shrugged. "Maybe you just aren't a high enough level or something? Brutus keeps going on about your *Mana Mastery* and control range, after all." She then stooped to pick up the rusty blade, grunting slightly. "Damn this piece of junk is heavy. How does Brutus fight with these things?"

"That could be it!" Finn exclaimed.

"What are you talking about?" Julia asked in confusion.

"You saw the blade move, and the channel effect definitely indicates that this *should* work. So maybe it has to do with the weight of the weapon."

Moving quickly, Finn yanked the dagger that Julia had given him from its sheath and set it on the floor. He then went through the same steps, flames soon wrapping around the blade of the knife. He held his breath and commanded the weapon to rise, his fingers twining through the requisite gestures.

The dagger lurched and then began to drift away from the floor until it hung suspended in the air, fire curling around the metal. It wobbled slightly before stabilizing. Finn was straining to hold the blade aloft, and it responded more sluggishly than his *Fireballs* and the small orbs of flame he used to practice his *Mana Mastery*. Maybe with some practice, he could get faster.

Julia stared at the blade. "Huh?" she muttered. "I'll be damned."

Finn was already considering the possibilities. "I'm limited to using unenchanted metal right now, and the damage increase is sort of negligible. A *Fireball* can do almost 300 damage, but the dagger is doing more like 30-40."

Julia shook her head. "That doesn't matter. It's not about the damage of an individual strike. The game world is pretty realistic, so it's more about *where* you strike. Certain parts of the body like the throat and eyes can provide massive damage bonuses, and cutting major arteries can cause severe bleeding damage. You can also cripple opponents. For example, cutting the tendons in your opponent's leg can slow or incapacitate them..." She trailed off, half-talking to herself.

Then she grabbed one of her throwing knives and tossed it on the floor. "Can you do a second one?" she asked him, her eyes challenging.

Finn's brow furrowed in concentration, shifting the channel to his left hand and casting *Imbue Fire* on the throwing knife. The cast time took a bit longer, a function of having a single hand and using a journeyman spell. However, a moment later, the second blade began to rise. The metal was lighter, and it glided upwards more smoothly, the knife awash in flame.

I need to practice casting the spell more quickly, he thought to himself. He would still be vulnerable before he had the *Imbue Fire* spell in place.

A glance at the UI in the corner of his screen indicated that channeling both spells was also draining his mana fast. The double-channel was costing him 40 mana per second. Accounting for his regen, his current mana pool, and the initial casting cost, he could only sustain both blades for less than a minute. A few seconds later, his mana depleted, and both daggers fell to the floor – the clang of metal resounding through the room.

Despite the limitations of the spell, Finn felt a flush of triumph wash through him.

This was the sort of thing that could give him a solid edge. He couldn't maintain the blades for long, and his control range was limited, but he suspected that could be improved with practice. Similarly, leveling the spell would likely increase his damage. If he could increase his mana pool and regen, that would also help a lot.

This newfound ability made it easy to allocate his remaining stat points. He needed more health and more mana, regen, and damage. Finn went ahead and dumped another 30 points into *Vitality* and added the remaining 45 to his *Intelligence*. Then he pulled up his Character Status.

Character Status			
Name:	Finn	**Gender:**	Male
Level:	40	**Class:**	Fire Mage
Race:	Human	**Alignment:**	Lawful-Neutral
Fame:	1050	**Infamy:**	0
Health:	895	**H-Regen/Sec:**	3.30
Mana:	1295	**M-Regen/Sec:**	26.00
Stamina:	1125	**S-Regen/Sec:**	9.30
Strength:	47	**Dexterity:**	71
Vitality:	70	**Endurance:**	93
Intelligence:	170	**Willpower:**	30

Affinities			
Dark:	2%	**Light:**	8%
Fire:	41%	**Water:**	5%
Air:	3%	**Earth:**	10%

The extra stat points had increased his mana pool by about 200 points and reduced the net channeling cost to 12.5 mana per second, increasing the total duration to 89.6 seconds – accounting for the initial mana cost. So, he could continuously maintain the channel on two blades for over a minute right now.

"Now this is going to be fun," Julia murmured.

"Maybe with a little training," Finn replied hesitantly. "I'll need to level the spell and try to continue to increase my control range. I also need to find ways to increase my *Intelligence* further so I can improve the duration and damage." He grimaced as he realized he might need to take a brief break from dueling to get a jump start on that training. At least this was a relatively slow time of day in-game.

He looked up to find a broad smile painted on his daughter's face, an evil glint in her eye. "I don't love that look..." he murmured. "That was the same expression you had when I told you I'd let you use the car after you got your license. You remember how that went..."

"I keep telling you, that guy hit *me*. Besides, you should be thanking me. I know an easy way to help you with both of your problems," she explained, daggers appearing in either hand. "First, you're going to let me kick your ass for a bit."

Her smile widened further as she stalked toward him. "Then, we get to go shopping!"

Chapter 28 - Thrifty

"I feel like I just got hit by a truck," Finn muttered as he limped down the hallway. It was taking a while for his natural health regeneration to heal his injuries.

"Oh, hush, you big baby," Julia retorted, a smile flashing beneath her hood. "I only stabbed you a few times. It was actually kind of cathartic for me..."

Finn glared at her. A "few times" had been more like two hours straight, with Julia only allowing him brief pauses to recover his waning health and mana. Although, he had to grudgingly admit that training against her was useful. Julia was deadly fast, and she struck with pinpoint precision, requiring him to use *Imbue Fire* with remarkable accuracy in order to block her attacks.

The real mystery was how Julia had gotten so damn fast. She had been circumspect about revealing her class and level, which left Finn to wonder what she had gone through during the beta. Had she started in Lahab? Traveled there? How had she learned *Sneak* or to fight like some sort of ninja? Every time he asked, he had just been met with another hail of knives. Eventually, he had wisened up and learned to keep his mouth shut.

Either way, Finn felt like he had improved during their sparring session. By the end, he had even managed to nick Julia once or twice. Finn glanced at his system UI, reviewing his notifications.

> **x6 Spell Rank Up: Imbue Fire**
> **Skill Level:** Beginner Level 7
> **Cost:** 130 Mana
> **Effect:** Imbues a weapon with fire mana, increasing the weapon's base damage by INT x 8%. Can only be used on unenchanted metal weapons.
> **Channel Effect:** Allows user to control the weapon within his control range at a cost of 23 mana/sec.

Leveling *Imbue Fire* was responsible for most of his

progress.

It had become much easier to control the blades as he ranked the spell. The knives still weren't as agile as his *Fireballs* or the orbs he summoned to practice *Mana Mastery*, but they were fast enough to be dangerous. Finn was not only capable of blocking attacks and striking at Julia with his blades, but he had also begun weaving in his own unarmed melee attacks and leaning on his *Magma Armor* to occasionally block a strike in order to open Julia up for an attack.

The downside was that the channeling cost of *Imbue Fire* increased with each level, lowering the already-short duration. If he only channeled one blade, his mana regenerated at a measly 4 mana per second, which meant it was hard to refill his mana pool if he kept a dagger up. However, this at least allowed him to slow the mana drain.

By the end of their training session, Julia had become much more wary of Finn – which was really the highest compliment she could have paid him.

The requisition hall soon came into view, mages streaming in and out of the room. Novices filled the outer hallway, making it difficult to navigate the crowd without accidentally bumping into someone. Julia spared Finn a wary expression, pulling her hood down and making certain that her arms were concealed by her robe.

"Geez," Julia muttered. "Why is this place so crowded?"

"It seems we're not the only people looking to purchase some gear," Finn replied quietly. It seemed that business was booming for Charlotte with the ongoing competition.

It took a few minutes for the pair to manage to wind their way inside the requisition hall. As soon as Finn stepped across the threshold, an assistant popped up in front of him. In contrast to his previous encounter with Charlotte's staff, the man looked harried, and deep circles hung under his eyes, as though he hadn't slept in days.

"Hello-and-welcome-to-the-requisition-hall. How-the-hell-can-I-help-you?" He asked in rapid-fire sequence. Finn cocked his head, noting that something seemed off, the man glaring at them. It seemed like staff morale might have dropped off.

"Novice fire mage. We need small bladed weapons, cloth or leather armor, and some rings and amulets," Julia explained, unperturbed by the aide's tone and listing the items on her fingers.

"Aisles-A1-F5-and-K4. I-hope-you-die-in-a-fire," the aide snapped, and then he promptly turned to the next mage that had walked through the door, not offering to lead them to their destination.

"Great customer service they have here," Julia commented dryly. "Anyway, let's go find you some shiny new gear!" She set off with a singular goal in mind and headed toward the aisles in search of loot. Even the other novices seemed to pick up on Julia's focus, moving out of her way as she stalked through the rows of equipment.

Finn just eyed Julia skeptically before following her, marveling that this was possibly one of the strangest experiences of his life – his daughter helping him shop for magical equipment in a video game.

That thought was short-lived as Julia began handing Finn an assortment of gear. Their first stop was a set of weapon racks. Julia immediately homed in on the more mundane knives and daggers, dismissing anything that had a magical glow. With the restrictions of *Imbue Fire*, Finn was limited to unenchanted weapons.

She had soon reduced the choices down to two options. One was a larger pair of daggers that were a bit longer than Finn's forearm. They were more like smallish short swords than small blades – at least to Finn's eye. The other option was a pair of more modest knives with an 8-inch blade. The knives were a bit larger than Julia's throwing knives but were smaller than the loaner dagger she had given him.

"Slower, but more damage and easier to block," Julia observed, holding up the daggers. "Or lower damage, but faster and more agile," she added, gesturing at the knives. "Which do you want?"

Finn chewed on his lip for a second before pointing at

the smaller knives. Right now, speed and control were more important than damage. Maybe at some point he could control flaming swords or the like, but he definitely wasn't there yet.

Julia promptly tossed him the knives with a casual indifference for the people around them and set off in search of more gear. Finn stumbled forward, grumbling under his breath and snatching the blades out of the air before they could hit other people.

He inspected the knives as he trudged after Julia.

Masterwork Dueling Knife
A solidly crafted, although mundane blade. This knife is designed for up-close-and-personal combat and is precisely balanced, allowing the blade to be tossed in a pinch.
Quality: D
Damage: 15-21 (Pierce)
Durability: 45/45

Imbue Fire added about 15 damage with his current *Intelligence*, which put the damage closer to the 30-46 range – not accounting for strikes against critical areas, of course. That was respectable. Finn idly considered that the spell basically converted *Intelligence* to damage instead of raw *Strength*.

When Finn looked up again, he found that Julia had led them to a row of armor. She immediately dismissed anything with chain or metal reinforcements, her gaze focusing on light leather and cloth. Of the cloth options, Julia also cut out anything with flowing fabric, opting instead for a tighter fit. He suspected she was prioritizing speed and agility over defense.

His daughter grimaced. "This is tough," she murmured to herself, holding up some equipment as she inspected it. "The leather has a higher defense, and it'll hold up better when you're taking damage, but the stats are mostly *Dexterity* and *Endurance*."

Julia pointed at some nearby robes, glancing at Finn. "The cloth is more caster-friendly. Most comes with high

Intelligence and *Willpower* stats. Although, it won't really offer any protection and most look like mystical ballgowns," she grumbled.

"Take this one, for example. Who the hell designed this? Seriously, this thing is a deathtrap for idiots," Julia added, holding up a wrapped garment with multiple flowing layers. It was made entirely of a thick velvet material, and Finn saw filigreed gold embroidery along the hems. "What is this supposed to be for? Are we going into battle or to a prince's ball?" She looked around in confusion. "Maybe it comes with some crystal slippers or something?"

Another nearby novice had just picked out a similar robe, feeling the fabric. At Julia's comment, he looked at her with a mixture of surprise and anger. She caught the player staring. "Oh, I didn't mean it looks stupid and impractical on *you*." Julia gave him a thumbs up. "Great purchase."

She leaned close to Finn, whispering a bit too loudly. "Terrible choice. He's going to die in that ballgown, but at least he'll leave a fabulous-looking corpse." The player let out a huff and stormed off.

"Is there anything in here that wasn't designed by Versace?" Julia called out, yelling at one of the nearby aides and stalking toward the harried-looking man. When he saw Julia approaching and the determination in her eyes, he looked like he wanted to run.

Meanwhile, Finn took a cautious step away from Julia, noticing the way the other players – particularly the *male* players – were now glaring at her. Apparently, they didn't love her pointing out that they were basically wearing a dress.

Even if there was some truth to that…

Finn picked his way down the aisle to put some distance between himself and Julia, occasionally picking up or inspecting a piece of armor. Despite her lack of etiquette, Finn quickly realized that Julia was right. The leather wasn't a great fit if Finn was prioritizing mana and mana regeneration. And most of the robes were sort of impractical. His sparring matches with Julia and the duels had emphasized the importance of speed and flexibility. That was also one of the primary advantages of his *Multi-Casting* compared to the other weapon styles.

As Finn approached the end of the aisle, he noticed a set of robes tucked away on the far end of a rack, partially obscured by the nearby clothing. He held them up to inspect them. Instead of thick flowing fabric and velvet, they were made of more practical and sturdy cloth. The robes were also designed to bind more tightly around limbs, limiting the amount of flowing fabric or the risk of the fabric getting caught on something. The color choice was also neutral, emphasizing brown and gray. Finn was okay with that. He didn't love the idea of broadcasting his affinity or accidentally revealing his location with gaudy colors.

He ran his fingers down a sleeve, noticing that it stretched up and across the wrist, partially obscuring his fingers. *This would also help conceal the Seer's tattoo and my spellcasting*, he thought to himself.

Now the only question was whether it gave him the stats he needed.

Battle Monk Robes (Full Set)
These robes were designed by a sect of caster monks who specialized in the art of combining magic and unarmed fighting. As a result, the robes are designed with practicality in mind and have been enchanted to enhance both a caster's mystical abilities as well as their innate speed and balance.
Quality: C
Defense: 35
Durability: 75/75
+30 Intelligence
+15 Dexterity

"I like it," Julia suddenly declared, glancing over Finn's shoulder. "Good pick."

Before he had a chance to respond, Julia had already paced off down the aisle, players scurrying to get out of her way. "Now we can go look at jewelry!" she called over her shoulder.

Finn sighed, draping the robes over his arm and

chasing after her.

Mercifully, choosing rings and an amulet proved to be rather straightforward. Julia picked rather mundane jewelry, opting for plain steel bands and muted gemstones over the flashier merchandise. She seemed to be of a similar mind as Finn. It was better to wear equipment that didn't glimmer or reflect light. With the game's heightened realism, there was no sense in accidentally revealing his location with ostentatious jewelry.

A quick inspection revealed the following stats.

Novice Ring x2
A simple ring designed for a fledgling caster. The metal has been enhanced to improve the caster's Intelligence.
Quality: C
+5 Intelligence

Novice Amulet
A simple amulet designed for a fledgling caster. The metal has been enhanced to improve the caster's Intelligence.
Quality: C
+10 Intelligence

They were a simple and practical choice.

"Okay, time to go pay for everything," Julia said, adding the jewelry to the pile and tugging at Finn's sleeve. She led him over to Charlotte's counter and put them in line with the other players.

Finn noticed that the other mages eyed them curiously, although he didn't understand why they were drawing attention. They were just shopping. Maybe it was because of Julia's rather boisterous behavior earlier?

Shaking his head, Finn decided to focus on his new equipment, doing some quick mental calculations. With the additional *Intelligence* from the armor and jewelry, he would be able to increase his *Intelligence* by 50 points. After the increase to his mana pool and regen and accounting for the initial casting cost of *Imbue Fire*, that would allow him to channel both daggers for nearly two minutes straight.

I can work with that, he thought. Presumably, he could purchase more powerful equipment once he rose in rank, allowing him to channel his spells for even longer.

"Hello, what are you purchasing?" Charlotte muttered in a bored voice as they finally approached the counter.

"All of this," Julia offered, grabbing the merchandise from Finn and dumping it on the countertop.

Charlotte's eyes snapped to the large pile of equipment; her brow furrowed in surprise. It was at this point that Finn suddenly realized that the other players in line were usually purchasing a single item – like a weapon or ring. None of them were carrying an entire ensemble, which possibly explained some of the weird looks they were getting.

Charlotte's gaze shifted to Julia and then to Finn, a glimmer of recognition in her eyes. "You're Brutus' sponsored, aren't you?" she asked.

"Yeah," Finn replied. "You helped me purchase some novice spellbooks a few days ago."

"It seems that you're moving up in the world," she observed, gesturing at the pile of equipment. "I assume you have the points to pay for all of this?"

A token appeared in Julia's hand, and she offered it to Charlotte. "He should have more than enough," she explained.

Finn glanced at the token in confusion. He patted at his pocket and bag, suddenly realizing that his stone chit was missing. When had Julia stolen it?

Charlotte just arched an eyebrow. "I suppose we'll see." She snatched at the stone chit and ran it across a pedestal beside her counter, looking at a display that Finn couldn't see. "Finn. Fire mage novice. Current point total... 2,030," she reported, shock evident in her voice.

She glanced at Finn, looking him over from head to toe and focusing on his starting equipment. "What rank are you?" Charlotte asked bluntly.

"He's currently number four among the novices," Julia reported.

This was met with a few hushed gasps behind Finn, the other mages in line murmuring amongst themselves. For some reason, he kept hearing them use the phrase "A-lister," although he wasn't sure what that meant. Finn also thought he caught the word "cheater" used a couple times and he frowned. Well, let them think that. It would make his life easier if the other mages continued to underestimate him.

"So how much does he owe you?" Julia demanded.

Charlotte glanced at the equipment, inventorying the items. "930 points should do it," she said finally.

Holy crap, this is expensive. That was 93 wins right there! The stat bonuses were nice, but he could probably live without them. Finn was about to suggest they put the equipment back, but Julia beat him to it.

"No problem," she said. "Go ahead and charge it."

Time seemed to slow for a second as Finn saw Charlotte's eyes gleam and her hand swipe through the air, running his token across the column. He could feel a pit form in his stomach. In just a few fleeting seconds, Julia had spent the better part of a day's worth of work. And for what? A few low-quality items?

A moment later, Julia was ushering him off to the side and shoving the equipment into his listless hands. "93 wins," Finn murmured to himself – still in shock.

How many ranks had that dropped him?

"Snap out of it," Julia barked, forcing him to focus on her.

"You have to spend money to make money. You need the stat bonuses, and the added defense will help a lot," she explained. "You were already starting to struggle against people like that air mage, and you can bet your ass they aren't skimping on their equipment."

"How many spots did that drop me, though?" Finn asked, still reeling from the cost.

"At a guess, I'd say you're in sixth or seventh place – based on the last rankings I saw anyway," Julia observed, her tone unapologetic. "But just like you, the other A-listers are going to have to purchase their own equipment, assuming they haven't already. No one is going to get away with dueling in rags as we approach the finish line. So that should even out over time."

"A-listers?" Finn asked in confusion.

Julia just stared at him. "Seriously, I'm with Kyyle here. How can you be so observant and yet so oblivious at the same time?" She sighed as she saw him shrug. "That's what the other novices have started calling the top-ranked students."

She shook her head. "But none of that stuff matters." She dropped her voice to a whisper, "You now have at least two minutes' uptime on your knives." She noticed his expression. "Yes, I can do math too, and I was paying attention earlier. That's a looooong time in a duel, and it will only improve as you continue to level.

"Right now, all you need to think about is the duels," she added. "Your new ability is going to take this homicidal mage prison by storm. No one here is going to be running a similar setup."

An excited smile stretched across Julia's face, and she held up Finn's token. He could see that the surface glowed – indicating that he had been summoned to a duel. "They're never going to know what hit them."

Something in Finn responded to his daughter's excitement. She was right. He knew he needed to update and overhaul his fighting style if he was going to be competitive for the remainder of the duels. Which meant updating his equipment too, even if it cost him a small fortune in points. That's why he had started down this path in the first place. Instead of focusing on how much progress he had lost, he should be thinking about making up for lost time.

His eyes centered on the glowing token. He was also curious to see how his new abilities would perform in a real fight. Finn could feel his mana respond to both the excitement shining in Julia's eyes and the sudden adrenaline spike that typically accompanied a duel. The warm energy seeped into his bones, and that familiar sense of boundless enthusiasm pushed aside his anxiety.

Finn snatched the token from Julia.

"That's the look I was waiting for," she said, observing

the flames that now danced in Finn's eyes. "Now, let's get out of here and go kill some people."

Chapter 29 - Subtle

After purchasing the gear, Finn darted into the changing room in the requisition's hall, quickly donning his new attire while Julia tapped her foot impatiently outside the stall. Afterward, he discovered that leaving the requisition hall proved just as difficult as it had to get inside, students crowding the tight space.

By the time they had made it out of the room, Finn had already burned several precious minutes, and he didn't have much time to reach the dais. As they hit the hallway, he and Julia broke into a light jog, aiming for the guild's central courtyard.

Julia glanced at the corner of her UI before turning to Finn. "We're going to have to pass through the abandoned section if we're going to make it in time," she huffed.

Finn grimaced. He knew she was right, but that also increased the odds of them getting ambushed. The players had grown more daring and had even begun attacking novices at random. A death was costly, even if the player hadn't been summoned to a duel yet. Frankly, he was surprised that the faculty hadn't caught wind of what was happening. Or perhaps they simply didn't care.

On the other hand, after spending a small fortune on his gear, Finn couldn't afford to lose any more points by missing this duel.

"Fine," Finn grunted. "Let's just be careful."

At the same time, he summoned Daniel, the elemental flashing into existence beside him and easily keeping pace. "Scout ahead," Finn ordered.

"As you wish," the AI replied in a slightly sullen voice, grumbling to himself as the AI's fiery form darted forward and illuminated the dark hallways. Finn swore he heard Daniel complaining – something about not even managing a "hello."

He suppressed a grimace. Daniel's mood swings were a problem for another time.

Shifting course, they took the next branching hallway.

Polished and well-swept stone soon gave way to dreary, half-forgotten halls filled with dust and cobwebs. Finn and Julia slowed slightly, changing their pace so that their footsteps landed more softly against the stone floor.

Seconds ticked past, Finn eyeing the shadows and adjoining hallways cautiously, anxious for a surprise attack. They had almost cleared the abandoned section when they heard a familiar alarm.

"Danger. Two players ahead," Daniel shouted, his voice echoing through the hallway. A moment later, the AI's light winked out. Finn suspected that Daniel had been destroyed – which just mean that Finn would need to wait an hour to re-summon him.

"Damn it," he muttered. With a quick swipe of his wrist, he pulled up his map. This hallway had no branching paths. It was either push forward or circle back. He glanced at his clock. They didn't have time to backtrack.

Finn's and Julia's eyes met. They wordlessly communicated the same message. They were going to have to fight this one out – and quickly.

Julia immediately dropped into *Sneak*, sliding back into the shadows, and disappearing from sight. Meanwhile, Finn bit at the inside of his cheek, his mind racing as he tried to decide how to handle this. Julia would focus on scouting the nearby area, ensuring that there were no witnesses. They had long ago decided that this was safer. They didn't need any players claiming there was a thief in the guild hall.

Which meant that Finn would need to handle the two players himself. To make matters worse, he didn't have much time. Maybe another 30 seconds before the players were on him - at least judging from Daniel's last location. As he eyed the hallway, an idea came to him.

He pulled his new daggers and carefully placed a blade on each side of the hall before backtracking slightly to give himself some additional room. With his enhanced HUD active, he made sure to keep the hidden blades within the translucent circular arc that now denoted his control range.

Then he waited.

Less than a minute later, two men sauntered down the

hallway. They must have known this hall had no connecting paths, and there was no easy way for their quarry to escape. The obvious deduction was that this was a regular ambush location for them. They each carried a staff and wore the gaudy style of robes that Julia had just been making fun of only a few minutes earlier. That indicated that the pair had some points to spare but were relatively inexperienced.

Amateurs then, Finn thought to himself.

"Well, well, well, what do we have here?" one of the players taunted. "Why are you wandering these vacant halls? Don't you know it's dangerous?"

Finn stayed silent.

The other player chuckled. "He looks confused," the other player taunted. "Maybe we surprised him."

"Or maybe he's just stupid. Where's your friend?" the first mage asked, some of the humor bleeding from his tone.

Finn's brow furrowed. How did they know about Julia? The answer came to him quickly. They must have hidden a scout further back, and he was relaying information using the in-game chat. Finn's estimation of the two players rose slightly. That was clever.

Hopefully, Julia would be able to address that problem.

"The silent act is getting a little old," the first player said, taking a menacing step forward. "Where did the other mage go?"

"Perhaps she ran away after their pet shouted an alarm?" the other player offered. "No matter, I doubt she'll get far. Keep this one busy while I tell the other group."

The first mage nodded, his hand moving as he cast an *Ice Bolt*, the frigid shard forming in the air beside him. The other mage then swiped at the air, presumably to pull up his chat window. Finn immediately connected the dots. This was a habitual ambush spot for these novices. Their scout stayed hidden and relayed information to the two mages ahead. Then the group used a pincer-strategy, trapping unwary mages in the hallway by striking from the front and back simultaneously.

Which meant Finn needed to act quickly.

Finn bowed his head, using his hood to keep his eyes concealed as he summoned his mana. He also folded his arms and his fingers began to twine slowly through a series of gestures, the movements concealed by his robes.

He murmured the incantation softly, keeping his lips as still as possible. He had developed this little trick after training with Julia. His daughter was just a bit too observant. While she couldn't understand the words, she had trained with him often enough that she could recognize the spell he was casting by the sounds. He had been forced to adapt.

As he neared the end of the spell, Finn realized he needed a brief distraction.

He addressed the two players, "You have no need to worry. My friend didn't run away," he said calmly.

They were now focused on him. One snorted. "Well, she's not here. Face it. She bailed on you."

As Finn saw the telltale flicker of orange flames rising behind the two mages, he shook his head, feigning sadness. "Ahh, I see the confusion. Let me clarify. She did leave – you're right about that – but she isn't running away."

He looked back up, his eyes now glowing a vibrant orange. "She's just making sure there are no witnesses."

The players' eyes widened, and the water mage moved to release his spell.

He was too slow.

Finn's twin blades launched forward, the burning metal simultaneously stabbing through the back of each player's neck. The tips of Finn's daggers emerged from the front of their throats, crimson blood bubbling around the wounds. At the same time, Finn stepped to the side. The water mage released his spell reflexively, the shard of ice flying past Finn and smashing into the nearby stone wall.

Then he stood calmly before the two players, his eyes glowing orange and the warmth of his mana thrumming in his veins. Their throats were impaled by his daggers, and he imagined the feeling was excruciating – simultaneously unable to breathe and the fire burning through their vocal cords.

They let out a faint gurgle, clutching at their throats in

vain, and their eyes bulged. Finn took pity on them. With a jerk of his fingers, the blades retreated, leaving gaping holes in their wake. Blood fountained from the wounds. Between the critical damage and the blood loss, their health drained at a frightening rate, both mages dropping to their knees.

Finn moved forward with unhurried steps, dismissing his *Imbue Fire*.

He watched impassively as the life fled their eyes, staying silent. If they looked back on this footage, Finn didn't want to give away any hint of who he was or how he had killed them. A moment later, both bodies lay still, cooling upon the stone floor.

"Oh, damn," Julia said from behind him, looking at the corpses.

Finn whirled, a tantalizing mixture of adrenaline and fire mana still surging through his veins. "Hey, it's just me," Julia replied, raising her hands. "We're good, and you can drop your mana."

That was easier said than done. Finn had to force himself to push aside the fiery energy, reluctant to look at what he had done without the cauterizing effect of the mana. After a moment of struggle, he managed to release the energy, his body feeling weaker and more lethargic as the mana fled his limbs.

When Finn looked back at the bodies on the floor, he felt his stomach writhe. Thick soupy blood pooled beneath each player. Yet their throats were worse. The flames had partially cauterized the wounds, leaving a charred, ruined mess of flesh and blood, their vacant eyes staring at him accusingly.

I did this? he thought to himself.

Under the effects of his fire mana, the horror of combat was burned away. Even in the duels, he usually didn't give himself time to linger or look at the bodies, choosing instead to simply grab the player's token and return to the guild hall. However, he couldn't avoid the sober reality of what he had done here.

He had brutally murdered these two people.

And he hadn't even given it a second thought.

Finn shook his head, tearing his eyes from the corpses and trying to clear his dark thoughts. "You okay?" Julia asked, concern tinging her voice.

"Yeah... I'm fine," Finn replied. "They mentioned scouts?"

"Already took care of them. It seems this group had a higher-ranked mage helping them. They set up a little scouting position and concealed it with an illusion. They dropped it once these two gave the signal. Never saw me coming," she added with a chuckle.

Finn just nodded, retrieving his new knives and wiping the metal off on the robes of the dead mages. He steadfastly refused to look at their wounds.

"Are you sure you're okay?" Julia asked again.

"Yeah, it's just harder to stomach when I'm not summoning the mana," Finn said softly. Although, that was only part of the truth. Finn didn't want to acknowledge the real problem. That panicked look in their eyes reminded him of his nightmares – of Rachael, a hand outstretched toward him.

"You don't have much time left," Julia said softly, waving at the glowing stone chit in Finn's pocket.

He grunted in response, rising to his feet and sheathing his blades. "What about the bodies?"

"Don't worry about it," she replied with a grimace. "I'll clean up this mess. Probably move the corpses into a nearby room and then clean up most of the blood."

She rested a gentle hand on his shoulder. "It's alright," she offered. "These assholes had it coming to them. They would have done worse to us. Besides, it's not like it's real."

She might be right, but it sure *looked* and *felt* real. Finn wondered if he had become so focused on winning – on beating the next opponent or learning the next spell – that he had lost track of why he was doing this in the first place. That intense drive and singular focus were familiar. Yet the last time he had given himself over to his passion, it hadn't ended well – which was probably the understatement of the century.

Are you repeating the same mistake here? a nagging voice whispered in the back of his mind. The problem was that he wasn't sure how to answer that.

Finn shrugged off Julia's hand. "It's fine. But you're right, I don't have much time left. I need to go take care of this duel. I'll see you in a bit." With that, he took off down the hallway at a run.

Julia's eyes followed Finn's back. The humor had fled, and she stared after him, her expression a chaotic mixture of emotion. There was pain there. And sorrow. For only a moment, she was just a girl, standing beside a pair of fresh corpses, watching as her father walked away.

Then she shook it off, the hardness returning to her eyes as they focused once again on the bodies. The blood had pooled and left a giant mess, and she was already imagining what a pain in the ass it was going to be to drag the bodies into a nearby room. Especially if she wanted to avoid getting blood all over herself.

"Damn it," Julia muttered.

Chapter 30 - Infamous

Finn breathed in, letting the warmth of his mana pool in his chest until the pressure built and expanded, threatening to overflow.

He exhaled, and his fingers danced.

Mana flowed out of Finn's body in an excited rush, as though anxious to be set free. He channeled the energy into the orbs of flame that whirled through the air of the courtyard in a complicated pattern. Even with his eyes closed, he could visualize the concentric rings. He sent the spheres spinning outward until they hit the edge of his control range before the pattern inverted and they were sent spiraling back toward Finn.

"Uh, what exactly are you doing?" a voice asked.

Finn's eyes snapped open, and he saw that Kyyle loomed over him where he sat cross-legged on the dais in the center of the guild's courtyard. The young man's gaze jumped between Finn and the four orbs that were floating above the platform. Meanwhile, the other novices hovering near the dueling columns had given Finn a wide berth, shooting him the occasional odd glance.

"Practicing," Finn replied with a shrug.

The rhythm was effective for training his *Mana Mastery*. Finn had been able to slowly increase his control range by repeating the same cycle over and over. He could now use his abilities within fifteen feet, his mod updating automatically to reflect his enhanced range.

"I think he means *showing off*," Julia snorted from beside him. She lounged on the stone, looking bored. She had rarely left his side since the attacks had escalated, only taking the occasional break to return to the real world.

"It seems like you're making people nervous," Kyyle observed, gesturing at the other novices that littered the dais. Despite the crowd, no one dared approach Finn and Julia. "What did you all do?"

Finn grimaced, trying to decide how best to frame his response. It was more about what Finn *hadn't* done.

Specifically, he hadn't let the other novices kill him.

The attacks had escalated drastically over the last few days in-game. The encounter in the hallway had just been the first skirmish of many. At this point, he was getting attacked almost every time he left a public area, regardless of whether he had been summoned to a duel. The attacks also seemed to be targeting him now, as though there were groups of students stalking his every movement. Maybe the other novices were trying to slow him down.

At the same time, their attackers had gotten smarter and more tenacious. It was no longer easy for Finn and Julia to avoid the encounters. Which often left only one option for dealing with the attacks – as well as quite a few corpses. Not that Finn was going to openly admit that to Kyyle, of course.

As a result, it was now far too risky and time-consuming to return to their training room, especially if they needed to be discreet about dispatching their attackers. That delay cut into Finn's points. So, he and Julia had taken to camping in the courtyard. Although, this unsettled the other mages for a different reason...

"Haven't you heard?" Julia drawled when Finn didn't respond immediately. "Finn here is a no-good cheat. That's how he's managed his current rank."

She heard a nearby player let out an irritated grunt of agreement, and a grin tugged at Julia's lips. She met the player's eyes. "Although, I'm sure Finn would be more than happy to *prove* his abilities if anyone doubts them," she declared loudly. "Any takers?" The player choked back a response and stepped away slowly.

"I thought so," she muttered with a smirk.

Finn let out a sigh. While her posturing was amusing, Julia was right. His newfound abilities were not well received. Claims that he was "cheating" had only gotten worse after he had begun using his daggers in the duels – with most of his opponents dying from unseen – or rather, *unnoticed* attacks. He was sure this had probably helped instigate the frequent attempts on his life.

"It's just a madhouse," Finn acknowledged. "We get attacked every time we leave this damn podium now, but no one here wants to acknowledge that the novices are attacking each other." Finn met Kyyle's eyes. "Frankly, I'm surprised that you haven't experienced this problem. Julia said you're in fifth right now."

Kyyle rubbed at his neck. "I've been sticking to public areas. Plus, *Dissolve* is pretty helpful, and I've discovered that the hallways aren't completely warded. I can usually box my attackers into a section of the hallway and take a detour."

Finn nodded. *Not a bad plan.*

He noticed Zane enter the courtyard, surrounded by a group of other novices. The large man had managed to hold on to his number two position for a few days now, and he walked everywhere with an entourage of at least five other mages. Finn also knew that Vanessa was currently in first and had apparently made friends with a few higher-ranked mages. She rarely left their side. In a nutshell, the other top-ranked novices seemed to be experiencing some of the same issues – although, perhaps not as keenly as Finn.

Kyyle followed Finn's gaze, observing Zane and the massive two-handed hammer that he lugged around now. The burly man nodded in their direction. Finn returned the gesture, wondering what it would be like to fight him. Zane's gang had likely helped him maintain his position, but he was still winning the duels by himself.

Kyyle edged closer to Finn, lowering his voice. "Putting aside the attacks for a second, have you noticed that the top-ranked players haven't been matched together?"

Finn hesitated before nodding slowly. "I have, although I thought maybe it was just me."

Kyyle shook his head. "I've been keeping careful track of my own matches, and I spoke with a few of the other A-listers. None of them have faced each other yet."

"It could just be a coincidence."

"And if it's not?" Kyyle replied.

"Are you suggesting that the matches aren't random?" Finn asked.

The younger man shrugged. "I'm just saying that it seems odd and my data is showing an unusual pattern. And then there are these attacks... Does it seem reasonable that the faculty really doesn't know what's going on?"

Finn's brow furrowed. Kyyle raised some interesting points. The implications were also... troubling. What could be the purpose of allowing the in-fighting among the students or actively manipulating the matchmaking? Was someone trying to affect the outcome of the champion selection? Finn supposed that made sense. The residents of this world would have a large stake in that outcome, including the faculty.

But what did they hope to gain?

And, perhaps more importantly, who were they backing as their top pick?

Kyyle gave Finn a knowing look, and he realized that the young man must have reached a similar conclusion. Perhaps there was a deeper game being played here than they realized.

"I don't—" Finn stopped abruptly as Julia's hand landed on his shoulder. She motioned across the courtyard, where Finn saw Brutus approaching with a number of guards armed with wickedly curved swords. The fire mage met Finn's eyes, his expression grim.

Ahh, shit. This doesn't look good, Finn thought to himself.

"I think this is your opportunity to get the hell out of here," Finn murmured to Kyyle. "I have a sneaking feeling Brutus is here for me." Kyyle grimaced but quickly retreated.

Finn spared a glance at Julia. "You too. Get going." Finn didn't need to explain his concerns aloud. Julia might be able to trick the other students, but she was here illicitly – a fact that could be determined by a quick inspection of her arms and a test of her affinity. The last thing they wanted was the faculty to discover that Finn was aiding and abetting a thief.

"I'll keep an eye on you," Julia whispered. Finn just nodded, and his daughter swiftly disappeared into the crowd, likely dropping into *Sneak*.

Finn sat there calmly as he watched Brutus and the other mages approach, the group making a beeline for his position. The crowd around the dais had now caught sight of the group and its target, and the circle around Finn had widened.

"Finn," Brutus grunted as he neared.

"Brutus," Finn replied calmly. No sense giving anything away until he discovered what this was about. Perhaps some students had claimed that he had attacked them?

"I'm going to need to ask you to come with me," the fire mage master said, his voice loud enough to carry across the courtyard. They now had quite the audience, dozens of students watching the exchange.

"Can I ask why?" Finn replied.

"Several of the students have reported that you are cheating in the duels. They also claim that you refuse to leave the dais – using this as a way to intimidate other novices into not entering the competition." Brutus' severe expression cracked for a moment at this last statement, shaking his head incredulously. He didn't even seem to believe what he was saying.

Not that Finn blamed him. That sounded absurd. Although, he noted that many of the players around him nodded in agreement with Brutus' declaration.

Ahh, the joys of being in the public eye, Finn thought dryly.

He moved to rise to his feet, and the other mages and guards around Brutus shuffled nervously. It seemed Finn's reputation had spread to the faculty and staff. Finn might not be topping the leaderboard, but he supposed the mystery surrounding his wins lent him a certain murderous charm.

"Well, let's go talk to the faculty then," Finn declared, keeping his expression neutral and his limbs relaxed. If this was a show, he might as well put on a performance.

He saw a glint of respect in Brutus' eyes as he gestured for Finn to lead the way. The guards soon encircled Finn, keeping a watchful eye on him as they exited the courtyard. The eyes of the other students followed them, and an excited buzz filled the air of the courtyard.

This certainly isn't going to help my reputation, Finn thought.

Despite his stoic façade and internal attempt to stay

calm, Finn's stomach was a roiling mass of nerves. He wasn't sure what he was about to walk into. Was he about to lose all the progress he had made? Have his mana purged? Get exiled? Would they try to pin the attacks on him? The questions boiled in his mind, and he had to tamp down on the urge to summon his mana.

The image of those first attackers came to him then, ragged holes carved in their throats and their thick soupy blood staining the dusty stone floor. The memory was accompanied by the same misgivings he had experienced a few days earlier. A doubting voice in the back of his head whispered to him, this time posing a new and different question.

Would it really be such a bad thing if the faculty stopped him here?

Chapter 31 - Cheater

Finn soon stood in a large circular chamber deep within the bowels of the Mage Guild. After depositing Finn in the center of the room, Brutus had taken a seat with the other staff. The guild's faculty were arrayed around him, sitting behind a wooden bench that ringed the room except for a small sliver near the doorway.

Abbad hovered against a far wall, although he hadn't acknowledged Finn when he entered. His face was a perfect mask. It appeared that the librarian was undeserving of a seat with the other faculty.

Meanwhile, the mages' eyes followed Finn, weighing and judging even before a word had been spoken. The silence in the air was tense and heavy.

For his part, Finn stood still, forcing his muscles to relax and to keep his posture loose and unconcerned. He had done enough public speaking to know a few tricks. Although, he could honestly say that he had never participated in some sort of magical trial and his life wasn't usually hanging in the balance during a tech conference or seminar.

Finn's eyes slid to the room's single exit, guards hovering near the doorway. He hadn't missed the fact that everyone had been disarmed upon entering the chamber – both himself and the faculty.

If it came to a fight, he might have a slight edge with his *Multi-Casting*. Although the prospect of fighting multiple master mages seemed futile.

In the center of this scene sat Nefreet, tattoos curling around the base of his neck and the headmaster's sharp eyes drilling into Finn, as though trying to uncover his secrets. Despite the combined gaze of the faculty, Finn could only focus on Nefreet. He had almost forgotten the headmaster's cold, impassive gaze and the measured precision with which he moved and spoke, as though every action was carefully planned, weighed, and considered.

"Hello, Finn," Nefreet greeted, his voice almost cordial. The rest of the faculty remained silent, merely observing. Finn could make out every cough and shuffle of their feet in the otherwise-still room.

Finn simply bowed his head, resolving to speak as little and as carefully as possible.

"It has been some time since we last saw one another. A few weeks at least, although it feels longer," the headmaster commented.

"I believe it was during my induction ceremony," Finn replied.

"Ahh, yes," Nefreet said, his eyebrow arching. "You refused the gift of Veridian, if I recall correctly." He glanced at Abbad. "It seems that you took to your studies with enthusiasm – passing your initial classes, earning yourself a sponsor, taking the leaderboards by storm..."

There was a moment's hesitation. "It's almost too much to believe."

The statement hung in the room – the implication clear. How could a novice traveler have not only learned Veridian within the span of two weeks but also risen to become one of the most powerful mages among the new group of students?

"Why don't we address the accusation directly instead of dancing around it," Finn said abruptly. "You believe me to be a cheater." It wasn't a question.

This statement earned Finn some murmurs among the faculty, their eyes widening at his directness. Although, Finn noted that Nefreet was unflustered. If anything, he seemed mildly amused by Finn's reaction.

"That is indeed the claim that has been leveled at you by the other students. Some members of our faculty have also expressed suspicion about your *abilities*," Nefreet added, sparing a look at Lamia to his right. The water mage didn't react to the gesture, although her cold expression already told Finn volumes.

Fucking perfect. Finn may have been cautious about revealing his ability to craft new spells, but Lamia had at least some evidence. He had blown up her classroom, after all. He could still remember her accusation that Finn was a foreign mage who had somehow infiltrated their guild. Even if they didn't believe him to be a spy, Abbad had been clear that the guild did not take kindly to powerful, upstart mages.

He needed to be extremely careful here.

"What is more," Nefreet continued, "the novices claim that you have attacked them and harassed them in an effort to bolster your own score in the duels. They say you frequent the condemned northern section of the guild hall and use these opportunities to attack others without leaving any witnesses.

"Given what is at stake in this competition, I'm certain you can understand the gravity of such an accusation," Nefreet offered, waving a hand. "The champion of these duels will not only represent the guild in the Emir's competition but could also potentially rule Lahab as a whole. The integrity of our participants is imperative."

The headmaster paused, gazing at Finn with unblinking eyes.

"How would you answer these claims?" Nefreet asked, gesturing for Finn to speak.

"I am aware of the importance of the duels – particularly in light of the Emir's decree," Finn began, choosing his words carefully. "I can also assure you that I have not done anything to undermine this competition. My accomplishments are merely the result of hard work, as I am sure my instructor and faculty sponsor can attest," Finn said, gesturing at Brutus.

All eyes turned to Brutus, and the fire mage gave a curt nod of agreement.

Finn took a deep breath. This next part was going to be a gamble.

"As for the attacks, I have not *initiated* any hostile action against the other students outside of the duels," Finn declared.

"Your word choice is telling," Nefreet observed, with an arched eyebrow. "Perhaps I should rephrase. Have you harmed any other novices outside of the duels?"

Damn it. There was no way to wiggle out of that question without lying, which meant Finn was going to have to double down on his position.

"Yes," Finn replied evenly, refusing to back down or

show contrition. The faculty murmured amongst themselves in shocked surprise, some of them gesturing at Finn.

Lamia's cold voice rose into the air. "He openly admits to breaking the guild rules, Nefreet. This is the only evidence that you need. He should be expelled." She received a few murmurs of agreement from the other faculty.

Finn could feel a burning kernel of anger flare in his chest. What was this lady's problem? Yet he forcefully shoved it aside. He needed to stay calm.

He raised a hand, interrupting the murmurs among the faculty. "You may certainly decide to expel me. But that would be unjust. If you will let me elaborate?" This last question was directed at the headmaster, and Nefreet gestured for him to continue.

"I have been using the old warded crafting rooms on the northern side of campus to train without disturbing others or damaging guild property. Unfortunately, this also makes me vulnerable. Many of the other students have begun waylaying and ambushing the top-ranked novices in the halls – usually in unoccupied portions of the guild."

"To what end?" one of the faculty asked in an incredulous tone.

"Assassinating someone who has been summoned to a duel forces them to default, which costs them points," Finn explained. "And killing one of our kind prevents us from engaging in a duel again for nearly an hour."

Many of the faculty were staring at Finn in shock, although he noticed that more than a few appeared unsurprised by this revelation. Maybe Kyyle had been on to something. It seemed at least a few members of the faculty knew about the unspoken competition taking place in the guild's halls.

"In short, many of your students are attempting to influence the rankings," Finn continued. "I have merely been defending myself. In fact, these attacks have escalated to the point where I cannot leave the courtyard without being assaulted. This is why I have taken to sitting upon the dais – not to intimidate the other students, but to avoid constant assassination attempts."

"This is absurd," Lamia spat. "Are we to believe that this novice is important enough that the other students would stoop to trying to kill him and him alone?"

"This problem isn't isolated to me, and it is easy enough to prove," Finn replied calmly. "Simply ask the other A-listers. They have all taken to frequenting public areas or traveling in groups."

Nefreet frowned then, his eyes drifting down to his hands. To Finn's surprise, he then looked toward Abbad. The librarian simply gave a single curt nod in response.

What was that? Why would Nefreet look to Abbad for confirmation?

"Hmm, well we will look into the matter of these attacks," Nefreet offered. "If the situation is as dire as you claim, then we will need to investigate and expel those responsible."

Finn's brow furrowed. He suspected that wouldn't help in the slightest. There was a potential solution to the assassination attempts, but it was a much bolder option. "I would propose that you go much further than that," Finn offered tentatively.

"Oh, really?" Nefreet asked with an arched brow. "What do you suggest?"

Finn took a deep breath. "The faculty should remove the restriction on students attacking one another – at least among the travelers."

This was met with a resounding silence, the faculty members all staring at him.

"The only way to avoid or deter these attacks is to allow students to defend themselves," Finn offered. "I could have addressed this problem long ago if I were not concerned about being punished for acting in self-defense. It would have only taken a few... *examples* for the other students to learn to leave me alone."

Nefreet seemed to be weighing this suggestion, although many of the other faculty looked aghast at the possibility.

"What you are suggesting is chaos," Lamia snapped. "Students would be fighting in the halls. The guild hall couldn't withstand this sort of infighting."

Brutus finally stepped, letting out a derisive snort. "I think you overestimate the novices. Their spells have been carefully doled out to them for just that reason – concern over their ability to cause large-scale damage. What are a few scorch marks or puddles of melted water going to do to warded stone?"

Another instructor spoke up, the same bald monk that had sponsored Kyyle. He spared Finn a measured look before addressing the faculty. "Finn's suggestion *is* consistent with the sense of competition the Emir wishes to foster among the students. While this rule has been our policy in the past, with the introduction of so many new travelers, perhaps it is time to adapt. If the infighting is already as bad as Finn suggests, this may be a way to release the growing pressure."

As their bickering continued, Finn focused his attention on Nefreet. The headmaster's gaze was distant, as though performing a complicated calculation that Finn couldn't see.

"You lot would act without even knowing whether Finn is telling the truth?" Lamia snapped, her voice rising above the crowd. "A *novice* stands before you – an accused cheater who has not proven his innocence." She glared at Finn. "For all we know, this could just be some sort of trick. He may be at the center of these attacks and making this change could simply allow him to advance further in the duels."

She scowled at the other mages. "Or do you really believe that a single novice is capable of easily dispatching several other students? Because that is the claim that this man has made – a wild, unsupported boast." Finn saw the faculty acknowledge this point, a few mages nodding in agreement.

Nefreet's gaze snapped back into focus at that comment. "Lamia raises an interesting point," he said, the faculty immediately hushing at the sound of his voice. "The issue is indeed one of *credibility*."

The headmaster looked to Lamia. "How would you suggest that Finn prove himself?"

Finn's former instructor paused, as though surprised

by the question. Lamia looked toward him, and a cruel twinkle flashed in her eye. "I suggest we put Finn to the test. If he truly believes himself capable of fighting multiple novice mages, then certainly he could withstand a master for a short time."

Finn didn't back down, holding her gaze evenly. He could feel the ember of anger in his chest flare and grow. It seemed the time for hiding his strength was over. "So be it," he replied. "However, why don't we sweeten the deal? If I can stand against you for sixty seconds, the faculty will permit the travelers free rein to fight outside the duels."

A sudden silence descended upon the room. Even the most vocal members against the change were hesitating. Finn could practically see their thought process. How could a novice hope to stand against a master for a full minute?

Nefreet stared at Finn, his head cocked to the side. "I find the rules of the challenge satisfactory. Finn shall defend against Lamia for one minute. If he fails, then he will be exiled. Do we have an agreement?" This last question was directed at the faculty.

They all nodded, and it was decided.

Without ceremony, Lamia rose from behind the bench and stalked into the center of the room. She looked at Finn dismissively, gesturing at one of the guards that ringed the room. "Bring me my staff," she ordered.

The guard looked to the headmaster for permission. "You may retrieve her weapon. The novice's equipment as well," Nefreet instructed the man.

A moment later, Finn and Lamia had their equipment returned to them and faced off in the center of the chamber. At a gesture from Nefreet, Abbad summoned a semi-translucent globe of air around them, the surface shimmering slightly. His hands kept moving even after completing the spell, likely channeling his mana into the globe to prevent any wayward spells from striking the headmaster or other faculty.

Finn stared down Lamia. He had sheathed his blades, and his hands remained empty, hanging limply at his sides. The water mage master seemed slightly confused by his nonchalance, as well as the fact that Finn wasn't carrying a staff or wand. She smirked at him, likely thinking he would be easy to break.

Strangely, Finn didn't feel nervous. Instead, a tantalizing mixture of excitement and anger raced through his veins, and it was all he could do to contain his mana and keep from summoning it. This was his chance to face Lamia again, this time on much more equal footing. The last time he had stood in this position, he hadn't known a single spell. That almost felt like a lifetime ago.

Now he had hundreds of duels behind him.

"The rules are simple," Nefreet explained. "Finn need only *survive* for sixty seconds. He cannot harm Lamia during this period of time. All skills and spells are permitted unless they would cause damage or injury to the room or the faculty." This last statement was directed at Lamia, and she grimaced slightly.

Great. At least she can't drop some sort of ice meteor on top of my head, Finn thought.

Actually, this scenario was optimal for Finn, which was why he had suggested it. They were close, Lamia only standing a few feet outside his control range. Not only that, but the tight quarters and witnesses ensured that Lamia would need to use smaller and more controlled spells. There was likely a limit to Abbad's shield.

"Are you ready?" Nefreet asked.

Lamia nodded, her eyes suddenly turning a dark blue as she channeled her mana.

Finn finally let his own mana run free, the energy bucking at the reins like a wild horse. It surged through his body in a torrent, until even the tips of his fingers felt warm to the touch. The familiar manic excitement bubbled and frothed in his mind.

"And... begin," Nefreet called out.

Lamia's hand began moving immediately. In contrast to their last fight, she didn't hold back this time. Nearly a dozen shards of ice formed beside her, pulling the moisture out of the air, and leaving it feeling dry and brittle. Finn suddenly realized that she was going for massive, slow-casting spells since she didn't need to worry about being attacked.

Finn was ready for that, however. He didn't bother casting *Magma Armor*. He didn't have enough time to get the defense spells in place while also getting his blades in the air. His hands darted through a rapid series of gestures, his fingers moving so quickly that they almost seemed to blur. Within moments, his daggers slid from their sheaths of their own accord.

He didn't need to wait for Lamia to launch her attack.

Instead, Finn darted forward, sprinting directly toward the water mage to ensure that she was within his control range. Her eyes widened slightly, but she continued to cast instead of attempting to stop him. Finn couldn't harm her, so why bother to stall his advance?

Then her spell completed.

Finn's blades lanced through the air at a blazing pace, leaving a trail of fire in their wake. The knives neatly sliced through two bolts before they could move and took out another five before they made it to Finn, tumbling and rotating in the air in a dizzying display. The remainder of the missiles were manageable after hours spent dueling with Julia. Finn leaped over one bolt and dove into a roll, letting the other shards stream past him.

Lamia stared in shock as she saw that her barrage had been neatly avoided, leaving Finn close and unharmed. However, her surprise was short-lived as her eyes darted to the other faculty. Finn couldn't embarrass her here – not with the others watching.

Cold anger suddenly burned in her eyes.

Her hand was already moving again. This time, a blizzard of cold energy began to swirl around Lamia in a vortex. Fragments of ice appeared in the maelstrom and pelted Finn, cutting at his skin and armor, and leaving thin red trails of blood. The small missiles were no real danger yet, but they were growing larger. Finn had never seen this spell before, but from the incantation he assumed it was some sort of nova – drawing in moisture and then expelling it outward. It would leave him with no room to dodge, and his daggers would be ineffective.

It was smart.

But Finn was no longer an amateur.

Normally, Finn would attack, but he couldn't physically harm or attack Lamia. Which meant he only had one option to avoid the spell.

His daggers slid back into his sheaths as he dropped the spell, summoning two *Fireballs* in their place. Instead of forming the spheres beside himself, Finn used his extended control range to form them right beside Lamia's head in the pocket of clear air inside the growing blizzard – holding the channel and feeding mana into the spells. This was difficult to keep up, forcing Finn to stand within the growing nova of ice and sleet in order to maintain his *Fireballs*. But he ground his teeth together and withstood the barrage, shards of ice cutting through his robes and skin.

Lamia sneered at the flaming orbs dismissively.

Finn's fingers urged the *Fireballs* to move, forcing them to carve a circular pattern around Lamia. They moved slowly at first, picking up speed until they whirled around Lamia's head in an orange blur.

For a long second, the spell had no effect, and Finn felt the maelstrom grow denser. A shard of ice pierced his arm, blood trickling down his fingers where they maintained the channel. Another lance cut a line across his stomach. Yet he forced himself to keep going, enduring the flashes of pain that riddled his body.

Then Lamia coughed, her incantation faltering.

Within only a few seconds, she was forced to drop her channel, groping at her throat, and gasping for air like a fish out of water as she glared at the two *Fireballs*. Between the flames and the vortex created by the swirling movement, Finn had funneled most of the oxygen out of the air, leaving too little for Lamia to breathe.

It was a trick he had considered after watching Abbad's spheres. The technique was somewhat impractical in a duel – where his opponent was moving and trying to kill him. But in this context, with Lamia standing still and committed to a large-scale spell, the combination was devastating.

Lamia clutched at her throat weakly, her eyes frantic now. Without enough oxygen to complete the incantation and her hand maintaining the requisite gestures, her spell began to falter and fade. She also had no easy way to summon more mana to dispel the *Fireballs* as they curved around her in a blur of orange and her stamina was swiftly draining away due to the lack of air – leaving her unable to break free.

Lamia dropped to her knees, her staff rattling against the floor as she clutched at her throat with both hands now. She was barely visible behind the tornado of fire, yet Finn could still see her glowing blue eyes bulge in panic.

"Time," Nefreet called out.

Finn immediately released the two spells, the fiery twister breaking apart with a whoosh of hot air that drifted through the room and eliminated the last traces of Lamia's spell. The faint fragments of ice were vaporized, causing a faint mist of warm vapor to drift through the room. A heavy silence hung in the air as the faculty looked on in amazement, the quiet broken only by Lamia's desperate heaving gasps.

"It appears that Finn has won," Nefreet offered. Finn looked up to see the headmaster staring at him with the same appraising expression.

Brutus let out an amused snort, crossing his arms and smirking at the other faculty. "Of course he did. I guess this means you lot are satisfied that Finn isn't cheating? Kind of insulting if you ask me. Why would I sponsor a cheater in the first place?"

"Indeed," Nefreet said. "Although, it does raise the question of how Finn learned both *Imbue Fire* and *Multi-Casting*," he commented dryly.

Finn held his breath. *Oh, shit.* Brutus hadn't taught him *Imbue Fire.*

Brutus' gaze darted to Finn before he turned back to Nefreet. "Faculty are permitted to provide their sponsored with special training. I didn't break the rules – even if he did learn to use his spells creatively."

"Hmm. That is a rather *flexible* interpretation of the rules," the headmaster retorted. He let out a sigh. "Nonetheless, Finn won. Let us consider the matter closed then – for now, at least."

Nefreet's gaze shifted to Finn. "As per our agreement, the students now have free rein to fight outside of the duels. A public announcement shall be made within the hour. Let us hope that is sufficient to quell these irritating accusations."

The headmaster paused for a moment and glanced at Lamia, who was still gasping on the floor. He tapped his lips with his fingers, deep in thought, before sparing one last glance at Finn. "You are dismissed."

Taking that as his cue to get the hell out of there, Finn headed toward the door. It was all he could do to keep putting one foot in front of the other, droplets of blood dripping onto the floor in his wake. The guards backed away quickly, giving him a wide berth and keeping a watchful eye on Finn and a hand on their weapons. It appeared that they were cautious with a novice who had bested a master.

As he passed through the door and it slammed shut behind him, Finn suddenly leaned against the nearby wall, breathing hard and letting his mask finally drop. He could feel his pulse pounding in his ears, and his palms were sweaty. Dozens of cuts and scratches riddled his body, and he let out a hissing breath as he yanked a particularly large shard from his forearm. Finn saw that his health was on its last legs, his natural regeneration barely keeping him standing.

Damn, that was close!

He felt no rush of victory as he stood there. Instead, Nefreet's expression lingered with him. In many ways, Finn had just heavily tipped his hand. Brutus had covered for him – something he expected he would have to account for later – and he had just bested a master water mage in front of the faculty, even if that victory had been narrow, and a result of the unique rules of their duel. He doubted that Lamia would let that go.

Local Area Notice: Mage Guild
Due to the recent escalation in attacks within the guild hall, the faculty has decided to amend the guild's rules regarding infighting.

> Travelers are now permitted to attack and slay one another within the guild hall without reprisal. Egregious damage to guild property and attacks on residents and faculty will still be punished with expulsion.
>
> Victory or death, we fight and train for the glory of the Emir.

"It seems you've been busy," Julia observed, dropping from *Sneak* nearby and swiping away the recent notification. She eyed Finn's injuries with some worry. "I take it the meeting went well?"

"I guess you could say that," Finn replied with a snort of amusement.

"So, what now?" his daughter asked.

Finn hesitated. He needed to get back to the duels. They only had a few more days left, and he still wasn't in first place. However, for now, that could wait. The larger problem slowing him down was the attacks by the other players, and he expected they would only become more aggressive now that the restrictions had been lifted.

There was only one way to deal with that problem.

Finn raised his eyes to meet Julia's, flames flickering in his irises. "First things first, we need to send a warning."

Chapter 32 - Vengeful

Finn sat cross-legged in a room in the abandoned portion of the guild hall. He'd been forced to clear enough room to sit comfortably amid the clutter.

He assumed this section must have originally been a large-scale workshop; several hallways branched away from the room, leading to a destroyed furnace and various testing rooms. In its heyday, he expected he would have seen mages bustling about the brightly lit space, crafting new and extraordinary weapons and armor. Now, the workbenches were little more than rotten husks, creating trash and debris that littered the floor.

At least the room could still serve a purpose. It was large, spacious, and had several entrances. All of those variables were helpful for what he had planned.

With a swipe of his wrist, Finn pulled up his chat window. He tapped an option to send an area message, typed out a clipped sentence, and hit send.

Then he settled in to wait.

Only a minute later, Julia popped out of *Sneak* beside him. "There are at least a dozen novices incoming on this location," she reported, her tone sounding worried. "Are you sure you don't want me to help?"

Finn shook his head. "There's no sense giving away that you are inside the guild illicitly. Plus, for this to work, I need to do this myself. We need to deter these people from attacking us."

"I guess I'll say it one more time, although you don't seem to be listening," Julia added in a dry voice. "This seems like a bad idea."

Finn looked at her, noting the way her fingers hovered on the hilts of her blades and the nervous expression on her face. "Weren't you the one advocating for me to send a warning a few days ago? Besides, what other choice do we have? We can't keep going with these constant interruptions. Not if we want to win this competition. This is about deterring future attacks."

Julia shook her head, biting at her lip. "Or – and hear me out – you could start a small-scale war within the guild. This has escalated out of control," she bit back. She met his eyes, adding quietly, "And are you sure you really *want* to win this competition? Like this?"

Finn winced, Julia's words echoing some of the same doubts that had begun circling at the edges of his thoughts over the last few days. Julia was usually his voice of chaos, urging him to try new things and disrupt the status quo. She had been that way since she was just a little girl. She had always been the one who came up with games and activities for the other kids – as well as getting them into a buttload of trouble. Hell, she was the one who had encouraged him to start playing AO!

If she was urging caution and restraint now...

He shook his head.

Despite his reservations – and Julia's – he didn't see another way. It was just math. The time he lost dealing with these attacks cost him points. He would never catch up to Vanessa and Zane at this rate.

Finn's fingers clenched around the small object in his hand. He just hoped his plan would work – both that he was capable of taking on this many opponents and that this sort of demonstration would really act as a deterrent.

He glanced at Julia, a grin tugging at his lips. "It isn't like you to be worried about me," he commented. "What happened to egging me on? Trying to stab me? Or is it only fun when you get to kill me yourself."

She met his teasing with a smile of her own – although it was a weak, sickly thing. "What can I say? I like my exclusive stabbing rights."

She hesitated. "Your thin attempt at deflection aside, it's just..." She shook her head, struggling to find the words. "I don't know. It feels like things have changed." Julia looked at him. "Like *you've* changed. I told you before, there's something weird about this game. It does things to people."

As he glanced at her, Finn couldn't help but be reminded of Rachael again. Julia had inherited so many of the same features – even capturing that concerned look that seemed to say he might be just a little crazy. Maybe that was part of the reason he had pushed Julia and Gracen away after Rachael...

Finn shut down that thought hard, closing his eyes to blot out the image it conjured.

The bottom line was that he had also noticed the changes Julia mentioned. He had started to become numb to the violence, despite the realism. He hadn't even hesitated at the idea of fighting one of the faculty. On more than one occasion, Finn had also questioned why he was still doing this. Did he even really *want* to win this competition? Or rule a city?

The answer seemed like a definite *no*.

He had the sudden urge to summon his mana – to revel in the excited glow that always accompanied his spellcasting. He knew that sensation would drive away the doubt that Julia's comment had created. The mana washed away his hesitation, sorrow, and despair and replaced it with boundless energy and focus. For just a moment, he could forget the pain he had lived with for nearly a decade.

His mana was almost like a drug.

Yet he sure as hell didn't want to admit that.

Finn's eyes snapped open. "It will be okay," he murmured. "It's just this one tournament. Once we get past this, things will calm down." His words felt flimsy even to his own ears, and he didn't have to look at Julia to know that she was staring at him skeptically.

Fortunately, Finn was saved from this conversation as he heard shuffling and voices coming down several of the connecting hallways. He glanced at Julia. "Go. It won't be safe for you inside the room."

Julia gave him a grudging nod and then disappeared.

Then Finn waited. He lasted only a few more seconds until he gave in, summoning the warm mana. Within moments, his blood seemed to simmer in anticipation of what he planned to do – his doubt evaporating.

The first of the players soon emerged from the hallway, instantly spotting Finn. They strode in almost casually – as though he presented no danger – until they encircled him. As

Julia had indicated, there were at least a dozen, all wearing the basic robes and staves available for sale in Charlotte's requisition hall. So, they were veterans of the duels.

Even better.

"You're Finn, huh?" a nearby player grunted, clearly the ringleader. "Why did you message the zone with your location?" he demanded. "Did you decide to just give up or something?"

"Not exactly," Finn replied quietly, his eyes pulsing with orange energy and his hands hidden from sight, his fingers already slowly tracing a complicated pattern. "I'm just tired of being attacked."

"Ahh, so you plan to beg for mercy then?" the player retorted, glancing at the other novices in amusement. "See, I told that mage it was just a matter of time before he caved!"

Finn's brow furrowed. "What mage?"

The player laughed at him. "You don't even know, huh?" He shook his head. "You've got some enemies in high places. Along with that other bunch of A-listers."

"Someone instructed you to attack us?" Finn asked again, his thoughts swirling. "Who?" His thoughts immediately jumped to Lamia. She certainly had the motive to conscript other travelers to attack him, even before he embarrassed her in front of the other faculty. Although, why would she want to attack the other students? Perhaps to distract from her real target? Possible… but it felt tenuous.

The player's smile widened, and Finn noted that he had shifted his weight, his fingers clutching at his staff. "Ahh, too bad you won't live long enough to find out. We're going to kill you again and again and again until you stop logging back in."

Damn it. It looked like question time was over.

Finn looked up at the player, his eyes shining with orange energy. "Fair enough, but first I have a present for you," he said. Then he threw the small object at the player and squeezed his eyes shut.

The man barely caught it in time, holding up a cloth pouch about the size of his fist.

"What the hell is—?"

He never got to finish that sentence.

One of Finn's daggers, that he'd subtly summoned behind the other players, suddenly rushed through the room. The knife sliced through the pouch and the flames immediately ignited its contents. A blinding flash of light illuminated the dark room, accompanied by a howl of pain as the contents burned into the flesh of the player's hand. The blade kept going, whirling and twisting about the room as it ignited more of the packets carefully hidden in the debris, buying Finn time to get his second knife in the air.

Finn could feel the wash of heat and see the light behind his eyelids, his blood boiling in anticipation. He had discovered something interesting after exploring the abandoned sections of the guild hall. Specifically, a barrel filled with saltpeter. After locating the guild's cafeteria, it hadn't taken him long to find a bit of sugar as well. A few minutes of tinkering had resulted in the small, makeshift flashbang grenades – which left a nasty burn and generated a lot of smoke.

Finn's eyes popped open, and he saw that the players were staggering about, rubbing at their eyes and hurling spells at random. The room was filled with a dense black fog that drifted toward the ceiling, the thick stone walls containing most of the smoke. Although, from his position on the floor, Finn could still barely make out the feet of each player as they stumbled around. Sitting in the center of the room, Finn's control range encompassed almost the entire room. The players were all standing well within the small translucent line that was displayed in his HUD.

He didn't give them a chance to recover.

His fingers danced, and his knives sliced through the air, flames curling away from the metal blades. The novices naturally assumed that the weapons were attached to a living hand – a rookie mistake. They shot off spells in the direction of the burning knives, but they simply whiffed and slammed against the room's walls.

A shout of pain went up as Finn cut through the back of a player's leg, severing the tendons neatly. As he fell, the player's torso came into sight. Another quick stab to the kidney left the player bleeding out on the ground, groaning and unable to move.

Then the knives moved on.

Finn's blades cut a swath of devastation through the room, aiming for tendons, arteries, and major organs with each stab and slice – Julia had taught him well. He considered idly that his *Fire Nova* would have been easier. But that would have also defeated the point.

He wanted them to remember this fight.

Finally, the smoke slowly began to clear, rifting down the adjacent halls. The bodies of nearly a dozen players littered the ground, groaning and whimpering in pain. At this point, Finn rose and stepped toward the ringleader, who lay on his back, clutching at his ruined hand while blood leaked from cuts along his inner thigh and arms. It seemed Finn had nicked a couple major arteries. The player didn't have long left. Finn needed to use this time wisely.

Finn crouched beside the man, meeting his eyes. They were desperate and panicked. The player reached for his staff, and a quick gesture from Finn impaled the man's forearm with a burning blade. "Tsk tsk, no quick movements," Finn murmured.

"What the hell are you?" the player croaked.

"An A-lister and someone you shouldn't have messed with," Finn murmured in reply. He leaned in close. "This was a message. My hands were tied in the past, and I was going easy on you. However, as you can see, I incapacitated all of you within minutes. Alone. This time, and *only* this time, I'll be merciful and end the pain."

At this statement, Finn's fingers jerked, and a nearby player's whimpering immediately stopped as a blade slid across his throat. The ringleader's eyes widened further, but he couldn't turn to look.

"Next time, I'll take my time," Finn said, his voice heavy with the implied threat. "I'd like for you to spread the word. If you understand, just nod once."

The ringleader nodded, the movement jerky and uncoordinated.

Then, with a few quick strokes, Finn put them all out of

their misery.

His goal complete, Finn's blades slowly slid into their sheaths, and he released the spells, his fingers slowing and then finally stopping their movements. He surveyed the player at his feet, feeling a momentary pang of guilt despite the warm energy that flooded his veins. He knew from firsthand experience that the game's pain feedback was bearable, even if it wasn't particularly pleasant. Even so, this strategy had been... cruel.

A sudden gust of wind tugged at Finn's robes, and the smoke rushed down a nearby hallway, soon leaving the room clear of the thick fog. He looked over to find Abbad entering the chamber, the man's eyes glowing a vibrant azure. Julia stood beside him.

The librarian's eyes skimmed across the bodies, and his gaze was impassive. Although Finn saw his eyebrow twitch slightly. Even Julia looked a little squeamish at the blood that now drenched the stones.

"What was this?" Abbad asked.

"My attempt to prove a point," Finn replied quietly, forcing himself to release his mana. Just as he expected, the warmth was immediately replaced with nausea as he looked at the bodies, and he glanced away quickly. "The attacks should lessen once word spreads of what happened here."

Abbad looked toward Finn. "Does this not seem harsh?" he asked, cocking his head.

Finn ran a hand through his hair, recalling Julia's words before he had initiated the ambush. He may have changed, but his actions were always logical.

"Perhaps, but it was also necessary." Finn met Abbad's eyes. "I've rarely found that the best course of action is easy."

He saw something in the librarian's gaze then. A faint flicker of doubt maybe. The emotion was hard to pin down and vanished as quickly as a breeze.

Although, this was a good time to press Abbad for information. "The players mentioned that someone had asked them to attack the travelers. They indicated that it was another mage," Finn offered. He saw Julia's eyes widen in surprise. "You wouldn't happen to know anything about that, would you?"

The librarian just shook his head. "This is the first I have heard of it. Perhaps another rival novice?"

Finn hesitated. The player hadn't indicated that it had been another competitor. He had mentioned "enemies in high places," which seemed to imply that the mage was higher-ranked, or possibly...

"I think it might be a member of the faculty," Finn murmured. "Perhaps Lamia? She seemed extremely resistant to the idea of allowing fighting within the guild hall. She could have been trying to preserve her plan to manipulate the rankings," he said, thinking aloud.

"A bold step," Julia muttered. "What if one of these travelers ratted her out?"

"Water magic is capable of forming illusions," Abbad observed. "For someone of Lamia's skill, that would have been an easy deception. If she is involved, then the travelers could have thought they were speaking to anyone. Either way, I will be attentive. Perhaps the traitor will be revealed in time."

Finn arched an eyebrow. "We'll see. Speaking of which, what are you doing here?" he asked.

The librarian hesitated for a moment, before turning his attention back to Finn. "I wished to speak with you after the confrontation in front of the faculty. However, I was not expecting this sort of red-carpet treatment," he observed, pointing at the blood staining the floor.

"Oh, look! The book robot makes jokes now!" Julia commented in an amused voice. "It's almost like he's a real boy." Abbad simply ignored her.

"Well, here I am," Finn replied, rolling his eyes at Julia. "What did you want?"

"I spoke with Brutus after the fight, and he indicated that he had not taught you *Imbue Fire*. Which raised the question, how did you learn to cast that spell?" Abbad asked, his penetrating gaze now observing Finn carefully.

Finn eyed the librarian warily, his thoughts racing. He could feel Julia's eyes on him as well, although she stayed silent, letting him choose how to proceed.

Should I tell Abbad about my spellcrafting?

After everything he had been through and the ringleader's reveal of some sort of deep-seated conspiracy against the A-listers, Finn wasn't exactly in a trusting mood. Even Abbad himself had warned him to be careful who he trusted. There was no sense giving away information if he could help it. And so, despite the librarian's help over the last few weeks, Finn decided to hold his tongue.

"I actually saw two higher-ranked mages sparring in the courtyard," Finn replied, trying to affect a casual demeanor. "One used that spell, and I was able to pick up enough of the hand gestures and incantation to cast it myself. I guess it must be a function of my *Learning* skill."

Abbad eyed him for a moment, his face neutral. Then he gave a curt nod. "That does indeed make sense. Although, most novices likely wouldn't have been quite as *perceptive*. I will be sure to inform Brutus of this."

Finn nodded, turning his attention back to the bodies. Julia was already picking through the corpses, retrieving a few items, and stowing them in her bag. As she caught him watching her, she raised an eyebrow. "What?"

"What are you even going to do with that stuff?" Finn asked.

Julia shrugged. "I certainly can't sell it here in the guild, but this equipment is still valuable outside these walls. I can just make a trip to one of my contacts in Lahab. Besides, if your goal is to send a message, stealing all their stuff will certainly help."

Finn shook his head. First, Julia urged him to exercise caution, and in the next breath, she was talking about fencing stolen mage equipment. The irony wasn't entirely lost on him.

"Although, you don't have time to stand around giving me judgmental looks," Julia offered, her fingers snatching a crystal-encrusted wand. "Your token is glowing again."

Finn looked at his pocket and could make out the glimmering symbol through the fabric of his robes. With a sigh, he pulled out the token and started toward one of the vacant hallways, heading toward the courtyard. "Alright, well I guess I'll see you in a bit."

He met the librarian's gaze as he passed, giving him a curt nod. "Abbad." The mage returned the gesture but remained silent.

As Finn exited the room, Abbad and Julia shared a look, not a word passing between them. Then they both turned to watch Finn's back as he strode down the hallway, concern etched on their faces.

Chapter 33 - Violent

The last two days in-game had been... interesting.

The new mandate meant that full-fledged fights were now permitted within the guild hall as long as the damage was relatively contained. Finn had often wondered what would happen in the real world if people were given free license to release some of their pent-up frustration.

You know, your typical *purge* situation.

He had always thought that the vast majority of people wouldn't act out – at least not if there was a considerable risk to themselves. If there was one universal rule he had discovered in his many decades on Earth, it was that people always acted in their own self-interest. Perhaps if the government in the real world had issued a similar decree, Finn might have been proven right.

Except AO wasn't the real world. And, more importantly, death wasn't permanent within the game.

The result was complete bedlam.

Finn turned a corner, stopping short as he witnessed a skirmish being waged in the hallway. An *Ice Bolt* slammed into the wall nearby, and it fractured into dozens of pieces. Meanwhile, spikes of earth speared into the air, erupting from the stone floor further down the hall. As he observed the chaos, a *Fireball* came hurtling through the air, which he neatly sidestepped.

A few days ago, this might have been a disconcerting scene. However, at this point, Finn just sighed, stepping back behind the wall and rubbing at his temples for a moment. At least six novices were going at it, and a glance at his map confirmed that doubling back would cost him 5-10 minutes. He had thought the ambushes were distracting and time-consuming, but these battles made it almost impossible to navigate the school.

Which left a more expedient option...

Finn's fingers wound together, and a short time later, *Magma Armor* slid down both of his arms. Since he had reached Intermediate Level 1, the armor had grown thicker, curling up across his shoulder and a spike of molten energy emerging from his elbow. The increased coverage was quite helpful, even if it made the armor a bit more cumbersome.

A few more seconds and Finn's knives glided from their sheaths, the blades bathed in flame. He squeezed his eyes shut, visualizing the hallway.

Three have their backs to me. At least three opponents on the far end of the hall. I need to strike hard and fast. A three-on-one fight was doable. Six-on-one was another matter entirely, and Finn didn't want to waste any more of his makeshift grenades on this. It was too time-consuming to make more.

Taking a deep breath, Finn dashed forward.

He raced down the hall, his blades dancing around him. A knife stabbed through the back of one mage's throat, blood spraying the air as he toppled forward. However, Finn didn't have time to reflect on that, diving into a roll to avoid another stray *Fireball*. He came back up in a crouch, the other two mages standing a few feet away. They had just seen something happen in their UI, their teammate's icon likely flashing gray as he died, and they slowly began to turn.

Finn's second knife sliced through the air, neatly cutting the tendons in their ankles. The two men toppled, and then two burning daggers swiftly ended their lives. The blades drifted back into the air, fresh blood sizzling and evaporating along each blade and filling the air with the muted, sickly-sweet smell of burnt flesh.

Finn rose back to his feet. There were still three more mages – the opponents that the deceased novices had been fighting. They all turned to stare at Finn, his eyes glowing a brilliant orange and two blades hovering beside him, the flames causing the air to ripple and warp above each weapon.

The novices glanced between Finn and the corpses, and he saw recognition in their eyes. "Finn," one of the mages croaked. "Oh, shit..." The other two looked like they wanted to run.

"I'm in a hurry, so I'll be merciful today. If you leave now, I'll save you a 45-minute respawn timer," Finn said, stalking forward with slow, ponderous steps.

"You have five seconds to decide," he added.

Then he began counting down. "Five, four..."

He never made it to three. The mages turned on their heels and bolted down the hallway like the devil himself was following them. As Finn released his mana and his blades slid back into their sheaths, he supposed that wasn't too far from the truth.

The last few days had taken their toll on him and left him feeling... Well, he wasn't sure how to describe it. Even now, he couldn't force himself to turn to look at the corpses behind him. He knew what he would find – jagged burned flesh and seared blood.

No, it was better – and easier – to simply keep moving forward.

With the brief respite, Finn decided to take a moment to regroup.

"Daniel," Finn said aloud.

A moment later, the AI flashed into existence. A brief pause as Daniel took in the sight of the dead bodies. "Um... how can I help you?"

"Scout the nearby area. Make sure no one sneaks up on me," Finn ordered. The glowing orange ball started to speed down the hall and Finn called after him. "And try to be discreet!" Daniel pulsed once and then disappeared around a corner.

Finn tapped at his UI, re-enabling his system notifications. While the other mages no longer seemed to be gunning for Finn specifically, skirmishes like the one he had just interrupted were now far too frequent. Between the duels and these small-scale battles, he had continued to level quite quickly. It was sort of like he was living inside a dungeon, except instead of monsters, he kept fighting respawning players.

x17 Level Up!
You have (85) undistributed stat points.

x2 Spell Rank Up: Magma Armor
Skill Level: Intermediate Level 3

Cost: 100 Mana
Effect 1: Creates a damage shield capable of absorbing 340 damage (170 damage if water/ice).
Effect 2: Damage absorption increased by INT x 35%.
Channel Effect: Repairs the shield at a rate of 60 damage/second at a mana cost of 20 mana/second.

x1 Spell Rank Up: Fireball
Skill Level: Beginner Level 10
Cost: 100 Mana
Effect: Creates a ball of flame that deals 200 + (INT x 50%) damage.
Channel Effect: Controls the Fireball within your control range at a cost of 10 mana/sec.

x3 Spell Rank Up: Imbue Fire
Skill Level: Beginner Level 10
Cost: 145 Mana
Effect: Imbues a weapon with fire mana, increasing the weapon's base damage by INT x 9.5%. Can only be used on unenchanted metal weapons.
Channel Effect: Allows user to control the weapon within his control range at a cost of 24.5 mana/sec.

x1 Skill Rank Up: Learning
Skill Level: Intermediate Level 1
Effect 1: 15% increased learning speed for skills and spells.
Effect 2: 1% increased experience gain.

x1 Skill Rank Up: Concentration
Skill Level: Beginner Level 9
Effect: Ability to split your focus between [2] tasks.

x2 Skill Rank Up: Multi-Casting
Skill Level: Intermediate Level 1
Effect 1: -42.0% casting speed on second spell.
Effect 2: -11% reduced channeling cost.

The stat gains had basically stopped since Finn had no time for training, but he was able to compensate for that stat loss with levels. With the additional *Intelligence* he'd gained, Finn could now maintain both knives for nearly five minutes without recasting. This had opened up more options, allowing him to weave in *Fireballs* and more easily cast or repair his armor while staying on the offensive.

Despite the chaos that the faculty's decree had created, Finn had benefited.

His thoughts were suddenly interrupted as a notification crashed down into his vision.

Local Area Notice: Mage Guild

The headmaster has called a general guild meeting in the courtyard in 60 minutes. All guild members are required to attend, and all duels that are not currently in progress have been temporarily suspended.

Please complete any task or duel that is underway and make your way to the courtyard promptly.

Finn felt a sense of unease settle in his stomach as he reviewed the prompt. It didn't take a genius to realize what this meeting would address. The obvious issue was the infighting between the mages – which had reached an unreasonable level within only a few short days.

Finn just hoped that he wouldn't be blamed for the fallout.

* * *

By the time Finn arrived in the courtyard, he was surprised to see hundreds of mages shuffling across the sands and filling the terraces that ringed the area. Even from the edge of the courtyard, he could see members of the faculty standing upon the dais, Nefreet taking a position front and center.

"There are more guards than I remember last time," someone commented from Finn's elbow, and he turned to find Kyyle standing beside him. The young man gestured to the soldiers that stood in the shadow of the terraces, armed with wickedly curved swords and bows and robed in heavy mail.

"And a few more experienced mages that don't look like they're here for the meeting," Kyyle added, pointing out robed figures that weaved through the crowd, their attention focused more on the students than Nefreet and the faculty.

Finn grimaced. "It's like they expect a full-fledged riot or something."

"I mean, is that really so strange?" Kyyle asked with a wry grin. "We've been killing each other for a couple weeks now, there are only three days remaining in the competition, and the faculty basically authorized us to slaughter each other outside of the duels."

Finn winced again. That had been a real winner of an idea...

"So, what he's saying is that it's time for you to tell me those three little words I love so much," Julia snapped, popping up beside Finn as she dropped out of *Sneak*.

Kyyle started slightly in surprise, his fingers twitching. However, he stopped himself from casting as he saw that it was just Julia. It seemed everyone was on edge lately. "What does she mean?" he asked cautiously.

"Oh, you don't know?" Julia interjected. "Finn here is the one that got the faculty to agree to let the novices murder each other. Brilliant idea, right? Truly a winner."

Finn glanced at the nearby students, noticing that more than a few had turned to look at him. "Hey, keep your voice down," Finn whispered at Julia. This just earned him an arched eyebrow in response.

Kyyle, for his part, was staring at Finn like he had grown two heads. "It seemed like a good idea at the time," Finn muttered in response to his unspoken question. "I was tired of getting attacked and not being able to fight back."

"Uh-huh," Julia replied. "And how is that working out for you now? Feel like the attacks have really died down since then? I bet that's why all the A-listers have beefed up their entourage of bodyguards," she offered, gesturing at Zane and Vanessa, who had entered the courtyard surrounded by other mages. "Oh, but you must be number one now, right?" she asked with mock innocence.

Kyyle chuckled. "Still number three the last time I checked. I have to say the mass murder decree didn't help my rank much either. I'm just a lowly number four."

Julia assumed an expression of mock disappointment, cupping a hand to one ear as she turned toward Finn. "Well, damn. I guess you were... what's the word again? *Wrong*? I'm ready whenever you are, though. Lay those sweet, sweet words upon me."

Finn muttered under his breath.

"Sorry, didn't quite catch that. You've gotta speak up."

"You were right," Finn grunted.

Julia closed her eyes and tilted her face to the sky. "It feels soooo good."

"Yeah, well let's hear what Nefreet has to say," Finn offered, crossing his arms defensively as the pair laughed at him. Although, they did at least turn their attention toward the podium as Nefreet gestured at Abbad. The librarian's hands wound through a series of gestures, and an unnatural breeze drifted through the crowd.

"Good afternoon," Nefreet said, his voice at a neutral volume. It sounded like he was standing right beside Finn.

Damn, that's still a cool trick, Finn thought. It would be incredibly useful for distracting people in a duel.

"As you are all aware, only three days remain in our competition to choose a champion to represent the guild in the Emir's contest," Nefreet continued. "We understand that this competition is grueling and has become increasingly competitive as each day passes."

He took a deep breath before continuing, "As you are all aware, a few days ago, the faculty met to discuss the attacks that had been reported by many novices. These students claimed that they had been waylaid in the hallways on their way to a duel. We determined that some students were working to manipulate the rankings, targeting high-profile competitors – specifically the top few ranked mages. I believe you all have come to refer to this group as the 'A-listers.'

"In response, the faculty decided to lift our policy banning violence within the guild hall – at least as it applied to travelers. The thought was that this would act as a deterrent, allowing the competitors to defend themselves."

Nefreet paused, his typically passive expression cracking briefly as he grimaced. Meanwhile, the crowd murmured, frustration and anger simmering among the sea of students. Clearly, most of the novices weren't happy at the full-scale war that was now being waged in the halls. Finn hunched his shoulders, trying to avoid drawing attention to himself. He could already imagine the angry mob that would be chasing him if they discovered that he had been behind that change.

"This policy, however, only served to further escalate the conflicts among the novices," Nefreet explained. "Understandably, this has created additional tension among our students. In fact, some of you have been quite… *vocal* about your displeasure with this policy.

"Unfortunately, there is little we can do to address these problems now. If we remove the restriction on violence within the guild hall, competitors cannot adequately defend themselves from nefarious acts. If we permit students to defend themselves, then we encourage a free-for-all that harms everyone," Nefreet explained.

"Which is why the faculty has arrived on a third course of action."

The air in the courtyard stilled as the students looked on anxiously. Even Finn could feel himself involuntarily holding his breath. What did a third option look like?

"At this point, the faculty feels that we have adequately ranked the novices among one another – at least with regard to identifying the most talented mages among the travelers and residents. Mathematically, it is nearly impossible for the closest competitors to surpass this group with the time remaining," Nefreet explained.

"Therefore, we have decided to alter the competition. As of this moment, the leaderboards are now frozen. Since we have only three days remaining, the top four students from among the residents and travelers will be selected to participate in a final tournament."

Everyone in the crowd stared at the headmaster in stunned silence.

"Among the travelers, the current top-ranked students are Vanessa, Zane, Finn, and Kyyle. Among the residents, the top-ranked students are Khiana, Quail, Sana, and Khan. Over the next two days, we will host a semi-final competition to select a champion among each group."

Nefreet glanced behind him at Lamia and received a curt nod. "In order to provide an educational opportunity for those who didn't make the cut, these competitions may also be viewed from the courtyard. This will give the remainder of you an opportunity to observe your peers and learn from them."

The headmaster's gaze swept across the crowd one final time. "With that, I will leave you to it. Consider the duels suspended until further notice. As for our potential champions, use this time wisely to prepare."

Nefreet abruptly stepped away from the podium, the faculty swiftly encircling him as they made their way out of the courtyard. Within only a few seconds, the crowd finally reacted, a ripple of sound sweeping across the players in a wave. It was a mixture of excitement, relief, outrage, frustration, and jealousy. A disharmonious cascade of noise that set Finn's teeth on edge.

"Well, shit," Kyyle muttered.

Finn glanced to the side to see the youth staring into space, his mental wheels already spinning. Finn idly wondered what it would be like to fight the earth mage, which immediately conjured the memory of Kyyle's conspiracy theory. He didn't actually know Kyyle's fighting style, or Zane's, or Vanessa's. Because the top-ranked students had never been paired together. Although it seemed that they would now get that opportunity.

It all felt too... *convenient.*

As Kyyle's eyes snapped back into focus, and he met Finn's gaze, he saw the same realization reflected there. It felt like this had been set up intentionally. Finn was beginning to question whether he had really convinced the faculty to lift the restrictions, or if this had been Nefreet's intention the entire time. But, if so, what was the goal?

"Well, this is going to be a real shitshow," Julia observed, her lips pursed as she watched the other students. "Now I need to find a good place to set up shop before the crowd moves in." She frowned in thought. "Maybe Brutus will let me borrow his umbrella, and I can find some beer somewhere. We can turn this thing into a magical tailgate..." She wandered off as she spoke, her eyes skimming the crowd for the large fire mage.

Which left Finn and Kyyle standing alone. "You know there's something else going on here, right?" Kyyle said softly.

"Yeah, I'm coming around to your theory," Finn replied.

Kyyle side-eyed him. "Our deal still hold?"

A grin tugged at Finn's lips. "Truce until we have to fight each other, I remember." He glanced at Kyyle. "But I'd be lying if I said I wasn't curious how you made it this far."

Kyyle snorted in amusement. "Says the guy who everyone claims is a cheater."

Then the young man's expression sobered, and he offered a hand. "I'll admit, I'm interested to see if I can beat you. However, I also don't want to be like these other assholes. Regardless of the outcome, I'd like to stay friends."

Finn looked at the hand for a moment, a strange feeling washing over him. Was this where he was now? About to shake hands with a goofy-looking college kid that he might have to murder tomorrow? It seemed like his entire world had been turned upside down and then shaken thoroughly. But he supposed he might as well lean into it at this stage.

Finn grabbed Kyyle's hand. "Sounds good to me. Good luck."

"You too," Kyyle replied. "I may as well go get ready. See you tomorrow, man." With that, the youth stepped away, making his way across the field.

As Finn's eyes followed the earth mage, he saw Zane and Vanessa lingering in the courtyard. They both eyed Finn, and he nodded at them. In contrast to Kyyle's reaction, he saw no goodwill in their eyes – only a cold appraisal.

The next couple of days were going to be interesting, to say the least.

Chapter 34 - Sturdy

When Finn returned to the courtyard the next day, it was a madhouse. The sands were packed with mages, their robed forms shuffling in one giant, brightly colored mass. The terraces weren't much better since many of the students had opted to set up camp on those balconies to get a better view.

Yet it wasn't the number of people that surprised Finn.

It was the object of their attention.

A massive circular pane of water, approximately thirty feet wide, now floated above the dais. The moisture was being suspended by at least a dozen water mages – staves held in hand – that ringed the platform. They each channeled a constant stream of water toward the circle, their staves glowing with a soft blue light.

Finn had no idea what he was looking at – although, the pane of water did resemble a screen. Perhaps the water affinity allowed some sort of scrying? That might explain Nefreet's comment about allowing the other mages to view these final matches. Although Finn had no idea how that was going to work.

He heard a sharp whistle and looked over to find Julia waving at him. "Hey, over here!" she shouted at him. Julia was standing near a familiar-looking umbrella, several glass chairs spread out under the canopy and a drink already in hand. It seemed his daughter had made good on her promise of a magical tailgate.

A minute later, Finn had managed to navigate through the mass of limbs and feet. He was greeted by the sight of a few familiar faces. It seemed that Julia had collected some friends while setting up camp in the courtyard. However, she didn't give him time to greet them, shoving a mug of something into his hand and herding him toward a chair before flitting off to talk to another mage.

She's not exactly keeping a low profile, Finn thought to himself.

"She roped us into this too," Brutus grunted at Finn, noting his confusion. Kyyle sat beside the fire mage and kept glancing not-so-discreetly in Julia's direction.

Finn just shook his head, his attention on the mages that filled the courtyard. "This seems like… a lot. I didn't realize there would be this many people watching."

"You nervous?" Brutus asked, side-eyeing him.

Finn rubbed at his neck. "I suppose so, although I'm not sure that matters. We're going to be competing whether I like it or not." This earned him an eye roll from the large fire mage and a snort of agreement from Kyyle where he sat nearby.

"Shouldn't we be on the dais?" Finn asked, directing the question toward Kyyle.

Brutus shook his head. "Don't worry about it. Nefreet's planning to choose the pairings at random. They'll call you lot up when your names get drawn."

Kyyle and Finn shared a look. For his part, Finn was hoping he didn't get matched with the young earth mage. He didn't look forward to the idea of trying to kill him. And he had come to learn that hesitation could be deadly in the duels. Many felt like he was playing a fast-paced and gruesome game of chess, with one wrong move deciding the fight.

"So, what's the deal with the big disc of water?" Finn asked as he slumped down into the chair, trying to change the subject and drain some of the tension from the air. He could already feel the antsy, nervous energy that preceded a major event humming in his veins. The best strategy was to try to distract himself.

Brutus grinned. "You'll see. Nefreet only pulls out all the stops for big competitions. It's a bit too energy-intensive for just any ol' duel." He waved at the dais. "Although it looks like you won't have to wait long to see it in action."

Finn turned to see Nefreet taking the stage, Abbad at his side. At a gesture from the headmaster, the librarian went through his routine, a gust of wind soon blowing through the crowded courtyard. The chatter slowed as the mages felt the familiar breeze on their skin, all eyes turning to the platform.

"Hello, mages," Nefreet greeted them.

"There is no sense beating around the bush. Today we will be conducting the semi-finals in our competition to choose a guild champion. The travelers and residents will each compete in their own elimination ladder. The travelers will go first."

"The rules will be the same as our regular duels. The participants will be teleported to a random location. The winner will be whoever manages to secure the other player's token and return first. Otherwise, anything goes."

Nefreet motioned at a nearby mage, and the man stepped closer. Finn could see that he was holding a large velvet bag. "We will be hosting two matches initially, with the winners of each match going on to fight in a final elimination round," Nefreet continued. "The initial pairings will be decided at random.

"With that out of the way, let's select our first competitors."

Nefreet dug into the sack beside him, and Finn held his breath, his hands clenching around the arm of his chair. The headmaster soon retrieved two glowing tokens. He turned to the crowd, announcing the first pairing. "Zane and Vanessa."

Finn let out his breath in a whoosh, noting that Kyyle had done the same. The pair glanced at each other awkwardly. While they might have gotten out of going first, the initial match-up meant that they would be fighting each other next.

Well, damn, Finn thought to himself.

"This should be interesting," Julia murmured, sliding into a chair beside Finn as she watched Zane and Vanessa both maneuver through the crowd to the stage.

Kyyle nodded. "It will be an even match given their spells and skill sets," he murmured, swiping at the air. Finn observed the gesture, assuming that the youth was accessing the journal he kept on the other students. He couldn't help but wonder what sort of notes Kyyle had on him.

Zane and Vanessa reached the podium a moment later. Zane wore simple cloth clothing, forgoing the typical robe. Oddly, he was equipped with only a single weapon, the massive two-handed hammer that he'd been lugging around for weeks. He barely looked like a mage. In contrast, Vanessa looked her part – dressed in flowing sapphire robes and carrying a staff adorned with a single, simple blue crystal at its peak.

The pair acknowledged one another but made no effort to speak or shake hands.

Nefreet handed each mage a token and then turned back to the crowd. "As one final note, these competitions will be carefully monitored using the scrying portal above me. This should give you all a chance to finally see the *A-listers* in action."

The headmaster nodded at Lamia, who stood nearby. The mage's hands twined through a complicated pattern, Finn's brow furrowing as he tried to track the movements and read her lips. Given the complexity and length of the incantation, he was guessing it was a master-level spell at a minimum.

A moment later, a ball of liquid materialized in the air beside Lamia, its form shifting and shimmering as though it were alive. The globe reminded Finn of Daniel. Perhaps this was an infant water elemental?

At Lamia's direction, the ball of moisture swept over to Vanessa and settled on her shoulder. Then Nefreet took a deep breath. "With all of our preparations out of the way. Let us begin the final elimination round of this competition!

"Zane. Vanessa. Good luck."

At this final statement, the pair touched their tokens together and abruptly vanished in a rift of multi-colored energy.

Immediately, all eyes turned to the disc of water floating above the field. The screen remained placid for several long seconds before the liquid began to swirl and spin, vague colors soon materializing among the waters. Then, all at once, a scene popped into focus.

The elemental had lifted from Vanessa's shoulder and was now floating above what appeared to be a mountaintop, recording the field below. Dark gray clouds lingered in the sky, and a faint smattering of snow drifted down on a flat plateau riddled with large rocks and patches of white.

Finn frowned in concentration, his nervousness forgotten as the analytical part of his brain kicked into overdrive. The field was compact, and he saw a sheer cliff edge on at least three sides. That meant Vanessa and Zane would be contained in this small, makeshift arena. The rocks strewn through the area also obscured line of sight. Notably, there were no environmental variables that would give one of the competitors an obvious advantage – at least not as far as Finn could see.

The elemental soon focused on the two contestants. They had been teleported in about 20 yards apart, their view of one another obscured by the massive boulders. Finn leaned forward as he watched their initial actions in this new arena.

Zane immediately started casting a spell, his fingers twining together. A moment later, his skin shimmered with a faint green light and then began to turn a solid, opaque gray, cracks forming in the once-normal flesh. It looked rougher and more durable than when Finn had watched Kyyle first cast the spell in Lamia's class.

"Hmm, intermediate *Stone Skin* at least," Kyyle observed. He noted Finn watching him and gestured at Zane. "That's what's letting him perform the full-body shift. Otherwise, he'd be limited to a single limb. It's a powerful defensive spell, although it has limitations. For example, it dramatically increases the weight and density of the mage."

Finn didn't have long to ponder on that. Because what Vanessa did next was far more fascinating. As she completed her initial spell, something drifted away from her stomach, as though her skin had turned to liquid. The blob grew swiftly and suddenly diverged, transforming into an eerily similar clone of the water mage.

Both Kyyle and Finn just stared. *What the hell was that?*

Brutus laughed at their expressions. "*Doppelganger* spell. Water mages can specialize in illusions. This typically makes it more difficult for them to cast hard-hitting spells since they have to maintain the illusion, but it can sure make them a real pain in the ass to fight. Also, that spell may be quite effective with this layout." His expression was thoughtful as he watched both contestants.

The pair started moving. Zane walked cautiously among the boulders, keeping his eyes peeled for an attack and holding his hammer at the ready.

For her part, Vanessa was less cautious. She shifted the channel for the *Doppelganger* to her staff as she cast *Obscuring Mist*. Finn recognized the gestures and incantation for that spell immediately – having studied the novice water spellbook. A thick mist soon rolled among the stones, further reducing visibility. At the same time, Vanessa gestured at her clone, sending it out among the boulders.

Zane slowed as he saw the thick vapor spreading, and he grimaced slightly. Finn could sympathize. Vanessa's strategy was smart. She likely knew she was less resilient than Zane, and she didn't know where he was yet. So, she was leaning into her advantage, further reducing visibility and trying to bait Zane into striking first to give away his position.

Vanessa suddenly stepped out from behind a boulder and Zane whirled. Moving with a speed and ferocity that left Finn stunned, the larger man sent his hammer hurtling through the air. Vanessa attempted to dodge, but it was far too late. The hammer smashed into her chest, and her body promptly exploded into globules of water that splashed against the ground. The hammer kept going, crashing into a boulder behind the clone, the force more than sufficient to crack the stone.

Zane didn't hesitate as he saw the clone break apart. He immediately dashed forward. His stone feet thundered against the ground, causing the soil to split and crack from his weight – Finn noting that he was indeed slowed by his *Stone Skin*. At the same time, that appeared to have some advantages. It seemed that Zane was able to use the additional momentum to empower his hammer throw. That would help to explain the force of the blow, at least.

Meanwhile, *Ice Bolts* pelted Zane's previous position. The water elemental's view shifted, showing that Vanessa had climbed atop one of the boulders, using the height to maintain visibility on the field and shower Zane with projectiles.

At first, Finn thought Zane was just trying to dodge the missiles, likely unable to see Vanessa while standing in the mists. In contrast, his movements made him easy for Vanessa to spot, each step causing the vapor to swirl and contract.

Although, if Zane was trying to avoid getting hit, he was doing a poor job of finding cover, the occasional stray bolt chipping away at the stone of his arms and legs.

Unless…

A smile tugged at the earth mage's lips, and his fingers twined through a rapid series of gestures. His weapon came hurtling back toward him out of the mists. In a single fluid movement, he spun and threw the hammer again, the weapon making a beeline directly toward Vanessa. She just barely scrambled off the boulder in time, the hammer crashing against the stone and letting out a thunderclap.

"He baited Vanessa into firing to figure out her position," Finn murmured.

"And found a creative use for the *Pull* spell," Kyyle added distractedly, his hands typing at his console. He saw Finn glance at him and elaborated, "Earth mages can control gravity as well as the density of objects. This is how we summon earth spikes, for example. *Pull* is a journeyman-level utility spell. In this case, Zane is using it to retrieve his hammer."

"Huh, that's clever," Finn replied, watching Zane. There was clearly a reason the man had made it this far.

Kyyle nodded. "The guy may be a dickhead, but he's good," he offered grudgingly. "Although, I don't think it's going to be enough…"

Finn could soon see what Kyyle meant.

Vanessa immediately reverted to a more defensive strategy. She summoned another clone, recast the mist, and then kept moving along the perimeter of the arena. She was waging a guerilla war against the earth mage. Her clone would pop out, reveal Zane's position, and then she would pelt him with a few *Ice Bolts*. Her attacks did little damage, but they slowly whittled away at Zane's health, carving off chunks of stone with each strike.

At the same time, Finn could see that the earth mage was becoming increasingly frustrated since he wasn't able to easily pin down Vanessa. His frown had deepened, and he was actively grinding his teeth together, the reinforced bone throwing off sparks.

"Come out and fight me!" Zane roared. Vanessa didn't respond or react, continuing her constant harassment.

What's her plan? Finn thought to himself.

"He needs to drop the *Stone Skin*," Kyyle murmured. Brutus just nodded in agreement.

When Kyyle saw Julia's questioning glance, he elaborated. "*Stone Skin* has an active sustain cost by default. Instead of a static shield with its own health, it reduces incoming damage by a flat percentage. Zane then relies on his natural health regen to recover any damage that makes it past the shield. Think of it like a defensive spell with a natural channel, I guess. My guess is that Zane put a lot of points in *Strength* and *Vitality* to compensate for the increased weight and to improve his health regen."

"Which means he's burning a lot of mana, and his pool isn't that large to begin with," Finn said aloud. Suddenly, Vanessa's plan clicked into place. She planned to wear Zane down so that he would remove his damage shield. That was why she was casting slowly and allowing her own mana to regenerate. She just needed to drag this out.

Zane seemed to realize the same thing, a grim expression settling across his face. "If you insist on hiding, I guess I'll just have to bring the fight to you!"

He abruptly dismissed the *Stone Skin*, or at least part of the spell. He maintained the spell on his chest and arms, while the remainder of his body regained its normal fleshy appearance. Then he re-called his hammer.

What he did next was plain madness.

Zane ran up one boulder, leaped over the edge and raised his hammer high into the air. The combination of his enhanced weight, momentum, and natural strength caused the weapon to strike the ground with terrifying force. The blast sent out a shockwave of kinetic energy that caused the ground to break apart and crumble, lancing forward in a straight line. The force of the blow was so powerful that it physically shoved the mist aside, carving a furrow in the vapor. As the shockwave hit a boulder, it smashed through the stone, causing it to crumble and crack before exploding apart in a shower of fragments.

Vanessa was forced to leap from her latest perch, hitting the ground hard and a whoosh of air escaping her lungs. Shards of rock cut at her face and arms, leaving small trails of crimson in their wake. However, she recovered quickly, recasting *Doppelganger* and sliding behind another boulder, staying along the outskirts of the field.

Yet Zane wasn't done. As the clone appeared, he repeated the same attack, smashing the ground repeatedly. Within the span of a few minutes, he had destroyed most of the boulders along the mountaintop and cleared a pocket amid Vanessa's mist. He soon stood there, his chest heaving and a layer of dust now coating his skin.

A sudden, eerie quiet now lingered through the courtyard as the students watched this impressive display of raw power. "Holy shit, we were supposed to keep up with this?" one novice a few feet away from Finn muttered.

Finn was less impressed. Zane had let his anger get the better of him. Kyyle must have been thinking the same thing, shaking his head sadly. Even as they looked on, the pair saw Zane's *Stone Skin* finally drop away as his mana bottomed out and he was forced to regen. That tantrum had likely spent most of his stamina as well.

Vanessa chose that moment to retaliate.

Ice Bolts sliced out of the mist, cutting bloody furrows in Zane's skin as he attempted to dodge the projectiles. Then Vanessa appeared, stepping out of the mists. Zane smirked at her, tossing his hammer almost casually. Yet instead of destroying what he must have assumed was a clone, Vanessa dropped to the ground into a roll and came back to her feet, her eyes glowing with a cold blue light.

A smile tugged at Zane's lips. He had found the real deal this time. Vanessa must have burned quite a bit of her own mana to maintain the illusions and constant barrage of *Ice Bolts*, finally forcing her to enter the fight personally. He rushed forward, his fingers twining through another series of gestures as he used his limited mana to recall his hammer.

The weapon came rushing back out of the mist and Vanessa side-stepped to avoid the returning blow, but the last-minute dodge put her off balance. Zane snatched the weapon from the air one-handed, rushing forward to capitalize on the water mage's moment of weakness. His left hook hit her squarely in the jaw, sending her stumbling backward.

The crowd of mages cheered, thinking that Zane was regaining the upper hand. Although, a frown lingered on Finn's brow. Something about that punch felt off, but he couldn't quite place his finger on why.

Vanessa backpedaled quickly to avoid Zane's follow-up swings, clutching her hand to her face, and her breathing ragged and panicked. Zane followed her, a mad grin painted on his face. The mists swirled around him with each swing of his hammer. Then Vanessa's foot landed wrong on the broken and uneven ground, and she was sent stumbling, falling hard on her back.

Zane approached her with measured steps as she struggled to crawl backward. A triumphant smile tugged at his lips.

Then Finn saw it. As Vanessa let her hand drift away from her face, there was no blood or bruising on her cheek.

"Oh shit..." he muttered.

All at once, the ground below Zane turned a dark blue, an intricate series of patterns etched into the broken stone. A series of icy spears launched from the ground in a flurry, each lance nearly as thick as Zane's forearm. They stabbed through his legs, arms, and torso as his body spasmed and jerked. Vanessa must have cast multiple *Grasping Cold* traps in the same location.

As the ice settled, Finn could see that Zane had barely managed to get off a *Stone Skin*, attempting to protect his legs. However, it hadn't been nearly fast enough. Lances were now embedded in the partially transformed skin of his legs and his unprotected chest. Even worse, he was trapped in place, half-suspended in the air and his blood leaking from the many wounds, staining the ice a bright red.

Then the image of Vanessa on the ground broke apart into a puddle of water, the real Vanessa striding calmly out of the mists, an *Ice Bolt* spinning in the air beside her. Her expression was calm and measured as she met Zane's angry and pain-filled eyes.

A swift gesture and the *Ice Bolt* embedded itself in the side of Zane's head.

And the fight was over.

A hushed silence had descended over the courtyard in the final moments of the fight. However, the tension broke soon after Zane died as an astonished cheer rose into the air. Finn ignored the noise, replaying the fight in his head. Vanessa's illusions were extraordinary. She had managed to make the clone react in an incredibly realistic manner. Not only that, but Finn's thoughts kept returning to Zane's punch.

She must have somehow increased the density of the clone's face to make it feel real, he thought to himself. Otherwise, the blow would have given away the gambit, passing through the clone's face or not offering enough feedback. Although, that indicated a terrifying level of control. It seemed the other A-listers had been just as busy as Finn.

He turned his gaze back to the floating screen. Vanessa stood beside Zane's corpse as the elemental panned around her. The water mage's eyes glowed a cold sapphire, and blood stained her robes as she observed Zane's body dispassionately.

If he made it through his own fight, this was what he would face.

As though reading his mind, Kyyle glanced at Finn, and their eyes met. They didn't need words to communicate what they were both thinking. They were up next. And if that match had been anything to go by, this was going to be one hell of a fight.

Chapter 35 - Soiled

"Finn and Kyyle," Nefreet called out, his voice echoing across the field.

Despite knowing that they were up next, Finn could still feel his stomach lurch at the sound of the headmaster's voice. He stood, forcibly shoving the emotion aside. He wasn't willing to give in to the enticing warmth of his mana just yet.

Both Julia and Brutus gave him a wordless nod as he met their eyes. There was nothing more to say at this point. Then the pair wound their way through the crowd, the other mages parting to let them pass and an excited hum filling the air as the students anticipated the next battle.

All too soon, Finn and Kyyle stood on the dais in front of Nefreet facing one another. The headmaster handed each of them a glowing token. Finn's thumb rubbed at the surface reflexively as Nefreet launched into another spiel, addressing the crowd.

Kyyle's eyes locked on Finn's. He offered a hand. "Good luck," he said quietly.

"You too," Finn grunted, accepting his grip but wincing internally. He really wasn't looking forward to killing one of the few tolerable people he had met in this magical prison.

Without warning, the earth mage tugged Finn closer, whispering into his ear. "Don't hesitate or go easy on me. I still think there is something weird going on here. My guess is that it has to do with you."

Kyyle stepped back, the gesture going unnoticed by the crowd. Although, Finn noted that Abbad was watching the pair closely. Finn looked at Kyyle with some uncertainty. He had to admit that some pieces still didn't add up, even with the last-minute setup of the final duels.

But what would make Kyyle think that Finn was at the center of this?

A more skeptical, jaded part of Finn's mind briefly considered that the young man could be messing with him, trying to throw him off his game. But that didn't really seem like Kyyle. Besides, he was explicitly telling Finn not to hold back.

Finn wasn't given time to consider this further. Nefreet's words suddenly penetrated the cluster of questions that swam through his head. "Now, without further ado, let us start the second competition of our semi-finals!

"Finn. Kyyle. Good luck."

That was their signal, and the pair reached forward. As their tokens touched, a flash of light enveloped Finn, and the world around him bled away, soon replaced by bottomless darkness.

*   *   *

It took Finn a moment to realize that he had arrived. He squinted, just barely making out the dark, blurry outline of the walls around him as his eyes tried to adjust to the sudden gloom. He resisted the urge to summon a *Fireball* and instead backed against what he assumed was a boulder, summoning his *Magma Armor*. There was no sense in giving away his position. The warm energy soon slid down both arms and glowed with a faint orange-and-red light – the dull glow hopefully too dim to draw attention.

In the time it had taken him to summon the spells, Finn's eyes had begun to adjust to the darkness, and he realized he could now see relatively well. He was standing inside a subterranean cavern, the ground a broken cluster of boulders, ravines, ridges, and large stalagmites. No sunlight trickled into the room. Instead, large patches of mushrooms and moss dotted the ceiling and walls, glowing with a sickly green-and-blue light. It was this bioluminescent fungus that made it possible to see.

As he surveyed his new battleground, Finn frowned.

His fire mana now simmered in his veins, and Finn was able to review his brief conversation with Kyyle with greater clarity. This cave lent some credibility to the young man's whispered words. The arena seemed to be tailor-made for an earth mage. It was possible it was simply a coincidence

– this cave *could* have been chosen at random.

But it sure as hell didn't *feel* like it.

Not that this did anything to help him with the current fight.

Finn stayed crouched down behind the boulder, giving himself a moment to think. Kyyle knew at least four earth magic spells – *Stone Spikes*, *Stone Skin*, *Dissolve*, and *Slow*. However, after watching the battle between Zane and Vanessa, it seemed safe to assume that Kyyle's sponsor had likely taught him one or two more journeyman spells. Finn also knew that the earth mage used a traditional staff, which gave him a single channel. That meant Kyyle would likely try to stay at a distance and use the environment to his advantage.

In contrast, Finn needed to get close and stay close to use his knives. He also couldn't be sure how much Kyyle knew about his abilities. Although one thing was abundantly clear – the kid was observant as hell. If Finn were a betting man, his money was that Kyyle knew at least part of Finn's abilities, either from studying him directly or by talking to the other students.

To make matters worse, anything that Finn could cast would make him stand out in the dark cavern. His eyes drifted to the glowing blue orb that drifted through the top of the cavern, recording the fight. Maybe he could wait and hope Kyyle made the first move.

However, as the seconds ticked by, Finn couldn't hear any movement from deeper within the cave. It seemed that Kyyle was waiting for him to strike first. Finn was also concerned that the earth mage could slowly terraform the environment if given enough time. It was possible that Kyyle might be able to use *Dissolve* without creating much noise.

I need to move.

"Daniel," Finn whispered.

The AI immediately flashed into existence nearby, a ball of flame that shone brightly in the dark cavern. "Go immediately. Fly through the cavern, winding through the boulders about four feet above the ground."

"Yes, sir," Daniel chirped and then sped away.

Then Finn started moving. He sprinted away from the

position where he had been crouched, trying to put as much distance between himself and the initial flash of orange light as he could. He likely only had a few seconds.

It wasn't a moment too soon.

Finn heard a rumble and looked back to see that a pit had opened up where he had been crouching. It seemed that Kyyle hadn't been fooled by Finn's ruse with Daniel. Instead, he'd focused on the original source of the trail. Finn could still see Daniel in the distance, winding between the boulders.

Damn, the kid is too smart for his own good. With his fire mana surging through his veins, this only amped up Finn's excitement. Now this was a real opponent!

However, he hesitated as he saw Daniel's light suddenly flash erratically, and then the AI flew up into the air, his voice echoing through the air. "Danger! Ambient mobs are present!"

It took Finn a second to see what the AI was yelling about. They were just dark blurs along the walls of the caverns, their bodies barely illuminated by the mushrooms. As Daniel flitted past one, Finn saw that it was some kind of beetle, except it was about the size of a large dog, its face adorned with cruel-looking pincers.

As Daniel sped past, the beetles seemed to sense him, turning to look in the AI's direction.

Infrared vision? Finn wondered. *Fuck.*

Starting in an underground cave was bad enough, but there were also giant heat-seeking beetles down here? This only bolstered Kyyle's conspiracy theory.

His thoughts were interrupted as he felt the soil give way below him. He acted quickly, his fingers gripping at the edge of the pit and vaulting over the edge in a single move – the reflex only possible after hours spent sparring with Julia. He glanced down in the hole and saw large spikes erupting from the bottom.

Dissolve and Earth Spikes make a pit trap. Noted.

Then Finn finally caught sight of Kyyle. The young man had found a small ledge on the far side of the cave, using that vantage point to survey the room, and cast freely. Meanwhile, Finn could see that the beetles were starting to swarm after Daniel, the AI floating along the walls and attempting to stay out of reach.

As more pits began opening around him, Finn started running, weaving between the boulders, and trying to throw off Kyyle's aim. A pit opened up in front of him, and he doubled back, perching behind a series of boulders to give himself a brief respite.

His thoughts were racing. This was a shit environment for him. If he used his abilities, he gave away his location more easily to Kyyle and would likely attract the beetles. Right now, the poor lighting was the only thing that allowed him these brief moments to pause. However, if he didn't do something soon, Kyyle would likely turn the whole damn room into one giant pit trap. The longer he ran, the worse it would become.

That meant he would likely only get one chance to attack Kyyle.

Finn saw Daniel flit past above him, and a plan began to form in his head. He needed to poke at Kyyle a little to get a better sense of his abilities, but he was going to need to be discreet. He doubted the earth mage had revealed his full hand yet. To top it all off, Finn should try to be as circumspect with his own abilities as he could. He still needed to fight Vanessa – assuming he somehow managed to win this.

Finn brought up his in-game console, dashing out a short message to the AI. Daniel's movements changed, and he began to weave an intricate pattern along the walls, staying a few feet away from the rock surface and out of the reach of the throng of beetles that now littered the walls. Finn didn't want a stray *Earth Spike* to take him out.

Then he swept the terminal aside. This next part was going to suck.

Finn's fingers wound through the gestures of a *Fireball*, the orb of flames soon igniting in the air beside him. Yet his hands kept going, summoning another until a pair of flaming spheres orbited him slowly.

Immediately, another pit began to form beneath Finn, but he was already moving. He dashed directly toward Kyyle, sprinting as hard and as fast as he could. The ground dissolved around him and Finn weaved from side to side to avoid the crumbling earth. As he closed in, he hurled the two *Fireballs* at the mage.

With a swift series of gestures, a wall of earth erupted from the ground in front of Kyyle, and the flames crashed against it, rolling across the condensed earth and charring the soil. A few seconds later, Kyyle broke apart the wall, providing line of sight on the cave once more.

Shit. Finn had no idea what to call that spell, but it seemed like the reverse of *Dissolve*.

Finn was already analyzing this new ability. It had taken Kyyle a moment to form the wall, and the *Fireballs* almost made it through the barrier. Yet within a few seconds, the soil had thickened, creating a nearly impenetrable wall about a foot thick. That gave Finn an opening – albeit a small one.

The ability to both dissolve stone and soil and erect new barriers also meant that Kyyle could terraform the environment at will. This had just gotten more difficult. Finn suspected that Kyyle had used that combo to win his previous fights. All he would need to do was drop the ground out from beneath a player. Even if the spikes didn't kill them, he could seal off the pit and wait until they suffocated.

Finn dove to the side as another pit opened up below him. He was going to have to change his plan a bit. He chucked another *Fireball* at Kyyle to buy himself a few seconds and then turned on his heel and sped backward away from the mage, making a beeline toward Daniel. He and the AI needed to regroup near the southern edge of the cave, but he also needed to make sure to keep his distance, or he might accidentally attract the beetles. He wove and leaped through the cavern as pits formed around him, all the while keeping a watchful eye on his stamina.

When Finn saw the telltale flicker of the AI in the corner of his vision, he changed course. He began weaving back through the room, staying on the one side of the cave. Meanwhile, Daniel started arcing back on the other side of the cave, each of them slowly circling their way back to Kyyle's ledge on the far end of the room.

The earth mage seemed to realize what was about to happen. He shifted his attention away from Finn for a moment, and the pits abruptly stopped forming. Finn couldn't see what Kyyle was up to in the gloomy cave – not while he kept up with his frantic pace.

As he neared Kyyle's location, his hands began moving. Flames soon wrapped around his knives as they slid from their sheaths. Finn's UI updated automatically, his control range now glowing in a circle around him.

He still needed to be closer – much closer.

Finn raced headlong toward Kyyle but slowed slightly as he saw an empty expanse of darkness now lingering along the base of the ledge. The young man had diverted his attention to create an effective moat around his location. The ravine was nearly twelve feet across, leaving only a sheer cliff face along the other side. This trapped Kyyle in place, but also made it a royal pain in the ass to reach him.

Damn it. Finn couldn't afford to stop.

His eyes darted to the wall to his right. Kyyle hadn't messed with that surface. He probably didn't expect Finn to suddenly turn into a spider. A crazy plan raced through Finn's mind and his mana burned in response. He could see Daniel arcing along the other side of the room – speeding along the path that Finn had fed him.

He didn't have time to second-guess himself.

He only had one shot at this.

Finn's world funneled until all he could focus on was each footstep and the flaming blades that drifted around him. The lip of the ravine approached swiftly, the stone floor ending in darkness. He had no doubt that some very sharp spikes rested at the bottom.

Finn leapt over a newly formed pit as he approached the chasm. He stumbled slightly, but quickly regained his balance, continuing his headlong sprint. He didn't slow down. He couldn't afford to.

As he reached the chasm, Finn didn't hesitate. He leapt into the air above the dark ravine, feeling the bottom drop out of his stomach at his sudden weightlessness. Then his foot landed on the hilt of a knife, the blade embedded in the stone wall. He leapt again, his other knife slamming into the cavern wall even as his first retracted and raced ahead of him, forming a makeshift staircase up the wall.

In his peripheral vision, Finn could see Kyyle's eyes widen, and his hands began to move. If he dissolved sections of the wall, Finn was going to have some problems. Yet the earth mage hesitated as Daniel sped past his head. The chitter of chitin striking stone was loud now, sounding like muted machine gunfire.

Kyyle turned and saw the horde of beetles sweeping across the wall behind him, chasing after Daniel. With a grimace, Kyyle was forced to shift strategies. His incantation and gestures changed subtly. Finn recognized them now. He had been watching the earth mage's movements as he dodged around the room. He was about to build some walls and let the beetles handle Finn – which was his best move.

Finn only had a window of a few seconds.

His foot touched another blade, and he pivoted, kicking against the cavern wall as hard as he could. Finn flew forward even as a new barrier of stone and dirt began to drift out of the ground around Kyyle. He tucked his head down and rotated so that his armored shoulder slammed against the earthen barricade that was still forming. It was just enough to punch a small hole in the wall.

And a single flaming blade sped through.

Finn's other blade stabbed into the wall of the cavern. Finn flipped backward off Kyyle's stone wall, barely managing to land nimbly on the other blade with one foot, wobbling unsteadily. He stood there, suspended precariously about twenty feet above the pit below, his muscles burning in protest and his stamina beginning to bottom out.

Yet his other hand hadn't stopped moving.

I'm sorry, Kyyle.

Seconds ticked past, the on-rushing horde of beetles still skittering forward.

Yet Finn waited.

A moment later, the earth mage's half-formed barrier began to crumble and break apart. What it revealed was Kyyle crumpled in the center of his miniature fortress, blood leaking from dozens of stab wounds and staining his robes a dark crimson. He let out a single gasping breath before going still.

Even with his fire mana surging in his veins, Finn felt a wave of nausea strike him as he looked at Kyyle. He hadn't been able to see inside the barrier, and so he had been forced to strike at random. The carnage was gruesome. Kyyle's face was awash in blood, and his unseeing eyes were still wide – staring directly at Finn.

Yet he couldn't stop now.

Finn clung to the warmth of his mana, letting it burn away the gnawing doubt and horror that twisted at his stomach. He forced himself to look away from Kyyle, only to see that the swarm of beetles was still approaching.

His eyes darted to Kyyle's body. He needed that token.

Moving quickly, Finn's other blade stabbed into the wall, and he jumped from blade to blade, running along the edge of the wall and directly toward the horde. Using the very last of his stamina, he dove forward, rolling across the ground. Kyyle's still-warm blood splashed his shirt and arms. Finn fumbled inside the earth mage's robes, his fingers slippery as he looked for that damnable token.

The chittering had grown even louder, the beetles only a few feet away now. They seemed to sense Finn's body heat, changing course until they were headed directly toward him, a roiling mass of chitin and gnashing pincers.

Then Finn's hand closed around a familiar object.

He ripped it from Kyyle's pocket, his hands drenched in blood. He managed to touch the token to his own just as claws sliced through his tunic, leaving a line of burning marks along his chest and neck.

Then the world disappeared around him.

* * *

Finn slumped to the ground, unable to stay standing. Aching lines of pain had been etched into his chest, his blood leaking onto the ground. Even worse, his stamina had finally hit zero, his muscles burning and unresponsive.

He gasped, a roaring sound in his ears.

It took him several precious seconds to realize he was still alive and that the roar wasn't his heartbeat. It was the cheers of hundreds of students – a flickering screen hovering above him. In his peripheral vision, he could already see green-robed mages rushing to tend to his injuries. His eyes drifted to his hand – his knuckles white. His fingers slowly unfurled. Two tokens rested in his palm.

He had won – if only barely.

Yet as his mana slowly receded and despite the pain and the cheers, Finn could only think of one thing. The image of Kyyle's bloodied face lingered in his mind's eye, burned into his retinas with painful clarity.

He had won.

But was it worth it?

Chapter 36 - Shaky

Finn sat in a small tent that had been erected along the side of the courtyard. The green-robed mages had tended to him, healing his wounds and handing him a tonic to help replenish his stamina. It seemed that Nefreet had anticipated some injuries, although Finn suspected that the tent was intended primarily to help treat the residents.

While Finn had been half-carried off the dais, he had heard Nefreet announce that the competition would move on to the semi-finals for the resident students. This would give Finn and Vanessa a chance to recover and regroup before their last match. Finn suspected he had an hour or two until he would be forced to fight the water mage.

Although he had mixed feelings about that.

The image of Kyyle's bloodied face had stuck with him. Usually, his fire mana made the battles easier, burning away his hesitation and replacing it with boundless excitement. With the other students, he was able to shake it off. Simply ignore what he had done and pretend that they were just faceless opponents.

Yet the warm energy wasn't enough right now. It was different when it was someone he knew. What had the young man experienced? Trapped inside those earthen walls, a self-imposed prison. The panic at feeling cornered. The burning sensation as the flaming blade stabbed and cut. The image of Kyyle's body returned then – that expression that lingered in his dead eyes – that was something Finn had seen before. It was the same look he had seen on Rachael's face right before...

"Hey, man," someone said, a hand clapping Finn on the back.

He looked up in surprise, nearly falling off his perch on the cot, to find Kyyle standing over him. A shaky grin crept across the young man's face, and he looked pale. Yet he was alive. In contrast to the real world, at least inside AO Finn's actions – or mistakes – weren't permanent. Although, that did little to ease the knot in his stomach.

"You look like shit," Finn observed with a grunt.

"Hey, that's my line," Kyyle retorted. He gestured at the cot. "You mind if I sit down?"

"Go ahead."

The pair sat there in silence, neither of them quite sure what to say.

"So, I'm starting to understand how you became an A-lister," Kyyle finally said, breaking the quiet. "I mean, I heard rumors, but..." He looked at Finn and shook his head incredulously. "Once those daggers are imbued with fire, you can actively direct them within your control range, can't you?"

Finn eyed the healers around them, lowering his voice. "Yeah. Apparently, fire magic is about controlling thermal energy. At least, that's how Brutus explained it to me."

"Did he also turn you into a ninja?" Kyyle asked in an exasperated tone. "Seriously, what the hell was that move at the end? You were leaping between daggers that were about an inch or two wide."

Finn rubbed at his neck. "Uh, well that one might have been Julia." At Kyyle's questioning glance, Finn elaborated. "She can be quite nimble... for a mage."

"For a *mage*?" Kyyle asked, skepticism lacing his voice. His implication was obvious. He didn't think Julia was really a student. Not that Finn blamed him. She never attended classes or participated in the duels, and she always kept her arms hidden from view.

Finn just shrugged noncommittally. "And what about you, huh?" he tried to deflect. "Just set yourself up with a little stone fortress. That combo is pretty deadly."

Kyyle grinned. "You gave me the idea after we tried to survive Brutus' golems. Manipulating the environment instead of attacking someone directly is pretty effective. You wouldn't believe how many people I've dropped into a hole in the ground."

"I think I would," Finn groused. He side-eyed the young earth mage. "Seriously, that was probably the most difficult fight I've had in a while."

"Not surprising. You were dropped into a poorly lit underground cave and forced to fight an earth mage who just happened to specialize in building walls and pits," Kyyle added with some sarcasm.

"You forgot about the heat-seeking beetles," Finn groused.

Kyyle barked out a laugh. "How could I forget!"

Then the earth mage's expression sobered, and he glanced at Finn. "Joking aside, you can't tell me that that duel felt genuinely random. It seemed tailor-made for me and weighted heavily against you."

Finn grimaced. The thought had occurred to him, and Kyyle's whispered words before their duel had stuck with him. "I'll admit it seemed a bit unfair." He looked at Kyyle. "But what you're proposing is one hell of a conspiracy. It would require rigging the rankings, the semi-final selection, and then tailoring the teleportation for that specific duel. You're suggesting—"

"That at least one member of the faculty is involved," Kyyle replied under his breath. "That's the most obvious deduction given the facts."

"It could be a coincidence," Finn offered weakly.

Kyyle just gave him a deadpan expression.

"Okay, fine. It seems like more than a coincidence at this stage," Finn acknowledged. "But what could be the goal of rigging these duels or messing with the students? And why would a member of the faculty be targeting me?"

Kyyle frowned. "That part is still a mystery to me. Maybe they don't want a traveler to control the city? The faculty are all residents, after all."

Finn grimaced. That did make a certain amount of sense. Someone could have been trying to undermine his score by targeting him for the assassination attempts. They might have also tried to rig the duels so he would lose.

But it still didn't address why they were targeting Finn specifically. If Kyyle was right and someone was trying to manipulate the duels, why would they have favored the earth mage over Finn? Were they just assuming that Finn was more dangerous or likely to win? While he certainly appreciated the indirect compliment, Kyyle hadn't exactly been a weak opponent. Besides, if the person's motive was to avoid having a traveler win, wouldn't they be focused on trying to discourage *all* travelers from participating in the duels?

It just didn't feel right. Finn rubbed at his temple, closing his eyes as these frustrated thoughts tumbled through his mind. He could see the "effects," but the "cause" was still elusive and hard to pin down.

Either way, it did little to address the larger question that kept bouncing around Finn's head. It had been something that had been nagging at him for a while but had only been driven home after he was forced to fight Kyyle.

"Are you going to keep going?" Kyyle asked softly.

Finn looked at him in surprise, suddenly wondering if earth mages could read minds now.

Kyyle grinned at his bewildered expression. "Come on. You've had the entire student body gunning for you for a couple weeks now, you've basically stopped logging out except to eat and shit, and there is clearly some sort of conspiracy against you." The young man hesitated for a moment. "Plus, unlike Zane, I don't get the sense that you enjoy hurting other people – even if it's only temporary."

"What, are you a psych major or something?" Finn grunted.

Kyyle's smile widened.

"Damn it, I should have known," Finn grumbled, glaring at him. Many of the signs had been there. Most earth mages focused on logic and deductive reasoning – peace through the absence of emotion – and Kyyle was no exception. Then there was the way the earth mage had carefully cataloged the other students.

"Hey, watching other people and figuring out what makes them tick is entertaining," the young man replied. "It's that sort of experience that also makes it obvious that you're trying to deflect again."

"Is this going to be a thing now? Just psychoanalyze me every time we talk," Finn muttered good-naturedly.

Kyyle arched an eyebrow.

"Okay, I'll admit I don't love these duels," Finn began. "I have some... well, some history I guess you could say." Even mentioning it tangentially caused a hollow pit to form in his stomach. Finn suddenly realized that this might have been one of the few times he had spoken about Rachael – even indirectly – to someone besides his children. Or a cryptic in-game deity that could read his mind, he supposed.

"I can't help but wonder if this is worth it," Finn continued, his gaze dropping to the floor. "Do I even really want to rule an in-game city? Compete in some super deathmatch after this one? Be the target for some ridiculous magical conspiracy?" He hadn't even mentioned that he had been conscripted into being the "chosen one" for a cryptic lady that claimed to be the god of fire.

Finn shook his head. "I've been so focused on just getting past the next hurdle and learning more about this world that I guess I never stopped to consider if this is even what I want."

As he always did, Finn had let his passion blind him. It was about the chase. The curiosity. The discovery. Yet the last time he had allowed his passions to lead him, he had lost everything. What would happen here? And for what? Some bragging rights in a videogame?

Yet even as he thought that it felt disingenuous. At this stage, he had experienced enough of this place to know it wasn't merely another game. Someone had created a living, breathing *world* here – replete with its own lore and people. It sometimes felt so real that Finn had difficulty remembering that he was plugged into a headset.

And maybe that was part of the problem. It wasn't just that he had been forced to kill Kyyle, or that it looked so damn realistic. What bothered Finn the most was how easy it had been – especially with the boiling energy surging through his veins. He had killed this kid with barely a second thought.

Finn suddenly realized he had lapsed into silence and looked back up at Kyyle, who was watching him with a sympathetic look. "I guess I don't know."

"That's fair. I certainly can't understand what you've been through and I'm happy that I don't have some huge magical bull's eye painted on my back," Kyyle replied.

He hesitated, meeting Finn's eyes. "But as someone who just spent two weeks grinding away at these duels and who just got a flaming dagger forcibly inserted into some really uncomfortable places, my vote is that you should keep going."

Kyyle glanced at Finn. "As I was walking over here, I was also eavesdropping on the other students. You know who they were talking about? It wasn't me, or Zane, or Vanessa. They were talking about you and that crazy batshit plan you just pulled off. How you backflipped off a damn wall twenty feet above a pit full of spikes. Oh, and you were casting at the same time – that point didn't go unnoticed."

Finn stared at him in surprise. Kyyle paused before continuing, shaking his head and his eyes on the floor. "There's something about you. Maybe the same thing your mysterious attacker sees as well. You approach this game much differently than the others – like it's real. There's something about the way you tackle a problem or challenge that is just... well... inspiring.

"If you want to call it, I understand. But if my input means anything, I'd love to see you standing on that platform at the end of this."

Kyyle let out a grunt as he rose from the cot and started heading toward the flap of the tent. Yet he paused after taking only a few steps and turned to look back at Finn. "Or maybe I just want to see someone knock Vanessa off her pedestal," he added with a grin. Then Kyyle walked out, leaving Finn to his thoughts.

He didn't really feel any better after the conversation, doubt still flitting at the edges of his mind. Although, Kyyle's words had softened the sting. He had to admit that he was curious to see where all this would lead. Why had the Seer chosen him? Who was tampering with the duels and why? And there was still a part of him that wondered how he would measure up against Vanessa.

Finn heard the roar of the crowd outside the tent, signaling that a resident duel had just ended. It seemed that he wouldn't have much time left to sit here and ponder on his life choices. Whether he liked it or not, his duel with Vanessa was swiftly approaching, and there was a horde of other students out there waiting to see the final duels. Hell, he could always decide to leave after he finished this silly competition.

So, Finn did what needed to be done. He swallowed his doubt, smacked himself a couple times, and got his tired, mopey old ass off the cot.

He had another battle to fight, after all.

Chapter 37 - Frigid

All too soon, Finn found himself standing on the stone dais, the gigantic liquid portal shimmering and shifting above him. Hundreds of students lingered about the burning sands and lined the terraces that ringed the courtyard, their eyes all focused on the pair of semi-finalists. An excited buzz of anticipation vibrated through the air. Vanessa stood beside Finn, although she had only given him a brief, dismissive glance. Despite her outwardly calm demeanor, he couldn't help but notice the way her hands were balled into fists, her nails digging into her palms.

Clearly, he wasn't the only one who was anxious about this next battle, although he doubted that Vanessa would openly admit that she was worried. Finn knew first-hand the pitfalls of pride. In his case, time and age had worn down that sense of ego. The world seemed to continually insist on showing him just how little control he really had over his life.

"Thank you to our resident novices for their great showing in the semi-finals," Nefreet announced, bowing his head at the small group of bloodied and injured mages that were being herded toward the healers' tent.

The headmaster's gaze turned back to the crowd. "Now we can move on to the last semi-final duel among the travelers. Vanessa and Finn will be facing off to decide which of the travelers will move on to the final elimination duel.

"The rules of the engagement are the same. Whoever returns to the dais first is the victor." Nefreet turned to Vanessa and Finn. "Are you ready?"

They each gave a curt nod.

"Then let the final duel among the travelers commence!" Nefreet announced.

Without any further ceremony, Finn and Vanessa touched tokens, and they both disappeared in a flash of multi-colored light.

* * *

The world suddenly snapped back into existence, Finn stumbling slightly. His feet landed with a splash and quickly sunk into thick mud. He immediately surveyed his surroundings and discovered that he was standing ankle-deep in what appeared to be a rice paddock – circular rings of water broken by thin, grassy knolls.

As Finn's gaze swept the field, he discovered that Vanessa had been dropped off only a few dozen yards away. Their eyes met, and they both stowed their tokens in a pocket before their fingers began winding through a lightning-fast series of gestures. Finn felt his doubt and hesitation melt away under the fiery effects of his mana. He immediately summoned his *Magma Armor*, the warm substance soon creeping down both arms.

It wasn't a moment too soon as Vanessa launched an *Ice Bolt* in his direction. Finn darted toward her, letting the bolt slide off his right shoulder – the ice carving a furrow in the molten substance that coated his arm. He needed to get close and stay close if he was going to have a chance of beating Vanessa. He remembered vividly how she had remained at a distance, using her clones to slowly whittle down Zane.

She must have been thinking the same thing since she abruptly changed tactics, and her fingers began to twine through the gestures of *Obscuring Mist*. A fine vapor was already beginning to form around her.

Shit, Finn thought. He knew her next step. She would slink back into the mist and then create her *Doppelgangers*. At that point, Finn would be at a disadvantage, his spells giving away his location and Vanessa able to attack at random.

He needed to beat her to the punch.

Finn ran harder, and his feet splashed through the water. The terrain was slowing him down and making it difficult to run, the mud sucking at his feet with each step. It was clear that this environment was better suited to his opponent. Again. However, he didn't have time to focus on that, continuing his headlong charge.

His daggers soon slid from their sheaths as he finished casting *Imbue Fire*, the blades rotating around him slowly. Vanessa hovered just outside his control range, and he ordered the blades forward to save himself a few precious seconds. The daggers rocketed through the air, heading directly toward the water mage. Her eyes widened slightly, but she didn't slow her casting.

Just as Finn came into range, Vanessa completed her spell. A nearly impenetrable mist exploded outward in an expanding ring, rolling past Finn and sweeping across the paddock. At the same time, Finn's blades lanced through the spot that Vanessa had been occupying a moment before, the flames barely visible amid the mist.

Finn saw no notification in his combat log.

He had missed.

He retracted the blades defensively. Finn could hear splashing in the mists, but the sound was muted and indistinct, making it difficult to identify Vanessa's location. Even more problematic, Finn could barely see his own hand in front of his face. Acting quickly, he repeated a trick similar to the one he had used with Lamia. He directed the daggers to spin around him, the combination of the movement and flames creating a miniature vortex that forced away the nearby vapor and created a small pocket of clear air.

It wasn't much, but it might give him a few seconds to react to an attack.

Finn went still, eyeing the mists, and quieting his breathing. He strained to catch any sound that might indicate that he would be attacked. He quietly ordered Daniel to stay close, the fire elemental hovering beside his shoulder. Finn couldn't afford to lose the AI. He needed someone to watch his back.

His thoughts were racing, trying to come up with a strategy for fighting Vanessa. This was a terrible environment for him. He was basically in a flat field with no obstructions that he could use as cover. On top of that, the water and mud greatly slowed his movements. Even if he dismissed his blades, it would be challenging to hide, each step causing the water to splash and ripple.

Finn suddenly saw a dark silhouette in the mist. Acting on instinct, he resisted the impulse to have his daggers attack the target.

"Attack from behind—" Daniel called out.

Finn ducked. The *Ice Bolt* sliced through the air above him and slammed into the ground nearby. The shard exploded as it hit the surface of the paddock, instantly freezing the water and creating a thick coating of ice about three feet wide. Finn stared in surprise at the point of impact.

A variant of Ice Bolt maybe? Or maybe she charged the spell before firing? Finn thought to himself. It seemed that Vanessa had saved some tricks during her duel with Zane. Perhaps some of her ego was justified after all.

Another *Ice Bolt* cut through the mists. This time, Finn intercepted it with one of his blades, slicing it in half. Surprisingly, the bolt didn't detonate this time. Perhaps the explosion only triggered on impact.

However, Finn's analysis was cut short as Daniel shouted another warning. His eyes widened, and he dove to the side, narrowly avoiding a third missile and drenching his tunic in the process. Soon, another patch of ice had been formed along the ground.

What the hell? Finn thought to himself. How had Vanessa cast those three spells in such quick succession? She should only be able to channel one spell, and he had observed during her fight with Zane that the cast time of her *Ice Bolt* was a couple seconds.

Unless she can channel two spells...

"Damn it," Finn muttered to himself.

"I see you're starting to understand your predicament," Vanessa called from the mists. The sound came from his right, and Finn turned slightly.

"Water magic really does have some interesting tricks," she continued. This time, the voice came from the other side. She must be using her doppelgangers to speak to him and keep the presence of the real Vanessa hidden.

To pull off that trick, Vanessa would likely need to be channeling mana into the clones as well. How was that even possible? That meant she was capable of a minimum of two channels or possibly three? Or maybe she shifted one of them to the clones after she cast the *Ice Bolts*?

He needed more information.

Finn didn't bother to respond to Vanessa. Instead, he immediately dashed toward the sound of the first voice. He soon caught sight of a dark silhouette and stabbed his blades forward, aiming for the legs. His daggers easily cut through the limbs, and the clone toppled to the ground, its torso already beginning to dissolve.

However, Finn had a chance to see Vanessa before the clone disappeared entirely. Clutched in her hand, was a wand that he didn't recognize. The entire weapon was crafted from a glimmering sapphire crystal, intricate runes carved into the base of the rod. At the top, a fist-sized gem had been fused to the weapon, glowing with a soft blue light.

That's new. Finn had never seen a weapon like that in the requisition hall, and his guess was that Vanessa had smuggled it into the duel in her bag. Finn could also vaguely recall one of his conversations with Brutus. His instructor had explained that there had once been staves and wands capable of channeling multiple spells. It seemed that Vanessa had found one – as a novice mage.

Or the far more likely answer was that someone was cheating.

Shit. Shit, shit, shit, Finn thought, gritting his teeth. He was in a terrible environment that seemed to be tailor-made for a water mage, and she somehow had a crazy rare wand? There was no way he could believe this was a coincidence – not at this point. Although, this realization did little to help him at the moment.

Another bolt speared out of the mists, and Finn cut it down with a stroke of his daggers. He glanced at the UI in the corner of his vision, noting that his mana had already dwindled by about 10%. He couldn't afford to keep up the channel indefinitely, and meanwhile, Vanessa was currently free to continue pelting him from the mists, giving herself time to regenerate her own mana.

Which meant that Finn needed to get rid of this damn mist. He had an idea for how to do that, but he would need some time, and he couldn't afford to let Vanessa continue to pelt him from every direction.

"Daniel," Finn murmured.

"Yes, sir?" the AI replied.

"Update my UI to show the rough trajectory of each bolt," he instructed quietly. "We can assume that Vanessa has a control range equal to mine or less. You should be able to triangulate her rough location based on the angle of the attacks." The AI flashed once in response.

Vanessa could only form the bolts within her control range. Right now, she was close enough to be able to fire at Finn from all directions. That meant he needed to create some distance. That would give Daniel a chance to home in on her location.

In short, this next part was going to suck...

Finn didn't give himself time to second-guess his plan. He sprinted toward one edge of the paddock, heading in the opposite direction from the previous bolt. As he ran, a rain of *Ice Bolts* sliced through the mist, Daniel shouting out the occasional warning. Finn dodged and wove, destroying the bolts where he could and only sustaining a few close scrapes.

Finn's UI continued to update, lines tracing the trajectory of each bolt. The angle of attack was narrowing the farther he ran. That indicated that Vanessa and her clones were all behind him now. Then Finn's UI finally flashed, and he glanced over his shoulder. Daniel had highlighted a rough circle about 10 yards behind him.

That meant she could only attack from one direction now.

Finn abruptly stopped and whirled, his daggers sliding back into their sheaths. He dropped to a crouch and raised his arms protectively, his fingers already twining through another spell as he held his breath. Flames began to curl through the air, the heat causing the ambient vapor to hiss and evaporate. Finn felt an *Ice Bolt* slam against his shields, the force of the blast causing him to stumble slightly and coating his forearms in ice. Yet the molten armor soon ate through the ice, freeing his limbs.

His fingers never stopped moving.

A veritable torrent of flames soon swirled around Finn, the heat so great that it was pushing back at the mists. Vanessa showered him with a flurry of bolts now, but the lances were half-melted by the time they struck his armor, the ambient heat acting as a shield.

Then Finn completed the *Fire Nova*.

Flames raced away from Finn in an expanding ring, burning across the field. The mists put up little resistance in the face of the inferno that blazed through the paddock, soon evaporating and drifting away in ghostly tendrils. As the flames finally cleared, Finn rose, keeping his arms up protectively. He resisted the urge to re-summon his blades, giving his mana a chance to regenerate.

Streamers of mist and steam drifted above the field and lifted off Finn's wet clothing. His *Magma Armor* was in rough shape, but he had managed to remove the *Obscuring Mist*. He found himself facing five clones of Vanessa that stood passively in the field, watching him with an appraising expression. At some point, she must have blasted the ground around her clones, creating a patchwork circle of ice. Her plan was obvious; she intended to fortify that position and make it difficult for him to approach.

Vanessa snorted, all five clones mimicking the movement perfectly. "An interesting strategy. You removed the mists, but that won't help you," they said in unison.

Finn just smiled, his eyes blazing with burning energy.

Actually, removing the mist helped a lot. The fact that there were so many clones and they were all perfectly mimicking her movements was proof of that. Vanessa must have recognized Finn's *Fire Nova* from their encounter with Brutus and realized that Finn intended to clear the mists. She couldn't stop him with his armor; therefore, she had cast more clones in anticipation of losing the concealing fog.

Finn had also made an assumption. Namely, that Vanessa's fancy new wand could only channel two spells. Concealed within the mists, Vanessa could use those channels to fire more bolts. But now she was forced to give up a channel to maintain the *Doppelgangers*. In order to maintain the illusion, Vanessa would need to be able to summon *Ice Bolts* near the clones within her control range. Otherwise, Finn would know which Vanessa was the real one. That meant devoting at least one more channel to her *Ice Bolts*. Plus, she was going to have to keep pressure on him now that he could see her.

He could work with that.

Vanessa frowned at the smile painted on Finn's face. In response, she started summoning more *Ice Bolts*. The clones followed suit, ice soon drifting through the air beside them as five bolts homed on Finn's position. She then shifted the channel to her wand and began summoning five more.

10 bolts. 8 are likely illusions, Finn reasoned.

"Keep track of the source of the bolts," Finn whispered to Daniel. "Maybe she'll mess up and won't vary the pattern among the clones." The AI flashed once in acknowledgment.

Finn didn't have much time to think after that.

He raced forward, his feet pounding at the water. At the same time, Vanessa began her barrage. Shards of ice sliced through the air in a torrent and Finn dodged and wove. His daggers soon re-emerged, flames curling around the blades. With deft fingers, Finn directed their movements as he ran, chopping bolts in half or knocking them off course. Most dissipated into harmless globs of water that promptly splashed back into the paddock.

The clones shifted, turning to follow Finn's movements. Despite his excellent defense, the barrage proved to be too much. One bolt slipped past his blades, and Finn barely raised his arm in time. The shard sliced through his fractured armor, and the molten armor finally failed. The missile exploded, icy shrapnel piercing Finn's skin. He could feel a dull ache in his shoulder and felt warm liquid running down his arm now.

That wasn't water.

Shit. "Daniel?" Finn managed to gasp as he ran.

"She is varying the pattern," the AI replied, his voice sounding harried. "I can't determine which clone is the real Vanessa."

It was worse than that. Finn couldn't keep this up forever. His stamina was already depleting swiftly just from trudging through the water and mud. Not only that, but the occasional missed bolt froze the ground, creating little islands of ice that made it even more difficult to traverse the paddock.

Running through mud and water was slow, but he also couldn't maintain his balance easily on the slick ice. If Finn kept this up for much longer, there would be more ice than water.

He needed to create some space and regroup.

Finn changed course again, putting some distance between himself and Vanessa. A smirk curled her lips as he retreated and she gave him a moment's reprieve, likely allowing her own mana to regenerate. She knew she still had the advantage.

Finn didn't spare her that much attention. He plucked a few half-melted shards from his shoulder, his fingers coming away slick with his own blood. His thoughts were racing, and his fire mana surged in his veins. He needed a way to identify the real Vanessa from the clones. That was the only way he was going to win this.

He inspected the circle of ice where the clones stood. There had to be something. Some tell that would give them away. What had he missed?

He noticed the clones shift as Vanessa took a careful step forward, avoiding the defensive patches of ice. Finn's brow furrowed. Vanessa hadn't managed to freeze a perfect circle in the ground, and some of the clones stood in ankle-deep water. If he had trouble maintaining his balance on the ice, then so should Vanessa – the real Vanessa. A clone, however, wasn't likely to slip and fall. That might offer a way to identify the real Vanessa. She would be the one that avoided the ice or exercised more caution.

The obvious solution was to throw a few *Fireballs* at the clones, forcing them to avoid the blasts and step onto the ice. Although, that would still require him to move closer and he would only be able to maintain one dagger. That wasn't going to be nearly enough to block all of the ice bolts.

Besides, that only addressed one problem.

Even if he identified the real Vanessa, he would still need to get within range to attack her. He doubted that he would be able to hit her with a *Fireball* outside his control range. His daggers would work best. However, that would put him at the edge of the circle of ice or inside it, and Finn was also skeptical that she would give him time to deal much damage before she retreated. If she gave up the clones, she could also re-summon *Obscuring Mist*. Which meant he would only get one shot – and his window would likely only be a few seconds.

If only there were a way to win without killing her…

Finn froze as a desperate, stupid gambit flitted through his mind's eye. If he could identify the real Vanessa – even for a moment – it might work.

"This is going to hurt," Finn murmured to himself.

"Sir?" Daniel queried.

"Change of plans," Finn said quietly. "Instead of focusing on the trajectory of the missiles, look at the movements of the clones. I'm going to circle Vanessa and pelt her with *Fireballs*, forcing the doppelgangers to change position. Any clone that steps onto the ice without hesitation isn't real. Highlight the fakes in my UI."

Finn glanced at the glowing orb of flame. "Got it?"

"Without both of your knives and given the data from your previous attempt, you will likely only be able to withstand the assault for 90 seconds. This doesn't seem…"

Finn frowned. Was that worry he detected in the AI's voice? "We don't have time for a debate. That's the plan," he snapped.

"Yes, sir," Daniel replied reluctantly.

Then Finn turned to face Vanessa. She was watching him passively, her mana likely near full already. His eyes skimmed to his own UI, noting that his stamina had replenished along with most of his mana. He had lost 15% of his health on that first try, but it was slowly beginning to regenerate. He was glad he had chosen to invest a few points into *Vitality*. He quickly recast his *Magma Armor* along each arm.

He had to hope this would be enough.

Then his eyes locked on Vanessa, and Finn felt his mana surge. Liquid fire was flowing through his veins and the energy swept away his own doubt. He almost felt too anxious to stand still.

So, he decided to give in to the sensation.

Finn raced forward, taking a path diagonal to Vanessa's position and heading in the opposite direction of the small field of ice that he had created after his first attack. Vanessa just shook her head, summoning another barrage of *Ice Bolts*. She was likely thinking he intended to repeat his previous tactic.

That was fine. Finn preferred that she underestimate him.

His fingers began twining through a rapid-fire series of gestures, and a single dagger slid from its sheath and a *Fireball* soon erupted in the air beside him. Without any hesitation, Finn launched the ball of flames at Vanessa and her clones. He wasn't focused on hitting a clone, only on the angle of attack, trying to force each version of the water mage to step onto a patch of nearby ice.

Finn saw one version of Vanessa step back onto the ice without any hesitation, and her foot didn't slip on the slick surface. Daniel immediately highlighted the clone in Finn's UI, and he felt a moment of triumph. He could do this; he just needed to keep it up.

However, that proved to be tough. With only one dagger and with the water of the paddock slowing his movements, Finn was struggling to fend off the barrage of *Ice Bolts*. Identifying the clones also did little to help since Vanessa would randomly select a version of herself as the origin of a real missile. He was forced to take the occasional hit or use his armor to deflect the blows.

Within less than a minute, Finn's body was riddled with scrapes, and more than one shard of ice was embedded in his skin, a product of a series of close calls. His *Magma Armor* wasn't in much better shape. One arm was now completely exposed, and the armor on the other was already crumbling, but he didn't have the time to recast it. The silver lining was that four clones had been highlighted in Finn's UI, indicating that the real Vanessa stood in the center of the group.

He eyed his health bar in the corner of his vision. He had 60% health left. It would have to be enough for what he had planned next. He felt his fire mana surge through his body in a fiery torrent – responding to the sudden spike in adrenaline as he prepared for one last headlong dash.

Finn abruptly changed course and sprinted directly toward Vanessa. At the same time, he summoned his second dagger, the flaming blade sliding from its sheath. Vanessa just smiled as she watched his charge, perhaps assuming he had given up or was making one last-ditch effort.

Good, Finn thought to himself.

Finn dived under a bolt, sliding across a sheet of ice even as more missiles slammed down around him and exploded in a shower of ice. Then he was back on his feet, continuing his mad dash. He was almost within range, keeping a watchful eye on the translucent line that marked his control range. As the real Vanessa came within range, Finn launched a blade forward. However, he aimed for a clone instead of the real version.

The clone didn't bother to dodge and soon dissipated into a harmless glob of water. Meanwhile, the remainder of the group started to backpedal out of the circle.

However, Finn wasn't done. He arced the blade through the air directly toward the real Vanessa while attacking with his second blade from behind. One blade went high, causing her to duck under the attack. The second went low, but she managed to twist away in time, anticipating the attack. The second blade cut through her robe at the waist but left only a thin trail of blood in its wake.

Finn grimaced but was unable to follow up on the attack as another hail of *Ice Bolts* rained down on his position. He gritted his teeth as he felt a bolt slice through his arm, and frozen shrapnel embedded itself in his thigh. Gritting his teeth, he pushed through the pain. He had to keep moving forward. He needed to make it to the center of the circle. Vanessa and her clones had completely relinquished the protective ring of ice now and were blasting away at Finn.

He barely deflected another *Ice Bolt* in time, but it was a fake, the bolt crumbling into water. The momentary distraction allowed a real bolt to slip past his defenses as Vanessa changed the angle at the last moment.

Finn's eyes widened, and one of his daggers lanced

forward, just barely knocking it off course. However, the missile landed beside Finn, and he was caught in the edge of the blast. The water began to freeze, and Finn promptly stumbled and fell to his knees with a splash. As the ice fully hardened around his leg, it locked him in place.

Red notifications were flashing in his peripheral vision, and Finn knew he was on his last leg – both literally and figuratively. His health was red-lining, and his mana and stamina were nearly empty. He was approaching the end of the line.

He heard a clucking sound and looked up to see four Vanessas watching him with the same familiar smirk. Another eight *Ice Bolts* already drifted around her clones. "This is the almighty Finn that people keep talking about?" she taunted. "You don't seem so tough."

Finn didn't say anything. While Vanessa spoke, his hands had been moving under the water. He could see that ice was slowly creeping through the water as it continued to expand and it was growing colder by the moment. He needed to hurry, but he forced himself to keep his movements slow and deliberate.

She cocked her head. "In fact, that last charge was probably the stupidest thing I've seen in a long time – even if you did manage to figure out which of the clones was real. Zane put up a better fight!"

Finn needed to buy himself a bit more time. He would have to prey on one of Vanessa's weaknesses. It wasn't her spellcasting this time. It was a flaw he knew well.

He'd have to take advantage of that pride that shone in her eyes.

"And people think I'm the cheater," Finn retorted, shaking his head mournfully. "I wonder how you came to have that wand. You wouldn't be able to pull off half of those spells without that weapon."

Vanessa's expression warped into anger. "How dare you? You think I cheated here? This was skill, talent, and hard work. I *deserve* this win. I fucking outplayed you."

"Ahh, it seems like I touched a nerve." Finn gestured at the water elemental that floated above the field. "Don't worry. I'm sure the rest of the students will agree with me. It's okay to admit that you got carried by your gear."

Vanessa's eyes skimmed to the elemental, and her eyes flashed a brilliant sapphire, her anger evaporating under the effects of her mana. She snorted. "Or are these the empty taunts of a man that's frozen to the ground and half-dead.

"If this guild has taught us anything, it's that only the *results* matter. A win is a win."

Finn's fingers found a hard object beneath the water's surface. His face was haggard, his body drenched with a mixture of water, mud, and his own blood. Yet his eyes raged with a blazing, triumphant fire as he met Vanessa's gaze, a grin tugging at his lips.

"I'm glad you feel that way," Finn replied. "That makes this easier."

He lifted his arms from the water, revealing Vanessa's token in his right hand and his own token in his left. Vanessa's eyes went round, and she patted at her robes, feeling the gash in her pocket where Finn's blade had sliced through the fabric.

"How...?" she began.

"To use your own words, you were *outplayed*," Finn replied simply.

Vanessa realized what Finn was about to do. Moving quickly, she tried to stop him, launching her *Ice Bolts* forward and the hail of missiles barreling toward Finn's position. The bolts exploded on impact, creating a frozen nova that showered the area and created a massive block of ice. As the debris cleared, Vanessa scanned the area anxiously.

However, she was too late.

Finn was already gone.

Chapter 38 - Hesitant

When Finn reappeared in the courtyard, he immediately slumped to his knees. Red notifications continued to flash in his peripheral vision, as though he might have somehow forgotten that he was half-dead. Frozen fragments of ice were still embedded in his skin, his left leg was encased in ice – which blessedly helped numb the pain – and blood trickled down his arms and dripped from his fingers.

Even more strange was the silence. It was a heavy, palpable thing – the hesitation of hundreds of onlookers who stared at Finn's broken body with a mixture of admiration, disbelief, and anger.

Then a single cry rose from the crowd. Even with his vision swimming, Finn could see Julia leap from her seat. "Finn!" she cried, pumping her fist into the air.

It was like she had opened a release valve, giving voice to the pressure that had been building. A roar rippled across the courtyard, cascading down from the terraces before sweeping across the crowd of mages. The wall of sound was almost tangible as it struck Finn, shaking his bones and rattling his teeth. The vibration caused the icy shrapnel to shift in place, and Finn let out a hissing breath.

The noise soon condensed into a rhythm, and it took Finn a few seconds to realize that he was hearing a chant.

"FINN! FINN! FINN!"

His eyes swept across the crowd. They were chanting his name. Despite his injuries, his fire mana immediately began to respond, an ember burning in his chest and faint tendrils of flames curling in his irises. Yet he forcibly dismissed the mana. It wasn't the time. Besides, he hadn't exactly managed to beat Vanessa; he'd just relied on a simple trick to help even the odds a bit.

"Congratulations to Finn!" Nefreet said, his voice somehow carrying over the cries of the crowd. "He has bested all of the travelers and will move on to the final match."

Despite his tone, Finn noticed Nefreet glance at him, a

faint frown tugging at the corners of his lips. It seemed the headmaster was forced to acknowledge the win, despite the fact that Finn hadn't actually killed Vanessa. The rules of the duels had always been clear. The winner was whoever *returned* first.

Finn didn't shy away from Nefreet's gaze, meeting it evenly. Despite his strong words to Vanessa, he suspected most students wouldn't appreciate how rare and powerful that wand had been. Yet the headmaster couldn't plead ignorance. However, Finn noted no trace of guilt or hesitation in the man's eyes. He simply turned back to the crowd.

He knows. He knows someone is tampering with the duels, Finn thought feebly.

He could see green-robed healers rushing to his side as Nefreet turned back to the crowd, raising a hand to quiet their chant. "That concludes the duels among the travelers. We will move on to the final elimination round among the residents, and then tomorrow we will have one final duel to choose a champion to represent the guild in the Emir's competition.

"I suspect many of you have questions regarding this final duel. For example, how will we pit a resident against a traveler?"

A pause. "In short, tomorrow's final duel will be to the death."

Finn's eyes widened slightly. *What? I'm going to have to kill a resident?*

"Since the travelers cannot truly die, the faculty has decided to impose additional constraints in order to even the stakes. If Finn loses, his mana shall be purged, and he shall be exiled into the sands." Nefreet looked back at the other instructors and Finn could see Lamia glaring at him like he had just kicked her dog. Apparently, even this penalty didn't seem sufficient for some of the faculty. "We have decided that this should give both our contestants appropriate *incentive*."

An incentive to permanently kill a resident? Finn thought bitterly. He also hadn't missed that his punishment gave the faculty one more chance to get rid of him for good.

"With that out of the way, let us focus on our final duel

among the residents..."

Finn had difficulty paying attention to the remainder of Nefreet's speech. His vision swam, and his body felt like it had been run through a woodchipper. Since he couldn't easily stand, Abbad approached Finn, and his hands wound through a rapid series of gestures. Finn soon felt himself rise from the ground, green-robed healers hovering nearby and tendrils of healing energy wrapping around his wounds. The group then started moving off the dais, the librarian maintaining his spell.

Finn closed his eyes, his thoughts racing. He wasn't sure what tomorrow would bring, and he still didn't know who was manipulating the duels, but he felt relatively certain about one thing. The final duel tomorrow wasn't going to be a fair and even match.

* * *

A few hours later, Finn sat on the dais in the center of the courtyard. His eyes were closed, but he knew that twilight had come to the Mage Guild. The sun had finally sunk toward the horizon, and the blistering heat gave way to the promise of chill desert air. The crowd of mages had long ago dispersed; only a few pockets of students lingered nearby in the sands.

Globes of fiery energy swam around Finn, the spheres weaving an intricate pattern that revolved out toward his maximum control range before spiraling back toward Finn – only to repeat in an endless loop. At this stage, the pattern was almost like breathing, an undulating, natural rhythm. He didn't even have to watch the dancing orbs to know what was happening.

"Is that Finn?" someone murmured as they passed through the sands of the courtyard.

"Quiet," another novice hissed. "Just avoid him. You saw what he did to Kyyle and Vanessa."

"How did he learn those spells, though? Is he really even a traveler? How could he have planned that fight against Vanessa with such precision?" another asked, their voice incredulous.

Finn had heard many of these comments while sitting

upon the dais. Even more strange were the stares and murmurs as he passed in the halls. Students went out of their way to avoid him. It seemed he had only added to his reputation. Most of the other novices no longer claimed that he was a cheater – although that theory seemed to have been replaced with a new one. Apparently, he was some sort of robot?

He supposed that was an improvement.

Finn's brow furrowed as he felt one of his orbs whisked away. It felt as though the sphere had struck something solid – although that was impossible. Finn hadn't detected any sound of someone approaching. He also didn't hear any shout of alarm or pain. His eyes snapped open, burning with a soft orange glow and training on a spot a few feet to his right where the sphere should have been.

As he stared at that spot, Finn thought he could detect a strange irregularity – as though the air was warped. It almost looked like the ripple of heat radiating off hot pavement. Acting on instinct, he directed the remainder of his orbs to that spot, encircling the space. Simultaneously, they all struck something solid, and the flames were soon blown away.

A moment later, the air rippled more forcefully, and it was like a mirror slid away, revealing Abbad standing upon the dais.

"That's a neat trick," Finn observed, trying to keep his tone neutral. "You're manipulating the air, aren't you? Creating a reflective bubble around yourself?"

"Indeed," Abbad replied and stepped over toward Finn, sinking down onto the dais until he was sitting beside him.

Despite his calm demeanor, Finn was processing the implications of Abbad's invisibility spell. If the librarian could walk around the Mage Guild undetected, he might be aware of far more than he let on. Combined with his ability to project his voice and several other potential applications of air magic – listening, sound dampening, etc. – he would have free rein to explore the school without being detected. He could listen in on practically any conversation.

As he sat there, Finn was already thinking through a

few ideas for how he might detect that invisibility bubble. Tracing an area with his orbs was a start. Maybe he could create a default pattern to sweep a room or large area. At this point, he could summon up to four of the globes, and they moved quite quickly. Some sort of smoke bomb might also work, giving away Abbad's location with ease.

Although, this all begged the real question. Why was Abbad here?

"Come to check on me before tomorrow?" Finn asked, finally breaking the silence.

Abbad tilted his head in thought, his eyes sweeping across the courtyard and following the handful of novices that drifted through the sands. "I suspect what you wish to ask is how long have I been watching you?"

"I'll admit, I'm curious," Finn acknowledged.

"Since the beginning," Abbad responded bluntly. He looked at Finn then, his eyes sharp and piercing. "I watched as you studied. As your thief friend reached out. As you trained with Brutus. As you slaughtered the other students among the halls. And as you learned to create your own spells."

Finn swallowed hard, too caught off guard to mask his reaction.

"You seem surprised," Abbad noted. "However, you weren't the first to discover *Spellcrafting*. I noticed that you reviewed several of Bilel's original workbooks – what we offer to the other students as *novice spellbooks*. You and Bilel share many similarities, you know. He was also a creative soul, one far ahead of his time."

Finn's mind was practically buzzing with questions, and he was having difficulty deciding what to ask first. Although, one question rose to the top of the heap. "Why aren't there more spellbooks? Why was *Spellcrafting* forgotten?"

"The simple answer? Control," Abbad said. He glanced at Finn. "The guild carefully regulates the information it doles out to its mages, using the duels as a mechanism to reward its students." He waved a hand at the courtyard. "It is all a distraction. An attempt to slow down and impose order upon the masses."

Finn chewed on that. Abbad had said something similar in the past. Although, now that Finn was aware that the librarian had been watching for some time, that also raised additional questions. And Abbad had already implied an answer.

"You knew about the infighting among the students, didn't you? Which means the other faculty must have been aware of what was going on long before I was brought before Nefreet and the other instructors." Finn looked at Abbad. "Was that a form of control as well? Were the faculty intentionally permitting the assassination attempts?"

A ghost of a smile tugged at Abbad's lips. "Indeed. It served multiple purposes. It identified the strongest among the students and the most creative. It also provided an additional dash of celebrity. As I said, the goal is partly to distract. It is easier to supervise a prisoner who is eyeing the other inmates instead of the guards."

"And these duels are more of the same then?" Finn asked.

Abbad gave him a questioning glance.

"Matching me against Kyyle first. Teleporting me into environments that heavily favor my opponent. And I certainly didn't miss the fact that Vanessa was wielding one hell of a wand. Is this more of the headmaster's *influence* at work?"

Abbad let out a soft snort. "Do you really believe that? What could be Nefreet's goal in manipulating the duels or stacking the challenge against *you*?"

Finn didn't have a good answer for that question. It was one he had been struggling with for days – even during his last discussion with Kyyle. The problem was one of motive.

"Individual motivations are a tricky thing," Abbad murmured, mirroring Finn's thoughts. "The mob acts in uniformity. It is predictable. Like the tides of the ocean. Yet the individual is a chaotic mass of emotions that often defies easy prediction.

"Nefreet is intelligent and observant – and my talents

certainly assist him. However, the rest of the faculty are also ambitious. This is a problem that the guild has faced for the last hundred years. We have a system that regulates and controls our students, but what about our instructors – those we raise above the others and reward with valuable and powerful abilities?"

"Are you suggesting that one of the instructors has gone rogue?"

Abbad shrugged. "I do not offer any conclusions, only observations. Although, if I were to add one more, I might suggest that you focus on *who* among the travelers managed to reach the top of the heap, stay there, and, in your own words, *wield one hell of a wand*. That fact might be telling, in and of itself."

Finn's eyes widened slightly. Abbad was talking about Vanessa. Since the water mage had been sponsored by Lamia, that suggested that the water mage master *was* behind the attacks and manipulation. Finn had suspected as much for some time. Lamia had made it clear she had little love for the travelers, and she was in a position to influence the duels since she had taken charge of monitoring the event. She also likely had a personal vendetta against Finn after he had embarrassed her in front of the other faculty.

At the same time, that explanation felt slightly off. It felt too neat – too obvious. Something pre-packaged for Finn's consumption. He chewed on the inside of his cheek. On the other hand, he didn't have any reason to believe that something more was going on here and Abbad had as much as admitted to the situation.

More importantly, this all led to the single question that seemed to rise above the rest of the pack, taunting Finn.

What the hell was he going to do about it?

He let out a soft sigh, rubbing at his eyes. Finn felt tired. He had been grinding away at his training for weeks now, with little sleep and few breaks. It also appeared that one or more of the faculty had it out for him. To top it all off, tomorrow he either needed to kill a resident – permanently – or lose all of the progress he had made so far. He didn't relish either option. From his experience, this world's residents were exceptionally realistic. Somehow the prospect of killing someone like Abbad or Charlotte felt... wrong.

Each resident was a full-fledged person, with their own history and motivations. Did they have families? Loved ones? Hopes and fears? Even if they were just a digital illusion, the prospect of destroying one of them left a bad taste in his mouth and a knot in his stomach.

Abbad had been watching him. "As I said, individual motivations are a tangled web. Do you plan to fight tomorrow?"

Finn glanced at the librarian in surprise. Indeed, the librarian seemed adept at reading others – even when he wasn't invisible. Although, he supposed there was little to gain in lying to him, not when Abbad had been so forthright with him.

"I honestly don't know," Finn replied, shaking his head, and his eyes drifted to the sands. "I have little interest in being part of some larger conspiracy among the faculty. I've experienced more than my fair share of intrigue over my life. I also have some reservations about killing a resident and the fairness of the duel tomorrow."

Abbad just nodded, letting a heavy silence linger in the air.

"Have you ever wondered about my affinity?" Abbad asked finally.

Finn glanced at him, confusion sweeping across his face.

"Let me rephrase. What is my motivation?" Abbad asked bluntly. "Air mages are supposed to foster happiness. As I'm sure your instructors have told you, many in my field find joy by living in the moment. They encourage randomness and chance to accomplish that goal." Faint amusement tinged Abbad's voice at this last statement.

Finn frowned. Now that he thought about it, that did seem strange. The reserved and stoic librarian didn't seem like the type to gravitate toward air magic. "Happy" wasn't exactly the first word Finn would have used to describe him.

Abbad met Finn's eyes. "As a young man, I thought life was a competition, a straightforward race to the finish line.

Systems like the one the guild adopts encourage this linear view of the world. They provide a concrete goal and place us in direct competition. However, you and I are no longer young men. We have lived a sizable portion of our lives. What have you learned from that experience so far? Does life seem like a race to you?"

Finn snorted in amusement. "Only if the race has no clear finish line, no rules, and most of the contestants don't seem to know that they're participating," he replied dryly.

A rare smile swept across Abbad's face. "Indeed. Life is chaos, no matter how much we might try to impose structure and order upon it. If there is any singular goal or finish line, it is only what we create for ourselves or let others impose upon us. We set ourselves a task, a goal, or an achievement, and then we struggle towards it – often doubling back, circling around it, and, on occasion, getting lost entirely."

Finn simply watched the librarian, noting the sober expression that lingered on the man's face. "For me, *that* is happiness. That chaos. It is the freedom to choose a goal, to pick a path. To stumble, to fail. To rally and step up on the podium, a crowd chanting your name," Abbad offered, sparing a glance at Finn.

"That is the dream I have for this place, and for these students. I wish this to be a school – a real school – not simply a disguised prison," Abbad murmured wistfully.

He laughed softly. "That's always the first question that we face. What is your goal? In some ways, that is the easiest part. Once you choose a goal for yourself, this invariably leads to a second and more problematic question. What are we willing to sacrifice to make that dream a reality? Because *everything* has a cost."

Abbad trailed off, his eyes distant. Finn could feel his own thoughts swimming. He saw some truth in what Abbad was saying. After Rachael, he had lost his direction. He had lost purpose. AO had helped him regain some of that. It had thrown these complicated and cryptic problems at him. It had given him a goal to strive toward. Yet in many ways, Finn was now struggling with that second question.

Was it worth it? Should he keep going?

Before the... *incident*, the answer had always been easy for him.

His thoughts returned to the fight with Vanessa – recalling how she had been willing to go to any lengths to beat him. "A win is a win," she had said. Finn had been like that once. He had been willing to do nearly anything to accomplish a task – forgoing sleep, and friends, and family. Yet that attitude had ended up costing him everything.

What was worse, he wasn't certain that he had really changed. Maybe that was why he had been so cautious about re-engaging with the world. Fear that he would repeat the same mistakes. Had his actions inside AO really been any different? He had endured the extraordinary to make it to this point, and this was just the beginning.

What was his limit?

Brutally murdering strangers? His friend?

Not only that, but this world kept asking for more and more from him – as though it were testing his limits. Maybe permanently killing a resident and getting embroiled in some conspiracy was too much. Even if he won, what would the competition among the guilds entail? He suspected that the other organizations that ran this city would have a strong incentive to meddle. And the pinnacle? Control of this city and the responsibilities that would entail. Was he willing to do what needed to be done to accomplish that goal?

As the silence lengthened and stretched, Abbad shrugged and slowly rose to his feet. "Unfortunately, these are questions that don't have a 'right' answer. We have to decide for ourselves what we wish to strive toward and the price we are willing to pay," he observed quietly, glancing down at Finn.

"I, for one, can only hope that you choose to continue with this competition. You could do good here, in this world," Abbad offered. In many ways, the librarian's words seemed to mirror what Kyyle had said to him – encouraging him to keep going.

Why do these people keep placing their faith in me? Finn wondered.

Abbad turned to leave, padding quietly across the stone platform. One last question occurred to Finn then, and he was calling after the librarian before he realized it. "What are you willing to sacrifice for your goal?"

Abbad hesitated but didn't turn around. "Everything," he answered simply.

Then the librarian's fingers wove through a complicated pattern, and a mirror of air swept in front of him. Within just a few seconds, Abbad had disappeared and only faint streamers of sand swept across the platform.

Finn was left sitting there, feeling even more confused than he had before. The conversation had only served to reinforce and highlight the doubts that had been lingering at the forefront of his mind for the last few days. It had also made one thing abundantly clear.

He wasn't certain whether he wanted to keep going.

Chapter 39 - Final

When Finn arrived at the courtyard the next day, he discovered the true size of the Mage Guild. It seemed news of the final competition had spread among the travelers. Hundreds – if not thousands – of mages were crammed into the field and ringed the terraces. The crowd had spilled over into the halls, novices struggling just to make it to the sands of the field to catch a glimpse of the duel. The massive water portal that still hung in the air and rippled and reflected the harsh sunlight that beat down on the courtyard.

The other novices, residents and travelers alike, were forced out of the way by Finn's entourage – a collection of guards that had appeared that morning to summon him to the field. Although, Finn wasn't certain whether the stone-faced and heavily armed men were there for his protection or to ensure that he showed up. Either way, they now created a pocket around Finn, shoving at the other mages roughly. It only took a few minutes for the other students to catch on that one of the competitors was entering the courtyard, Finn's name suddenly drifting above the crowd like a whisper.

Through it all, Finn felt numb.

This was usually the moment he should be filled with nervous excitement and a hint of nausea, forced to pace off the excess energy somewhere as he tried vainly to focus on something else.

Yet he just felt... nothing.

The events of the last few days lingered with him. He had been forced to butcher his friend, go to extreme lengths to defeat Vanessa, was the focus of some sort of deep-seated conspiracy, and now had to go kill another student – permanently and on live-magical television. The worst part, however, was the conversation with Abbad the night before.

After a sleepless, anxious night, Finn still wasn't certain how to answer the librarian's questions. If he were being honest with himself, he wasn't sure what his goal really was, much less what he was willing to sacrifice to accomplish it. It was like Abbad had finally put into words a battle that had been raging in Finn's mind for a long time – perhaps even before he stepped foot inside AO.

"Hey," a voice said to Finn's left, and he jumped slightly, startled by the interruption. He turned to find that Julia had appeared inside the circle of guards. Finn waved off the burly men as they noticed the rogue in their midst and reached for their weapons.

"Hey back," Finn replied in a tired voice.

Julia looked at him, noting the circles under his eyes and the weary droop of his shoulders. "You don't look like you slept at all."

"Nerves, I guess," Finn grunted.

Julia arched an eyebrow. "Uh-huh. I'm not sure I believe that. What's going on?"

Finn opened his mouth to respond but hesitated. What exactly could he say? That he was having second thoughts? That this game had forced him to confront a series of questions that he would have much preferred to take to his death bed, happily ignored. That he was wondering what would happen if he ran right now. How far could he make it before the guards hauled his ass kicking and screaming up onto that platform?

Yet his daughter was still looking at him expectantly, her normally jovial expression cracking slightly and worry shining in her eyes. "I'm not looking forward to killing a resident," Finn offered weakly. "They seem far too real."

Julia tilted her head, and he wasn't sure that she believed him. She didn't press the issue, perhaps sensing that now wasn't really the time to talk about this, with hundreds of excited mages squeezing in around them.

"Okay," she said softly, almost inaudible amid the buzz of the crowd. "Well, I brought you something," Julia offered, thrusting a leather bundle into Finn's hands.

Finn glanced at her in surprise, but she offered no explanation, only gesturing for him to open the package. He peeled back the thick leather as they walked, discovering that Julia had handed him a bundle of razor-sharp throwing knives, each blade carefully sheathed.

"Figured you might need a few extras," Julia offered as

Finn stared at the blades. A hopeful, expectant look lingered on her face. Even though a fully grown woman now stood before him, Finn could still remember a similar expression on the face of a young girl as she brought him some spaghetti art she had made in class.

Something clicked in Finn's head then, his gaze panning back and forth between the blades and Julia's face. With the sensation came a wash of guilt. His children represented a reason to keep going – a purpose. In fact, they were the reason he had even started playing this damnable game. Finn had done little to foster those relationships over the years. Instead, he'd chosen to wallow in his own misery after Rachael had passed. Despite that, Julia had stayed steadfast with a ready smile and a forceful nudge.

Before he realized what he was doing, Finn hugged his daughter, wrapping his arms around her. She stiffened as though confused, but he felt her muscles ease after a moment, and she hugged him back.

When Finn withdrew, he noticed that her eyes were a bit glossy. He wasn't quite able to decipher the look on her face though. "Good luck," she offered, not able to meet his eyes. "I'll be rooting for you."

Before he could reply, Julia had vanished, slipping between two of the guards and almost instantly disappearing among the crowd. His eyes followed her, the brief exchange only serving to add to the chaotic, swirling thoughts that rebounded through his head.

Finn didn't have long to dwell on the encounter as his group neared the dais. The crowd parted to let them pass, and soon they were free of the throng of mages. Finn stood upon dense, hard stone once more and his eyes took in the massive crowd that filled the courtyard and terraces.

Streamers of multi-colored energy wound through the air, the students summoning their own mana in dazzling displays. Finn saw water dance and spiral and flames flicker and fade, the combined energy of dozens of students spelling out the names of the competitors. He saw his own name emblazoned in flame, painted several times across the field.

"Mages, students, and teachers," Nefreet's voice

whispered through the courtyard. The crowd stilled and quieted. "Today is the final duel. A battle that will determine the strongest from among our novices. A final competition to choose a mage to represent our guild in the Emir's competition."

Nefreet turned back to the stage, waving at Finn. "From the travelers, we have Finn. A fire mage of exceptional talent and skill." Finn noted the way the headmaster's eye twitched slightly at that comment. Apparently, he didn't enjoy admitting to Finn's abilities.

"From among our residents, we have Khiana, an air mage with the speed of a striking python and the power of a chimera." Finn looked over at his opponent, although the man made no effort to acknowledge Finn's glance. Khiana was a slender man, wiry muscle rippling beneath practical robes. Instead of a staff or a more typical weapon, bandoliers filled with knives crisscrossed his chest.

Because of his injuries, Finn hadn't had a chance to watch the resident semi-final duels, although Kyyle had offered some insight into his opponent. It seemed Khiana had yet to lose a duel and had struck down both of his opponents within only a few minutes. He had barely taken a scratch. This man was much more deadly than the other air mages Finn had faced before – and even those fights had been rough.

As Nefreet continued his announcements, Finn's eyes swept the dais. Brutus stood to the side with the other faculty, and his instructor gave him a nod as their eyes met, his irises flashing with fiery energy. Finn returned the gesture as he continued to observe the mages crowding the platform. Something felt off, but it took him a moment to realize what was missing.

Lamia was nowhere to be seen.

Water mages still ringed the dais, but the water magic master wasn't present among the faculty. Finn had a sinking feeling in his stomach. He had long ago given up fighting Kyyle's conspiracy theories, and Abbad had as much as admitted that a member of the faculty was gunning for him. Now his number one candidate was missing? He had a bad feeling about this.

"These duels are a lesson – even for those not standing upon this dais!" Nefreet called out, interrupting Finn's thoughts. "They sort us and define us. They allow the strong to rise to the top. More than that, they give us *purpose*. A goal to strive toward even as they harden our bodies and our minds to the rigors of our craft.

"These two champions represent the culmination of this grueling gauntlet, mages forged of fire, ice, wind, and earth. They represent the strongest among us, not just in the fury of their magics but in their strength of will."

Nefreet waved at Finn and Khiana. "This is the lesson that the Emir has encouraged us to instill in our mages for the last hundred years. Victory or death!"

As Nefreet spoke this last line, a rippling roar rose up from the crowd, crashing across the courtyard like a tidal wave until it vibrated Finn's core. His fire mana responded to that passion, yet only weakly, his own reservations holding him back.

"Now, we shall commence this final duel to choose a champion for our guild!" Nefreet announced.

With that, the headmaster turned back to Finn and Khiana and handed each of them a familiar stone token, a glowing symbol emblazoned on its side. With the ceremonies out of the way, the two competitors turned to face each other. Finn saw no doubt or hesitation in Khiana's eyes as he stared back with calculating precision, as though he were analyzing a table or a chair – not a living breathing person.

He wasn't certain that the same resolve shined in his own eyes.

Yet there was nowhere to go but forward. Before Finn knew it, their tokens tapped against one another and the world abruptly faded away in a flash of multi-colored light.

Chapter 40 - Compelling

When Finn opened his eyes again, he wasn't standing in a field, or an underground cave, or a muddy rice paddock. This was no foreign field of battle. Instead, he was somewhere... *familiar*.

The leather walls of the tent billowed and flapped behind him, snapping taut as a breeze rippled across the structure. This gust of air caused sand to spill inside the tent, twisting and swirling in the air and shifting the streamers of silk that hung from the ceiling. He remembered those decorations, how they had slapped him in the face as he wheeled himself through this same tent. Although, that seemed like an age ago.

Oh, what the hell is going on now?

Finn's eyes panned across the tent until they rested on the tapestry near the back of the room. The scene had changed. The former phoenix was gone, only ashes remaining. In its wake, an egg now rested in the center of the tapestry, awash in flames. From this shell, Finn could see the tip of a fledgling firebird's beak just barely emerging, as though it were struggling to break free. He felt himself drawn to the image, and he swore – for just a moment – that he saw the flames flicker.

"We meet again," a familiar voice spoke from behind the tapestry. A moment later, the Seer moved into sight, thick silks wrapping her body and leaving only her eyes visible. The black python slithered up her arm and wound around her neck, its eyes watching Finn.

"What is this?" Finn asked. "This isn't the duel."

The Seer gave a faint shrug. "Consider this a brief *intermission* – the others won't even notice that you're gone." As she noted his sour expression, she continued. "If your opponents choose to stack the deck against you, then you need to keep an ace up your sleeve? Fight fire with fire? Pick your favorite metaphor, the result is the same. If they choose to cheat, then we should feel free to bend the rules ourselves."

She gestured at the table where she had given him his

reading. "Or simply look at this as a brief respite. I am just asking that you sit and chat with me for a while."

Finn hesitated. He doubted the god had good intentions or that she was truly on his side. As Abbad had said, individual motivations could be tricky, and it wasn't clear what the god hoped to gain from him. Yet, Finn also supposed he had little choice. She was right that he wasn't anxious to get back to the duel, so he reluctantly slid into the seat. He eyed the stack of nearby tarot cards suspiciously. However, the Seer made no move to pick them up.

Instead, the fire goddess leaned forward and inspected Finn carefully. The scrutiny felt invasive, in no small part because he knew the goddess was capable of rifling through his thoughts as easily as she was able to examine his body. Her fingers touched at his wrist, shifting the fabric back and revealing the guild tattoo on his left arm and the cards and roiling mass of flames that now adorned his right.

"You have come a long way since you first entered my tent," the Seer murmured. "You have struggled and overcome. Found challenges in this world, unlike anything in your own." Her eyes centered on his, and he saw a glimmer of flame in her irises. "For a time, I felt your passion spring free and unbridled, burning with a warmth and brightness that I have not seen in ages."

Her expression flickered, the muscles around her eyes tightening. "Yet I sense doubt now. Hesitation. Passion muddled and confused."

Finn ground his teeth together. "You dropped me in some sort of magical prison, which is pretty obvious despite Nefreet's fancy speeches. Now I'm participating in a deathmatch and have been forced to kill others – brutally. If that didn't bother me, I'd probably be a sociopath."

The Seer watched him for a moment before shaking her head. "That isn't it – at least, not entirely. I see in your mind that the mages explained to you the nature of fire magic. It is about *passion*. For many, their passions are mundane. Family. Loved ones. Hobbies. A career.

"However, in others, those passions are more nuanced. More difficult to pin down."

She inspected Finn as though expecting him to speak, but he stayed silent.

"I initially thought that the act of creation alone would be enough to illuminate the void in your soul. Indeed, it sparked a flame, which continued to build and grow – at least for a time. It began to blaze so brightly that others strove to touch it, to stamp it out, to steal it for their own."

Her eyes flashed. "Yet that flame has dwindled and faltered since then, and it is now barely an ember of its former glory. That means I was incorrect. You want something more."

The Seer leaned forward, her eyes glowing with a soft orange light. "What is it that you *want*, Finn? What is the secret passion you hold close to your chest like a jealous lover?"

Inadvertently, Finn's thoughts immediately turned to Rachael, her face hovering in his mind's eye. There was a reason there was a hole in his heart; her loss had put it there. However, he forcefully shoved aside that thought. It was impossible. Only pain could be found by walking down that path.

"Ahh," the Seer murmured, leaning back and watching him. "You set your eyes on the heavens and would attempt to steal the stars. Your wife. A lost love. Is that what you need to feel complete? To give you purpose?"

"You can't offer me that," Finn snapped, unsettled by how easily the woman had picked up on his surface thoughts.

The Seer tilted her head, her eyes flashing again. "Can't I?"

Out of the corner of his eye, Finn saw something settle on the table. It was a simple coffee mug covered in ones and zeros. The cup was familiar. One of his favorites, actually. It was the mug that Rachael always brought him when he was lost in a new project.

A hand touched his face then, skin sliding against his own, and he felt warm breath in his ear. "You're almost at the Finn-ish line," a voice whispered.

Finn froze, his mind faltering. Rachael had always said that to him – his wife, a hopeless fan of puns. It had actually been part of her wedding vows. As they stood in a field in the middle of nowhere beside that silly dilapidated barn, she had told him, their friends, and their family that he was her "Finnish line." She had even managed to keep a straight face – sort of. That had morphed over the years, becoming her mantra when he was sucked into a new project.

Tantalizing hope bloomed in his stomach, mixing with the dread certainty that this wasn't real. It couldn't be real. Finn turned to find Rachael hovering beside him, smiling and her eyes shining. His heart lurched. Before he knew what he was doing, Finn reached for her. Yet as his fingers touched her skin, they passed through her cheek, and the image broke apart into streamers of smoke, blowing away.

Finn was forced to choke back at the lump in his throat. It took him a few seconds to muster the words. "Why are you torturing me like this?" he finally croaked.

"I am not torturing you," the Seer replied in a calm voice. "I have the power to give you what you want. You would like for your wife to be returned to you, no?"

Finn glared at her, anger flaring in his chest. "No one has the power to return the dead. I don't know how you picked out that memory, but that wasn't my wife."

"Not yet," the Seer said firmly. "But it could be."

Finn froze, confused by the certainty in the goddess' voice and doubt pushing back at the anger that bubbled in his chest. "What? What are you talking about?"

"Do you remember how you built your last creation in your own world?" the Seer asked. "The one that cost you your heart?" she whispered.

Finn's brow furrowed. His last project had been to design the AI that ran the autonomous driving program for Cerillion Logistics. In many ways, that had been his life's work – a culmination of decades of training.

The project itself had seemed absurd at first. Finn had been tasked with designing software that could handle billions of decisions in real-time, with an infinite variety of variables – weather, speed, visibility, weight, cargo, traffic density – just to name a few. With so many moving parts, the AI needed to be able to make judgment calls that no programmer could possibly anticipate. It needed to be flexible, dynamic, and self-improving.

In short, he needed to design a human mind in a digital space. He had spent years and countless sleepless nights with little progress.

"Do you remember what finally pushed you over the edge?" the Seer murmured. "That spark – that moment of inspiration."

Rachael. Finn felt his heart pounding in his ears.

His wife was a doctor – *had been* a doctor, he corrected himself. She had given him the push he needed. He remembered the moment vividly. He had been pacing his office, frustrated at another failed attempt when Rachael came in. She had sat with him, listening to him rant about how the project was impossible. She had stayed silent the entire time, and when he finished, she had posed a single question.

"If you're trying to design something that works like a human mind, why not start there?"

She had asked this as if it were obvious. And maybe, to her, it had been. Yet it had started him down a bottomless rabbit hole of research and discovery. Between Rachael and the company's pull, Finn had gotten permission from her hospital to use their MRI and imaging equipment. And when the moment came to choose someone to examine, Rachael had even volunteered herself.

They had spent months – years – in that lab, monitoring every aspect of her brain activity. They had collected audio samples of her voice, transcribed and recorded the electrical signals in her hippocampus and cerebral cortex as she had explored her own memories, and had forced her to solve progressively more challenging puzzles and tasks while they monitored her.

And the result had been a new type of AI controller – the first of its kind. Finn had modeled it using Rachael's mind, her memories, and her passion.

"You built something extraordinary in her image," the Seer murmured. More softly, "Perhaps that is why it hurt so badly when she passed – or rather *how* she passed."

Finn looked away, rubbing at his eyes. The invention

Rachael had helped him build had ended up killing her. Maybe the Seer was right. Maybe that was why he had fought so hard to get the program canceled – even if it was far too late. There was a sort of macabre irony to how those events had unfolded.

"Why are you dredging this up?" Finn asked, his voice cracking. He swallowed hard against the sudden lump in his throat. He preferred to keep these memories buried.

"Because you know what that invention was capable of – its true potential," the Seer replied. She waved at the tent around them. "How do you think this world was created?"

Finn stared at her – this digital goddess who was spelunking through his mind as though she was flipping through the pages of a picture book. He saw the way her body language was smooth, flawless really; her dialogue was dynamic. Finn knew that if he attempted to administer a Turing Test, he likely couldn't tell the difference between the Seer and a living, breathing person. He had picked up on these details the moment he had started playing, but he hadn't appreciated the obvious deduction...

"They used my AI," Finn gasped, disbelief coloring his voice. He should have known. Of course George had taken what Finn had built and iterated upon it. Finn could even guess who he had used to work on the project.

"Indeed," the Seer replied with a nod and a knowing look, waiting for him to connect the dots. "So, you know what I am offering."

Finn understood what the Seer was saying, even if he couldn't truly believe it. If this world was created using the original AI kernel that he had modeled using Rachael's mind, then his wife might still be here – at least her core memories and thought processes.

"I have the power to bring her back," the goddess said. "Not a ghost or an illusion, but Rachael herself."

Finn just stared at the Seer, his mind awash in confused chaos. "It-it wouldn't be her, though," he retorted, struggling with the idea. "It would be a ghost, a carefully crafted simulation. It wouldn't be *Rachael*."

The Seer laughed then. "Why ever not? If the

memories are the same, the behavior identical, what is the difference?"

There was some truth to the Seer's words, but they still felt... *wrong*. "What about her soul?" Finn demanded. "That wouldn't be the same woman I married."

"Can you define the soul?" the Seer asked. "Weigh it? Measure it? Even begin to describe what it is? Show me your own soul. Point it out for me."

Finn struggled to frame a response but came up empty-handed.

"You can't," the Seer continued, her eyes flashing as she leaned forward. "In the absence of that definition, the soul could be *anything*. What's to say that her 'soul' then isn't merely a function of all the things that make Rachael herself. Her memories. Her wants. Her hopes. Her fears. The nervous gesture she made when she was worried. The way she always double and triple-checked the locks on the doors before you left the house.

"You have seen this world now – tasted it. Can you say without doubt or hesitation that the residents of this world aren't 'real' by any definition of the word?" the Seer demanded.

"It's not the same," Finn muttered, his eyes dropping to the floor.

How could he know that the AI – that the residents – truly felt emotion? That they weren't merely acting?

A heavy silence hung in the air as Finn tried vainly to gather his own thoughts. They kept returning to one moment, that instant when his entire world had changed.

"The day that Rachael died, I remember the weightlessness," Finn murmured, speaking slowly as though feeling out the memory. "The terror of being trapped in a metal can with the person I held most dear in the entire world. I knew I couldn't run, or flee, or fight. That sense of hopeless, inescapable dread is something I will always remember. I watched as my heart was ripped away from me. I realized then with perfect clarity that my kind... we all die and we die alone.

"I knew true fear then."

Tears budded at the corners of Finn's eyes as he raised them to look at the Seer. "As bad as that was, you know what was worse? Afterward. The pain. The loss. The lack of control. I felt... I felt lost, and I wanted so badly to end it. To leave that world and just give up. You know what held me back? That same fucking fear. I was too damn terrified to take that leap.

"I was too weak."

Finn was glaring at her now – his gaze insistent and demanding. "Can you tell me that you understand that? That fear of dying? That inescapable terror that clutches at your heart and holds you paralyzed? Because that's part of what it means to be real. To be *alive*.

"Can you *show* me that you understand that feeling?"

The Seer looked away from Finn then, and the world seemed to stutter – just a faint flash, so quick that Finn almost thought he had imagined it. When the Seer looked back at him, her expression had changed subtly. She looked different in a way that was hard for Finn to identify. Her gaze held an almost-palpable weight, sorrow lingering there.

"I can understand what you're saying," she offered quietly. "I can appreciate my own mortality. Yet the challenge is indeed *proving* to you that I can."

She continued, holding his eyes. "What tears or theatrics or words could I offer that would show you that the emotion was genuine? No matter my behavior, you could claim that it was an illusion – a perfect lie. You are asking me to prove the impossible.

"But let us reframe the question. How do you know I'm *not* real?"

Finn felt himself floundering to come up with a rebuttal. He had experienced similar misgivings over the last few weeks, and that was partly why he hesitated at participating in this last fight. He didn't relish the idea of killing a resident. Despite his own reservations, the faintest flicker of hope bloomed in his chest.

Could it be possible?

Finn shook his head. He didn't know. He *couldn't* know. And maybe that was the goddess' point.

"Well, consider my offer. I can bring your wife back. I can bring Rachael back," the Seer declared.

Finn let out a harsh laugh then. "Brutus and others call you the Crone. He warned me of making a deal with you. He said that nothing comes without a price. Even if I believe that it was possible, what would this *resurrection* cost me?"

The Seer's eyes flashed again, now glowing with a soft orange light. "I wish to reclaim my place in this world. To do that, I need an avatar. Someone who can build the pyre and set it aflame – that can inspire passion in others. The first step is to win this competition and take control of Lahab."

She grimaced. "Yet you aren't ready. Until now, you have been working with self-imposed handicaps. Your doubt, your despair, and your self-recrimination still weigh you down. You must decide to set down those burdens. To embrace your passion. Embrace this world. Launch yourself into the flames with abandon and let the fire consume you completely – let them forge you into something new.

"Stop holding back."

Finn could only stare at her, feeling himself falter under the force of her words. In many ways, he knew she was right. In those moments where he had given himself over to his mana, he had done extraordinary things – and he had reveled in the sense of freedom and power that had come with those accomplishments.

Yet it also scared him. And, more insidious, he felt as though he didn't *deserve* it. Maybe the pain was his punishment for failing Rachael.

"As you did before, you'll have to decide for yourself whether you are willing to take the leap," the Seer continued, her voice not unkind. "If you wish to accept my offer, you need only give yourself over to the flames – body and soul. I will know."

Finn simply sat there in silence, unable to move or speak. He heard the legs of the Seer's chair rustle the thick carpet, and he soon felt a hand rest on his shoulder, comforting and warm. As he stared at the ground, Finn saw flames beginning to ignite along the floor around him – the start of a blaze that he knew would soon consume him.

"I will send you back now. Think upon my offer," the Seer said.

Then the fires enveloped Finn. He willingly sunk into their warm embrace, the world fading from view and soon replaced with merciful, dark oblivion.

Chapter 41 - Blazing

The world lurched back into focus far sooner than Finn would have preferred. He found himself in a frigid field, brisk wind snapping at his robes. His feet sank several inches into thick snow, and he could already feel an inadvertent shiver shake him as the cold sank into his bones. Ridges of ice and snow lingered on either side of the field, creating a shallow, makeshift valley. With practiced movements, Finn immediately began casting *Magma Armor.* The response was more instinct than conscious thought at this point.

Which was good, because Finn was having difficulty focusing. Between the conversations with Abbad and Julia – and the offer now posed by the Seer – his mind was a chaotic whirlwind of emotion and half-formed thoughts.

"So, we meet at last," a voice called out.

Finn raised his eyes to find Khiana standing in the snow a few dozen paces from him, his arms crossed, and his posture relaxed. The water elemental had already risen into the air, assuming a vantage point above the field.

For his part, Finn wasn't certain how to respond. Should he say something snarky? Simply attack? He just felt confused. He wasn't even sure that he wanted to fight.

"Staying silent, huh?" Khiana observed. "You did the same in your previous duels. Barely a word unless you were speaking to your pet."

The man stretched casually and glanced at the water elemental drifting above them. "I can't say that I blame you. It's difficult to speak candidly with so many watching." He sighed. "In that case, we may as well go ahead and get started."

As he finished speaking, the air mage's fingers began to wind through a complicated pattern. Within only moments, forks of electricity arced through the air around him, condensing to a fine point before exploding forward. Despite his jumbled thoughts, Finn was prepared to avoid the attack – to dodge to the side or raise his armored limbs to block most of the blast.

However, he stared in surprise as the lightning arced wildly, spearing directly up into the air. The bolt struck the water elemental directly, and the blast blew apart the globe of water, creating a shower of electrified droplets that rained down upon the snow with a sparkle of energy.

What the hell?

Khiana was now staring at Finn, his eyes glowing with a brilliant azure light. Yet he made no move to attack. Instead, he stood still, as though he were waiting for something.

Finn didn't have to wait long to discover Khiana's purpose.

The snowbanks on either side of the field shimmered and shifted, the illusion melting away to reveal two rows of mages. By Finn's estimate, there were roughly twenty of them, and they represented a wide range of affinities – at least if the multi-colored glow around their staves and wands was any indication. From amid the pack, Finn saw a familiar face emerge.

Lamia.

The water mage master strode forward until she stood with Khiana, staring coldly at Finn as her eyes blazed with sapphire energy. "You did well," Lamia said, laying a hand on the air mage's shoulder. "And you will be rewarded for your efforts."

Finn barked out an inadvertent laugh, the sound echoing harshly through the icy field. It just seemed so silly and obvious. Of course, Lamia had been rigging the competition. He had suspected it all along. And now her plan was obviously to slay Finn here, allow Khiana to emerge the victor, and finally achieve whatever grand scheme she had in mind.

After everything he had endured, it was just too much.

The water mage's eyes widened at his reaction, suddenly uncertain.

That only served to make Finn laugh harder. After his exchange with the Seer, the whole thing seemed absurd.

"I don't know what you find so amusing," Lamia snapped at him. "You will die here in this field and then you will be stripped of your mana and expelled—"

"Into the sands, I know," Finn interjected, wiping at his eyes. "Believe it or not, I've heard that line before. From you. Several times. If you're open to accepting feedback, I'd try to think up a new threat. Vary it a little, you know."

Rage flickered across Lamia's face, barely contained. "It is just this sort of arrogance that proves why the travelers cannot be trusted to represent the guild – to represent *our* kind."

Finn's brow furrowed at her words, but he was watching Lamia's face – her body language. He wasn't even certain what he was looking for. Maybe some sort of clue that would give away that this was just a digital illusion? His thoughts kept returning to his conversation with the Seer. Was this all scripted? A play acted out for his benefit? Or was Lamia's xenophobia genuine?

"What right do you have to our world? To rule over our people?" she demanded, becoming angrier as Finn held his tongue. "Have you lived here? Grown up here? Struggled for power and earned your place among us?

"You are invaders. Arrogant and stupid. Ignorant of our ways and yet demanding of our gifts and knowledge. We cannot *accept* this," Lamia snapped at him, gesturing at the other mages. As she grew more upset, fragments of ice began to materialize in the air around her, the mana sliding through her veins automatically responding to her emotions.

Finn couldn't tell if Lamia sincerely felt that anger or not. There was no obvious tell that gave away her inhumanity. No repetitive dialogue. No twitch or stutter. And he had to admit that her reasoning did make sense. As she spoke, he also observed the tension in the other mages. The way they tightened their grip on their weapons, the way their eyes skittered between him and Lamia. Their chests rose and fell as they breathed. Their feet shifted anxiously in the snow. These were human movements and human reactions.

Is it *real*? That question kept rebounding through his mind. That was all that mattered to him right now. Not Lamia's betrayal. Not his imminent death.

The answer to that question was more important to

him than anything.

"What is wrong with you?" Lamia barked. "Why do you stand there quiet and unconcerned? You are going to die here. Everything you have worked toward will be stripped from you."

Finn just shook his head. "I've already lost everything," he murmured.

Lamia snorted derisively. "Fine. Then you certainly won't mind if we take your life."

At her signal, the two rows of mages began to conjure a legion of magical projectiles – flaming balls of fire, arcs of electricity, and shards of ice were soon pulled from the air and began floating beside each caster. The missiles were all targeted at Finn, a lone man standing against a firing line of mages.

Finn knew he should feel afraid, angry, upset. But he only felt *confused*. His fire mana simmered in his veins, but it felt weak, barely more than embers of its former fiery glory. It seemed to be affected by his doubt and uncertainty.

The first wave of projectiles launched forward, the energy rippling and contorting in the air and the elemental energies crashing into one another in their headlong rush toward Finn. Weeks spent in relentless training had his fingers moving on their own, summoning his daggers and slicing the missiles from the air as he danced through the snow.

He dodged and shifted, his feet kicking up a fine, cold powder. Finn ducked one missile, sliced another in half, leaped into a roll and landed back on his feet, turning to absorb a blast of lightning along his shoulder. He felt the shield being blown away, the energy arcing around his armor, searing his robes, and leaving burning welts along his skin.

Finn felt the pain, although it was dull. Muted. Not as sharp or biting as the real thing. That was a tell. It was a giveaway that this was all fake.

At the same time, was that really good evidence? He knew that was intentional. That was simply a rule of this world. Like gravity or entropy – a natural law programmed into the fabric of this universe.

Besides, regardless of degree, was the pain he experienced in his world any less 'real?' It was the same response. Neurons firing somewhere in his brain. The same could be said of his sight, his hearing, his sense of touch and smell – the heat he felt as a *Fireball* raced past or the flash of light from a blast of electricity.

Was any of this less real than what he experienced in his world?

Another shard of ice rocketed toward him, and Finn barely avoided the frozen lance. The missile cut a line across his cheek, blood welling from the wound. He spun and twisted to avoid a spear of earth and stone that suddenly jutted from the ground, kicking off the column of rock to avoid another *Ice Bolt*.

The back of his hand wiped at his face and came away wet with his own blood. It felt warm on his skin. It wasn't enough. His senses could be manipulated. They wouldn't give him the proof he needed – give him the *answers* he so desperately needed.

His eyes centered on Lamia and the other mages. What was going on behind their eyes? Did they think, feel, care, love, and fear? And yet he knew that this was a hopeless exercise. The Seer was right. He was asking her to prove the impossible – to prove a negative. He wanted her to show him that she *wasn't* fake.

The barrage of magic relented for a moment, and Finn stood there, breathing heavily. Half-melted puddles and columns of earth littered the area around him. The snow had been blasted away from the force of the elemental energy that had been hurled at him, creating a circular patch of muddy water and stone. Finn's body was covered in injuries. Blood trickled down his cheek and dripped from his fingers. His armor was nearly gone, only a few fragments of the molten energy still clinging to his left arm.

"Just give in," Lamia's voice called out. "Give up. This is hopeless."

Finn looked at her with bleary eyes, trying to decipher her words. That was indeed how he had felt after Rachael was taken from him – and exactly what he had done.

He had given up.

Instead of answering Lamia, Finn recast his *Magma Armor*, the warm substance sliding down his arms as he reassumed a defensive stance and his knives orbited him slowly. The mages in the field shuffled in the snow, eyeing each other uncertainly. Finn wasn't really fighting back, but at the same time he had survived their combined barrage. He could see their thoughts painted on their faces. This wasn't how this was supposed to go down.

Finn was supposed to beg. To plead. To succumb to their power.

Lamia ground her teeth together. "So be it. We'll do this the hard way."

Another gesture and the mages around her began to summon a second barrage of missiles. This time, they didn't hold anything back, the energy soon growing so dense that Finn could only make out indistinct flashes of orange, yellow, and blue. He knew he couldn't dodge everything they planned to throw at him.

As he stared his death in the face, the Seer's question echoed in his mind.

How do you know I'm not real?

The truth was that he didn't.

Tears budded at the corners of his eyes and Finn squeezed them shut. It was just too painful to admit that. That meant that it was *possible* to bring Rachael back.

He had gone so long without hope that even the faintest ember burned to the touch. What if he was wrong? Could he endure that sort of pain again? Or would it finally break him beyond redemption?

He knew he had a choice to make. Right now.

Was he going to attempt to live again? To fight to reclaim Rachael – or whatever version of her that the Seer might offer. Or would he give up right here? His character might die in-game, but he knew with sudden certainty that his death would be real.

Before he had entered this world, he hadn't been

living. He had merely been *existing*, a robot walking through the same mechanical steps each day. Had he been any different than a machine? The NPCs in this world were more alive than that husk of a human being. Going back to that was as good as death – a self-inflicted purgatory.

As that thought echoed through his mind, Finn felt something shift inside him. A sudden resolve flared in his chest – a willingness to try. To give life one more shot.

Behind his eyelids, he saw a small spark ignite in the darkness. That spark turned to a flame, fragile and tender at first, licking at the air cautiously. He could hope again, it whispered. He could love again. It was a chance. A possibility.

I could see Rachael again.

So, he took a breath and leapt.

Finn grasped at the flame with everything he had, focusing on that lone point of light amid the darkness. He fed the flames his memories of Rachael and he didn't hold back this time. The pain at her loss. His rage, anger, and frustration. His regrets for days spent on work instead of with her. Lost plans and untested futures. He fed the flames his *love*.

He gave himself over to the fire – heart, body, and soul.

The flame soon grew, the inferno expanding outward until it had driven out the darkness. The energy burned through his veins until it felt like his blood was boiling, and his entire body was on fire. When he felt like he couldn't take it anymore, he opened his eyes, and they blazed with a fire so hot that it burned bright white.

For a moment, Finn was confused. The elemental missiles still hung in the air, but the mages stood frozen and unmoving, simply staring at him.

Finn suddenly realized what they were looking at.

His robes had burned away, the tattoo on his right arm scorching through the fabric and the ink twining across his skin and creeping across his torso. At the same time, the lines had changed color, now glowing with a white-hot light.

"The Mark of the Crone? It can't be..." Lamia murmured.

A notification suddenly crashed down into Finn's vision, the notice itself engulfed in flames that seemed to pulse in time with his heartbeat.

> **System Notice: Mark of the Crone**
>
> You have accepted the Seer's offer, embracing the flames. They have purged and purified your mind – giving you renewed purpose and freedom from the shackles of your old life. You have been reborn in fire, forged in adversity, and let loose upon this world as the avatar of flame.
>
> The Mark of the Crone has been activated, feeding off the passion you have inspired in others and empowering you for a short time. However, all gifts come with a price. If the flames are not released within five minutes, they will consume you, destroying your body.
>
> +500 Intelligence
+500 Willpower
+200 Dexterity
Increased Fire Magic Affinity (temporarily set to 100%)
All skills temporarily set to grandmaster
>
> "Consider this a token of good faith – a taste of what you could become. Eliminate your enemies, burn them where they stand, and let your flames roar into the sky, sending a message for all to see." – The Seer

"Kill him," Lamia screamed at the other mages, knocking them out of their shocked stupor. As one, they released the barrage of missiles. A rainbow tidal wave of destruction rippled across the landscape, rolling and tumbling. It burned, crackled, and hissed. When it struck, a massive explosion of energy fountained into the air, causing the clouds overhead to swirl around the column and creating a vortex of loose vapor.

As the energy slowly cleared, the mages held their

collective breath.

A ball of molten lava stood where Finn had once been, like a fiery egg laid upon the frozen plain. Slowly, the shell unfolded to reveal that Finn hung suspended inside. The magma shifted and retracted until it slid back up along Finn's arms and his feet touched the ground once more. As the substance finally settled, spikes of magma still dotted his limbs and caused the air to ripple and warp from the heat.

"Daniel," Finn murmured, his eyes blazing.

The AI flashed into existence beside him, although he seemed to hesitate in shock at Finn's transformation. "Um... sir?"

"Highlight all targets in my UI and then get out of the way," Finn instructed. The AI didn't argue this time, flashing once and backing away quickly.

Suddenly, all of the mages on the field were illuminated in a soft blue glow. At the same time, Finn muttered another word, "Icarus."

It was his turn to retaliate.

And he knew just how to do it.

Finn unfurled the package that Julia had given him, a bundle of throwing knives that landed on the ground with a thump. Then he began to create something new – his mind frothing with excitement. His fingers blurred, moving so quickly that the friction caused sparks to form in the air. This was a grandmaster spell, eight full lines of incantations highlighted in his system UI – the word cloud on the right side of the interface struggling to keep up as Finn picked out the phrases.

As he brought a new spell into the world, pockets of flames began to erupt in the air around him, dancing and spinning in a dazzling display. The other mages looked on wide-eyed at the amount of mana being funneled into the air.

"Stop him!" Lamia shouted, her hands already moving as a massive meteor of ice and snow began to collect in the sky above her. "Attack before he casts."

They summoned more missiles, and the air mages among them dashed forward, trying to teleport into range in a vain attempt to interrupt Finn's spell. Yet the heat around

Finn had grown oppressive, the air practically boiling and forcing them backward. More mages shot missiles in his direction, but Finn knocked aside the few that made it past the aura of heat with a casual grace, his armor easily deflecting the blows.

Then Finn finished his new spell, and his UI prompted him for a name.

"Last Dance," Finn whispered.

Fire suddenly engulfed all the throwing knives, at least two dozen blades lifting into the air simultaneously and drifting around Finn in a whirlwind of steel and flame. Unlike Finn's standard *Imbue Fire*, they glowed white, the heat so intense that it was melting the metal of the blades. They wouldn't last long at this rate.

But Finn didn't need them to.

He raised his head to look at the other mages, and he saw more than one stumble backward, fear shining in their eyes. Yet he was beyond caring about that anymore. He was committed. He had embraced the flames. He had a goal now, and nothing and no one would stand in his way.

Finn didn't even need to move.

He directed his blades forward, the faint translucent line that marked his control range now ringing the entire field. The blades arced forward in a blaze of flames – racing through the air like miniature meteors. They struck at the mages with a ferocity and strength that was terrifying. More than one mage struggled to block the attacks, summoning walls of earth or ice. Yet the blades simply skittered around or blasted through these obstacles before cutting into flesh. They severed limbs and melted bone.

Screams soon rose into the air, a discordant symphony of pain and fear as Finn cut down the mages around him to the flash of flames and the spray of crimson blood. A knife stabbed through one woman's throat. Another decapitated a fleeing mage – the flames immediately cauterizing the wound. Another absorbed a blast of lightning while a second cut the offending air mage's hand off at the wrist. Finn cut and burned until nothing was moving, and stillness descended upon the field.

Within the span of minutes, only two people remained standing.

Lamia looked to her side where Khiana struggled on the ground. His arm had been severed at the shoulder – his knives now strewn about the ground. He sucked in a sharp breath as another of Finn's blades embedded itself in his chest, burning his lungs from the inside out. Then he went still.

The blade slowly retracted and spun back through the air to rejoin its brothers where they orbited Finn in a slow-moving sphere of steel and flame. The blood coating the blades was soon washed away by the fire – purified by the flames.

Finn walked toward Lamia, noting the panic that filled her eyes. She looked around the field, searching for a way to escape or to fight back. Yet her eyes only found the dead and dying. Dozens of bodies littered the ground, many still smoldering.

"You are making a mistake," she said as Finn approached. "You don't understand the game that is being played here."

Finn said nothing, his gaze impassive as he continued forward.

"The Crone will deceive you. She always does. She preys on people's passions. Just like the flames, her gifts never last," Lamia pleaded. "But I can help you. Just tell me what she offered you and I'll match it."

Finn shook his head. "I'm sorry, but you can't give me what I want."

As he finished speaking, his blades all stabbed forward at the same time.

Lamia raised her hands, tried to cast a spell, but it was far too late. The blades cut into her, her body spasming as they all struck simultaneously. The combined heat was so great that the fires began to consume her – incinerating her while she was still alive. She tried to scream then, raising her head to the sky, but no sound escaped. Within only seconds, a pile of ash was all that remained of the former water magic master.

And Finn stood alone.

He was struggling to concentrate. He knew he should release the fire – he had read the warning in the prompt. But it was a struggle. The power was intoxicating. With the flames permeating his body, he felt no pain, no hesitation, and no loss. He felt free – fully free in a way that he hadn't experienced in more than a decade.

Yet it also felt *wrong*.

In a flash, he saw Rachael's smiling face in his mind's eye. "You are almost at the Finn-ish line," she had murmured in his ear.

But he wasn't there yet.

He had a concrete goal now – one he intended to accomplish.

A reason to keep going.

Mustering all the willpower he had left, Finn forcefully released his fire mana. Yet this time, he couldn't simply force it back into his mana pool. This power had come from the Seer and was far too great to contain. He had to release the pressure somehow. Acting quickly, Finn did the only thing he could. He set it free.

The energy exploded outward, creating a wave of flame nearly ten feet tall that rolled across the field, melting the snow and burning away the corpses that littered the field, leaving only charred bones in its wake.

As the energy finally fled him, Finn dropped to the ground. He felt suddenly weak – almost too feeble to move. Notifications flashed in the corner of his vision, but he was having difficulty focusing on them. As his vision swam and he began to lose consciousness, Finn remembered that there was one last thing he needed to do.

Amid the nearby pile of ash, he saw a familiar glowing token. The edges were singed and crumbling, but the warded stone was otherwise intact. He struggled toward it, crawling along the ground and using the last vestiges of his stamina. As his fingers curled around the token, the darkness finally began to claim him, the world bleeding away. Finn gave himself over to it willingly – too exhausted to fight any further.

Chapter 42 - Triumphant

Finn blinked blearily. His throat felt raw, and it hurt to swallow.

His fingers clawed at the ground, coming away wet. As his eyes began to focus, he realized that his hands were covered in a mixture of frigid water and mud. He forced himself upright, groaning at the effort. Notifications were still flashing in the corner of his vision, but he didn't spare them much attention.

His focus was on the field around him.

It looked like a meteor had struck the mountainside, obliterating the snow and leaving muddy, charred dirt and stone. Amid this scene of devastation were dozens of corpses – little more than blackened skeletons now. The memories came flooding back then.

His encounter with the Seer. The ambush. His decision.

"Rachael," Finn croaked.

Finn had done this.

Well, technically, the Seer was primarily responsible. From the explanation he had been given of the magic system and the goddess' words inside her tent, his guess was that the goddess harvested mana. The Emir's competition had likely created a whirlpool of passion – students dedicated to winning the duels. Perhaps Finn's own infamy had helped, creating a nemesis that pushed the other students to ever more-extreme heights.

Either way, it seemed like that had been a one-time deal.

Notifications still flickered in the corner of his vision. Likely indicating levels gained and skills upgraded. However, Finn wasn't interested in that right now. There was only one thing he was curious about.

Finn pulled up his mod. The UI soon flickered in his vision. As he opened his spellbook, he could see what he had created. The incantation was long and complicated – far more complex than anything that Finn had cast before. There were also no gestures linked to the spell. He must have been acting entirely on instinct. He doubted he would be able to recast it again – at least not any time soon. Although, the Seer's message to Finn had been clear. Someday, he might be capable of harnessing that sort of power.

A spell capable of obliterating a small army of mages.

Finn shoved himself to his feet, feeling the crisp winter air drift across his bare chest. He looked down at the Seer's mark. The tattoo had receded and was now only emblazoned along his right arm. Although, Finn could have sworn the flames had grown slightly, almost touching his elbow now. He couldn't be certain what that meant.

He shook his head; that question could wait for another time.

His eyes drifted to his hand, where a familiar stone token rested in his palm. The surface glowed with a faint light. He needed to return to the guild. He couldn't be certain how much time had passed in-game – he certainly hadn't had a chance to check his clock before massacring the group of mages and passing out.

Finn pulled his old tunic out of his bag, tugging the garment over his head. Perhaps he could at least conceal the tattoo along his right arm. Although, as he surveyed himself, it was still obvious he had been through hell. He grimaced as his eyes skimmed to Lamia's remains. The water mage's death would likely raise some questions – especially since Khiana had destroyed the water elemental and hadn't returned. Perhaps Finn could at least clean himself up and hide any obvious details that might allow someone to identify the water mage. With a sigh, he got to work.

A few minutes later, Finn was as prepared as he was going to be.

He pulled out the two tokens. He had no idea what he was going to face when he returned, but there was nothing for it. Not giving himself time to hesitate, Finn tapped the tokens together, a miasma of rainbow-colored energy tearing open around him and the world drifting away.

* * *

In an instant, Finn was back in the guild courtyard.

What he witnessed was pure chaos. A massive crowd still filled the field, hundreds of angry and confused voices drifting through the air. The portal of water still hung over the dais, but the picture was blanked out, the surface only reflecting the sunlight that beat down on the courtyard. At some point, several earth mages had created a rough barricade around the dais, securing it against the crowd of onlookers.

Finn glanced to the side and saw Nefreet huddled with a group of water mages and other faculty – likely trying to figure out what the hell had happened and how they could re-secure the connection to the water elemental. Although, strangely, Abbad was nowhere to be seen. Usually, the librarian was attached to the headmaster at the hip.

Okay, so it doesn't look like too much time passed...

A cry went up from the field as someone caught sight of Finn, still haggard and bloodied. He saw that it was Julia standing on her chair and screaming at the top of her lungs, "Finn has returned. Finn won!" He could see Kyyle standing beside her, the youth soon adding his voice to the chorus of cheers that had begun to erupt from the crowd.

That got Nefreet's attention, and the headmaster met Finn's gaze. For an instant, Finn saw something that resembled surprise flit across the man's face. Although it was gone in an instant. Had he known about Lamia's deception? Suspected it? Maybe the man was just surprised at Finn's abrupt return. He had thought the conspiracy might have died with Lamia, but something in the headmaster's reaction gave him pause.

Or perhaps he was just becoming paranoid...

Nefreet gestured at an air mage, and a breeze soon drifted through the crowd. Then the headmaster's voice whispered among the other mages. "Finn has won his duel against Khiana! Look on, mages, and behold your new guild champion! May he fight for the glory of the guild in the Emir's competition!"

At the same time, a notice slammed down in Finn's vision.

Local Area Notice: Lahab
The Mage Guild has completed its competition, and the traveler named Finn has been declared the guild's champion!

A roar of sound met this announcement, the crowd letting out a resounding cheer. Amid this riotous wave of noise, Finn felt a large hand clap him on the back, and he turned to find Brutus grinning at him. "Well done, kid! I knew you had it in you."

"I'm not a kid," Finn replied sourly. "We've been over this a few times now…"

The fire mage just ignored him – his excitement getting the better of him. Before Finn could ask him what he was doing, Brutus' hands had started winding through a series of gestures. A fountain of flame suddenly speared into the air, mages diving out of the way to avoid the blast of heat. The large man continued to pour more and more mana into the column, and other fire mages soon joined him.

Flames rocketed through the air as dozens of mages channeled their mana simultaneously. The flames continued to expand, the column widening until it had forced everyone from the dais. The fire grew, twisted, and spiraled, fountaining up into the air until the column towered nearly a hundred feet. The flames then arced back toward the courtyard and embers rained down upon the crowd – twinkling like fireflies.

Finn had mixed feelings as he watched the flames. The column was almost certainly visible throughout Lahab and loudly announced Finn to the other residents and travelers. He could also feel his own mana respond to the passion in the crowd's cries and the roar of the fire, but he didn't let himself give in to the sensation.

Despite the cheers and his victory, Finn didn't feel a true sense of triumph. This was just one step along a long and twisting path. A path that he hoped would eventually lead him back to Rachael. As the Seer's illusion had whispered to

him, this wasn't the end.
    It was just the beginning.

Chapter 43 - Resolved

Finn opened his eyes, taking in the rumpled, chaotic texture of the drywall along the ceiling. He had been awake for some time. He lay there without moving, savoring the calm and refusing to give in to the dark thoughts that lingered at the edges of his mind. He knew he didn't have long, maybe a minute at most.

On cue, Daniel's blue form soon flashed into existence nearby, his voice far too cheery for the hour. "Good morning, sir."

Finn just rubbed at his face without responding.

"Are you alright?" the AI prompted a few seconds later.

"Yes, Daniel," Finn replied tiredly. This was their familiar ritual – part of a sequence of steps that comprised Finn's morning routine. At his reply, a soft chime echoed through the air, and a chair wheeled into the room, gliding over toward the edge of the bed.

"Would you like any help, sir?" Daniel asked.

"I'm good," Finn grunted, as he did every morning.

Finn gripped his legs, feeling nothing as his fingers touched the bare skin. After days and weeks spent in-game, it was his real-world body – heavy and useless – that had begun to feel foreign to him. He maneuvered the limbs over the edge of the bed and then lifted himself into the chair, grunting from the effort.

He refused the AI's assistance again when he offered to help roll him into the bathroom. Instead, Finn palmed the wheels with practiced movements. Then he set to work, throwing himself into his routine to quiet those damnable thoughts and questions. He brushed his teeth and took a shower – the most exhausting step. Most importantly, he took his time. He was in no hurry today. In fact, the routine was calming – a welcome distraction.

1 hour and 58 minutes later, Finn was finished.

He wheeled himself into the kitchen, yet again refusing Daniel's help. Today, there was no telltale smell of cooking food or impromptu visit from his children. Only cold tile and polished countertops stared back at him. The room felt chilly, although he knew that Daniel carefully regulated the temperature in the house. It was the same as it was yesterday, and it would be tomorrow.

"Please adjust the household temperature up 1 degree," Finn ordered. Although, a part of him knew that it wasn't the house's AC that bothered him.

"Of course, sir," Daniel replied, pulsing softly.

Then, with a sigh, Finn set to work, snatching some food from the fridge and going through the motions of cooking himself breakfast.

Another 47 minutes later and Finn set the last of the cooking instruments in the dishwasher. He sat there, looking around the room and searching for another task. Unfortunately, there was nothing left. He was washed, dressed, groomed, and fed. His laundry list of commonplace tasks was complete.

"Would you like for me to prepare your office?" Daniel chirped from nearby.

Finn grimaced. He had been putting that off. He had been trying to distract himself from the inevitable with the mundane. Yet there was nothing for it.

With deliberate movements, Finn wheeled himself down the hall and into his office, hovering in the doorway for a moment. His eyes rested on a familiar helmet that sat upon on the solitary table in the center of the room. The dark plastic seemed to absorb the fluorescent light like a black hole. Or maybe that was just his imagination.

He pushed his way into the center of the room, and screens flickered to life, orbiting him slowly. A news feed drifted across one screen – proof that he was still connected to the public network. That was yet another change from the norm. Another display showed half-written code: some experiments and tweaks for his in-game UI.

Finn observed the screens, finally letting the chaotic thoughts return.

The training. The fighting. The invention.

The blood and fire.

The offer.

Awaken Online.

"Sir, are you alright?" Daniel prompted.

Finn started and glanced at the AI. This instanced version of Daniel represented Finn's original coding. He was a mechanical puppet pulled along on well-defined digital strings. Yet his voice and behavior now sounded quite different than his fiery cousin in-game. The orange fire elemental had changed since Finn had introduced his code into AO. He had become surly when he wasn't summoned, expressed emotion – even challenged Finn's judgment. The fiery form of Daniel showed a semblance of autonomy.

A stray thought tugged at the edges of Finn's mind. That was something he could address right now. Something he could control.

And perhaps something that could quiet the chaos that still lingered in the back of his head – the questions that had returned in full force once he'd pulled off that headset.

With a swipe of his wrist, Finn brought up a keyboard, the translucent keys projected in the air in front of him. His fingers danced, and the floating screens shifted and disappeared. In their place, a new image materialized, hovering in the air and rotating slowly. It showed a softly glowing blue cube. Finn tapped it, and the object expanded, breaking into dozens of smaller cubes that hovered around a central core.

This was a visual representation of Daniel's original codebase. The simple household AI Finn had built represented a set of core processes and ancillary modules that had been added to handle specific tasks. Despite the familiar structure, he still reviewed the model carefully, looking for any anomalies.

Finding nothing, Finn flicked the structure away.

Here was the moment of truth.

Finn pulled up the code for the in-game version of Daniel.

A new image popped into existence, this one glowing with a bright orange light.

"What is this?" Finn murmured in shock.

A fountain of orange energy had sprung to life in front of him. There was a single column, the edges at the top blurring and arcing – curling back in on themselves and reattaching at the bottom of the cylinder. Finn pinched at the air and zoomed in. That was when he realized that the fountain was actually composed of millions of the smaller modular blocks. Even as Finn watched, they shifted and changed and reformed, flowing through the structure and evolving with each pass.

Finn recognized what he was looking at, but it still seemed impossible. It mimicked the structure he had initially used for the AI he had developed for Cerillion Logistics, but someone had gone much, much further. The structure represented an infinite recursive loop, with the program designing new modules and improving the others with each subsequent pass. The code was overhauled, destroyed, and reborn as it flowed through the column.

Even more spectacular, the AI was improving on its *ability* to make improvements. The flow and twist of the code was changing even as Finn watched. It was actively evolving and adapting. The modular code almost looked like blood passing through a living creature, pulsing and throbbing like a heartbeat with each rotation.

It almost looked… alive.

"It's possible," Finn muttered to himself. "It's actually fucking possible."

When confronted by the Seer and then Lamia, Finn had made a choice. He knew that. He had grasped at the *hope* that the goddess could deliver on her promise – that the people he had met inside the game were real. That the Seer could bring Rachael back.

While Finn might not be able to prove that the AI felt or experienced emotion, the orange image flickering in front of him offered a different kind of evidence. It indicated a codebase so complex that Finn was having trouble dissecting it. It was something so close to a living mind that he wasn't certain he could tell the difference.

It's possible.

That thought kept rebounding through his mind.

Finn pulled his attention away from the image reluctantly, shifting his gaze to the table beside him where a familiar plastic helmet sat. His fingers reached out tentatively, feeling at the hard material and tracing the faint scratches along its surface.

With trembling hands, Finn lifted the headset, staring at it. He could do this. This was a chance. He could accomplish the Seer's task and finish the Emir's competition. And at the finish line, Rachael might be waiting for him.

At that thought, the lingering doubt and hesitation faded, replaced with a steadfast resolve. Abbad's words returned to him then – the librarian's questions hovering in his mind. Finn could answer them now.

His goal was to bring Rachael back.

Finn tugged the helmet over his head, his vision quickly obscured by darkness, and the sounds of his office muted behind the thick insulation. Immediately, a splash screen popped up in his vision, the emblem for Awaken Online emblazoned in front of him.

Abbad's second question rang through his mind.

"What are you willing to sacrifice to accomplish your goal?"

"Everything," Finn whispered.

Epilogue

An eerie quiet lingered atop the mountain. The harsh clang and sizzle of battle had given way to the faint whistle of frigid wind. The air suddenly shimmered and shifted, taking on a yellowish hue. Then it was as though a screen had parted, the shield of air sliding away. Two men stepped out of the rift, their feet crunching in the snow as they made their way down into the small valley below them.

One of the pair hobbled forward more awkwardly. He leaned heavily on an ornate staff composed of gold, adorned with bands of multi-colored crystal that spiraled up the shaft. His skin was wrinkled and aged, pockmarked and stained, and he let out a wheezing breath with each step, as though the effort cost him.

"Lend me a hand, Abbad," the older man said, gesturing at the librarian.

"Of course, my Emir," was the terse reply. Abbad let the older man lean on his arm as they made the short trek down into the valley.

As they reached their destination, the pair maintained their silence. Their eyes skimmed across the field. A faint dusting of snow drifted down around them, but not enough time had passed for the snowfall to obscure the visible signs of the battle that had been waged across this mountaintop. A massive circle had been carved in the snow, filled with a mixture of mud and water and the remains of the fallen – brittle, dark skeletons, their limbs frozen in a panicked, frenzied state. They remained where they had fallen. Where Finn had slain them.

Abbad took in this scene with implacable, calm precision – although he could feel disquiet whispering in the back of his mind. He noted the locations of the bodies, the damage to the underlying bone. If he hadn't witnessed the massacre himself, he would have had trouble identifying the cause of death and angle of attack from the fractured bone.

"A right mess he made of this lot," the Emir croaked. "Such a waste."

Abbad forced himself to stay quiet – his will like iron.

The Emir poked at Lamia's remains. "Although, this one at least served some use in the end." He glanced at Abbad. "That was clever of you to use her. How did you know the ruse would work?"

"Lamia has not been discreet with her distaste for the travelers. Placing Finn in her class was a simple matter. I may also have had other students and faculty... rile her antipathy. After that, it only took a few careful nudges to set her along the desired path."

The Emir barked out a hoarse laugh that led into a short coughing fit. "Ahh, I see. Does the Marked One suspect you?"

"I do not think so," Abbad replied, bowing his head. "He believes me to be a simple librarian and a trusted advisor. He suspected that Lamia was behind the attacks by the other travelers – a point that was surely confirmed by her ill-fated ambush. I also told him that it was typical for water mages to use illusions. Even if the students could somehow identify my involvement, that should insulate me from suspicion."

"Perfect," the Emir murmured with a knowing glance at Abbad. "When I appointed you to head the Mage Guild, I wasn't certain of your reasons for hiding behind that puppet, but now I see that I underestimated you."

"As I was taught, the foolish charge from the front. The wise wait in the shadows," Abbad answered simply, bowing his head. He hesitated, uncertain whether the Emir might view his next question as impudence. "Was this necessary?" he finally asked in a clipped voice.

The Emir raised an eyebrow as he glanced at the so-called librarian. "You think I take an unnecessary risk?"

Abbad tilted his head. "You saw for yourself the power of the Marked One. By pushing him like this, I wonder if we risk creating a force that cannot be contained."

The old man's eyes went distant as he looked at the skeletons that littered the field. "And so, the Marked One shall rise above the others of his kind, his flames consuming the bodies of the fallen," the Emir recited. "You know the Crone's prophecy as well as I. We are merely encouraging events to unfold as they were meant to."

"And the competition among the guilds?" Abbad asked. "I don't recall that described in prophecy."

The Emir's head swiveled to face Abbad, his eyes flashing dangerously. "Take care, Abbad. Your loyalty and skill earn you some measure of lenience. But my patience is not infinite."

A brief silence and then the Emir continued, his tone more even, "As the Crone herself knows, people are blinded in the pursuit of their passions. Competition, rivalry – they keep the sheep blind and docile, looking for predators in the shadows when they should be watching the shepherd holding a blade behind his back.

"No, the competition is necessary. We will continue as planned. With our champions nearly assembled, they need only form their parties, and then we shall send them into the abyss."

"We won't be able to monitor them easily there," Abbad replied.

"Ahh, and that's where your little *nudges* will become useful. The board has been carefully set – our pieces arranged. We must simply wait to see how the game unfolds."

"At the risk of testing your patience further, I feel compelled to remind you of our *arrangement*," Abbad said. "Parts of what I told the Marked One were true. My goal is and always has been the freedom of my kind. I expect to call my debt when this is finished."

"Indeed," the Emir said, his eyes turning back to Abbad. For an instant, they flashed with multi-colored energy. "A compact has been made."

The End

Thank you for reading!

First off, I hope you all enjoyed the story! This was a blast to write. I typically fall in love with a character as I write a book, but there's just something about Finn... equal parts heartache and awesome, I suppose.

I'm tentatively planning to write two more books in this storyline – which will bring us roughly current with Jason & company. I already have both books outlined and plotted. I'm just wavering if I want to take a few months and knock these out before we return to our favorite necromancer. I know a bunch of you are impatient to get back to Jason. Although, I think finishing this arc first might be more satisfying since Finn will be relevant in the larger storyline moving forward – if you haven't caught that already!

Anyway, I'd love to hear your thoughts and if you'd like to see more of Finn!

Please leave a review!

I can't overstate how important these reviews are to ensure other people get a chance to read my stories. I would also love to hear your thoughts – positive, negative, or anything in-between.

Please feel free to email me directly at **tbagwell33@gmail.com** if you have any questions, comments, or suggestions. If you see any errors, please let me know, and I will fix them immediately!

For all the latest info on my writing projects, check out my **blog,** and sign up for my **newsletter.** We also have an awesome **Facebook group** and **Discord server** if you want to hang out with fellow members of <Original Sin>. We do regular giveaways, and this is a really cool group of people. If you would like to help support me, please feel free to stop by my **Patreon** – where I typically publish early chapters of my latest work.

Finally, if you want to find new books or talk about other Gamelit/LitRPG, feel free to check out this **group**.

Acknowledgments

I'd also like to give a shout-out to everyone who helped me write *Awaken Online: Ember*. Like most great things, it takes a village to write a book. Or at least one that makes sense and is (relatively) error-free. Thank you all for your help and support!

- Ashley Anderson (Editor)
- Krista Ruggles (Artist)
- David Stifel (Narrator)
- Celestian Rince (Proofreader)
- Stephanie Fisher
- Cynthia Bagwell
- Phillip Bagwell
- Alex Teine
- Arthur G. Davidson
- Christopher Brink
- Christopher Wible
- Evan Moore
- Gareth Warner
- Jonathan Decker
- Kyyle Newton
- Megan Woodyard
- Robert Wierzbicki
- Whistleknot
- All of my Patrons. You guys are awesome!

Printed in Great Britain
by Amazon